D0860876

Unfinished Business

JUL - - 2017

Unfinished Business

BRIAN CLARY

WILLIAMSBURG REGIONAL LIBRARY
7770 CROAKER ROAD
WILLIAMSBURG, VA 23188

UNFINISHED BUSINESS

Copyright © 2016 Brian Clary.

All rights reserved. No part of this book may be used or reproduced by any means, graphic, electronic, or mechanical, including photocopying, recording, taping or by any information storage retrieval system without the written permission of the author except in the case of brief quotations embodied in critical articles and reviews.

iUniverse books may be ordered through booksellers or by contacting:

iUniverse
1663 Liberty Drive
Bloomington, IN 47403
www.iuniverse.com
1-800-Authors (1-800-288-4677)

Because of the dynamic nature of the Internet, any web addresses or links contained in this book may have changed since publication and may no longer be valid. The views expressed in this work are solely those of the author and do not necessarily reflect the views of the publisher, and the publisher hereby disclaims any responsibility for them.

Any people depicted in stock imagery provided by Thinkstock are models, and such images are being used for illustrative purposes only. Certain stock imagery © Thinkstock.

THIS BOOK IS FICTION AND THE PERSONS, ENTITIES, LOCATIONS AND EVENTS DESCRIBED IN THIS BOOK ARE LIKEWISE FICTIONAL AND NOT BASED ON ANY ACTUAL PERSON LIVING OR DEAD, OR ANY PAST OR PRESENT BUSINESS ENTITIES.

ISBN: 978-1-5320-0759-0 (sc)
ISBN: 978-1-5320-0760-6 (e)

Library of Congress Control Number: 2016918682

Print information available on the last page.

iUniverse rev. date: 11/11/2016

Dedication

Though have strove for the gentility of Ben Digby, I have often acted with the petulance of Joseph Pitzmyre. I am nevertheless blessed with a wife, Nina, that claims the best attributes of Emily Digby. I have two sons, the oldest of which favoring Cookie Harrington's gentle giant demeanor and interest in the culinary arts, while my youngest is strikingly similar to Mungo Thibodeaux, and I would not have it any other way. This book is dedicated to them.

Ackowledgements

Special thanks goes to my longtime friend Gerald Cothran for taking the time to read this manuscript and providing his thoughts and encouragement. I am further grateful to Frank Deloache for offering his editorial expertise.

Preface

Let's let the dead skin of broken dreams, be shed. Begin anew the pursuit. Cause those broken dreams aren't really broken. They're just unfinished business, so let's make them our business and close the deal. **ZAIM RICOCHET**

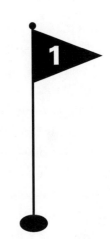

The First Hole

(Bozeman, Montana October 30, 1997)

*T*he Lone Wolf Country Club was built among the foothills of the majestic Gallatin Mountain range of Southern Montana. The heart of the club was a long rectangular one-story brick building with locker rooms on the west end, a pro shop in the middle and a café to the east. The picturesque sloping fairways of the 18-hole golf course sprawled to the south of the building, and an asphalt topped parking area lay at its north.

The centerpiece of the pro shop was a long oak showcase, akin to what one might have encountered in a nineteenth century general store. It had slanting glass panels, similar to a candy counter, except in the stead of confections, lollipops and rock candy, this counter displayed, golf caps, towels and gloves baring the Lone Wolf emblem, and new and used golf balls and tees. Atop the counter sat an old brass lamp, a cash register and a slotted wooden box used to receive the golfer's signed scorecards. Three long rows of racks and shelves dominated the middle of the pro shop, displaying merchandise ranging from clothing and shoes to a wide selection of golf clubs and golf bags, all available for sale at a discount to members.

All interior walls of the building featured darkly stained oak panels, each original to its 1949 construction. Plaques adorned many of these panels, celebrating a near a half-century of club champions, each with an etched, brass plate bearing the winning member's name and the year of their victory. On other panels, hung framed black-and-white photographs attesting to the celebrities who had visited Lone Wolf to dine, or play a round or two of golf, while passing through the scenic town of Bozeman. These photos featured legends of golf, such as Hogan, Snead and Sarazen, luminaries from the realm of politics, including Truman and Eisenhower, as well as stars from Hollywood, the likes of Gleason, Crosby, Hope and Fonda.

The powerful and famous were photographed there, during an era when Lone Wolf was the jewel of the mountainous expanse, separating the established East Coast, from burgeoning West. However, with the proliferation of commercial air travel, the construction of the interstate highway system and newer more desirable golf venues in the region, the Lone Wolf Country Club had experienced a long steady decline in membership and revenues. That loss, coupled with the gradual attrition of the old guard members, relegated those that remained only to reminisce about the club's better days. Three years earlier, and in order to bolster the finances, the club's Board of Advisors reluctantly voted to allow non-members to play the course, on a daily fee basis, and to purchase items in the pro shop—at retail. Dues-paying members continued to receive preference on tee times and had exclusive access to the locker rooms and the club's café.

On this evening, the door to the Lone Wolf pro shop swung open rapidly, compelled in large part by a stiff Northeasterly wind. Chuck Duval, the young and capable pro shop attendant, was intrigued to see Benjamin Digby's slight five foot six inch frame emerging from the dusky conditions. The clothing on the racks in the pro shop flapped rapidly until Ben turned, fought against the wind, and managed to force the door shut.

"It's really howling out there, isn't it Mr. Digby?" asked the tall, thin Duval as he tossed Ben a dry towel.

"Yes, and it's beginning to snow harder," Ben answered as he labored to breathe.

"Accumulating?" Duval asked.

"Only ice in the tree tops, the course itself is holding up."

"I didn't think anyone was still out there—what took so long?"

"I played twenty-seven," Ben said catching his breath, "and man does the sun fade quickly in October."

"Believe it or not, tomorrow's Halloween, and November's only a few hours away."

"It feels every bit of November out there now—I almost froze to death," Ben said, as he unwound his scarf, then removed the gloves from each of his numb hands, and began rubbing them back and forth on the towel, hoping to restore feeling.

"I guess golf's about done for this season," Chuck said.

Ben looked up at him remorsefully, and said, "That's why I pushed for the extra nine."

"Well, today is just an appetizer, and the entrée arrives tomorrow."

"What does that even mean?"

"I saw reports that a strong Canadian front is coming down, and it's due to hit late morning tomorrow," Chuck explained. "You're lucky you got in the extra nine, because I'm told we won't make it beyond tomorrow afternoon."

This was dreadful, but not unexpected news to Ben who except for his stint in the Army, had lived in Montana his entire life. He marked each year by the turn of the seasons and, through the decades had come to associate them, as one might regard old friends or relatives. Each season had attributes he disliked and others that he coveted, but when each visited, as with relatives, some always seemed to overstay their welcome. This was especially true for brother winter, and with his impending arrival, Ben knew his coveted golfing routine was on borrowed time.

In Montana, the end of a golf season does not occur based on a preselected date on a calendar, but rather in the form of a gradual deterioration in weather conditions until the utility of staying open, was outweighed by declining interest or ability to play. Local courses would typically remain open through the first few snowfalls, with only intermittent and limited shutdowns. With moderating temperatures and some maintenance, the courses could persevere the early assaults, before inevitably succumbing to the elements.

Each fall, a strong weather system would roar down from the north, arriving with such a severity that it imposed a definitive—nondiscretionary—absolute closure of the course until the spring thaw. Learning on this afternoon, that Bozeman was on the precipice of such a storm deflated Ben, who treasured his three to four, rounds per week, and the arrival of winter to Ben was comparable to how schoolchildren regard the end of summer.

"You'll be out of a job soon, huh?" Ben asked, as he managed to unzip and shrug his way out of his old duck down quilted jacket and brush away the melting flurries.

"Yes sir, but I'll have a couple of weeks of down time, and then I'll go over to Bridger Bowl."

"Ski instructor?" Ben asked.

"I wish—they make the big bucks. No, I just work the lifts and fill in at the ski shop when someone's sick."

Ben leaned toward the brass lamp on the showcase, placed his damp score card under its light and squinted to read and mentally tally his scores. With the lamp light highlighting Ben's wind-chapped face, Chuck asked, "Say, how'd you get those?"

"Get what, son?" Ben asked.

"The scars on your cheek and neck. Did you have some sort of an accident?"

"Oh those … no … I got them over in Europe in forty-four," Ben replied.

"Were you there on one of them college exchange student deals, or something else?"

Ben looked up from reading his card and replied, "Something else."

"So what'd you shoot?"

"Let's see here, ninety-two on the first eighteen and forty-six for the extra nine," Ben said as he signed the card and handed it to Duval for purposes of maintaining his handicap rating.

"If nothing else you're consistent," Duval said.

Ben was a steady nineteen to twenty-two handicapper who had long since ceased trying to lower that number, but always strove to remain as close to that range as he could. Each passing year brought new challenges, and maintaining was in his way of thinking, winning.

"I'm curious about something, Mr. Digby. You don't play in the club tournaments or compete against anyone these days, so why bother with keeping the handicap?" Chuck asked, while sliding Ben's scorecard in the slotted box.

"I compete with myself in a way," Ben said.

"I don't really understand, but we're certainly happy to keep the tally for you."

"You'll learn that when it comes to golf, it's important to play honest and legit and to challenge yourself, more than worrying about challenging others."

"Huh, I guess I never thought about it that way."

"You know Chuck, traditional stroke play golf is relatively unique in the world of competition. It's a sport where you play for yourself, and not on a team, and where your play doesn't influence the play of others."

"What do you mean by the last part?" Chuck asked.

"Think about it. On defense in baseball, you are trying to pitch balls that are thrown well enough that they can't be hit. Similarly, tennis players hit balls to their opponent that they hope won't be returned."

"And in football, boxing and hockey, they're just trying to kill each other!" Chuck said.

"There's truth in that, all right," Ben said. "However, golf is different, considering its rich history of sportsmanship and the personal struggle involved in learning to play and striving for improvement. You see that man right there," Ben said, pointing to one of the framed photos on the wall.

"Sure, that's Bob Hope."

"Right and he once said *if you watch a game, it is fun. If you play at it, it's recreation. If you work at, it's golf.*"

Fellow club member, Mungo Thibodeaux overheard the exchange, and as he passed, he added, "Mark Twain called golf *a good walk spoiled.*"

"Hello to you too, Mungo," Ben said and Mungo waved and entered the café.

Chuck stared curiously at Ben, and asked, "What does the quote mean?"

"Hope's or Twain's?" Ben asked.

"Both, I guess."

"I think they're essentially saying the same thing. Golf is hard, and represents a labor of love of sorts, and I confess that I've struggled with it mightily for decades."

"But you don't practice much and have never taken lessons—at least not since I've been here."

"It's true that I'm a self-taught golfer, and that's not a wise thing. When you do it that way, you learn many bad habits, and they are hard to overcome. If I could go back in time, and start over from scratch, I would do things differently, but can't and have had to suffer all the complications that come with that."

"All the more reason for lessons, right?"

"No, not necessarily," Ben said. "Several years ago I came up here alone to get in nine holes, and got paired up with a golf pro from Bismarck. As we played, he graciously gave me some pointers, adjusting my grip and my stance and he insisted that I had to take the club back on a different plane."

"Did it help?"

"No! It took me over two months just to break a hundred again," Ben chuckled. "But I do focus on the fundamentals, at least as I understand them. I work hard for improvement, but not for praise or trophies, or to end up on one of those plaques on the wall, I do it for myself. I realize it's hard for a young man like you to grasp, but in a way age is my competition, and as the years go by, my opponent is getting fierce."

"Huh, I've worked here for four years and never thought about golf in that way."

"Chuck, I've always regarded the game as a microcosm of life. There's a civility and discipline to the game, things like hitting in the proper order, not talking or moving when someone else is hitting, and letting the group in front of you clear sufficiently before driving your ball."

"And tending the flag while someone's putting," Chuck added.

"Exactly, and you've seen it with your own eyes—people who don't obey those rules and lack the required etiquette on the course, and they usually make for bad folks off the course."

Chuck leaned over to Ben and whispered, "Yeah, like some of the newcomers. I've seen them interfere with the play of others, including their own friends, like clearing their throats during back swings and walking the green while someone's putting."

"Golf is a gentleman's game, though some men that play it aren't so gentlemanly," Ben said. "But if you work at it, and you're honest, and focus on the important things, everything else will take care of itself—both on the course and off."

"It's funny that you brought this up. We had this big muckety-muck from one of the large oil-and-gas companies come to speak to my business management class. You know what he does when he needs to hire a new executive?" Ben shook his head. "He does two things, first he takes them to a nice restaurant, but only for dinner. He prefers an evening meal over lunch to, among other things, see if the prospect drinks and if so, how much and how they handle it."

"It seems it might be more telling if the candidate drinks at lunch," Ben said.

"That's true, but he covers that on the second thing, but while dining he monitors the alcohol intake and its impact on the candidate. More importantly, he watches to see how the prospect interacts with people, not so much with him or even other folks at their table, but rather how they interact with the restaurant employees. If the prospect is rude or unkind to the maître d' or the wait staff for example, that's a big red flag to him. He figures if the candidate will treat strangers that way, in front of him, then he or she may not treat subordinates or coworkers at his company well, and might become what he calls a *cancer* inside the organization."

"Makes sense to me, what's the second thing?"

"He takes them to play golf," Chuck said.

"Really?" Ben asked, intrigued.

"Yes, and he said that whether they're good or bad at the game is irrelevant. More than their score, he observes how they approach the game and watches them to see if they get angry when hitting bad shots, and whether they throw clubs or use bad language. He also pays close attention to see if they follow the rules, and *then* he offers to buy drinks on the course to see if they'll accept."

"Is that a bad thing if they do?" Ben asked.

"Not necessarily. It's the amount they drink and how they handle it that counts."

"Sounds like a smart man, Chuck. I've always felt that you can learn a lot about a fella in a fox hole and on a golf course."

"But Mr. Digby, don't you miss playing golf with those friends of yours?" the young man asked. "I remember my first season here, that you had a few fellas that you golfed with from time to time."

"I miss them, all right," Ben said, "but like I say, I still have my opponents, it's just that you don't see 'em and they don't pay dues."

"I think I'm starting to understand that now," Chuck said, and he returned to his duties of closing down the pro-shop for the evening.

As Ben was apt to do following a round, he headed with his jacket, scarf and plaid thermos in hand, toward the club café for a refreshment. Though the café had offered a full bar for the past three years, Ben was a teetotaler, and on this day hot chocolate would be his beverage of choice. He made his way into the café and over to his longtime friend, café proprietor and fellow Army veteran, Carl Harrington. Carl, better known to the members as *Cookie*, was a career Army cook who served in Korea and Vietnam before spending the balance of his twenty-six years of service in the Officer's Mess at Fort Harrison.

Following his discharge from the service, Cookie hired on with the longtime owner of the café, Alf Perry. He worked hard under Perry's direction for a number of years and gradually learned the business. When Perry elected to retire five years earlier, Cookie negotiated a price and bought the café, and assumed all responsibilities, calling on Alf only on certain occasions to fill in. Himself a widower, Cookie found operating the café a suitable way to occupy his time and to ply his hard-earned culinary skills, while supplementing his military retirement.

With Alf's occasional help, and that of part-time waitress, Katrina Daly, Cookie had cover during unusually busy times and for occasional absences for funerals, VFW hall functions, doctor's appointments and rare bouts of illness. Katrina, affectionately referred to as *Kat* worked part-time as a Bozeman 911 dispatcher and moonlighted at the café. She had flaming red hair and faint red freckles on her cheeks, and was tough and capable. She could at all times hold her own amongst the café's male dominated clientele, but when need be she could also be a charmer. These attributes served her well, both at the Sheriff's Department and at the café. She was proficient enough to assume kitchen duties when needed, but her forte and meal ticket was serving spirits, an occupation that could yield nice gratuities.

The café featured a sizable dining area, with booths along the walls and numerous tables with gold-speckled, white Formica tops filling the middle. The highlight of the room was a large picture window, through which patrons could see portions of the scenic golf course, with the eighteenth fairway and green front and center. Adding to eye appeal were the snowy peaks of the Gallatin Mountains showing strong and tall in the background. Directly across the room from the window was a door opening, giving customers passing by a view of the kitchen. Similar to that found in old Pullman train cars, this kitchen featured a stainless steel stove, grill, griddle, counter top, refrigerator, freezer, wet bar and sink. Wooden shelves were fastened to the walls, and atop some sat condiments and seasonings, while others featured a wide array of liquors, liqueurs and mixers.

As a member of the golf club for decades, Ben Digby had fond memories of the café and the countless times that friends had gathered there to exchange stories and for fellowship. In the earlier years, the golf club regularly teemed with members, including those that no longer played golf, but refused to abandon their communal connections. They frequented the café, alone or sometimes with their friends or families to dine and take in the enduring scenery. These club denizens once represented a community within a community, comprised of those with deep roots in the region, each sharing a reverence for its ethos, history and culture.

As this old guard dwindled, Bozeman experienced a largely unwelcome transition, with folks arriving there from various parts of the country, whose only stake in the area was money and commerce. The locals had early on labeled them as, *outsiders* or *newcomers*, they were generally regarded as petulant, and lacking the civility and decorum that historically characterized the community.

The majority of those migrating to Bozeman did so at the behest of their employers, primarily national or multinational corporations, specializing in the retail and service sectors. These companies transplanted their key management level personnel to Bozeman, with a mission to compete against the established local businesses. To the chagrin of Ben, and many of his contemporaries, a growing number of these newcomers joined Lone Wolf as members, entitling each to all of the club's privileges and amenities, including access to the café. Some regarded this change as progress, but the older folks saw it differently, and suppressing their sentiments proved a constant challenge.

This clash of cultures was especially difficult for Cookie, who over time had arrived at the realization that the newcomers represented more and more of the revenues of the Café. Though Cookie was a large-framed, barrel-chested man, weighing in excess of 250 pounds, he was an amiable fellow who was hard to push to anger. This proved to be an asset, considering that he, more than most any other established Bozeman resident, had to endure the conduct of the outsiders. On this afternoon, Cookie was dressed as he was every day, in thick-soled black work shoes, sturdy black denim pants, and a white chef's shirt with offset, tarnished brass buttons on the chest. Cookie kept several such shirts in his wardrobe rotation, though each were threadbare and mottled with light stains that persevered repeated attempts to bleach them. He capped off his uniform with a white disposable paper hat that concealed a perfectly level, salt-and-pepper crew cut.

The newcomers' patronage of the Lone Wolf café was more a matter of convenience than an interest in the club itself or the game of golf. Two years earlier, a real estate developer opened Kirkaldy Estates, a subdivision situated in the Gallatin Valley. It was an elite community targeting the affluent professional class migrating to Bozeman, and featured large custom-built homes constructed on half-acre lots. The major artery connecting Kirkaldy Estates to downtown Bozeman, brought commuters directly past the entry to the Lone Wolf Country Club. Cookie's café represented one of the only eateries on that route and more importantly, the only one offering a full bar. Some of the newcomers grabbed breakfast there on the way into town or occasionally chose the café for lunch, but for many the café had emerged as their preferred watering hole.

When Ben entered the café on this evening, he noticed the presence of a number of newcomers, including a group sitting around three tables, haphazardly strung together in the center of the room. They were drinking cocktails and beer, and talking boisterously, and as Ben walked past their table, he overheard one of the men say under his breath, "Hey, guys check out those pants—I think they're corduroy."

The speaker was Clive Jacklin, and if there was a ringleader for newcomers, it was he. Unbeknownst to Ben, Jacklin ran the local branch of Accel Bank, an out-of-state financial concern that was among the newer additions to Bozeman's business community. Accel Bank leased space in the Pitz-Smart department store, a major nationwide retailer that also represented Accel's principle depositor. Considering the foot traffic and visibility afforded by being located in the popular discount department store, Accel soon had other Bozeman area banks and credit unions reeling, despite negative press reports describing their high interest rates and a predatory approach to competition and lending

Ben glanced toward Jacklin's table, but opted to ignore the commentary on his outer layers, which also included a well-worn sweater above his corduroys, and below them were his weathered, black golf spikes, which he had repaired many times over many years. By contrast, these newcomers sported designer casual wear, with pressed slacks and colorful golf shirts, and two of them stylishly draped heavy cashmere sweaters about their shoulders.

"So what'll it be Ben?" Cookie asked cheerfully as he spied his friend approaching.

"Hot chocolate, please."

"I heard you talking to Chuck and thought you would, so I already have some heating for you," Cookie said. He carefully poured a cupful from a simmering pot on the stove, and then added a generous splash of half-and-half, just as Ben liked it. "How was it out there?"

"Very cold and very windy," Ben said.

"I bet," Cookie, said as he handed Ben the thick, brown ceramic mug filled close to the rim. Ben lifted the cup to his wind-chapped face and blew a couple of precautionary breaths across the brown frothy surface, before venturing a sip. The drink was hot, but with the addition of the half-and-half, it was not so much so as to burn his tongue, and it delivered a soothing warmth to his throat as he swallowed.

"How'd you know I would want the hot chocolate?" Ben asked.

"It's black coffee when you go out on the course and also when you arrive back—unless the temperature is below forty degrees, and then it's hot chocolate."

"I guess I'm pretty predictable," Ben said, as he took a seat at a table, and enjoyed another sip from the mug.

"I've just come to know you well, after all these years," Cookie said joining Ben at his table, "so, how does it taste?"

"Perfect, Cookie, thank you."

"Are sure you don't want to try an espresso or a latte next time?"

"A what?" Ben asked curiously.

"I can now fix you an espresso or a latte—if you prefer," Cookie explained.

"The last time I heard of anything like that was in Paris during the war," Ben said, "are you really making 'em?"

"Darn right! That's what the new guys want, and this thing makes them," Cookie said, directing Ben's attention behind him, and to the large chrome dispenser sitting on a table against the wall.

"I noticed that thing sittin' over there, but just thought it was a fancy coffee urn," Ben said, "so when did you get that contraption?"

"A while back, but I had it in the kitchen until I could find time to rig it up out here."

"Looks expensive."

"Very expensive, but it's the top of the line," Cookie bragged.

"I've noticed some of the newcomers drinking from those dinky little cups, but I didn't think much about it."

"That's the way you serve some of the drinks this thing makes," Cookie explained, and lifted one of the small cups from the side table, set it in front of Ben, and leaned close to him and whispered, "Do you know that I charge those knuckle heads two dollars and fifty cents a pop for that this size cup?"

Ben recoiled, as if he had heard a gunshot, and stared down at the cup incredulously. "You gotta be kiddin' me!"

"No, that small one there is what they call a demitasse, but some of the drinks this thing makes are larger, and they're a buck more."

"Three-fifty, huh?" Ben asked.

"Yes, and they're glad to pay it, too. One of those dudes from California said that the joint he goes to out there would charge double what I do. And if you think that's high, you ought to see what I charge for those cocktails their tippin' back," Cookie said.

Ben shook his head in disbelief, and then leaned down to tie his left shoelace.

"Check out those shoes," Clive Jacklin said to his coterie, but loud enough to for Ben and Cookie to hear.

Clive's friend and colleague, Billy Auchterlonie, glanced over in Ben's direction and added, "Hell, those things should be in the Smithsonian."

"Don't engage them, Ben," Cookie said under his breath. "Just take 'em with a grain of salt."

Ben nodded, rose from the table and said, "Thanks for the delicious drink."

"No problem, my friend."

Ben took another sip from the mug, poured the remainder into his thermos, and said, "I'm pleased to know I can buy three more for the price of one of those little ol' dinky drinks."

"I don't blame you for leaving, though," Cookie said as he walked him to the door. "I'm sorry that they—"

"Don't worry about it. It's not your fault, plus I'm beat from playin' twenty-seven."

"You know that the golf's about over for this year?"

"That's what Chuck said, we're getting a pretty big one tomorrow, huh?" Ben asked.

"Yeah, but look on the bright side," Cookie whispered, glancing at the table of reveling outsiders, "maybe less of them will be coming up here."

"Don't bet on it. After all, it's not golf that most of them come here for."

"That's true, plus I don't think these guys are fond of the cold weather, either," Cookie said.

"Apparently, just look at their clothing. They must just go from one climate-controlled environment to another, and they don't wear thermals or even try to properly layer. If they got out on the course on a day like this—dressed like that—they'd get frost nip, frostbite or worse, before they reached the second tee."

Ben reached to open the exit door, but stopped when Clive Jacklin asked sarcastically, "Hey, old man, did you break the course record today?"

Ben turned and replied, "No, the only thing I broke today was a taillight on one of those foreign cars out the parking lot, when I accidently reversed my golf cart into it."

The table of newcomers looked at each other with alarm, simultaneously rose and scurried past Ben and though the exit door, each anxious to see which one of them was the victim. Ben winked at Cookie as he followed the outsiders to the parking lot and hopped into his 1971 olive green, Chevrolet pickup truck. As he drove out of the parking lot, Ben grinned broadly at the sight of each of the shivering newcomers surveying their snow-dusted imports for nonexistent damage.

The Second Hole

"*I* was worried about you, Benjamin," Emily said, as her beleaguered husband walked through the front door of their home and began removing his layers in the entryway. "Why'd you stay out there so long—it's snowing you know!"

"So I've noticed," Ben, teased as he dusted the white flakes from his old quilted jacket. He then removed his sweater, and hung it and the jacket in the entryway closet, before walking to their living room.

The love of Ben's life was born Emily Anne Vardon to a career carpenter and an elementary school teacher. The two were high school sweethearts and they married in 1943 during Ben's two-week furlough from the European Theater of Operations. After receiving a bachelor's degree, Emily followed her mother's example, by teaching English in the Bozeman public school system, a position she held for twenty-eight years. The couple had no children, and after her retirement from the district, Emily immersed herself in civic activities. She focused on fundraising for various causes, including the local VFW post, where Ben was a long-time member, the Methodist church and the PTA. In her spare time, she wrote sonnets and poetry, keeping them all in boxes, rarely sharing them with anyone beyond Ben. She was a thin woman with long undyed graying hair, and she had a kind face featuring soft, silky skin and endearing light-blue eyes. She looked remarkably similar to the way she did when they first met, except for subtle changes and a few facial lines, brought on by the passage of time.

"Look at your hands," Emily said, staring at Ben's chapped and scaly skin.

"They're fine," Ben responded dismissively, seeking refuge in his old leather recliner.

"Ben, your hands look as bad as the arms on that beat up old chair," she said, pointing to the recliner's cracked leather that offered glimpses of the hardened and crumbling yellow foam cushioning underneath.

"Really Em, I'm fine."

"I don't think so—I'll get the lotion."

He sat up straight. "*Please* don't do that!"

"Why? Look at what golfing in that frigid air has done to your already frail skin."

"Em, I wear gloves on both hands to play at this time of year," Ben defended.

"What kind of gloves, those thin, flimsy ones with the pinholes in them? Do you really think they protect you from this kind of weather?"

"They're thin, but don't have the holes like the summer gloves do, and between shots I put my hands in my jacket pockets."

"I'm surprised you don't have frostbite," Emily said.

"You can't wear mittens or leather work gloves and expect to grip the club."

"You shouldn't have been out there at all in weather like this—I'm gonna to get the lotion."

"Hang on now!" Ben pleaded. "I don't want you to do that."

"Why not? You obviously need something on that skin, and my lotion will help."

"Your lotion makes my skin feel ... well ... slimy."

"That's how you know when it's working," she countered.

"It makes my skin crawl and it stinks too."

"I've heard you say many times, that you like the smell of my lotion when I use it."

"It smells good on you—it stinks on me," Ben said.

"Fine, go ahead and live with those alligator hands. The bottom line is, what you see out there is not the kind of weather a man your age, or any other age for that matter, should golf in."

"Calm down old woman," Ben said, relaxing at having repelled the lotion threat, "one more day of golf, and I'm all yours for the winter."

"One more day?" she asked and Ben nodded. "Oh, I don't think so! They should've closed that place down weeks ago," Emily argued, while wiping her hands on a dishtowel. "I swear, as God as my witness, they keep that course open longer and longer every year. My theory is that they're trying to kill off all of you old heads, in order to make room for that younger and wealthier crowd."

"That's the plan, huh?" Ben asked.

"Sure, and those your age that manage to elude the icy hand of death out on that golf course, will get their comeuppance in the form of a heart attack, stroke or some form of diabetes from all of that terrible food up there!"

"Are you referring to Cookie's grub?"

"I like Carl very much, and you know that, but his food is deadly I tell ya, what with fatty breakfast sausage, biscuits, cream gravy and hash browns."

"You just covered the four food groups," Ben said.

"Excuse me?"

"The four food groups, meat, bread, dairy and vegetable," Ben said, counting them off on his chapped fingers.

"That's a tortured interpretation, don't you think?

"Well, I just—"

"Under that logic, fried okra, onion rings and potato chips would be a vegetarian diet."

"Well, what do you know, I could actually become one of those after all."

"Might as well, I'm sure that's not much worse than what Mr. Harrington feeds you down at the cafe."

"You really think Cookie's a part of the conspiracy to wipe out us old guys?"

"Maybe not consciously, but that's going to be the end result," Emily insisted.

"But the rich newcomers eat there too."

"I know, but there's a latency for these things, and they're only at the beginning of their own personal poisoning. Their more immediate doom there just might be the demon alcohol, I've heard that those newcomers spend like drunken sailors up there at Carl's place."

"I've known plenty of drunken sailors and comparing them to the newcomers is insulting to the drunken sailors," Ben said.

"You know what I'm talking about," Emily replied. "I hear they saunter up there each evening and toss back the hooch for hours on end."

"How'd you hear about such a thing?"

"Katrina Daly—for one. The other day I was at the beauty shop, and Kat told us girls that the newcomers routinely run up over thirty dollar bar tabs—each!"

"Really?" Ben asked.

"That's what she said, and Doris Price also said it was true."

"I can understand how Kat could attest to that, but how in the world would Doris know anything about it?" Ben asked.

Emily pondered. "That's a good question, you don't think she's been ... you know ..."

"Do you actually think Doris Price is tipping back a few at Cookie's place?" Ben asked dubiously. "Granted I'm not there much in the evenings, but I've never seen or heard of her, or any other woman, for that matter, drinkin' up there."

Emily dismissed the notion, saying, "Oh, it couldn't be, after all, Doris is Southern Baptist."

"Em, do you know why if you're going to take a Baptist fishing, you always take a minimum of two of them?"

Sensing a groaner coming, Emily rolled her eyes. "I give, why?"

"So you can go off in the woods to pee and no one will drink your beer!"

"That's awful," Emily said as she popped his shoulder with the dishtowel. "But Kat raises a good point though, I guess the newcomers do bring a lot of money into the community."

"Perhaps, but wouldn't we all be better off without the newcomers and their money?" Ben lamented. "Take the Pitz-Smart store for example, is our community better off with those guys setting up shop here?"

"Please tell me you're not going to start in on them. There are a lot of other companies that have brought businesses here besides Mr. Pitzmyre," Emily said, referring to the Pitz-Smart department store chain founder and CEO.

"I know, but I just use them as an example because—"

"Of your resentment?" Emily finished and Ben hung his head. She smiled lovingly at him, and added, "I'm not fond of their kind either. They are haughty and they drive those little sports cars like maniacs, and they act like they own the place, but all I'm saying is that their presence here hasn't been all bad."

"It was bad enough for us," he said, while feeling around the crevices of his recliner cushion for the remote control, "I wonder if there's a football game on."

"My lord, isn't there always one on this time of year?"

"No, not always—unfortunately. Say, what's the heater set on?" Ben asked.

Emily darted her eyes back and forth. "Why do you ask?"

"Because I'm freezing in here, that's why."

"It's on sixty-nine," she said.

Ben glanced up to her. "No wonder I'm not warming up in here."

"Have you seen the cost of heating oil?"

Ben sensed from her tone that he had struck a nerve and asked contritely, "No ... is it high?"

"*Very* high. It started after Labor Day, when I noticed that the rate was higher than last year, and it's already gone up three times since."

"I see," Ben said. "But what's the price of a doctor's appointment, if I catch cold just sitting in my own home?"

"Benjamin—Taylor—Digby!" Emily responded, making Ben wince at his own poor choice of words. "How dare you complain about contracting *any* climate-related illness in here, when you went out *there* and played eighteen holes in that weather," she said, pointing out the window toward the flailing icy tree limbs of the aspens in their backyard.

"Twenty-seven."

"Excuse me?"

"Holes, I played twenty-seven," Ben confessed, and Emily gasped. "But look, the season's almost over and I just—"

"Please tell me you're not seriously thinking about playing again. The weather out there is terrible now, and the news says that it's getting *much* worse tomorrow."

Considering his heating oil faux pas, Ben knew that he needed to regroup, and choose his words carefully if he were to have any chance of squeezing in the one last round. "I heard about that storm too dear, but I also know that it won't get bad until mid to late morning. So, if I get out there early, I can finish before it hits. It's the last round Em, and then I'm all yours for the *whole* winter." Emily did not deny him out of hand, and seemed to consider the request, providing Ben a measure of optimism, and he tried to close the sale. "Don't deprive me of this one final chance to play and to bid farewell to the course for the next six months."

"You should have bid farewell today."

"Come on Em, it's just one more round?" Ben pleaded like a child at a park wanting one more trip down the slide at sunset.

Emily took a seat on the worn right arm of Ben's recliner. "I can't talk you out of this foolishness, can I?" she asked rhetorically. "Ben, you're going to die out there someday, but you go ahead and risk your life. After all, if you don't care about your own health and well-being, then why should I?"

"I'll be careful."

"Fine—I want you out early and back early, and no twenty-seven holes, you hear!"

"Yes dear," Ben said and returned to searching for the remote control.

Emily acquiesced in part, because she was well aware that in a matter of hours, Ben would have to suspend his golfing until spring, but she also desperately wanted Ben diverted from the topic of Pitz-Smart and the newcomers.

"Sorry to nag, but it's only because I love you, Benjamin Digby," Emily said, and Ben nodded.

Rarely did she refer to him as Benjamin, limiting the use of his full first name to chastisement for his occasional off-color language or an audible belch—or worse. At other times, she used the long form out of genuine concern, or sentimentality and this reference represented the latter. Emily remained perched next to him and rubbed his back while Ben, having located the remote control, sat scanning through the channels, searching for a football broadcast. He managed to locate one, and was pleased, but just as he did the network cut to a commercial break.

"Darn it!" he said, turning down the volume on an ad featuring men's fashions offered by a new out-of-state haberdasher. "Look at that—I bet that's where they shop."

"Who?" Emily asked.

"The outsiders, that's who. Based on their appearance at the club, I'm sure they get their clothing from some fancy schmancy place like that. You ought to see 'em in those flashy outfits, struttin' around the club and driving around in those damn European ..."

"Benjamin!"

"Sorry! Darn European cars—including German models—how soon we forget."

"The war ended over fifty years ago," Emily said and Ben glanced up to her, nodded and returned his attention to the television. "But I agree that they *do* like to dress up," she conceded.

"Yes they do. Slick, shiny designer slacks, silk shirts, and some even wear cashmere sweaters and argyle socks!"

"They dress that way to play golf?"

"That's just it. They pay dues and come up there most every day, but they rarely actually step out on the course, especially this time of year."

"Oh, so they're flashy *and* wise," she teased. "But I guess that's the way they dress in New York and California, and I'm sure they think the residents here don't dress right either."

"Perhaps you're right, considering that they made fun of my outfit today."

"Oh? Was it that raggedy duck down jacket you insist on wearing?"

"No, they haven't made fun of that—at least not that I know of."

"What was it then?" she asked.

He glanced up to her and said, "My corduroys."

"Oh, really?" Emily said, feigning dismay.

"I see ... you don't disagree with them, do you?"

"Please don't take this the wrong way, but those are a little ... let's say ..."

"Out of style?" Ben interjected.

"I was going to say dated, but yes."

"Fine, I'm dated then, but I like what I like, and I wear what I want to wear. I find corduroys to be comfortable, warm and durable."

"They're certainly durable all right," Emily said, knowing how long Ben had owned this particular pair.

Ben frowned. "I would've thought you'd favor durable. After all, durable means longevity, and longevity saves money."

"Honey, you're turning red and need to calm down," she said soothingly, and pulling his head over to her side.

"I'm sorry, Em—I know you're right. I'm old fashioned and just don't take to change well."

"The heck you say," Emily said facetiously, drawing a belly laugh from Ben. "But dear, things *do* change, and I don't like most of it any more than you do, but it's our reality. Do you think I like standing in those long lines at Pitz-Smart just to buy a pound of ground beef or a pike fillet?" she said and immediately regretted it.

"You're shopping at Pitz-Smart?" Ben asked and she nodded. "Oh no ... I don't understand. When did you quit buying meat at Whitcombe's?"

"I'm sorry I brought it up," she said, "just enjoy your football game."

"I'm entitled to know why you're not tradin' at Whitcombe's," Ben demanded.

She took a deep breath, exhaled and explained, "Whitcombe's went out of business six weeks ago. I didn't tell you right away, because I knew you'd be upset."

Ben instantly empathized with the family-owned meat market, and said, "What's Dan and Sandy going to do? They're young, and they've got two kids approaching college age."

"I guess you should hear this from me, and not find out on your own," Emily said. "Dan Whitcombe is cutting meat up at Pitz-Smart and Sandy is a cashier there."

Ben's expression turned to one of deep despair. "Why would they do that?"

"You said it yourself. They have a long way to retirement and two teenagers. At least when this happened to you—"

"Us," he corrected.

"When this happened to us, you were where you could retire."

"Not the way we planned," Ben lamented.

"I'm fully aware of that," Emily said, "but you retired none the less, and I'm glad you're having a chance to do something beyond working yourself to death. I mean how many men have you known, that that toiled for decades only to die suddenly without ever enjoying the fruits of that labor?"

"We've known several, unfortunately."

"Right, and how many times, over the years, did you tell me that you dreamed of a time when the only decision you needed to make each day was *scrambled or fried—walk or ride*?"

"I see where you're comin' from, but retirement should be voluntary and not compulsory," Ben said. "It wasn't time, and I hadn't got things to where I wanted them to be."

"We live *very* well," Emily said.

"Not well enough to avoid frettin' over heating oil prices."

"Stop it, will ya!" Emily said playfully. "We're fine."

"Poor Dan," Ben said, shaking his head. "He was the third generation in that meat market."

"Fourth," Emily said.

"Even worse," Ben sighed. "Say, is shopping at Pitz-Smart the reason that the toilet tissue seems so thin?"

"I suppose so."

"Everything's just so upside down these days," Ben said.

"I know, but if you'll recall, our parents felt the same way about our generation."

"What do you mean?" Ben asked.

"Don't you recall their reaction to leather jackets, ducktails, pitchin' woo and let's not forget the dreaded rock and roll."

"You're right," Ben said, as fond memories filled his mind. "Man, my dad was at the end of his rope with it all. He was convinced that Elvis was the anti-Christ, and Jerry Lee Lewis was his arch angel."

Emily laughed. "You see, it's just change."

"I guess," Ben conceded, "but I don't have to like it."

"It's not all bad though," Emily said. "It's easy to reflect on the things from the past that make us nostalgic, but there were many things that weren't so good back then, and things that are much better now."

"How do you figure?"

"Remember polio and tuberculosis? Then there were the wood burning cook stoves, and when we were kids, we chilled our food with a block of ice in a wooden box. We now have refrigerators, microwave ovens and over thirty-five channels on the TV instead of three. All I'm saying what's happening today is not the end of the world."

"It is for business owners like the Whitcombe's."

"They're still plying their trade, but it's just at a different location," Emily countered.

"It's not the same as running your own business," Ben said. "These local owners are our friends and neighbors, and now they've surrendered to Pitz-Smart."

"I know well how you feel about them sweetheart," Emily responded, desperate to console him, "but the prices are really good there, and low prices really help those who are struggling, whether it's large families or seniors on fixed incomes or college students. What's more they create jobs too and look what they do for the seniors?"

"I've heard about that too. I'm told they call them *hosts* and they make 'em wear those red T-shirts and hand out the shopping carts and fliers and such—I think it's demeaning."

"Ben, I agree with you on many of your complaints—I truly do. But you've anguished over this for years now, and may I remind you, that we had a deal to put this Pitz-Smart stuff behind us."

"You're right ... and I'm sorry," Ben conceded and noticed the game back on the screen. "But if only I could've just held on long enough to get us down to El Dorado."

"Not that too!" Emily groaned.

"I can't help it—El Dorado was our future."

"Ben my dear, mentioning El Dorado was *also* a part of our agreement."

El Dorado was a fledgling Arizona real estate development when they discovered it in 1982, while attending a convention of Ben's military comrades at a resort hotel near Scottsdale. While on this junket, sales people offered the convention attendees tickets to a nearby arboretum in exchange for taking a tour of the property. They had a free afternoon one day and, accepted the offer, and took the tour. Their plan was to endure the presentation, only for the tickets, but the beauty of this subdivision in the Sonoran Desert struck them equally.

Built around a picturesque golf course, the El Dorado homes featured Spanish inspired designs, with limestone veneers, orange cement roofing tiles and vibrant green lawns. The golf course of the same name, featured vibrant, rolling and perfectly manicured fairways, each bordered by vast expanses of bright white desert sands, dotted with sego palms and large saguaro cacti. Emily was drawn to the warm, dry climate and Ben fancied the concept of winter long access to golf.

The couple toured four model homes and afterward, the resort facilities, and while in the gift shop at the latter, Emily thumbed through brochures, while Ben selected a picture post card from a wire rack. He gazed at the card, which provided an aerial view of El Dorado's golf course and the surrounding subdivision, and quickly purchased it. He folded the card, scenic photo to the inside to protect it, and tucked it in his billfold. The couple formulated a plan whereby they would purchase a home there, and spend their summers in Bozeman and winters at El Dorado. Ben made Emily a solemn pledge that day to work hard, and save even harder, in order for them to have a second home in this self-proclaimed *Eden in the Southwest*. When they returned to Bozeman, Ben continued his practice of working long hours during the week, and even longer on Saturdays, with his eyes unblinkingly on the prize. When Ben felt tired or discouraged, he would remove the post card, gaze at the photo and it served to encourage him to work longer and harder.

"So you forgive me?" Ben asked.

"For us not getting us a place at El Dorado?" she asked and Ben nodded. "There's nothing to forgive, and besides, Montana is our home."

"What about the weather?" Ben asked. "Look at the conditions out there and how it affects your arthritis, in contrast today's paper said the high in Scottsdale was seventy-four."

"Ben, why are you checking weather reports for Arizona, for goodness sake?"

"I, uh … I just … happened to notice it."

"What was it yesterday?"

"Seventy-six," he blurted before thinking and Emily shook her head. "Look—I just like to know, that's all!" Ben defended, then pointed his nose up and sniffed several times. "Say, what's that I smell?"

"It was going to be a surprise, but I made you some Texas red," Emily said and turned toward the kitchen.

"Chili!" Ben said, perking up. "Why didn't you tell me about that when I came in?"

Emily stopped and asked, "Why?"

"If I'd known that, I wouldn't have gotten into all that maudlin Pitz-Smart stuff."

After his return from the European Theater in 1945, Ben spent four months at Fort Hood. Emily joined him in Texas for three of those four months, and chili became, and remained, one of Ben's favorite indulgences. For Ben, the mere mention of his favorite dish, coupled with the football broadcast, quickly reversed his somber mood, activated his salivary glands, and brought an immediate sense of serenity. Everything burdening his mind vanished the moment Emily returned and sat a steaming bowl and a handful of crackers on the tray table in front of him.

"Thanks, it looks and smells great! Are you going to have some?"

"Maybe, after I clean up the kitchen, but you go ahead." she said. "Since you can't be dissuaded about tomorrow, when you're done eating, slip off the corduroys. I'll get them and your other clothes in the wash, then in the dryer before I go to bed, so they'll be ready for you in the morning."

When the last second of the football game clock ticked off, Emily was asleep in their bed and Ben was dozing in his easy chair. He rose and turned off the television, crept lightly into the bedroom, and prepared himself for bed. He then set the alarm for 5:45 a.m., switched off the nightstand lamp, then crawled between the cool sheets and covered himself with a heavy blanket. He eased over toward Emily in a fetal position, until his body warmed the sheets enough so that he could slowly straighten out his arms and legs, and then closed his eyes.

The Third Hole

*B*en woke the next morning before the alarm, and disarmed it before it pierced the quiet and roused his slumbering Emily. Anticipating a challengingly cold day, he layered his clothing carefully, starting with a full-length set of thick thermal underwear. He then visited the clothes dryer, added his heavy sweater, and his clean brown corduroys over the thermals. He next stepped over to the front closet, and slipped into his old duck-down jacket. For his neck and face, he opted for his thickest plaid scarf, and for his head, he selected his wool-lined corduroy hat with insulated flaps to protect his tender ears. He returned to the bedroom, and sat on his side of the bed pulling his boots over two layers of wool socks, when Emily stirred.

"Are you really going out there today?" she asked in a raspy voice.

"Yes."

"You hear that, don't you?" Emily asked, referring to the clanging wind chimes on their back patio. "It's already starting to blow."

"It's been coming and going, since three," he responded.

"Have you been awake that long?"

"Off and on," he replied, cinching the laces of his boots. "I'll keep a close look out on the conditions, and one way or another, I will be home for lunch."

"You better, Mr. Digby," she said, rolling over and returning her head to her pillow.

Ben grabbed his golf spikes and walked out of their bedroom, through the living room, and toward the front door. He turned on the porch light, and eased his head outside to check the rusty Coca-Cola thermometer hanging next to their doorbell. Squinting, he saw the mercury stood at twenty-six, and knew that it represented close to the high for the day. He switched off the light, glanced upward and took heart when he saw stars from horizon to horizon.

When Ben pulled his truck onto the Lone Wolf parking lot, he still needed his headlights, but the eastern horizon showed a faint orange glow. He looked around the lot and saw Cookie's truck, but also present were a couple of other vehicles he did not recognize. The prospect of other golfers being present concerned him, and he scurried with golf bag, thermos and shoes in hand into the clubhouse looking in all directions for anyone who might threaten to beat him to the first tee. When he entered the café, he relished the smell of coffee brewing and the sound of Cookie's metal spatula clanging on the griddle.

"Good morning!" Ben said.

Cookie poked his head out of the kitchen, and said, "Hey there! So she let you out of the house, huh?"

"Reluctantly. It was touch and go for a while, but she made sure the life insurance was paid up and relented."

Cookie grinned. "How 'bout some coffee?"

"Yes, please. In fact, make it a large for my thermos—I think I'm going to need it," Ben said and began swapping his boots for his golf shoes.

"You're really gonna play?" Cookie asked.

"Yes. There's no other golfers here, are there?" Ben asked.

"Not that I've seen."

"Good," Ben said walking back to the kitchen and placing his boots in the corner. "Is it okay if I leave these here for now?"

"Sure thing," Cookie said, and handed Ben his tall cup of coffee.

"Just be careful out there, it's already windy and according to the weather service, it's going to get *real* nasty *real* quick. This thing is speeding straight down from Alberta, and according to the news you've got a couple of hours—tops."

"That should be enough. Say, it looks like you've got a slow leak over there," Ben said, observing water dripping from the kitchen faucet, into the stainless steel sink.

"Yeah, I know. Day before yesterday, I got Kat to look after things here and dashed over to that Pitz-Smart store to get a washer and seat for it. I looked all over that place, but never found where they kept them. I searched every aisle in their so-called *hardware department* for someone to help me, but I couldn't find soul."

"There's no sales people in their hardware department?" Ben asked.

"There's no sales people period. They have employees that stock shelves and such, and if you corner one, they're not likely to know a faucet seat from the county seat. That's what I miss about your store, I could go there, and even if you weren't around, someone in short order could find exactly what I needed, and the whole visit wouldn't take more than a few minutes."

"But you'd pay more for parts in my store, wouldn't you? I mean, that's what I've always been told."

"Who knows, since it turns out Pitz-Smart don't stock seats and washers?"

"They have a hardware department that doesn't carry faucet parts?" Ben asked dubiously.

"That's right. They reluctantly offered to order them for me, but said it would take as much as three weeks to arrive."

"Did you order them?" Ben asked, while pulling on his golf gloves.

"Naw, by that point I was frustrated and running late getting back up here to prep for lunch, so I just left," Cookie said. "Want me to fix you something to eat before you head out?"

"Yes, I think a sausage biscuit will do the trick!"

"Biscuits aren't ready yet, is toast okay?"

"Fine, but make it quick, please," Ben said. "Listen—as far as the faucet is concerned, I still have a good supply of parts. I'll get the model number off it and bring you what I have next time I come in."

"You don't have to do all that."

"I want to," Ben said, wiping the chrome base of the drippy faucet with his sleeve to reveal the brand and model number. He wrote the information on the corner of a paper sack lying next to the sink, tore it off and placed it in his wallet. "I should have these, Cookie."

"I appreciate that, but won't it be a long while before you get to come back up here?"

"I'll get a kitchen pass every once in a while, plus this'll give me a good excuse to return."

"That's really nice of you, Ben," Cookie said turning a thick slice of pork sausage on the griddle.

"It's not a problem, after all I have no need for the parts at this point, but I better get goin' if I'm gonna have a chance of finishing. Say, wrap that sandwich up when it's ready, put it in a sack, and I'll be back in a minute."

"You got it, pal."

Heading into the pro shop, Ben spotted Chuck Duval coming out of the stock room, and said, "Good morning, Chuck."

"Hi, Mr. Digby. I kinda thought I'd see you here this morning."

"I want go ahead and tee off now if that's okay," Ben asked.

"It's still pretty dark," Chuck, said pointing out the window where the overnight spot light still illuminated the eighteenth green.

"I know, but can I go anyway?"

"Sure, go anytime you want," Chuck said.

Ben thanked him, and walked around the counter and rummaged through the bucket of the used golf balls in the oak showcase, searching for suitable candidates. Brand was a factor, but minimally so, as he usually selected balls that were reasonably round, fairly clean and free of dents or nicks on their dimpled coverings.

"Here Chuck, I'll take these," Ben said, placing six balls on the counter and handing him a twenty dollar bill.

"Why used ones, Mr. Digby? We're having an end-of-season sale on Titleist and Top-Flite."

"These are fine and still cheaper, and after all some of 'em were probably once mine anyhow."

The young man snickered, put the bill in the register and retrieved Ben's change. "Seventeen dollars," Chuck said, extending his hand holding a ten, a five and two ones.

"Keep it, young man. That might just be enough to buy you a meal at that fancy ski resort you're going to," Ben said.

Chuck stared wide-eyed at the bills. "Are you sure, Mr. Digby?"

"Positive. You do fine work here son, and I hope to see you next year when the course re-opens."

"Thank you *very* much!" Chuck gushed. "I am definitely coming back."

Ben nodded his approval, and asked, "Say, I saw a couple of cars in the lot, is there anyone else here for golf?"

"Yes sir. There's a foursome checked in and they're down at the cart barn trying to stay warm until the sun comes up."

This alarmed Ben and he walked to the window and saw four bundled up old-timers standing around a propane heater in the corrugated-sheet metal structure. Two of the men were holding drivers and taking practice swings, and he sensed he needed to act fast, and noticed two empty golf carts parked just outside of the pro shop door.

"Can I take one of those?" Ben asked, pointing.

"Sure thing," Chuck responded, "they both have plenty of juice."

Ben scampered back toward the café, and Cookie met him in the doorway with the paper bag in hand. "Here you go," Cookie said, and Ben took the sack and noticed that two newcomers had arrived and were sitting in separate booths, and one was tapping his finger impatiently on the tabletop and glaring at Cookie.

"Thanks Cookie, it smells great," Ben, said then saw that three more patrons were nearing the door from the parking lot. Though Ben sensed from their attire that their only interest was breakfast, he could not risk it, and was even more anxious to get started.

"Don't let this storm sneak up on you Ben," Cookie said.

"I won't," Ben said, and started back toward the pro shop, but stopped when he overheard the impatient newcomer ask, "Hey, can I get a little service over here?"

"Just a minute, buddy," Cookie responded and he turned back to Ben. "If I didn't need this café for my retirement, I'd give him the what-for."

"Easy, Cookie," Ben, warned, "Don't rouse the MPs."

Cookie smiled and nodded, and Ben threw the strap of his golf bag over his shoulder, then with his breakfast sack and thermos in one hand, he used his free hand to throw his long scarf around the front of his neck, over his left shoulder and back around again. He marched out the pro shop door and toward the two electric carts, and seeing that both had keys and operable plastic wind guards, he secured his golf bag on the back of the closer of the two. He took the driver's seat and pointed the cart down the path that led to the first tee, just as the dusk to dawn light over the eighteenth green switched off.

As he drove, he glanced down the slope to the cart barn, and confirmed that the four men were still biding their time, but as he drove passed the barn, he again glanced in that direction when he heard a loud clanging sound. Ben saw that the wind was now lifting and dropping a loose corrugated panel on the roof of the barn, and surmised that it must have been occurring for a while, since the old-timers were ignoring it. Ben continued unabated, until he skidded to a stop at the first hole. He exited the cart with driver, ball and tee in hand, and rushed up the slope to the tee box. He quickly teed his ball and wasted no time in driving it smartly down the dimly lit fairway, then jumped back in his cart, accelerated down the cart path, and started on his breakfast as he drove.

For the first few holes, the rising sun provided sufficient light and a modicum of warmth, but as Ben progressed on the front nine, the morning sun ceded to a foreboding line of gray clouds delivering gusty northeasterly winds and falling temperatures. Despite the declining conditions, Ben played exceptionally well and at better than desired pace, but the temperature continued to drop, the grey clouds turned darker and the strength of the wind gusts steadily rose.

When Ben completed the ninth hole, and was making the turn toward the tenth, he noticed numerous empty carts now parked near the clubhouse and that several golfers were steering theirs off the course to join the others. *Do they know something I don't know?* Ben asked himself, while sailing past the clubhouse and toward the tenth hole. He parked at the tee, took two sips of coffee from the thermos before commencing the back nine with another solid drive. The ominous clouds were pitch black and seemed to follow him down the path, and a light but steady snowfall commenced.

When Ben finished the twelfth, he was unaware that he represented the lone golfer remaining on the course, and by the time he reached the fifteenth, the weather worsened. The accumulations of ice in the treetops were now straining the boughs and branches and snow was now beginning to stick on portions of the fairways and the edges of the greens. He estimated that the wind gusts were topping twenty miles per hour, and realized he was playing on borrowed time. As he marked his score for the sixteenth hole, the wind now blew constant and hard, and the velocity was enough that he had difficulty balancing himself over the ball and it forced him to take more time than he desired to execute each shot. Despite the declining conditions, Ben continued to post remarkable scores and he pressed on.

Back at the club café, the golfers that had abandoned their rounds exchanged accounts of what they experienced and how far each had made it, before surrendering. As the breakfast rush subsided, Cookie and Chuck walked out onto the covered deck overlooking the golf course. Cookie had curtailed his smoking to three to four cigarettes per day and coveted most, the post-breakfast smoke. With their heavy coats on and the building shielding them from the wind, it was tolerable on the deck, but more snow was falling, making them wonder about Ben.

"I'm gettin' concerned," Cookie said, cupping his left hand around the cigarette dangling from his lips. He lit up, took a long drag, and blew the smoke upward and away from Chuck. "Ben's still out there and this weather ain't gettin' any better."

"Yeah, playing eighteen by himself on a normal day, he'd be through by now," Chuck said.

"You're right, but this certainly ain't no normal day," Cookie said, as the wind suddenly shifted directions and a snow-laden gust knocked each man off balance and extinguished Cookie's cigarette.

They instinctively hustled back inside, and Chuck spoke for both of them saying, "Gosh, it's just terrible out there! Do you think Mr. Digby finished or quit and just headed straight home?"

"Maybe," Cookie said, "but he always turns in his card."

"He wouldn't if he didn't finish, though."

"Good point," Cookie said and walked to the pro shop door, and peered through the window toward the parking lot. He spotted Ben's partially snow covered truck and said anxiously, "He's still out there!"

"Should I go look for him?" Chuck asked following Cookie into the café.

"That's not a bad idea. I'd do it myself, but Kat's not here yet," Cookie said while glancing out the picture window, and witnessing the wind hurling both ice and snow across the eighteenth fairway. "Can you bundle up quickly and get on out there?"

"Sure, I'll get my layers on, and all I'll need is an insulated hat," Chuck said.

"Want to borrow mine?" Cookie offered pointing toward to his heavily stained Russian trooper's hat hanging on a hat rack.

"Uh ... no thanks, I'll just borrow one off a display mannequin," he said and Cookie followed him back to the pro shop and watched as Chuck selected a new red insulated hat with earflaps.

"I'll keep an eye on the pro shop," Cookie said, "and you be careful out there, you hear?"

"Yes sir," Chuck said, "I'll just take a cart out past the eighteenth green and keep back tracking until I find him."

Once sufficiently clothed, Chuck trotted out the door and took the nearest vacant cart, that was unimpeded by the abandoned ones on and near the cart path. He was making his way through the driving wind, toward the eighteenth, and found that the cart's plastic wind guard provided little protection from the stinging, wind driven, ice and snow, and as he passed the eighteenth green, Chuck flinched when the nighttime floodlight suddenly switched on.

As Chuck neared the eighteenth tee, he saw an outline of a figure and slowed the cart. Through the elements, the apparition revealed itself as a small man, and stopping his cart on the path, Chuck cupped both hands around his mouth and yelled, "Mr. Digby! Is that you?" With his scarf partially covering his face, coupled with the driving wind, Chuck's voice was muffled, and accordingly, he received no response. He exited the cart and walked further toward the tee, and confirmed it was Ben and that he standing with his back turned to him, holding his driver. "Mr. Digby! Are you okay?"

This time Ben heard him, and turned to see Chuck standing with his arms folded in front of him, panting and worried. Ben bent down to tee up his ball with his right hand and motioned Chuck away with his left. He then stood erect over the ball and yelled, "I'm all right, but I have to play the last hole."

"You've gotta come in, sir!" Chuck pleaded as the wind gusted and he raised his arms to his face to fend off the pelting ice.

"You don't understand—I *must* finish!" Ben shouted, as he struggled to position himself for the tee shot. His small frame swayed in the wind, forcing him to spread his feet wider for balance, as he straddled the ball. He started his back swing, just as a sudden gust reeled him and he stumbled backward and to the ground, landing next to a wooden stand that in the summer held an insulated water cooler. Chuck rushed to his aid and pulled him up to his feet, then picked up the tee and ball and handed them to Ben, and he placed them in his pocket.

"Are you hurt?" Chuck asked.

"I don't think so," Ben gasped, then coughed hard, three times.

"Come on Mr. Digby, let's go in! Since your stuff's on your cart, let's take it in and I'll come back and get the other one later."

"I can drive my own cart," Ben said, returning his driver to his golf bag.

"No, let me drive—please," Chuck, insisted and Ben acquiesced.

With Ben seated silently next to him, Chuck slowly maneuvered the cart around his vacant one, by veering onto the icy grass. With rear wheels spinning on the slippery turf, they slowly passed the parked cart, and he maneuvered theirs back onto the concrete path. Anxious to deliver them from what could now be considered a blizzard, Chuck fully depressed the right pedal. However, Ben sensed a calming of the wind and quickly craned his neck out of the cart and stared upward at the treetops. Confirming an easing of the conditions, he reached over and turned the key, bringing the cart to a halt.

"What are you doing?" Chuck yelled in protest.

Ben placed the key in his pocket, and said, "Bear with me son, I think there's an opening to finish."

"Please Mr. Digby, let's go in."

"Just sit tight and let me give it one more try," Ben pleaded, and after retrieving his driver, he struggled to walk back to the tee box, however, as he bent down and teed the ball, the winds returned with a vengeance, and it rocked him. Undaunted, he recovered and steadied himself over the ball, but before he could commence his backswing, it gusted harder, and this time he heard cracking limbs and saw accumulations of ice and fresh snow toppling from nearby treetops to the ground. Included was a large compacted mass that fell along with the thick branch that had been supporting it, and struck the turf between the two men, with a force that they each heard with their covered ears and felt through the soles of their shoes.

Chuck again intervened, "Come back to the cart!"

"Chuck, I only have the one hole left," Ben demanded in a voice that was now weak and barely audible.

"*Please*, Mr. Digby! You're gonna to get us killed!"

Chuck's reference to *us* resonated with Ben, and he realized that more than his own safety was at stake. He stared down the fairway and glanced back to Chuck noting his frightened expression, and relented. He walked wearily back to the cart, then sat silent, winded and weak as they made their way on the cart path, past the illuminated eighteenth green, and up the slope toward the clubhouse.

The Fourth Hole

*S*eeing the approaching cart through the café window, Cookie poured a fresh cup of hot chocolate, sat it on a table and rushed into the pro shop to meet the two men, just as they emerged from the darkness through the door.

"What in the world happened?" Cookie asked as he observed Ben standing breathless, with his eyes clenched shut. Ben tried to speak, but found that he was too winded to utter a word. He next tried to open his eyes to look at Cookie, but found the pro shop's lights were far too bright. "Chuck?" Cookie asked anxious for answers.

The young Duval likewise struggled to catch his breath, but interjected between gasps. "It's just ... awful ... out there ..."

Cookie turned back to Ben and said, "I poured you a cup of hot chocolate, so why don't you come with me into the café and grab a seat?" Ben nodded, and Cookie led his reeling friend by the arm toward the dining area, with Chuck following behind them. Ben coughed several times as they walked, further challenging his already labored breathing, but when they reached the café, and Cookie settled him into a booth, Ben's breathing stabilized and he fully open his eyes. Cookie slid the mug of hot chocolate in front of him, and the café patrons, including those who had much earlier abandoned their rounds, stared on curiously, as Ben unwound his scarf, revealing his red, chapped face, no one uttered a word—not even the outsiders.

By then, Katrina had arrived for her shift, and seeing Ben struggling, she grabbed a clean, dry dishrag. She was particularly fond of Ben and as she handed him the towel, she asked, "Are you okay Mr. D?"

"Yes, and thank you for this," Ben said lifting the rag.

"Sure thing Mr. D, can I get you anything else, sweetie?" she asked. Ben shook his head and applied the rag to his face and then to his duck down jacket, wiping the snowflakes that were now mostly beaded drops.

"Crap," Ben said. "Only one lousy hole left!"

"Were you trying to finish up out there?" Cookie asked.

"Oh yes, he was!" Chuck intervened. "I found him on the eighteenth tee, and the weather was goin' nuts, but even with that, he was *still* trying to tee it up to play, and I practically had to force him off the course!"

Cookie stared curiously at Ben, as several patrons gathered around the booth sporting their own perplexed expressions, and all present, old timers and newcomers alike, wondered what compelled Ben to play on so long past reason.

"Did you try to finish, because it's the last round of the season?" Cookie asked as Ben managed a sip from his cup, then shook his head. "Then what was it? Everyone else got off the course an hour ago."

"Dang it, Chuck!" Ben said. "I left a perfectly good ball and tee down there."

"Even if it's under a foot of snow, I'll try to get 'em when I fetch the other cart," Chuck said.

Ben nodded and lifted his insulated hat from his head and placed it upside down on the Formica tabletop. Despite the frigid temperatures outside, Ben's sparse strands of silver hair were sweaty and clinging to his scalp. Next, he removed both gloves, and eased the numb and tingling fingers of his right hand inside his jacket pocket and retrieved his crumpled, damp scorecard. He sat it on the table and stared at it, but his audience stood wondering what significance it represented. Ben tapped the card with his index left finger and said, "Have a look."

Cookie lifted the card, unfolded it, and pressed it out flat on the table as more patrons rose from their seats to get a glimpse. Cookie looked at Ben, then back down at the card, expecting to see something conspicuous that would explain Ben's foolhardiness, but all he saw was the marked scores of the seventeen holes Ben did complete.

"I don't get it—what's the big deal?" Cookie asked.

"Total 'em up," Ben, replied.

Cookie trained his eyes initially on the scores of the first nine holes and counted under his breath, then said, "Wow, an even par thirty-six on the front?" Cookie asked, and Ben nodded and took another sip from the mug. Cookie made the same mental calculation for the backside, and a wry grin spread across the chef's face.

Clive Jacklin, dressed in a bright red jacket and black leather pants, rose from his table and, broke the silence. "So what's the big damn deal?"

"It's unbelievable!" Cookie said. "An even seventy for seventeen holes? You've never shot like that before in your life, have you?"

"No, not even close," Ben confirmed, while gripping his warm mug with both hands.

"Did you say he shot a seventy with one hole to play?" Jacklin, asked.

"Yes, it's all right here," Cookie, said displaying the card to him.

"It's too bad you didn't get it in, but you weren't going to shoot worth a damn on it in this weather," the smarmy Jacklin asserted.

"What do you mean, Clive?" Cookie asked.

"I think he definitely should've tried to finish, but just look at it out there!" Jacklin said pointing toward the picture window and the near horizontal snow racing across it. "If he had tried to play it, he couldn't have possibly done well!"

Ben shrugged and said, "Maybe or maybe not, but the weather for the first seventeen was no walk in the park, either, and I might add, I could have shot a ten or more on eighteen and been well under my best round."

"You tell him Mr. D," Katrina encouraged as she glared at Jacklin for what she regarded as hassling her friend.

"It's too bad you blew your big chance by quitting," Clive's friend, Billy Auchterlonie said.

"Just one lousy hole away from the best round of your life what a pity," Cookie lamented while shaking his head.

"Yeah, you should've done everything you could to complete it," Auchterlonie added, "I wouldn't allow bad weather to stop me from finishing the last hole of *my* greatest round."

"You don't know what it was like out there!" Chuck intervened. "When I found him on the eighteenth tee, limbs were breaking, and the ice was blowing out of the trees, the fairway was getting covered and you could hardly see the putting surface, even with the dusk to dawn light on. Heck, I don't know how Mr. Digby played any of the back nine in these conditions!"

"Suit yourself, but Billy's right. An old dude like you doesn't get a second chance for something like this," Clive Jacklin said. "If it were me, I'd get right back down there and find a way to play it out."

"The course is closed," Chuck said.

"No, it's not!" Jacklin countered. "He has a right to finish if he wants!"

Stewart Spindler, another outsider who happened to be the manager of the local Pitz-Smart department store, rose from his table and joined the discussion. "Clive has a point. You came in here for refuge due to this rotten snow storm, and that's no different than coming in here or into the cart barn until a thunderstorm passes." Spindler was a pudgy thirty-seven -year-old, with thinning blonde hair that always seemed disheveled. He had a washed out pale face, except for perpetually rosy cheeks, and his blue eyes sat unnaturally close to each other, and his eyelids often blinked rapidly, for no apparent reason.

"I think Stewart's right!" Cookie said. "And like any other round with a weather delay, you have a right to resume when it lets up!"

"The course is closed," Chuck Duval said, "but even if it wasn't, this isn't just any other bad weather day, and it's *not* gonna let up."

"Oh don't be so sure about that Chuck. We've all seen winter storms hit with a vengeance, only to calm some once the brunt passes," Cookie said.

"That's a great point," Billy said, "hell, there's at least another six hours before the sun goes down, and anything can happen between now and then."

"Yeah Ben, you only need a five to ten-minute window to get back down there and finish it," Cookie encouraged.

"Hey, let's see if it's lettin' up some now," Billy said and he and several others rushed to the picture window to assess the conditions.

"It doesn't matter," Chuck said emphatically. "My orders from the Board of Advisers are *very* clear! When the last golfer finishes, that means the golf course is closed for the season. Mr. Digby was the last off the course, so we're officially closed."

"Dude, you said when the last golfer *finishes*, and the old man here didn't get to finish, thanks to you I might add," Clive argued.

"When the course became unplayable, he gave up and came in here, and that means he finished," Chuck said.

"That's crazy. What if he came in here just to get a beer, or to take a leak, you wouldn't say he was finished then, now would you?" Clive asked.

"No, but he didn't come in for that, he came in because he was through."

"He wasn't through!" Clive argued. "You said yourself he was still trying to play, and *you* forced him off the course and in here against his will. Now you want to use that to say he voluntarily terminated his round?"

"Under that line of thinking, all these other guys in here would have the same right, and that's a nightmare!" Chuck said.

Jacklin scanned room and asked, "Any of you others here with incomplete rounds interested in going back out there to finish?" As expected, there were no takers, and Jacklin said, "Nightmare solved."

Before Chuck could respond, Billy had a weather update. "Hey old man, look out here!" he said pointing. Ben turned and saw that the outside conditions had changed and though the wind continued, it had slowed and the blowing of ice and snow had eased. "I think you've got that window of opportunity right now!" No sooner than Billy ended his sentence, the wind quickened, and those present heard a loud noise from the outside. All eyes trained on the window, and those closest to it, saw that the loose corrugated metal panel on the roof of the cart barn, had torn from its rivets, and had taken flight. Like a six-foot by four-foot whirling ninja star the panel soared toward the clubhouse, and everyone cringed as it passed the window and sunk itself deeply in the trunk of a nearby pine tree.

"I think that window just closed," Katrina said.

The group again congregated at Ben's table and Billy asked, "Say, just how old are you anyway?"

Ben grinned, but the protective Katrina bristled and asked, "What kind of question is that? Do you think Mr. D *forgot* to play the last hole?"

"Easy Kat, the man asked an insightful question," Ben said, "I'm seventy-four years old."

"Dude! You could've done it!" Billy said.

"Done what?" Cookie asked.

"He could've shot his freakin' age, but he blew it by leaving the course with only one lousy hole to play!"

"I tried to finish, I truly did," Ben defended, "but the snow and ice was pelting me *real* bad on seventeen and the wind was getting' down right fierce. When I hit my approach to the seventeenth green, which by then had a layer of powder on it, I was lucky to have only a two footer for a birdie. If I had to make a putt beyond a gimmie, I would have been in deep trouble. Fortunately, I could tap it in and dash for the eighteenth tee, and that's when Chuck saved me."

"Saved you? The dude screwed you!" Clive Jacklin insisted.

"Yeah, he should've let you finish the hole," Stewart Spindler said, and all eyes turned accusingly to Chuck, who sat at a loss for words.

"Wait just a second!" Ben intervened. "While Chuck and I were out there facin' this Canadian storm, you all were inside here sippin' those prissy drinks."

"Prissy drinks?" Clive asked indignantly.

"Yeah, those 'lah ti dahs or whatever the hell y'all call 'em," Ben said.

"It's a latte," Clive smirked.

"Oh, that sounds better ..." Kat, said under her breath.

"But this is history we're talking about," Billy pleaded. "If you would have just stuck it out, you could've been in the newspaper tomorrow morning!"

"Yeah, in the obituaries!" Chuck said.

"You know what I mean man, shooting your age is a big damn deal in golf!" Billy countered.

"I realize that," Ben said, "but it doesn't really matter because even if the wind and snow fall had abated, it's unlikely I could have played it out. As Chuck said, we could hardly see the fairway from the cart path since it was getting' covered with snow and ice. The only way to even detect the green was the up slope in the snow from the creek up to the putting surface."

"Have you ever come this close before?" Clive Jacklin asked.

"Shooting my age?" Ben asked and Jacklin nodded. "Heavens no, I shoot mostly in the nineties, sometimes worse."

"Nineties? You're that bad and almost shot your age?" Clive blurted and Ben nodded. "I'm not kidding—I would have risked *anything* to get in that last hole."

"Oh, really?" came a voice with a distinctly southern drawl. It was Mungo Thibodeaux, who, until that comment had been content to sit silently in the corner drinking his coffee and reading the Tribune, Bozeman's local newspaper. Mungo, had a thin frame, but was too short to be characterized as lanky. He had a long, thin face that was ruddy from years of working outdoors, and always had the expression of someone in deep thought. Despite his lack of formal education, Mungo was intelligent, well read and a hard worker. He was born in Texas, but decades earlier Mungo's father took a job with a fledgling oil exploration company in Montana and moved the family to the area when Mungo was a young teenager. Mungo quit school at age sixteen, lied about his age to an army recruiter and enlisted in the Army infantry. After basic training, he deployed to Vietnam, which qualified him for membership in the Veterans of Foreign Wars local in Bozeman. All members of the VFW shared the scars of war, some visible, some not, and Mungo's came by way of a failed training exercise that resulted in him having a metal plate inserted into his skull. Though it was not a debilitating injury to him, it was enough for the Army to award him an honorable discharge and return him stateside. Once home, he took a low-level position with the same oil company as his father, thrived there and worked his way through the ranks and into management.

"What do you mean by *oh really*?" Clive demanded of Mungo.

"You and your buddies haven't set foot on the course since the temperature dropped below fifty."

"Well I ..."

"Well, my ass! You dare to carp on poor ol' Ben Digby, an eighty year old man, who—"

"Seventy-four Mungo," Ben corrected.

"Sorry, Ben. A seventy four year old man who ventured out in a blizzard, played seventeen holes, and nearly made some sort of record, while you and your ilk didn't have the gumption to step up to the first tee!"

"How do you respond to that, leather pants?" Katrina asked of Clive.

"Look—barmaid, the men are talkin' so why don't you make yourself useful and bring me another beer," Clive said holding up his empty, green Heineken bottle.

"Comin' right up," Kat said retrieving his empty, and heading toward the kitchen.

"The point is that this old dude had a chance for true greatness, and didn't take it, that's all I'm trying to say," Clive defended and turned back to Ben. "Are you really that bad of a golfer?"

"Chuck can attest that I currently carry a twenty-one handicap," Ben replied, and Chuck nodded his affirmation. "I've only broken ninety a handful of times—ever and never have I broke eighty."

"Ben, it's certainly a terrific round, and no one can take that away from you," Cookie said.

"Thanks, I've always heard that if you play long enough, you'll get your day, and this was mine."

"What do you mean by *your day*?" Jacklin asked.

"You know, a stretch where everything falls into place, and you perform like you never have in your whole life. I think the athletes call it being *in the zone*," Ben explained.

"Yeah, like Don Larsen in the fifty-six World Series!" Cookie said.

"Or Roger Maris in sixty-one," said another.

"Then there's Wilt the Stilt's hundred-point game in sixty-two," Billy Auchterlonie contributed.

A man in the corner added in a thick New York accent, "What about DiMaggio's fifty-six-game hitting streak in forty-one?"

"Definitely in the zone," Cookie agreed.

A large man with a cheerful face rose. He had a thick five o'clock shadow and dark curly hair crowned with a Red Sox baseball cap, and said in New England accent, "Then there's Ted Williams batting .406 in forty-one."

"Boo!" replied the New Yorker from the corner.

"How 'bout Nicklaus at the eighty-six Masters?" Chuck asked.

"Good one!" Billy said.

"Then there's Mary Lou Retton's perfect ten in eighty-four," Spindler said, and the room fell silent, and all eyes stared uninspiringly at him.

"I liked that one, Stewart," Katrina said.

"I in no way, compare myself to any of those great athletes, including the gymnast, " Ben said glancing at Spindler, "but this was my moment, and I just happened to have it on a bad weather day."

"What's the big deal about shootin' your age anyway?" Spindler asked of Jacklin.

"Stewart, it's as rare as rare can get. At my club in California, which I might add has been open over sixty years, we have *never* had any member do it—not one! Only three ever got within a stroke of doing it, and their pictures are hanging on the locker room wall."

Then the New Yorker added, "At my club, one guy *did* shoot his age, and he's a legend. Hell, they almost renamed the golf club after him—and would have if his last name hadn't been Lipschitz!"

"Chuck, do you think the Board of Advisers could have a plaque or something made for Ben to hang in here?" Cookie asked.

"Whoa, guys!" Ben interjected, holding up his hands to stem the tide of comments. "This is all real nice and I'm glad to have had a good round, but it's over. I didn't make it, and that's the end of it."

"I know it's bad out there now, but why not try it again tomorrow after the storm blows over," Cookie suggested.

"Wait a just a doggone minute!" Chuck protested. "The course is closed, plus the hole is covered with ice and snow and three or more feet is supposed to fall by morning."

"So what?" Clive argued. "It's just one hole to play, and you don't even have to be here."

"You don't understand, the season is over, and that hole will be unplayable until the spring thaw."

"Chuck's right," Ben said, again trying for an end the debate. "The Montana winter has definitely arrived and is here for the duration."

Stewart Spindler rose from his chair and said, "Shelley wrote in *Ode to the West Wind* and I quote, *if winter comes, can spring be far away*?"

"Who-in-the-hell is this Shelley character?" Mungo Thibodeaux asked.

"Only one of the finest European writers in literary history—that's who!" Spindler retorted.

"The one that wrote Frankenstein?" Katrina asked.

"No! That was—"

"Whatever!" Mungo said, rolling his eyes. "All I can tell you is for this Shelley chick to write something like that, she must not have ever lived in Montana."

"The Shelley I referred to was a he, if you must know," Spindler said.

Mungo looked at Spindler curiously. "You're jokin', right?"

"No, it's true."

"Shelley was his first name?" Mungo asked.

"No, it was his last name," Spindler explained. "It's just that in literary circles he was simply referred to as Shelley."

"I damn sure would've sure put a stop to that!" Mungo said. "Being saddled with that last name is trouble enough, but lettin' people use it as first name, is beyond the pale."

"This coming from a man named *Mungo*," Jacklin said.

"Mungo is odd all right, but ain't Shelley!" Mungo defended.

"So what was Shelley's real first name?" Katrina asked, as she handed Clive his uncapped cold beer.

"Percy," Spindler said.

"Really?" Mungo asked and Spindler nodded. "Well—the fella just couldn't catch a break, now could he? Do you reckon he had a middle name he could've used instead, I mean his first and last were a tad troublesome?"

"Bysshe" Spindler said.

"No, it's true," Mungo, responded.

"No, I'm giving you his middle name—it was Bysshe, b-y-s-s-h-e."

"What kind of name is that?" Cookie asked.

"Don't know," Spindler said. "Perhaps it was his mother's maiden name."

"Wouldn't that make him a son of a Bysshe?" Mungo asked.

"Either way, I bet he sure could fight!" Katrina said.

"But back to Chuck's point, the fairways and greens are covered and will be like that for months, so what do we do?" Cookie asked.

"It was playable until a half hour ago, and it's not completely frozen," Clive responded, "we just need to find a way to get the snow off the fairway and green long enough for him play it out."

"The course is closed!" the beleaguered Chuck reiterated.

"We're not saying that you should leave the whole course open, just the eighteenth—for one player—now how tough could that be?" Clive asked.

"The ice and snow isn't going anywhere for a *real* long time!" Chuck said exasperated.

Ben finished his hot chocolate, grabbed his scarf and hat, and rose and walked to a chair by the kitchen. He sat and began swapping his golf shoes for the boots, as the debate continued on. Once done, Ben stood and started toward the exit with his clothing and golf shoes in hand until the café patrons noticed him departing.

"Don't go, old man," Clive pleaded, and Ben stopped in the doorway and turned to face him. "If the snow let's up, all we have to do is try to clear the hole long enough for you to play."

"And just how is that supposed to happen?" Ben asked.

"I've been thinking about that," Clive said. "How about everyone chipping in and renting a small snow plow and—"

"Whoa, Mr. Jacklin!" Chuck intervened. "That'll ruin the hole!"

"So what! You got all winter to fix it."

"We can't work on it in the winter, and besides the course is—"

"Closed!" came a chorus of voices.

Billy stood and said, "Don't let this drop, man—we got to think this through."

"What do you have in mind?" Cookie asked.

"I'm not sure," he replied, pondering.

"I got it!" Clive said. "If the snow stops, we simply melt off the accumulation."

"But, how do you do that?" Cookie asked.

"How 'bout a flame thrower!" Mungo said.

"What!" Chuck yelled.

"Don't shy away from it, Chuck. I know for a fact they got 'em down at Palmer's Army Surplus, and I damn sure remember how to use one."

"No!" Chuck said.

The newcomer from Boston rose from his table, and in his thick New England accent said, "I have an uncle who's in the road construction business in Salem. They have these large rolling pieces of equipment that have a horizontal platform of fire on the bottom that faces low to the ground. You see, the fire from the platform is used to heat and melt the tah and a large roller on the back of the machine flattens it out," he said then waggled his beer bottle toward Katrina to evidence its emptiness.

"One Sam Adams coming up!" Katrina said.

"What's tah?" Mungo inquired, of the New Englander.

"Excuse me?"

Mungo sighed. "You said the machine melt's the tah … what the hell's tah?"

"Hot tah," the man repeated

Mungo scratched his head and squinted. "Hot what?"

"Tah – t-a-r."

"Oh—why didn't you say so?" Mungo said rolling his eyes.

"So then what?" Cookie asked.

"So since it can melt tarrrr," the New Englander said with exaggeration, while glancing at Mungo, "this solves the dilemma, since this machine would clear that fairway and green in one pass!"

"Have I mentioned that the course is closed?" Chuck said in a voice that was now weary and hoarse.

Undeterred the room erupted into a cacophony of suggestions, ranging from laying artificial turf over the snow, to erecting an elongated canopy above the fairway and green and heating it, but Ben wasn't playing.

"Thanks fellas, but I think we've discussed this enough for today," he said, and again turned to leave.

"If you leave, the chance is lost forever," Clive admonished.

Cookie rose and asked desperately, "Isn't there something you can think of to do? I just hate to see the sun go down on this opportunity."

"Yes, I actually do have a plan," Ben said, the room fell silent and all eyes focused on him. "Here's what I think I'm gonna do. First,

I'm going to go home and take a hot shower. Then, I'm going to put on some dry, thermal underwear and my twenty-year-old, green, Terrycloth robe, and I'm going to watch TV, with a bowl of leftover chili and a handful of saltine crackers—or Fritos, if my bride has some, then I'll call it a day."

"Listen old man, you have an obligation here," Clive said.

"Oh?" Ben asked as he donned his hat and scarf.

"Yeah, you gotta think of the game!" Clive urged.

"What do you mean?" Ben asked.

"The game of golf! You owe it to the game to try to get this done," Jacklin insisted. "This isn't something you walk away from just to go eat!"

"What do *you* care about the game of golf?" Ben asked, now agitated. "I mean, do you and your buddies even play?"

"Sure they do, Ben," Mungo interjected, much to the surprise of all of those observing. "These guys play golf ... *if* you consider sitting indoors, readin' magazines, drinkin' fancy coffee and booze, and bitching about the stock market, all while wearing pristine designer clothes—playing golf!"

"Ha-ha, real funny," Clive said. "I'm just trying to help, but if you want to piss this opportunity away, it's your loss."

"Gentlemen, I appreciate all the interest in this, but there's no way to finish the round, and I'm goin' home now before they close the roads," Ben said as he exited through the pro shop, and rescued his clubs and thermos from the cold, icy golf cart and headed to the parking lot.

With the early winter storm still waging its wrath on the community, Ben guided his truck slowly and carefully down the treacherous mountain pass, and into the familiar surroundings of his neighborhood. After pulling his truck into the driveway, Ben parked and dashed briskly to the front door, pausing only to glance at the Coke thermometer before entering.

"I was getting worried about you dear, what took so long?" Emily asked.

"Sorry Em, I just got hung-up."

"You didn't play twenty-seven, did you?"

"Lord no, I didn't even finish the eighteen."

"I see, was it because of the weather?"

"Yes," Ben responded, while taking off his layers in the entryway.

"Give me those and strip down to your thermals, and I'll shake everything out in the laundry room and get them in the wash," Emily said and as Ben complied, she added, "but, I'm not surprised you didn't finish, that storm is a real doozy."

"It sure is, and it's now only three above zero."

"And to think that you insisted on going out in it at all!" she said shaking her head. "Have you had lunch?

"No, and I'm very hungry."

"What did you have for breakfast?"

"I plead the Fifth," Ben said.

"That means sausage or bacon, so I'll make you a salad for lunch."

Ben cringed. "I was kind of counting on a shower and then another bowl of your delicious chili."

"That's leftovers, Ben. Let me make you something fresh."

"Please, Em. Chili is one of the rare foods that's even better after a day in the fridge."

"But chili, two days in a row?"

"I'm truly fine with it, plus it'll help warm me up," Ben said, mustering all of his sincerity,

"Have it your way then," she relented.

Ben showered, donned his robe and devoured the bowl of left over chili at the kitchen table. Afterward Emily took him by the arm and led him toward their living room, noting how stiffly Ben walked and that he winced as he moved. "You're too old for this kind of foolishness."

"I know," Ben conceded, as he eased slowly down into his recliner and laid his head back.

Emily ran her hand through his thin silver strands. "I can tell you pushed it Ben, and you're exhausted. You're not thirty-five anymore, you know."

Ben looked up at her. "Would it make a difference that I was having a great round?"

The hand that had gently stroked his hair suddenly bopped him playfully on the top of his head. "What good is a great round if you die of pneumonia, huh? After all, do you want them to post your score on your tombstone if you keel over out there?"

"No, not particularly, but if they're going to include a round on it, I'd hope it would be this one."

"Fine! When you go, I will have the monument company etch the scores on your grave marker and add:

> *Here lies Ben, who loved his golf,*
> *Until a round too many bumped him off,*
> *Now he lays silent beneath this ground*
> *But, boy he was having a heck of a round!*

"Very nice, Em. It seems like you've got my demise all planned out," Ben said, smiling. He turned on the television, and soon thereafter, he closed his eyes and lapsed into a well-earned, afternoon nap.

The Fifth Hole

A s had become Emily's grocery shopping routine, the following morning she arose early in order to reach the Pitz-Smart store to claim the coupon-discounted merchandise before it was depleted. Ever the frugal shopper, Emily had dutifully clipped coupons throughout the week and carried her collection, neatly organized in a separate pouch in her handbag. When Emily left their house that morning, she knew from the local weather report that the snowplows had cleared the roads, and that only light flurries were falling, which was important to her, since she hoped to complete her shopping, and return home in time to prepare Ben's breakfast.

When Ben awoke, the first thought that sprung to mind, was golf. However, just as quickly he recalled the events of the previous day and knew that he had arrived at day one of the dreaded off-season. He now faced many months of completing domestic projects, although he would look forward to some of them, particularly those that called upon him to use his tools. Decades in the hardware business allowed Ben to accumulate quite the collection of hand tools and woodworking equipment, all of which was stored in a large workshop behind their house.

When he noticed Emily was already gone, he considered simply rolling over and going back to sleep, but he knew that procrastination was no remedy for the winter blahs. Consequently, he forced himself out of the bed, and immediately confronted the discomforts occasioned by the excesses of the day prior. His sore joints and muscles had him hobbling as he walked the short distance to their bathroom. Once there, he found a note from Emily leaning on the bathroom mirror, reminding Ben of her grocery-shopping trip and it concluded with a request for him to change three burned-out light bulbs, two inside the house and one outside.

"Let the chores begin," he said, as he commenced to lather his face for his morning shave. Though this initial slate of tasks was easily completed, Ben sensed it was penned in haste and would surely be expanded upon Emily's return. Soon his face and chin were smooth, his hair and teeth brushed, and he was dressed for the day.

What do I do first? Ben asked himself, knowing that his options had severely diminished from just twenty-four hours earlier. Feeling that he had plenty of time to tend to three light bulbs, and knowing that finishing any task too rapidly was an open invitation for more, he decided to put on a half-pot of coffee. While it brewed, Ben pulled on his boots and stepped, awkwardly and with great care outside, to fetch the morning paper. By this time of morning, he could usually find their copy of the Tribune, shoved in a plastic tube just below the mailbox, which stood at the curb next to their driveway.

He stepped high as he trudged through the snow, and saw that the sun was moving further away from the horizon. Despite the flurries, the weather proved far more tolerable than the previous morning, but when he arrived at the mailbox, he reached into the plastic tube, and came up empty. *The coupon bandit strikes again* he thought as he turned and ambled gingerly and emptyhandedly on his aching legs back to the house. Once inside Ben poured a cup of the coffee, and truly did not mind not having the paper on this morning, since he was content to relax in their sunroom, without the distraction of the scuttlebutt typically featured in the Tribune. He assumed a comfortable padded lounge chair, sipped his coffee and gazed at the winter landscape that included the snow-burdened trees greeting the rising sun. He thought it ironic, that the same snow and ice that proved his bane on the golf course, now provided him with such a splendid sense of serenity.

A second cup of coffee and a half hour later, Emily returned. "Ben, where are you? I need to ask you something," she called from the kitchen.

"I'm in the sunroom—need any help with the groceries?"

"No thanks, I've got them," she said, and Ben returned to the sight of the sun's rays glistening on the snow, now showing as a thousand tiny sparkling diamonds. Moments later, Emily stepped into the sunroom, and the sight no less captivated her, causing her to forget her reason for entering.

She stood next to Ben's lounge chair, and he took her hand and asked, "It's quite pretty, wouldn't you say?"

"Yes indeed. I don't care how many you've seen before, there's no match for the beauty of the first heavy snow fall," Emily said, taking a seat on the wicker loveseat to Ben's left.

"Well?" Ben asked.

"Well, what?"

"I thought you had something to discuss. If it's about the light bulbs, I'll—"

"Oh no, it's not that," she said, turning to face him. "It's about yesterday. What in the world did you do at the golf course?"

"You already know about the pork sausage."

"Not that, silly. What else happened?"

"I played golf, why?"

"Well, it was the strangest of things," she said turning toward him. "While I was shopping, two different people came up to me and remarked about something you did, but or the life of me, I could not figure out what they were talking about."

"What'd you say?"

"I didn't want to seem oblivious, so I just politely acknowledged them and continued on my way. All I gathered was that it had something to do with your golf round and what's weird, is they both seemed to kind of … well … feel sorry for you."

"Oh, I got it now. It was probably about my score."

"What about it?" she asked.

"Em—I was having the best round of my entire life yesterday," he said enthusiastically.

"In that weather?"

"Yes, and it was truly amazing."

"That's wonderful! Why didn't you tell me?" she asked.

"I tried to, but you bonked me on the head!"

"I'm sorry Ben, so what was your score?"

"That's the problem, it wasn't a complete round," Ben explained.

"Oh that's right, what a shame. That must be why those folks seemed so sympathetic."

"It was disappointing, considering I shot a score of even seventy for the first seventeen holes, and really wanted to finish," he explained.

"Seventy, huh? That must be good, I mean why else would people be asking me about it?"

"It's certainly good for me, I've never shot anything close to it—ever."

"It just proves that like fine wine, you're getting better with time," she said smiling.

"So, what's for breakfast?" he asked

"You're getting your favorite," she replied cheerfully.

"Bacon and eggs?"

"No, siree. It's that special oatmeal you like so much."

"Does *special* mean it's got meat in it?" Ben asked.

"Of course not, but it is the type you favor, remember? It's the brand with the cinnamon and raisins, and last time I bought it I asked you about it and you said you really liked it," Emily said, then noticed Ben's morose expression. "You did like it, didn't you?"

"Oh sure … it was fine … for oatmeal … I guess."

"That's good, considering I used a coupon from this morning's paper to stock up."

"You stocked up, huh?" Ben asked.

"Yes. I bought four boxes and got one free. We could have it every morning for a month and not run out."

"Oh boy," Ben said facetiously.

"Don't be that way. It was a good bargain, and besides, it's very healthy for the both of us."

"By the way," Ben said, "how do you suppose those people down at the store know about my round of golf?"

She pondered for a moment, and then said, "I don't know—it didn't come up."

Emily headed to the kitchen to put away the groceries and to heat up breakfast. A short time later she brought a tray, atop which sat a full bowl of oatmeal and the remains of the newspaper and placed the tray on Ben's lap. He continued to enjoy the scenery from the sunroom, as he grudgingly partook of his breakfast. By the time he reached the bottom of the bowl, some gathering clouds had dimmed the sun, diminishing the view and the room's ambient light. Ben switched on the floor lamp next to his lounge chair and lifted the Tribune section on top, but found it riddled with holes where coupons were once displayed, and sat it on the floor next to his lounger. Next was the sports page, and though largely intact, there had been no football games to report and it did not hold his interest. He sat the sports on the floor, and picked up the local news section, and found it had been spared Emily's couponing scissors, and as he perused it, he homed in on a second-page headline:

LOCAL GOLFER SNOWED OUT OF HISTORY

Benjamin Digby flirts with rare golfing record in weather-shortened round

Hmm, so this is how they knew, he thought as he read the article written by local reporter, Brian Cotton. The writer detailed

Ben's scoring success, how unusual it was for him, the travails he encountered along the way, and then how the round was interrupted on the eighteenth tee. Cotton based most of his account on interviews with Chuck Duval and Cookie Harington, and it concentrated on the disappointing nature of the turn of events. Cognizant of the importance of Ben's near accomplishment, the reporter concluded his article with an editorial flourish:

> *What a true shame it would be to allow the forces of nature to deprive a man of his shot at golfing greatness. Most golfers never get within a country mile of shooting their age, and this man draws within a short distance of the coveted goal, only to be rebuked by forces of nature beyond his control. A few hundred yards, 368 to be exact, separated him from the chance of reaching this rare sports pinnacle. The consensus around this newsroom is to let Mr. Digby play the final hole next spring when the course re-opens. Speaking only for this humble writer, and perennial duffer who is fortunate to occasionally break 100, I hope this gentleman seizes the opportunity to finish his round next year, and I, for one, want to be there when he does.*

Ben walked to the kitchen, placed his bowl and the tray in the kitchen sink, then said, "Well—Em, you might want to read this," he said, setting the Tribune section on the bar in front of her and added, "That Warhol fella was right—I'm famous for fifteen minutes."

She lifted the paper and smoothed it out, but without her reading glasses, she could only make out the headline. Seeing that the article involved Ben, she quickly retrieved her reading glasses from her apron pocket and read the piece in its entirety. "Oh, Ben! How exciting and what a nice report."

"He seemed to capture it all right."

"I'm sorry I didn't realize what you did was such a rare thing," Emily said, "and I can't believe I was so busy coupon clipping that I missed this!"

"Thanks dear, but I haven't done anything, since I didn't complete the round."

"But this reporter says you should finish it in the spring—you *can* do that, right?"

"It's much ado about nothing," Ben said dismissively.

"You're such a contrarian sometimes, why can't you open your mind to the concept?"

"I don't know if it would even be legit to do what they're saying, I mean the notion of playing a single hole of golf months later, and expecting it to count seems silly to me. One of the reasons I was later than I wanted to be in getting home yesterday, was all the crazy bantering about it at Cookie's place. Besides, it's a long way to next season, and frankly I'd rather change light bulbs and eat oatmeal, than to think about this."

"Suit yourself, but I'm going to cut this out and put it in the scrap book."

Early the next morning, Ben woke from the sound of a loud bump from the outside, and thought *what in the world was that?* Something had surely fallen, but Ben could not tell if it had landed on their house, his workshop, or perhaps the neighbor's home next door. Careful not to disturb Emily, he quietly put on layers, and still sore from his challenging golf round, he walked guardedly into the backyard. As he stepped onto the crunchy snow, his movement activated their security floodlight, and he relied on it to check for damage. Seeing none on their house, he inspected the workshop and found that an ice-burdened tree limb had broken off from one of the tall aspens, and landed on the roof.

He walked to the eave line of the shop, and on tiptoes reached and tugged at a hanging branch that was attached to the larger limb, and with a couple of yanks, he managed to haul the entire limb off the roof and down to the ground. Ben checked the asphalt shingle roof for damage, and seeing none from his vantage point, he unlocked the workshop door to check the roof from the inside. He entered and switched on the fluorescent lights suspended from the rafters and saw no obvious breaches in the plywood sheathing above him.

Thank goodness, he said to himself and selected a handsaw from a wall of hand tools hanging neatly on hooks. He walked back outside the shop and used its lights to see as he sawed the limb into sections, secured them with twine and left two bundles on their patio, where they would remain until heavy trash pick-up day. Ben returned the saw to its designated hook, and as he turned to leave, his hip bumped his workbench, rattling the numerous plastic, compartmentalized boxes resting atop it. A wide array of small parts, including faucet seats and washers, occupied those boxes, and it reminded him of his pledge to help Cookie with his leaking faucet.

He pulled the piece of paper sack from his wallet, glanced the model number, and consulted a binder of product manuals, in order to identify the correct part numbers. Once done, he plucked a corresponding seat and washer from one of the plastic boxes. He reached to turn off the lights, but stopped, and retrieved an empty clear plastic baggie from a drawer. He then returned to the same box of parts, emptied the remaining contents of into the baggie, and thought *that ought to keep him for a while.*

Ben switched off the lights, locked up the shop and returned to the house to start the coffee. By the time he entered the kitchen, the clock on their range read 6:25 a.m., and as the coffee percolated, he headed to the sunroom to watch the dawn. Before the coffee finished brewing, their ringing phone jarred him. Not wanting to awaken Emily, he rose and walked quickly toward the phone, but the ringing stopped before he could grab it. Figuring the caller had realized that they had dialed a wrong number and had hung up, he returned to the comfort of his lounge chair.

"Ben, it's for you," Emily shouted as she scurried into the sunroom. Dressed in her robe, she stood cupping her hand over the receiver of their cordless phone and whispered excitedly, "It's a news reporter."

"It's probably that Cotton fella from the Tribune, and he already wrote a story."

"Either way, I think he still wants to talk to you."

"Please tell him I have nothing to add to it," Ben said.

"Sir, my husband said he read your story in the paper, and liked it *very* much, but he doesn't feel he can add to it," Emily said, and Ben nodded his approval for her diplomacy. "I'm sorry? Did you say that you're *not* the one that wrote it?" Ben looked up at her curiously. "Oh ... I see," Emily said, and she extended the phone to Ben. "He says he's with ABC News."

"ABC News!" Ben said straightening to attention in a manner, he had not done since muster calls in the Army.

"That's what he said."

Ben took the phone, and uttered, "Hello."

"Mr. Digby, as I explained to your wife, I'm very sorry to phone so early, but this is Michael Hagen and I'm with the ABC affiliate in Helena."

"Okay," Ben said, as Emily pressed her ear close to the phone, straining to hear.

"I've been asked to do a story on your amazing round of golf and that's why I'm calling," the man explained and Emily beamed with pride as she clutched her hands at her breast.

Ben cleared his throat and asked, "Mr. Hagen, what could the people up there in Helena want to know about me and this golf thing of mine?"

"You should understand, the story is not intended for Helena," Hagen advised.

"I see, so it's for here in Bozeman?" Ben asked.

"No sir. The story is for tomorrow's episode of Good Morning America, airing direct from New York."

Ben flinched when Emily squealed with excitement, then she placed her hand over her mouth to contain any further unintended audible reactions.

"Good Morning America? You mean that program that's on our local channel thirteen?" Ben asked.

"Oh, so you're familiar with the show?" Hagen asked.

"Sure, I've watched it."

"Great, now to do this we—"

"Excuse me for a second," Ben interrupted. "How'd y'all find out about this all the way over in Helena?"

"The AP."

"The what?" Ben asked.

"The Associated Press. You see, some reporter did a piece on this, I presume it's the one your wife mentioned, and his paper sent the story to the wire. You see, when a reporter does a story that the editor senses has broader than local appeal, they will send it to a wire service like the AP or UPI. This allows other news outlets to see it, and if they like it they can run the original story as written, or follow up with their own and that's why I'm calling."

"But what in the world could be so interesting about this round of golf?" Ben asked, and Emily swatted him lightly on the arm, for trying to discourage the reporter.

"Are you kidding? This is a *great* story, one full of human interest and has the combination of the essence of sports mixed with the cruelty of nature. It's the proverbial thrill of victory and the agony—"

"Of defeat," Ben finished. "I used to watch that show too, and I think I know how that poor skier fella felt on the opening of it."

"Oh, it's not that bad, Mr. Digby. All we need is a simple interview, and the whole thing won't take but a few minutes."

"Just an interview, huh?"

"That's it. So what do you say?"

"Oh, I don't know. I just think that this is getting way out of hand," this time Emily elbowed Ben, and he gasped.

"Are you okay, Mr. Digby?" the reporter asked.

"Yes, but pardon me for a second," Ben said as he clasped his palm over the receiver. "What was that for?"

"Please don't turn this down. You deserve the attention, and it would be exciting for the community," she pleaded.

"I don't know Em, I mean it's just ... uh ... I think that ..." Ben stammered, but saw the heart-melting stare from Emily's pale blue eyes. "Mr. Hagen, I guess I'm willing to do the interview, but how am I going to make the hundred mile drive to Helena? I'm sure that the roads between here and there are very icy."

"Oh no, Mr. Digby, we'll come to you. We can get our equipment there without any problem," Hagen assured. "We want to capture the interview today, so there will be time to edit it for tomorrow morning's broadcast."

"Fair enough," Ben said. "Do you need directions?"

"No thank you. I looked you up and have your address right here, and can find it with no problem. We should be there around noon, is that all right?"

"That's fine," Ben said and hung up the phone. As quickly as he committed to the interview, he just as rapidly began regretting it. Emily, on the other hand, was nothing short of giddy, and reveled in the attention her modest husband was receiving.

Ben dressed and walked outside to shovel the snow from the driveway and sidewalk, while Emily spent a considerable part of the morning in preparation for their guests and carefully choosing options for Ben's attire for the interview. When Ben returned inside, she led him into their bedroom, and he marveled at the array of clothing splayed out on their bed. Each ensemble included a pair of pants, with the legs of each running across the bed and down the side and dangling toward the floor. A corresponding long-sleeve shirt or sweater laid flattened out above the waistline of the pants, and Ben noted no less than six combinations offering stripes and solids—colorful and drab—in light, dark and neutral hues. Though Ben's taste in clothing and for coordinating colors was questionable at best, Emily had always required his input for such decisions.

"So, which one of these do you favor?" Emily asked as Ben stood and stared at the selections. Though he truly did not care what he wore, he knew from experience that he could not escape offering an opinion, consequently he walked the bedside and began his assessment. The pressure was not as great on this occasion, since Emily herself had selected all the candidates, therefore he comported himself as if carefully evaluating each, before pointing to one particular ensemble.

Emily's expression immediately signaled disapproval. "Those, huh?"

Ben instinctively made mental pivot. "Yes, but now that I think about it, those right there would do just fine," he said putting his finger on a different option, and liked his odds now, considering that he had a third of the outfits covered.

"That's what I was thinking," Emily said cheerfully.

Well, even a broken clock is right twice a day he thought.

The winning selection was a pair of blue slacks and a red and white turtleneck. Though Ben thought the color scheme more suited for the Fourth of July, he dared not mention that, as any such comment was sure to spark a renewed search.

"Do you want me to put these on now?" he asked.

"Absolutely not," Emily said. "The reporter won't be here for quite some time, and you have not had lunch. I don't want any visible wrinkles, stains or spots."

"Speaking of lunch, what are we having?" Ben asked.

"It was going to be a surprise, but if you must know, we're having hot dogs." Ben did not know if the Fourth of July colors subliminally inspired that selection, or if it was divine intervention, but he was grateful nonetheless, and it eased his dread of going on camera.

After lunch, Ben changed into his designated outfit and Emily, in anticipation of the arrival of their guests, put out a few snacks. Ben watched a football game and dozed intermittently in his recliner, until a rapping at their front door brought him to his feet. Emily walked toward the front, with Ben trailing behind her, until he glanced out their kitchen window and stopped. From there he had a view of the side of their house where their driveway ran from the street up to their garage.

"What are you doing?" Emily asked, turning back to him.

"Take a gander at that!"

Emily joined him at the window and beheld a large blue-and-white van bearing the news network logo parked on their driveway. Atop the van was a telescoping antenna that inched upward into the grey winter sky and two men were hustling equipment out of the rear of the vehicle.

"What did I get myself into?" Ben lamented.

"Oh, it'll be fine," Emily, said encouragingly and they remained drawn to the activities on the outside, until a second knock reminded them of their guests. Ben hurried to the entry and opened the door, to find a tall man dressed in a starched white shirt, grey slacks, yellow tie and blue blazer, under a grey, full-length overcoat.

"Mr. Digby, I presume?" the man asked.

"Yes sir," Ben said shaking the man's outstretched right hand and noting a manila folder in his left. The reporter was a strikingly handsome, middle age man, with a dimpled chin and a full head of hair, which was jet-black except for wisps of grey near the temples.

"I'm Mike Hagen, we spoke on the phone."

"Yes sir, we've been expecting you. I am wife and this is my Ben ... Oh, crap! I mean this is—"

"I gotcha, Ben," the reporter said, and gently shook Emily's hand. "It's a pleasure to make your acquaintance, ma'am."

"Likewise sir, want you please come inside?" Emily invited.

Hagen followed the couple through the entry area and toward the kitchen and he remarked, "What a charming home you have."

"Thank you, Mr. Hagen," Emily said.

"Please, call me Mike."

She nodded and escorted him toward the kitchen table, where he politely declined an offer of the snacks and hot tea or coffee. Hagen was clearly ready to get down to business and stood leafing through the pages in his file, as Ben again glanced out the kitchen window.

"What in the world is that antenna for?" Ben asked.

"That's our satellite truck, and with that antenna, we'll be able to transmit the feed from the interview right back to the studio in New York."

"Did you hear that, Ben? You're going to be on satellite!" Emily said.

"It seems so," Ben said, and though he failed to grasp fully the technology jargon, the mere description of it contributed to his anxiety. "Don't we need to let those other fellas in?"

"No sir. Since snow is a part of the story, I thought it would be advantageous if we shot the interview outside," Hagen explained. "Is that okay with you two?"

"Em?" Ben asked and both men turned to her.

"Fine with me, if he'll bundle-up," she replied.

"Good," Hagen said. "The weather's not bad and we won't be out there very long, and I think the wintry background will cap it off nicely."

"Alright then, I'll get ready," Ben, said.

"Fine, and while you do that, I'll just look over my notes, and when you're ready, we'll go outside and get started."

The couple walked toward the front closet, and Emily selected her fleece-lined overcoat, as Ben instinctively retrieved his old, duck-down jacket from its hanger.

"Oh no you don't, Benjamin!" Emily said grabbing his arm.

"What?"

"You're not going to wear that raggedy old golf jacket on TV!"

"But Em, it's my—"

"Wait!" Hagen interjected while walking toward the couple. "Does that happen to be the jacket you wore that day on the golf course?"

"As a matter of fact it is," Ben, said.

"That's perfect!" Hagen said.

"Perfect?" Emily questioned.

"Yes ma'am. As I explained on the phone, this is a human interest story, and I think it's a fine choice for him to wear the same jacket that protected him on that day."

"By human interest, do you mean that he has to look needy?"

Hagen chuckled. "No ma'am, it's not that at all. You see, I sense that your husband is a real salt of the earth type—a man of the people as they say, and because of that the viewers are going to eat this story up. So, for the same reason I want to shoot this outside with the snow in the background—I favor him wearing that jacket."

Ben looked at Emily, and she reluctantly conceded. "All right, I give up."

"Are you sure, dear?" Ben asked.

"Yes, go ahead and wear it, if looking like a hobo helps with the *human interest*."

Ben struggled, but managed zip up the old jacket, and as they exited and walked down the sidewalk, Hagen said, "Though it's a little overcast out here, there will still be a glare and we'll need to put some face make-up on you."

"Face make-up?" Ben asked, as he stopped and looked anxiously back to Emily.

"Oh, don't worry," Hagen, said, "the purpose is not to make you pretty, it's just a light brushing of pancake makeup."

"I see," Ben said as they walked on.

"Also, do you see that crate over there?" Hagen asked pointing down at a wooden box resting on the ground. It was a half-foot tall, and showed wear, including chipped blue-and-white paint where the network logo once displayed. "It won't be in the shot, but I'll need you to stand on it during the interview to lessen the gap in our heights."

"I understand," Ben said.

One of the two men on the crew positioned Ben on the box and at the proper angle to capture the glistening white snow on the trees behind them as well as the long icicles descending from the eave of their home. The same man then dabbed Ben's ashy, chapped cheeks and forehead briskly with a small powder puff.

The other crewmember manned the camera, and Emily noticed

that next to him, sat a small, black-and-white monitor. It was mounted on a plastic tripod and displayed the images being captured through his lens, and she turned slightly so she could alternate her attention between, the live interview and the images depicted on the screen.

Hagen stood at an angle next to Ben, holding his long, thin microphone with a black foam ball on the end. Emily glanced over at Ben, and knew well by his expression that he was very tense, and she began to worry about how he would respond under the pressure. She called to mind a potluck dinner at their church where the pastor selected Ben to say the blessing before all the congregants in the fellowship hall, and recalled how it unnerved him. She had urged him into this interview and did not want him to be embarrassed, especially on television, and felt her own sudden sense of dread.

The crewmember returned the powder puff to a plastic box, removed a small mirror from it, and it handed to Hagen. The reporter stared into it, turning his face first left then right. He then checked his hair, and parted his lips, revealing near perfect, pearly white rows of teeth. Finding nothing to correct, Hagen handed the mirror back to the man and cleared his throat, and asked, "Ready, Mr. Digby?"

"I suppose," Ben, uttered.

"Okay guys," Hagen said, and with that prompt a bright glaring light atop the camera struck Ben's face.

"Dang!" Ben said and flinched.

"Sorry, Mr. Digby, I should have warned you about that."

"Yes!" Ben said, squinting and using his hands to shield his eyes.

"Now you know why we needed to put something on your face to avoid the shine."

"Yeah, and I feel like I need some suntan oil too," Ben said, lowering his hand and blinking several times until his eyes acclimated to the light.

"Alright, let's try that again," Hagen, said and after a moments pause, the camera operator nodded. "We're here in frigid Bozeman, Montana, to bring you a remarkable tale of the battle of man versus nature. Next to me is Bozeman native, Benjamin Digby, and his story has captured the attention of the whole community," Hagen said and when Emily noted on the screen that the tight shot on Hagen's face widened to include Ben for the first time, her heart fluttered.

"Earlier this week, Mr. Digby here, set out to play a seemingly routine round of golf, but two things made it anything but routine. As you can see in the background, a great snowstorm descended upon southern Montana, and did so as Ben struggled to finish his round. However, there was something else extraordinary about that day, right Ben?" Hagen said, placing the microphone close to Ben's face.

Ben froze and Emily's fluttering heart sank, as she watched her husband staring awkwardly at the microphone. Emily conspicuously cleared her throat and Ben glanced to her, and she nodded rapidly in an attempt to urge him to speak.

"Uh ... yes sir, um ... you see ... I was shootin' myself a darn good round, I mean ... at least a good one for me that is."

"You mentioned a good round for you, what do you normally shoot, Mr. Digby?"

"Oh, I'm pretty ... um ... standard in the mid-to low nineties, so ... uh, I was real lucky to have been doin' a little better on that day," Ben said, with an uncharacteristic nervous quaver in his voice.

"Don't be modest, Mr. Digby. You were shooting better than you had in how many years?"

"Better than I ever have actually. I've ... um ... I've played golf for decades and have *never* shot anything like ... uh ... I did on that day."

"And did it bundled in layers too, right?"

"Right, and with gloves on each hand," Ben added.

"So tell us about the weather?"

"It was, uh ... getting' cold and a windy when I started, and it worsened as I played the front side, and got down right terrible on the latter part of the back, but with all of that, I managed to shoot real well."

"Well enough to have a chance to accomplish something that few golfers have done, and that's to shoot your age."

"That's true, I got closer than I could have ever dreamed of," Ben said, and the nervousness seemed to evaporate from his voice.

"Now, you're seventy-four years young, aren't you sir?" Hagen asked.

"That's right."

"And you managed to complete the seventeenth hole, with a total score of seventy?"

"That's true, but I wasn't really thinking so much about that, as I was focusing on just trying to finish."

"I know from personal experience that the storm that blew through that day was a real humdinger," Hagen said. "Describe what it was like for you coming down those last couple of fairways."

"This thing was comin' in hard and fast and got worse as I played the sixteenth hole, but it was on the seventeenth where it started gettin' downright dangerous. The worst part of it was the wind, which had the ice and snow steadily flying and swirling around. On the eighteenth tee, it was hard to see and tough to stand still enough to even attempt a shot."

"I can tell you really wanted to get in that last hole," the reporter observed.

"You just don't know, Mr. Hagen. If I were just shootin' my usual score, I'd have knocked off around the twelfth or thirteenth, but even though I was tired and it was awfully cold out there, I played on."

"And you're wearing the very jacket you had on that fateful day, aren't you, Mr. Digby?"

"Why yes, I am," Ben said, glancing to the frowning Emily.

"Now, when you were trying to play the eighteenth, what was on your mind?"

Ben scratched his head, and said, "Just finishin' and not getting hurt in the process."

"The eighteenth is a par four, right?"

"That's right—a tough one at that."

"And all you needed was a par, and you would've shot your age?"

"That's correct."

"Mr. Digby, tell all of our viewers why you did not complete that eighteenth and final hole."

"Well sir, the temperature was plummeting, the wind was quickening, and the snow and ice began blowing around harder, and it wasn't just what was falling from the sky, it was also the accumulations being blown out of the tree tops."

"Sounds dangerous."

"It was, and the snowfall was so bad by then that it made it real hard to see down the fairway. Everything was becoming blanketed with the white stuff, and it was blowing like hell, and … oops!"

"That's okay Ben," Hagen said patting Ben on the shoulder.

"So I waited on the eighteenth tee, but it was scary bad, you see. I've lived here my whole life, and I ain't never been caught up in anything like it." Up to that point, Emily was unaware of just how dangerous the conditions had been for him, and how senseless Ben had acted. Nevertheless, she set that aside, and watched on as her now confident mate was hitting his stride.

"So I stood on the eighteenth, trying to decide what to do," he continued as Emily glanced at the monitor as the camera zoomed in on Ben. "I hoped for a hiatus, one where there would be a calming of the conditions long enough to finish it. I even hunkered down under a wooden water stand to try to wait it out and to catch my breath. I tried a couple of times to hit my drive, but with the wind blowing and tree limbs cracking and falling, I just couldn't get it done."

"Sounds like a frightening situation."

"It was, but fortunately the young fella from the pro shop, Chuck Duval, came lookin' for me and may have actually saved me. But that's why I didn't finish it and lost my chance."

"What a tragedy," Hagen said shaking his head.

"No mister, I'm a war veteran and as such, I know well what true tragedies are, and they're things like death and war, and the real heroes are the ones that never made it home. This was just an interrupted golf game … nothing more."

"Well said, and thank you for your service," Hagen said.

"My honor, sir."

"Here's the big question, will you try to complete that eighteenth hole at some point in the future? After all, you just need a par to make history."

Shrugging his shoulders, Ben said matter-of-factly, "The course is closed for the winter and won't reopen until next spring, so I don't see how I could. It was simply a nice round, but incomplete round."

"Ben!" Emily chided, and then immediately covered her mouth.

"It sounds like your charming wife here with us, might disagree," Hagen said to Ben, then turned to face the camera. "As you can see folks, Ben's a humble man, but I think that there just might be some excitement around Bozeman come next spring. Back to you in New York."

The camera panned back to include Emily's proud, cheerful face in the last shot, then the monitor faded to black. Hagen thanked them and bid farewell, and the couple returned inside. Through the kitchen window, Ben watched the crew working, as they packed the equipment back into the van, and the satellite antenna slowly retracted.

"Benjamin Digby, I think that you represented yourself and this community very well," Emily said, beaming with pride.

"Do you really think it went okay?" Ben asked. "I mean, I was real nervous."

"It was great! And the guys at the VFW hall are going to love that you remembered the *true heroes*."

"Oh, I doubt they'll see it, assuming it airs at all, but you really liked it—even with my old jacket and all?"

"Yes, even with the raggedy jacket. I do hate that everyone is going to see it on TV, but hopefully they won't notice how bad it is," Emily said. "By the way mister, I heard what you risked out on that golf course!"

"It wasn't so bad," Ben said.

"Really? Wind-driven snow and ice, and cracking tree limbs! What were you thinking?"

"Making you proud."

"For future reference, I'm plenty proud without you risking your life."

When they rose from their bed the next morning and dressed for the day, they decided to have their breakfast on TV trays in their living room. Emily switched on the console television, turned the knob to channel thirteen and while the television warmed up, they ate and waited together for the top of the hour.

Ben glanced at Emily's tense expression and said, "Please don't be disappointed if it doesn't come on."

"Hush, Ben. You're going to jinx it!"

"Jinx it? Don't you think the decision to run it or not was made long before now?"

"I don't know dear, but anything can happen, plus they're two hours ahead of us," Emily responded anxiously.

"What's the time zone got to do with it?"

"I don't know, you just need to remain positive, that's all!"

"Okay. I'll keep my mouth—"

"Wait, it's on!" she said, and they both focused on the screen as the network logo faded and the host began describing the morning's line up of guests and featured stories, and among them was a political scandal, a volcano eruption in South America, and a train derailment in India. The anchor finished by describing a man in Mississippi who was so large that the police needed to knock out an exterior wall of his home, to extract him in order to take him to the hospital. The broadcast switched to the national news and weather and then to the first commercial break. Ben finished his oatmeal, rose without comment and rinsed his bowl in the kitchen sink.

"I'm so sorry, dear," Emily said.

"That's all right," Ben, replied, "it was nice while it lasted."

Emily sipped her hot tea as the broadcast returned and the featured stories and guest interviews began. Not particularly interested in earthquakes, scandals and train wrecks, Ben began his first chore of the day—cleaning the ashes and unburnt scraps of wood from the fireplace. Emily rose and began washing the dishes but continued making wishful glances at the television, but as the program wound down, so did her hopes, but as she placed the final dried spoon in the drawer, something caught her ear.

"Finally folks, a story of heartbreak in the heartland, involving a man in Bozeman, Montana who had a date with destiny," the anchor said

"Ben, it's on!" Emily shouted, and Ben rose quickly from the hearth, so much so that he struck his head on the brick mantle. He winced and rubbed his head briskly, unwittingly getting the soot from his hands in his hair, and as he hustled toward the television, the anchor said, "We now go to Michael Hagen in Bozeman for the details." In a flash, the image of the handsome reporter appeared on the screen, with the snowy landscape filling the background. They watched the entire interview, which aired with minimal editing, and Ben was most pleased that Emily's cameo at the end made the cut.

Emily rose and hugged him tight. "That was great Ben, and I'm so proud of you, and I know the whole town is too."

"It was pretty good, wasn't it?"

"Yes, indeed, and you looked so strong and handsome!"

"Handsome, huh?" Ben asked.

"Yes, but not as handsome as you do now with your hair dyed black," she said with a chuckle.

Ben glanced curiously at the mirror above the mantle, saw his soot-tinged hair, and said, "Oh hell!"

"Language, Benjamin!"

"Sorry, Em, but I must say, I haven't seen something as lovely as you on a screen since we went to the Palace Theater and saw Doris Day in *The Man Who Knew Too Much*!"

"Oh ... so she's the one who does it for you, huh?" Emily replied playfully. "I thought all along it was a tossup between Sophia Loren and Grace Kelly."

"They're all fine, but none of them can hold a candle to you dear."

"That's very nice of you Ben, but it's not going to get you out of your chores."

Ben tried to go about his tasks that day, but was forced to pause several times to take calls offering kudos and well wishes from friends and family. Then, over the succeeding days, mail arrived from other acquaintances, and some from total strangers, but all were positive.

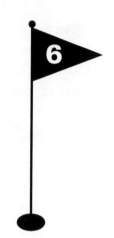

The Sixth Hole

*E*arly on the following Friday morning, Ben ventured outside to retrieve the paper, and found that the overnight snowfall had been minimal and according to their usually reliable Coke thermometer, the temperature had risen into the lower thirties. Feeling a bit stir crazy, Ben considered venturing to the club for breakfast and decided to float the idea to Emily. In advance of his plea, he mentally catalogued reasons to justify the high-calorie excursion, and among the rationales were giving the television interview—at Emily's urging, the improved weather conditions, his meritorious progress with his honey-dos and last but not least, his pledge to remedy Cookie's drippy faucet.

He made the pitch and won Emily's approval, and while veiling his exuberance, he bundled up. He then retrieved the plastic bag of faucet parts, placed them in his jacket pocket and paced cheerfully out the front door, down the sidewalk, and into his truck. Simply being outdoors, and in the crisp open air, delivered a sense of liberation, and that combined with the thought of an oatmeal-free breakfast elated him.

When Ben pulled onto the parking lot, he saw a surprisingly large number of vehicles already present, and to his chagrin, he noticed many models that most assuredly belonged to newcomers. Undeterred, he parked and walked briskly across the parking lot, and entered the café. Cookie glanced at him, did a double take, then wiped his hands on a towel and said, "Great to see you, Ben!"

"Ditto," Ben said, shaking Cookie's hand. "How are you?"

"Fair to middlin'."

"Business is good," Ben said as he surveyed the bustling dining area that was over half full.

"Yes," Cookie replied, then added under his breath, "Not necessarily the business I want, but good trade, nonetheless. Say, that was some interview!"

"You saw it?" Ben asked.

"I sure did, and the fellas around here have been talking all about it."

"Really?"

"Yes, and you did a great job."

"I appreciate that," Ben said pulling the baggie with the faucet parts from his pocket. "Before I forget, I brought you these."

"You remembered," Cookie said gleefully as he accepted the bag and took note of its contents, "and brought spares to boot?"

"Yes, that ought to take care of it for a while," Ben said and patted Cookie on the shoulder. "After breakfast, I can switch 'em out if you want."

"Thanks, but I can handle that part myself, now that I have what I need. What do I owe you?"

"Nothing," Ben said unwinding his scarf.

"Ben, these must have cost you some good money, so let me pay you for 'em."

"I have no use for them now and take pleasure in finding a purpose for them," Ben said.

"Much obliged," Cookie said.

"Well, look who's here," Clive Jacklin said swaggering toward the two men, as Ben unzipped and removed his jacket. "If it ain't ol' Ben, the television star—have you changed your last name to Hogan yet?"

"What do you want?" Ben asked, as his head disappeared into his sweater and he began trying to remove it.

"I keep up with the news, and saw an article on your television interview," Clive explained.

"I keep up with the news too, and saw all those scandalous stories about your bank," Mungo Thibodeaux said.

"Well didn't, and besides, I'm not talking to you," Clive said, prompting Mungo to shake his head and return to his breakfast.

"Can I get you anything else Clive?" Cookie asked hoping to intervene while Ben continued his struggle to remove his sweater.

"No, I just want to speak to the celebrity here, assuming he can find his way out of that worn out thing he's wearing."

Finally freeing himself, Ben laid his sweater on the table, and ran his fingers through his hair to smooth the dishevelment from its removal.

"Put 'er there, Mr. Hogan," Clive said mockingly extending his right hand.

Ben brought his hand down slowly, and placed it firmly in Clive's and said, "The name is Digby."

Jacklin's facial expression changed from a smirk to one of repulsion, as he removed his hand from Ben's firm grip, to find a layer of Ben's hair cream on his hand. Clive dared not risk soiling his designer casual wear and immediately pulled several napkins from the dispenser on the table next to him, and Cookie snickered. While struggling to rid his hand of the goo, Jacklin continued, "How do you feel to being the BMOC?"

"What?" Ben asked.

"You know, the big man on campus, the el hefe, the big cheese."

"I'm not following you," Ben said.

"You're what qualifies around this town as a celebrity," Jacklin said as he glanced around the room noticing many present, including his friends, were now watching the exchange and Cookie was getting worried.

"Look, I'm not trying to get cross with you, but I came up here to have breakfast and not to give another interview," Ben said. "So get to the point, assuming you have one … Mr. … whoever you are."

"You don't know?" Clive asked indignantly.

"I've seen you up here some, and Mungo doesn't think much of your business, but other than that, I don't know anything about you," Ben said.

"I'm Clive Jacklin, and I just happen to be the Vice-President of Finance at Accel Bank," he bragged.

Mungo again looked up from his breakfast plate. "Ben, have you ever known anyone that worked in a damn bank that wasn't a Vice President of somethin'?"

"Now that you mention it, no," Ben said.

"Right," Mungo said, "but I guess someone has to be in charge of the *vice* there, and Chive here seems to have risen to the task!"

"It's Clive," Jacklin said, and turned back to Ben. "The point is, I read that piece about your golf round from the other day and just wanted to talk to you about it, that's all."

"If you read the Tribune, you *must've* also seen some of those articles on your bank," Mungo interjected.

Clive grimaced. "For your information, I don't read that fish wrap that you all around here call a newspaper."

"I see, Mr. Vice President, so if you don't read the *fish wrap*, as you call it, in what paper *did* you read the story about Ben?" Mungo asked.

"Newspapers are *so* nineteen-eighties," Clive said smugly. "I choose to save trees, by getting my news—the *real news*—in ways other than the ancient method of a printed paper."

"Like what," Mungo asked, "smoke signals, carrier pigeon, tom-toms?"

"No, and I find newspapers to be as arcane as those methods."

Mungo looked at Clive suspiciously. "All right fancy pants, so just where do you get your so called *real news*?"

"If you must know, I read it from websites."

"Web what?" Mungo asked.

"Web—sites, you know, from the internet," Clive said and Mungo looked bewildered. "Don't you know about websites?"

"No, not outside the context of spiders," Mungo said glancing to

Ben and then to Cookie, and sensed they knew no more about what Clive was describing than he did.

Clive rolled his eyes. "It's the WWW, the world wide web, man! You know—the internet—they call it the *information super highway*. That's where you get the *real* news in the nineties."

Mungo stared at Clive and said, "You mean to tell me that you can't find those scandalous articles on your bank on that inter-web thing?"

"Of course not! They don't publish garbage like that!" Clive said.

"Hmm, sounds like your *information super highway* is really a one way—dead end—street," Mungo said.

"Good one Mr. T," Katrina added.

Clive bristled. "I didn't come here to talk to you little man, I'm talking to the celebrity."

Mungo would not be deterred. "But if you didn't read the corruption articles on your bank, how did you know about 'em."

"I was made aware of them by word of mouth, and just know that we may sue that lousy excuse for a newspaper for defamation."

"Look, guys, I just came here to eat breakfast," Ben said. "So what exactly do you want?"

"I'm just trying to tell you that this golf thing of yours is a pretty big deal," Clive said, "not big enough to deserve national news coverage, but it's still pretty damn big."

"Clive's right," Cookie added. "I can't think of anything bigger around these parts since the avalanche."

"Thanks fellas, but it's over," Ben said.

"Yes it is, and you should've stuck it out that day and finished," Clive said. "I warned you about it, but you blew it off and left anyway."

"Ben, you should know that most people around here think you should complete it though," Cookie added.

"The course is closed, and there's no way to play it. I mean, take look out there—even the pond is now froze over," Ben said referring to the small body of water adjacent to the eighteenth green.

"But the Trib and that TV reporter said you can finish it when the course re-opens," Cookie countered.

"That's a bunch of crap and they know it," Jacklin said, continuing to rub napkins between the fingers of his right hand. "That chance evaporated when the sun went down that day—end of story."

"Hardly seems fair," Katrina, said setting a cup of coffee in front of Ben.

"It's not fair and it's not true," Cookie said.

"Here we go again," Ben said, shaking his head, "Look—I just want to get my breakfast ordered."

"What do you mean it's not true?" Clive asked of Cookie.

"Just that. Since it's clear that he won't be able to do it this winter, he can play the eighteenth when the course reopens next spring."

"Next spring! You gotta be kiddin' me?" Clive said.

"What's wrong with that, Clive?" Cookie asked.

"It's absurd, that's what! I mean the thought of letting a man finish a round of golf, months after it started is nothing short of insane."

"Why do you say that?" Cookie responded. "Do you think you know more about it than ABC News and the Trib?"

"A lot more, and even the celebrity himself said the round is officially over!"

"No! Ben said it's over—not *officially* over," Cookie said, turning to Ben. "You haven't signed and turned in your scorecard, have you?"

"No, since the round was incomplete, it wouldn't go toward my handicap, so I just hung on to it."

"Good!" Cookie said and turned back to Jacklin. "So Ben can just keep his card open until spring."

Ben, wanting an end to the discussion, said, "I agree with the Vice President on this, and as far as I'm concerned, the round *is* officially over. I had my shot—the golf gods gave me the chance—and the weather gods took it away. Now, with that said, can I please order?"

"Hold on now—Cookie's onto somethin'," Mungo said, as he rose from his table and put on his Lone Wolf cap, wiped his mouth and joined the others at Ben's table. "Even on the pro tour they do this, and I know you've all seen it. The golfers are playing along, and the weather interferes or it gets too dark, and they resume the next day or whenever they can."

"Hey, the little man's got a point," Billy Auchterlonie said.

"Yeah, and it's hidden under his cap," Clive said.

Ben shook his head and said, "I'm sure that weather delay thing is for sanctioned tournaments, where they have TV coverage, sponsors, prize money, point standings and all that stuff to deal with, and even with all that, I've never seen them resume a round months later."

"Hey, in Massachusetts these delays happen to us a lot," the Red Sox fan with dark curly hair, said. "For us, it's usually fog or snow, and when the fog rolls in or we get a light snow fall that stops play, we mahk our balls, and wait to see if we can finish the hole later."

"You do what?" Mungo asked.

"Beg pardon?" asked the New Englander.

"Your balls, what did you say you do with 'em?"

"We mahk them."

"Look—I'm not trying to be difficult, but I don't get what you're saying," Mungo said.

"Mahk, mahk, m-a-r-k!" the man responded with frustration.

"Oh, why didn't you say so?" Mungo said, rolling his eyes.

"So we each marrrrk each ball," he exaggeratedly for Mungo's benefit, "and we wait, and if it doesn't clear up, we come back the next day, and if it's still bad, we leave our mahkers out there and keep coming back until it's good to continue."

Mungo stared skeptically at the New Englander. "So, you really leave markers out on the course until it clears up—no matter how long it takes?"

"Yes, of course!" the man responded. "What do you with your balls in bad weather?"

"Gettin' a tad personal, aren't you?" Katrina gibed.

The Red Sox fan blushed. "Come on, you know what I mean. How do you guys handle weather delays around here?"

"Speaking just for me. I use it as an excuse to come in here and drink," Mungo said, and Kat nodded her confirmation.

"Fine, but in Massachusetts, we mahk our spots and keep returning until we can finish the round."

"Sounds like a lot of trouble to me, but that settles it!" Mungo said, then proclaimed. "This chowder head is from the cradle of liberty and says Ben's got a right do it—so it must be so!"

"I appreciate all of that, but I'm done with all this nonsense," Ben said, but the crowd would have nothing of it.

"You're missin' the point," said the New Yorker from his corner table, "I've got an angle none of youse haven't even thought of."

"Use?" Mungo asked.

"No, youse," the man said.

"What?"

"Youse as in youse guys," the New Yorker said.

"Jesus!" Mungo blurted. "Ain't *any* of y'all from around here?"

"Let him talk," Cookie said, as the New Yorker took the floor.

"You paid a green fee for eighteen holes, and that entitles you to get to play all eighteen, got it? I'm a lawyer in Manhattan, and I can tell you straight, that constitutes a legally binding contract," the counselor said and pounded his fist on the table like a gavel for emphasis.

"I didn't pay a green fee," Ben said, "I'm a member."

"Sure you did. You just paid it upfront, in the form of dues and you have every right to finish!" the New Yorker persisted.

"Perry Mason here confirms it!" Mungo declared. "Ben, you have the constitutional right to play the hole."

"This is crazy!" Clive said.

"But Clive! It was you that was encouraging him to play the other day," Cookie reminded.

"Sure, if he could have gotten back out there that afternoon, but now we're now talking about months later!"

"Well, I got a newspaper, a major network, a patriot and a New York lawyer that says I'm right! So what do you have?" Mungo asked.

"What do I have?" Clive asked, as he walked over to Ben and placed his now-cleansed hand on Ben's shoulder. "I have the man that shot the round in my corner, and I don't think he believes it's any more legit than I do, so what do you say old man?"

"I say I'm hungry, that's what," Ben said as he studied the breakfast menu intently, despite knowing precisely what he wanted to order before he entered the café.

"See, he knows it's not legal!" Clive said.

Mungo shook his head. "Look, Chive, Ben didn't—"

"It's Clive!"

"Fine, but Ben didn't say that."

"It's abundantly clear that he's not interested and knows better than to even try," Clive said.

"Aw hell, Ben's just being modest," Mungo said. "He don't want all of this fuss, and I understand that, but ultimately it's his call on whether to play it or not. Though I think it's legit and that he ought to do it, I stand ready to honor his decision, so once and for all, what do you say Ben?"

"I say I'm not doing it."

"You can't do that!" Mungo yelled.

"Wait! You just said it's my call?" Ben protested.

"Well, it's bigger than you now," Mungo said. "Now look, Clyde, you know that—"

"Clive!" Jacklin corrected.

"Whatever, but you know for a fact that the pros get to resume rounds after a storm passes, and Ben shouldn't get anything less than that!"

"I hear what you're saying, but in case you haven't noticed, the storm *has* passed—days ago in fact."

"But not the effects of it! When the effects subside in the spring, then its show time for my pal Ben Digby!" Mungo said.

"It makes no sense that a man could start a round, abandon it and finish it months later. A day or two perhaps, but not months!" Jacklin argued as Pitz-Smart manager, Stewart Spindler entered the café.

"Who says?" Cookie asked. "I've been working around here day in and day out for years, and I've seen many a round resumed when the weather clears."

"That's right! This is just one, real long, weather delay," Mungo said.

"But it will resume in a completely different calendar year for crying out loud!" Clive countered and Spindler readily recognized the subject matter of the debate.

"So what, fancy pants?" Mungo defended, "what if Ben played the round on New Year's Eve and a storm flooded the course and forced him to quit. You just said you'd have no problem with him finishing in the next day or so right?" Mungo asked.

"I guess not," Clive conceded.

"Aha! So being in a different calendar year is *not* a barrier!"

"Fine, but a weather delay for almost a half a year? Come on man, that's crazy!" Jacklin asserted.

"Clive's right," Stewart Spindler said with his eyelids aflutter. "That's too long of a gap to expect it to count."

"Who asked you, Pitz-Smart boy?" Mungo asked.

"No one—but I have a right to speak, don't I?"

"First Amendment," the Manhattan lawyer called out from the corner.

"Right!" Spindler said, then added, "Another reason it can't be done, is that the conditions will have changed, and the course will be completely different when it re-opens."

Ben lowered the menu. "I've played this damned old course for decades. I played it before some of you guys were even born, and I can tell you one thing for certain, this golf course doesn't change—ever!" Ben said and a couple of old timers present nodded their agreement.

"Ben's right about that," Mungo agreed. "Plus, what's condition got to do with anything?"

"How in the world can you begin a round in one climate and resume it in a completely different one?" Spindler asserted. "I mean the man was playing in a snow storm when he reached the eighteenth tee, so how could he possibly go out and play it in the spring sunshine?"

"I can explain this," Mungo said, garnering the attention of the room. "Now listen carefully, and I'll tell you how this works. When the course opens next year, Ben goes to the eighteenth, tees up the damn ball and hits it—that's how!"

"That's funny smart ass, but a joke doesn't make it legal," Jacklin said. "Answer Stewart's question about the climate difference."

"Let's say Ben's round is flooded out mid-way through on a Sunday afternoon, and it didn't rain anymore that night, with me so far?" Mungo asked and Clive nodded. "When Ben would return on Monday to play, which you said he can do, the course would be drier and the sun might be shining, and that's okay, isn't it?"

"Sure, but—"

"Stay with me Clyde, so the course *would* be different."

"Yes—some, and the name's Clive."

"Right. Now snow is just frozen rain, correct?"

Jacklin rolled his eyes. "Yes—damn it, but what's that have to do with it?"

Mungo responded by singing in the manner of a children's song, "So, when the frozen rain goes away, then it's time for Ben to play!"

"This is bullshit!" Clive yelled. "And I agree with the celebrity, that this is only for tournament play."

"What's your basis for that?" Mungo asked. "I mean the damn rules are the damn rules! There aren't rules for tournaments and a separate set for the rest of us—so Ben gets to do what the tour guys do."

Clive shook his head vigorously. "I'm feel sure that this is against the rules for just casual—recreational—non-tournament play."

"Really?" Mungo asked. "So where do we find that rule? Is there a book called *Chive on Golf* that we ain't heard about?"

The red-faced Jacklin, responded, "It's Clive, and I bet you old hayseeds here have never even seen a rule book!"

Jumping to Clive's defense, Spindler said, "Yeah, I've seen the old guys here improving your lies and kicking balls out from behind trees."

"What's the matter with that?" Mungo asked. "My best club is the foot wedge!"

"See? See?" Clive said, now on the offensive. "It's true, you're all just a bunch of old, no-rule-reading cheaters."

Mungo looked sternly at Clive. "Now you hold on there, buddy. I'll tell you one thing about Ben Digby, he don't—"

"It's all right, Mungo—let it go," Ben interrupted.

"Sorry, Ben, but they need to be set straight on this. Ben Digby don't cheat! He plays it where it lies, counts every stroke and takes no Mulligans, and that's a fact that you can take to the bank ... well not your bank Clyde ... but a *legitimate* bank."

"What's a Mulligan?" Kat asked while making the rounds with a pot of coffee.

"For most of us, it's just a type of stew, but for these guys," Mungo said pointing to Clive and his colleagues, "it's a free pass on getting to re-hit a bad shot. Those inclined to play that way, decide how many each player gets at the beginning of the round."

"That doesn't seem fair. Is there a rule on that?" Kat asked.

"No," Mungo responded, "and ain't legit, but those that do it, routinely take one or two or twelve of 'em as they play their round."

"So are you trying to tell me that you sanctimonious old members don't fudge a little here and there?" Clive smirked.

"Oh, there's plenty of duffers like me that take liberties with the rules. Hell, I'm so bad at the game that I might be the only member that's had to get his ball retriever re-gripped," Mungo said. "But that's not Ben! He has always played it straight, and believe me, it drives us other guys nuts, but it's true. And might I add, I've seen you fancy pants types takin' more than your fair share of liberties."

Jacklin shook his head righteously. "Now you wait right there, I'm—"

"Oh please! Are you going to deny that you and your bunch fudge a little?" Mungo asked. "I've seen your ilk on the course, bending the rules and takin' more Mulligans than you'll find in a Dublin phone book!"

"Can I please just get something to eat?" Ben pleaded.

"Do you deny that?" Mungo pressed.

"Deny it? Why I take umbrage at it!" Jacklin said indignantly.

"You can take whatever you want at it, but it's damn sure the truth! I've also seen y'all, improving your lies, lifting the ball out of divots, and fluffing the fairway grass up to set the ball on."

"These fairways suck!" Jacklin defended. "What do you expect us to do?"

"Ha! So you admit y'all cheat!"

"No!" Clive said. "The tour allows for *lift and place* in shitty conditions, and the conditions here are *always* shitty."

Mungo flashed a devilish look. "So you otherwise play the game to the letter of the rules, do you?"

Standing erect and confident, Jacklin proclaimed, "Yes I do, and you should know that I consider myself a student of the game."

"Well, student of the game, you must have missed the class on *building a stance!*" Mungo charged.

"What are you talking about?"

"Do you remember the club tournament last Fourth of July?"

"Remember it? Hell, I placed fourth in it," Clive bragged, while glancing confidently toward his contemporaries.

Mungo commenced pacing back and forth in front of Clive, and asked, "You damn sure did, and as such you were paid a little prize money too, weren't you?"

"Yeah, they paid the top five."

"Right!" Mungo said, stopping abruptly in front of Clive. "Do you remember playing the eleventh hole?"

"Why do you ask?"

"Please just answer the question sir," Mungo demanded and returned to pacing.

"Let's see ... hmm ... number eleven is the par five, right?" Clive asked.

"Correct," Mungo said.

"Yeah, I recall it."

"Where'd you hit your drive?"

"I hit it through the fairway, into the rough, and it stopped under a fir tree," Jacklin said.

"Right!" Mungo said, pivoting abruptly toward Jacklin. "What'd you do for your second shot?"

"I played it *exactly* where it landed, if that's what you're getting at. I didn't pick the ball up, kick it out or even touch it for that matter."

"But why don't you tell this jury of your peers what you *did* do?" Mungo asked.

"What is this, some sort of a half-assed court trial?"

"Need my card?" asked the Manhattan lawyer.

"Please just answer the pending question," Mungo demanded.

"If it's not a trial, then what is it?" Clive asked, and beads of sweat formed on his upper lip and forehead.

"Objection, non-responsive!" Mungo snapped.

"Sustained!" said the New Yorker. "You should've hired me!"

"Now tell us, what you *did* do to hit the second shot—Mr. Vice President?"

"I swung and hit the ball, that's what. I don't get where you're going with all of this."

"Did you hit your second shot standing or kneeling, and don't lie because I was in the group behind you?" Mungo asked, leaning uncomfortably close to Jacklin, and all eyes, except Ben's, were glued on the two men."

"Because it sat under one of the limbs on that tree, I couldn't address the ball standing. So I knelt down on my knees to hit the shot, and I know for a fact that doing so is not against the rules."

"Would anyone mind if I just fix *myself* something to eat myself?" Ben asked.

"Mr. D is starvin' Cookie," Katrina intervened urgently, "want me to fix his breakfast?"

"No, I'll get it," Cookie said. "Sorry Ben, want your usual?"

"Desperately," Ben said, and Cookie trotted to the kitchen, but monitored the cross examination from there.

"So what did you do before you knelt—*sir*?" Mungo asked.

"I unclipped my bag towel and placed it on the ground and knelt on it. Then, I took a couple of practice swings, hit the ball with a choked up five wood, and hit it *very* well I might add, enough so to save par."

"Congratulations, but what you just described is defined as *building a stance* and it violates the PGA rules—Rule 13.3 to be exact."

No one in the café spoke a word, but everyone watched on as Jacklin's sweaty face turned red. "Look—it had *rained* the night before, and I didn't want to get my pants soiled, just for that cut-rate golf tournament!"

"So you didn't want to get your pants soiled out there *that* day, but probably just soiled *those* pants in here today," Mungo said pointing at Jacklin's slacks.

"You wouldn't understand this, but those were white, custom made, twill slacks, that by themselves probably cost more than your whole wardrobe."

"So if you had on, say pants like mine, you wouldn't have violated the rules?"

Clive surveyed Mungo's lime green polyester pants. "First off, I wouldn't be caught dead wearing pants like that, but if I had worn something like those, I would have felt no need to protect them from the wet ground. I would have knelt down, without the towel, hit the shot and burned the pants after the round."

"But since you had on your high-priced, hoity toity, designer pants, you built an illegal stance, right?" Mungo asked and Clive looked around room and seeing no way out of the situation, simply nodded. "I'm just curious, do you call them your *cheatin' britches*?"

"No!" Clive said. "And besides, that minor infraction—assuming it really was one at all—didn't change the outcome."

"Really?" Mungo asked staring suspiciously at Clive.

"Yes, little man. Even if I had taken a penalty stroke for that, I would have still placed fourth. I would have shot eighty-two, and the fifth place guy shot eighty-four."

"Did you sign your score card?" Mungo asked, stroking his chin whiskers with his right hand.

"Of course."

"Okay, student of the game, did you also miss the *signing of an incorrect score card* class?" Mungo asked and Clive sighed with disgust. "I thought so, but if you had attended that class, you would have learned PDQ that Rule 6-6 B says that you are DQed, and I don't mean Dairy Queen, and thus SOL—I rest my case!"

"Disqualified?" Clive asked dubiously, and Mungo nodded. "Fine, wise guy! I'll give back the five hundred bucks."

"With interest—at the rates your bank charges?" Mungo asked.

"No!"

"Hardly seems fair," Katrina, said as she bussed tables.

"I agree," Mungo said, "and what about the trophy?"

Desperate for a comeback Clive said, "Oh, you're so clever, aren't you?"

"I like to think so," Mungo, replied grinning.

"Oh yes, indeed, you *are* brilliant. As a matter of fact, I bet the rubes around here see you as the *sage of the sage brush*, the *guru of grits*, and the *master of manure*—yes, a true miracle worker," Clive said, as he began his own pacing.

"I accept the first three, but I think *miracle worker* is a tad too much," Mungo said.

"Oh no, don't sell yourself short—no pun intended," Clive said glancing toward his friends. "Why, I bet a miracle worker like you could even walk on water!"

"I could walk on that water," Mungo said, pointing out of the window toward the iced- over pond.

"You see! You see! It's true that he *is* a miracle worker!" Clive said with the voice inflection of a revival tent preacher. "What else can you do, huh? How about melting that pond and turning the water into wine?"

"No, I can't do that," Mungo confessed, "but there was a time in my first marriage when I turned the rent money into bourbon whiskey."

Even Ben chuckled at that one, but was troubled by the escalating tone of the debate. "Y'all cut this out, fellas. This all started because of my stupid golf round, and I'm done with it! All I've heard since I got here is this bantering and bickering, and I'm about to starve to death the process!"

"Coming right up, Ben!" Cookie yelled from the kitchen.

"Thanks, Cookie," Ben said then addressed the room. "I'll say this once and for all, the round is over and I'm through with all of this nonsense," he said firmly, and the tension in the room eased and everyone returned to conversing at their own tables.

The Seventh Hole

The following morning, Pitz-Smart founder and CEO Joseph Pitzmyre sat at his desk in his spacious California penthouse office, ignoring the panoramic view of the rising sun over the hazy Los Angeles valley. By that time of morning, he had already worked out in his private gym, showered, dressed and made it to his desk, before his office staff, and sat catching up on a backlog of recent financially related periodicals and newspapers. As he perused selections from the stack, one particular piece caught his eye and he decided to phone Stewart Spindler at his store in Bozeman.

"Pitz-Smart in Bozeman, how may I direct your call?" the store operator answered.

"This is Joseph Pitzmyre, get Stewart Spindler on the line."

"You're who?"

"Joseph Pitzmyre," he repeated tersely.

"Joseph what?" the girl asked.

"You gotta be kiddin' me ... it is Pitzmyre ... Pitz as in Pitz-Smart, and myre which rhymes with fire and that's what I'm about to do to you, if you don't get Spindler on the phone!"

"Okay—Mr. Piss-fire. May I tell him what this is regarding?"

"Unbelievable!" Pitzmyre said. "Tell him it's regarding replacing his store's operator."

"Please hold," she said calmly and recorded chamber music filled the silence.

"Spindler here."

"It's Joe."

"Hey Joe, How's everything out in—"

"I don't have time for that shit," Pitzmyre said. "What are you hiring out there?"

"Is this about my operator? She said you wanted to—"

"It's about me calling *my* store there and having whatever you hired as an operator interrogate me, to get to you!"

"She's new and is only human and I—"

"And how is it possible that you have an alleged human answering my store's phone who doesn't know the name Joseph Pitzmyre?"

"I'm sorry," Spindler, said contritely, "what else do you want me to say?"

"You could say that you resign, but with you being my sister-in-law's brother, I'm guessing that won't happen."

"Do you want me to fire her?"

"Oh no, Stewart. Based on you third-quarter numbers, I think she's tailor made for your store. Hell, I think you should promote her to upper management!"

"But Joe, our quarterly numbers were up," Spindler countered.

"Up from your disastrous figures from the year prior, but you're still scraping the bottom of the barrel nationally."

"I'm sure that we'll—"

"Screw it, Stewart! I don't have time to debate your failing store right now. I called because I saw an article featuring some old golfer out there who almost shot his age."

"Yeah, Ben Digby?"

"You know this guy?" Pitzmyre asked with interest.

"Sure. We're not buddies or anything, but I know him, and I golf at the same club where he shot the *round of a lifetime*, as people here are calling it."

"That's perfect! He is going to complete that round next season, right?"

"That's what they said on TV, but I don't think so," Spindler said.

"TV? I just read about this in a wire story, are you saying this dude got a television interview too?"

"Yes," Spindler said.

"What? Some public affairs program at airing before sunup on Saturday morning?"

"No, he was on Good Morning America."

Pitzmyre sprung to his feet. "You mean to tell me that this guy was on a nationally broadcasted show about this?"

"Yes, it came on a day or two after his incomplete round."

"But this guy *isn't* going to finish it?" Pitzmyre asked.

"The round?" Spindler asked.

"Yes, the round! Why is he not gonna to complete in the spring?"

"First of all, I don't think he likes all the fuss over this," Spindler said. "Secondly, do you know my banker friend Clive Jacklin?"

"Know him? Who do you think set those crooks up in business out there? Plus, who could forget Clive—rhymes with chive?"

"He and I told the people at the golf club, that it was crazy to think that completing a round months after it started could be legit."

"Tell me you didn't!" Pitzmyre said.

"What's wrong, Joe?"

"What if that kinda talk got back to that old fart ... Dingbat ... or whatever his name is?"

"It did, he was sittin' right there in the café when we said it."

"Are you crazy, Stewart?" Pitzmyre yelled. "You don't know the first thing about marketing and public relations, do you?"

"What's Ben's round of golf got to do with my store?"

"It's all about getting people in it, that's what! One way to do *that* is to promote *this*."

"What do you want me to do?" Spindler asked.

"Partner up with the old dude, and milk it for all its worth. People, like those out there gravitate to this kind of stuff," Pitzmyre explained. "Have you ever heard the saying, *there's a sucker born every minute*?"

"Sure."

"Well, I know suckers, and built an empire on the concept of having a store within fifteen minutes of most of them and to get them in the stores, you need marketing."

"So you want suckers in your stores," Spindler asked.

"Let me clarify, I want suckers shopping in my stores, but I don't want them running my stores or answering the damn telephone. Stewart, you've got to find a way to get this guy on board with playing that hole—and for our brand to be a part of it."

"That's another problem. It seems that Digby owned a retail store here in Bozeman, and he went out of business a few years ago, and word is he blames us."

"All the more reason to convert him, and all others who feel the same way," Pitzmyre said. "This grudge-holding mentality is not something to live with, it's something to combat and conquer. Once those people learn that our prices beat the hell out of the other stores there, they always come around. I'm sure it's this old-fashioned, lingering, nostalgia crap that has a lot of small competition hanging on in your area."

"But what's that got to do with Ben?"

"Stewart, this guy's golf round got national news coverage. How many times do you think someone in that town has ever done that? What's more, the article indicated that they might do a follow-up on this, and if they do, there may be another chance for national news, and we need to be a part of it."

"But Joe, the course will be closed for several months, so won't this whole thing just die and fade away over the winter?"

"It will if I leave you in charge of it! We have to fan the flames and make sure this stays relevant, and when it gets time to play the hole, we'll be side by side with this guy and have our name and logo all over it!"

"I never thought of it that way," Spindler said.

"Well there's some more national news," Pitzmyre sighed. "Look—Stewart, you have this gem of a story taking place right under your nose, and instead of seizing it, nurturing it and owning it, you and Clive spend your time trying to kill it! We've to get behind this, damn it!"

"What do you have in mind?"

"I don't know for sure, and I'll need to ponder on it, but in the meantime job number one for you is to convince the geezer that he needs to finish his round, okay?"

"Got it, but there's another problem."

"What—now?" Pitzmyre asked impatiently.

"Clive told me that out of spite, he was going to research the official rules and find proof that Ben can't do it."

Now irate, Pitzmyre's final words were, "Listen to me carefully, Stewart ... you tell that smug, underhanded, crooked Clive that if he does one thing to discourage this old dude, I'll pull every dime out of his third-rate bank, cancel their lease, and he'll be the newest caddy at that backward-ass excuse for a country club!"

The line went to a dial tone and Spindler had his marching orders. He needed immediate access to Ben, and the only way he knew to accomplish this, was through Cookie's café. Though he normally ate there once or twice per week, following Pitzmyre's challenge, he decided to make it his daily routine. He ate there every morning for a full week, without seeing Ben, and he grew more anxious and thicker around the waist with each unsuccessful trip.

One particular morning, weather reports forecasted the arrival of another strong cold front, and in light of those predictions, Spindler doubted that Ben would venture out to the café. Nevertheless, he dropped by there on his way to his store, and as he pulled onto the parking lot, he was exhilarated to catch sight of Ben walking briskly through the entrance of the clubhouse. Spindler parked his sedan, lifted a leather folio off the passenger seat, donned his heavy coat, and then scurried toward the entry gripping the folio in his gloved right hand.

Once inside the near-empty café, Spindler saw Kat re-filling catsup bottles at a table, and that Cookie had joined Ben in a booth. Playing it cool, Spindler took a seat at a table several feet away from the two men, removed his gloves and coat and arranged his papers in the folio. He ordered a coffee from Katrina, and bided his time while Cookie and Ben conversed.

"It's going to get bad out there again today," Ben said, looking out at the threatening skies through the picture window.

"Yeah, Mungo told me we're supposed to get a foot or two," Cookie said. "Hell—it all but killed the breakfast crowd."

"Speaking of Mungo, how in the world did he come up with all of those rules the other day?" Ben asked.

"Rules?" Cookie asked.

"You know the building-the-stance and the score-card disqualification?"

"Oh that," Cookie chuckled, then lowered his voice. "I wondered that myself, and after everything died down that day, I asked him about it. Ben—the whole thing was a setup."

"Oh?"

"Yeah, it seems that character witnessed Clive doing that towel thing last summer, and knew right away that it was a violation. It seems a few years ago, at a tournament at Torrey Pines, that big golfer ... what's his name?"

"Big in notoriety or big in size?"

"Both actually—he's a major champion and a heavy set fella—you know the one nicknamed, the Sea Lion or something."

"The Walrus—Craig Stadler?"

"Yeah, that's it," Cookie said. "Well, it seems Stadler did something similar to what Clive did, and Mungo knew that Stadler got disqualified for it."

"Why didn't Mungo raise it then?"

"That's the best part," Cookie whispered. "It seems that Mungo resents the newcomers so much, that he just couldn't do it that way— he said that wasn't *enough*."

"I don't understand."

"In Mungo's way of thinking, raising it right after the tournament would mean that it would've all been handled privately in the backroom here. It would have just cost Clive the five hundred bucks and a plastic trophy, and Mungo might have looked petty for even pointing it out. Instead, he researched the rules, memorized the rule numbers, and explained to me that he saved it for a time that he could—and I quote—*stick it where the sun don't shine.*"

"Really?" Ben asked with amusement.

"Yes, it wasn't enough to just cost him the money, he said that he wanted to *ruin* Clive in front of his friends."

"That's Mungo," Ben said with a belly laugh. "He truly is a genius, you know."

"That he is," Cookie said. "I'll get your breakfast started."

Kat sat Spindler's coffee cup in front of him, and turned to Cookie and said, "I'll get Mr. D's breakfast, if you want."

"Will you?" Cookie asked.

"Sure thing, if it's okay with Mr. D."

"Fine by me," Ben said.

"Want the usual, hon?"

"Yes, thank you, but can you scramble the eggs, though?"

"You got it, sugar."

Spindler, trying to act as nonchalant as possible, made his way over to the two men with his coffee cup in one hand and the folio in the other. He sat his cup on the table, pulled up a chair, sat on it and asked, "Good morning gentlemen, mind if I join you?"

"It looks like you just did," Ben said.

"Thanks. I didn't expect to see you here today, Ben."

"Likewise," Ben said, glancing at Cookie.

"Do you want to order breakfast now, Stewart?" Cookie asked.

"The coffee's fine for now."

Because of his position with Pitz-Smart, Spindler had to wear business casual or better on a daily basis. Unlike many of the other newcomers, Stewart's clothing was not acquired from a local or mail order haberdasher, but rather it represented off-the-rack selections from his own store. His typical attire included knit slacks and a cheap, button-up dress shirt, and a necktie. The ill-fitting shirts were such that when he would sit down, as he did on that morning, the portions of his shirt between each button bulged, exposing his blonde chest hair, and because of his awkward build, the shirts were routinely partially untucked at one place or another around the circumference of his belt line.

"I couldn't help overhearing you two talking about Mungo. He's quite the character, isn't he?" Stewart asked.

"Yep, that he is," Ben, responded.

"Ben, if you have a moment, I wanted to discuss something with you," Spindler said.

"Want me to leave?" Cookie asked.

"No, you're okay," Spindler said.

"What's on your mind?" Ben asked.

"I wanted you to know, that after all of that arguing the other day, I did some research on the golf rules," Spindler explained.

"Not that again," Ben said, shaking his head.

"Just hear me out, because I've got what I believe to be good news for you. You see, the rules say you *can* finish your round, and I've brought proof," Spindler said, producing a set of paper clipped pages from his folio.

"But you and Clive claimed it was against the rules," Cookie said.

"I was just going along with him, because I thought he knew what he was talking about—turns out he didn't."

"I think Mungo pretty much proved Clive is no rules expert," Ben said.

"Right, and that's why I began to think that he just might be wrong on this. Now I know that you're tired of the bickering over whether it is legit or not, but I just—"

"I'm the only one not bickering," Ben said, "I made it clear that the issue is closed."

Tensing at the comment, Spindler's eyelids starting to twitch, but he persisted. "I realize that, but I conducted my own research, and thought that with some clarity on the rules, it would allow you to make ... well ... an informed decision."

"I have made my decision," Ben said but Spindler, undeterred, laid the clipped papers on the table close to Ben.

"What exactly do you have there?" Cookie asked.

"The definitive answer, that's what!" Spindler said excitedly. "You see, it's all right here in black and white—straight from the R&A."

"The what?" Cookie asked.

"The Royal and Ancient Golf Club of Scotland," Spindler said, and Cookie leaned forward in order to read the top page of the papers. "They are the official authority on all things golf, and they say right here—and I quote: *A round interrupted by weather can be resumed the first day that the course is suitable to play.*"

"Well, I'll be damned," Cookie, said, "you mean Mungo was right about that, too?"

"Definitely," Spindler confirmed, nudging the papers even closer to Ben.

"You ought to at least have a look Ben," Cookie said.

Ben acquiesced, put on his glasses, and glanced at the highlighted portions of the pages, then began shaking his head. "I appreciate you going to all of this trouble, but I'm simply not interested."

"Don't say that—I mean this is too important to just walk away from. Of course it's your call, but what does it hurt to wait for next spring, and give it a go?" Spindler pressed as panic was setting in. "You're a par away from glory and the whole community is interested in you seeing it through."

"He's got a point," Cookie said. "I don't see why you wouldn't try, especially considering the rules allow for it. One way or another, you'll record the greatest round of your life and if you do par it, hell your name will mentioned around this place long after we're all gone."

"I think I'm getting mentioned around here enough as it is," Ben said.

"You're such a humble man," Spindler said, "so much so that I don't think you truly appreciate the excitement your round has already generated. I'm around the citizenry, day in and day out, and this *is* a big deal to them."

"It's certainly been the main topic of conversation around here," Cookie added.

"So I've noticed," Ben said.

"I understand where you're coming from, but it would mean a lot to the town and the fellas down at the VFW hall," Cookie said. "This kind of excitement doesn't happen around here very often, and they'd get a real kick out of you playing it."

"Now, Cookie, why in the world would the vets down there care about this golf round thing? After all, Mungo and I are the only ones that even play anymore."

"You should've seen 'em at the hall that morning you were interviewed. They were as proud as they could be, just seeing your face on that old console TV," Cookie explained.

"The guys saw it?" Ben asked.

"They sure did, and I popped over there and watched it with them."

"How were you able go to the hall that time of morning?"

"I asked Alf to come in and look after things, and between him and Kat, I was able to slip out for an hour or so. Since the hall's closer than my apartment, I just headed over there and stayed long enough to see it."

"How'd y'all even know it was even coming on?" Ben asked, and Cookie's expression changed. "Did Emily tip you off?"

"Yes, but I wasn't supposed to tell you."

"Hell, I should have known she would do that," Ben said with amusement. "So the guys really liked it, huh?"

"They loved it and when you mentioned the *true heroes*, the vets that could, actually stood and cheered."

"Cheered?" Ben asked dubiously, and Cookie nodded. "And the TV was workin'?"

"For that old junker, it was, I mean we had to jiggle the tubes to get it turned on, and you know that the picture is always terrible. So we had to have someone stand next to it and hold the foil on the rabbit ears, to fight the snow and the horizontal roll."

"Did that work?" Ben asked.

"Some, but no matter what you do, the screen is always a little fuzzy, but it's unwatchable unless someone's tending to the antenna. Since we didn't know when your interview would come on, to be fair we took ten minute shifts manning the rabbit ears. When one of us stood in the right spot and held the foil in just the right way, it didn't move too much and we'd get a decent enough picture. But when Mungo took his turn, it worked *real* well, until your interview came on."

"What happened then?" Ben asked.

"Mungo kept trying to move to where he could see the screen, and each time he did, the picture would go nuts."

"Why'd y'all use Mungo, after all he's so impatient?" Ben asked.

"It just happened to be his shift when it came on, but oddly enough he's the best at it," Cookie explained. "So when Mungo would stand still, the picture was tolerable. The snow that did remain on the screen, made it like that day Chuck retrieved you from the eighteenth. It looked like flakes were flying all around you and that reporter, and in an odd way added to the feel of the story."

"I guess, you take what you can get with that old Zenith," Ben said. "But, Mungo's the shortest, so I wonder why he's better at it steadying the picture."

"He thinks it's the metal plate in his head that gives him the edge," Cookie explained.

"You guys ought to know that we happen have a big sale on televisions this week!" Spindler interjected.

Ignoring the sales pitch, Cookie said, "The point is, there's a lot of excitement wound up in this, and I think you *should* finish the round."

"I hear what you're saying," Ben said.

Spindler perked up and asked. "So will you do it, Ben?"

Suspicious of Spindler's insistence and motives, Ben asked, "Just why do you care so much about this?"

"It's all about the community," Spindler adlibbed.

"Community? Pitz-Smart?" Ben asked dubiously.

"Despite what you believe, we *are* good for the community. I know there is hard feelings here, and we see that all the time, at least until the folks—you know—get used to us. But don't do it for us, do it for you, your wife and your buddies over at that club Cookie mentioned."

Ben seemed unpersuaded, and Cookie asked, "Stewart, would you mind giving us a second to talk?"

"No problem, I need to go to the john anyway," Spindler said as he rose and walked away from the table.

Cookie waited for the restroom door to close behind Spindler before saying, "Ben, you know how I feel about Pitz-Smart, but this could be really exciting for the men, and could mean a lot of publicity for the club here too. We need new members, and this thing could bring them in."

"Oh sure, let's get the word out and end up with more newcomers."

"They're a pain all right, but unfortunately the club needs 'em," Cookie said.

"I see your point, and I do empathize, but don't you think there's something fishy about all of this? I mean, why would Stewart take such an interest in this golf rigmarole, and why come up here carrying those rules?" Ben asked.

"I'm not quite sure, but come to think of it, he's been carrying around that leather notebook and hanging out here an awful lot lately," Cookie said.

"More than normal?" Ben asked.

"Much more."

"A part of me really wants to log a number on that scorecard for finality, if nothing else, but I'd just like to be left alone about it until then. When the course re-opens, I would be content to just quietly walk out there, tee it up, and let the chips fall where they may. But, the more I'm pushed, the more I feel the urge to resist."

"I can understand that, but your friends would like to be a part of it and see it too," Cookie said.

"Having people around when I do it would be awkward, maybe even be nerve wracking."

"Bottom line is you do want to complete it, right?" Cookie asked.

"I do, but all this attention really eats at me Cookie and Stewart's encouragement down right gives me the creeps."

"What do you think's going on?"

Ben shook his head. "I don't know, but Pitz-Smart must have something to gain, but can't put my finger on it."

"It's certainly odd, but why not agree to it to get them out of your hair and ignore everything else until the day comes."

"Perhaps you're right, after all, I'm not committed to doing anything beyond that," Ben reasoned.

"Right," Cookie agreed, "just set aside all of the—wait here he comes."

"So, what do you say, Ben?" Spindler asked returning to his chair.

Ben glanced over to Cookie, and at his hopeful expression, and said, "It's against my better judgment, but I'm leaning toward doing it."

Though less than a full commitment, the other men nodded their mutual approval, and Cookie asked, "So Stewart, you want to order now?"

"No, not this time, but thanks anyway," Spindler said, as he rose and walked hastily toward the exit, not wanting to afford Ben any opportunity to reconsider.

"Don't you feel like checkin' to make sure you still have your wallet when a guy like that leaves the room?" Ben asked and Cookie smiled.

The Eighth Hole

When Spindler arrived at his second floor office at the store, he wasted no time getting Pitzmyre on the phone.

"What do you want Stewart?" Pitzmyre answered.

"It looks like a done deal, Joe."

"What? You're resigning?"

"No, nothing like that," Spindler said. "It's about the golf thing—I spoke to Ben Digby."

"Did he commit to playing the hole?"

"I think so."

"You think?" Pitzmyre asked.

"Yes, we talked, and he's now leaning toward doing it."

"I need more than *think* and *leaning* to jump on this," Pitzmyre said with frustration. "I'm working up a deal—a big deal—one that could involve a lot of money, and I have to get a commitment."

"I didn't make him sign a contract or anything, but I really believe he'll do it."

"That's a good start Stewart, but I'm going to need something firm—something binding."

"I understand, but we can't push him too hard, or we'll run him off for sure. The guy's very skittish and more than a little suspicious, and he's real old."

"I can't help that last part, but if he continues breathing between now and the day that golf course re-opens, I need confirmation that he's on board. Tell me more about how the conversation went."

"When I first broached the subject, he was dead set against doing it, but as we discussed it, he seemed to soften and by the end the conversation, he came around to the concept. I really think I got through to him."

"That's good, so how'd you do it?"

"With everyone hassling him over whether the concept was legal or not, I—"

"Including you and Chive."

"Yes, including us, so I figured he needed some clarity on the issue to … you know … to encourage him. I went to a local library and read up on the official rules of golf, and lo and behold, they say his round *can* be resumed when the course becomes playable. So I made a copy of the rules, highlighted the important parts and presented them to him."

Pleased by this revelation, Pitzmyre said, "Nice job Stewart, maybe there's hope for you after all. The only thing more surprising than you getting this right is that place out there actually having libraries," Pitzmyre said. "All that matters now is making sure none of those yahoos out there, do anything to discourage ol' Dingbat, got it?"

"Got it!"

"Now, that brings us to step two, luring him into the publicity part," Pitzmyre said.

"I think I understand what you're getting' at, but Ben truly doesn't like us," Spindler warned.

"Stewart, if we can't market this, I don't give a shit whether he plays the hole or not."

"I get that, but I sense he's already suspicious of me urging him on."

"Fine, leave him out of it for now and work behind the scenes. I know this is going to take some finessing, but we're going to need some intelligence on Dingbat."

"Like what?"

"Ask around, and find out what makes him tick and learn his likes and dislikes."

"I already know what he dislikes—us."

"Damn it Stewart! I can't help the way he feels—that's his problem, and quit focusing on that, and find out what he's passionate about."

"I'm not sure I'm following you, Joe."

"Why am I not surprised? Look—do I have to come out there and handle this myself?"

"Come on, Joe—ease up a little."

"Look—the guy has to have some friends, so talk to them about his interests. Learn what civic clubs he's involved with, or if he goes to church, or the charities he supports and crap like that."

"He did mention a club he's involved with."

"Good, start with that and build on it."

The next morning, Spindler was driving out on the by-pass highway toward Pitz-Smart, when he happened to see Mungo Thibodeaux pumping gas at a corner convenience store. He U-turned, and pulled onto the lot, parked his car in a spot near the store's entrance, and pondered his approach as he walked from his car over to the row of gas pumps.

"Mornin' Mungo," Spindler said.

Mungo turned and saw Spindler, rolled his eyes and said, "'Mornin' Stewart."

"So, what brings you here?" Spindler asked.

"Trying not to run out of gas. How 'bout you?"

"Oh … uh I'm thinking of gettin' me some gas too," Spindler said, pointing to his parked sedan.

"I got news for you, you're gonna to have to move your car," Mungo advised. "They ain't got hoses that long."

"Yes, I'll do just that," Stewart said. "How was your Thanksgiving?"

"Rotten," Mungo said tersely.

"Why?"

"Too many relatives came up from Texas."

"That's a long way to come," Spindler said.

"Sure it is, but they like to ski, so distance and ice and snow don't stop 'em."

"So, what do you think about Ben Digby?"

"He's a great guy, why?"

"I know, but I mean about this golf hole thing."

"I think he ought to play it," Mungo said, keeping his eyes trained on the pump's rolling dials.

"Me, too. You were right about the rules, you know. I researched them and he *can* complete it when the eighteenth becomes playable—even if it's next spring."

"I know that, and if you haven't noticed, I've become quite an authority on them golf rules."

"Yes, and man you really put it on ol' Clive, the other day," Spindler said with a contrived chuckle.

"He had it comin'," Mungo said. "Hey, come to think of it, both of you guys were against Ben playing the hole—what changed?"

"I wasn't against it, I just didn't think it would be legit, so I researched it and learned that it is."

"Well, I hope he plays it and shoots his age—couldn't happen to a finer fella," Mungo said.

"You're pretty close to Ben, aren't you?"

"I think that's safe to say," Mungo said.

"I was wondering what Ben likes to do when he's not golfing?" Spindler asked.

Mungo thought for a moment, and said, "Well, he's really good with tools and enjoys doing woodworking projects, and he likes to bitch about your company—a lot, and that's about it."

"He really has a grudge with Pitz-Smart, huh?"

"Ben has a grudge with the Germans, but Pitz-Smart, now that's a whole 'nother level."

"Other than tools and woodworking, is there anything else he does?"

"Not as far as I know, I mean we're friends and all, but I don't hang out with him at his house or anything like that."

"Does he go to church?"

"Emily drags him over to the Methodist church from time to time, and on most all of the big days ... you know like Easter and Christmas, but that's about it."

"I see. Anything else?"

"Good grief!" Mungo said turning back to Spindler. "Are you writing his biography or somethin'?"

"No—I'm just interested in the guy—that's all, and was just wondering what he enjoys doing," Spindler explained and Mungo returned his focus to the pump dials. "Does he have any other interests?"

Mungo thought for a moment, and then said, "He's very involved with the VFW."

"I heard somethin' about that—does it involve wrestling?"

Mungo turned and stared at him scornfully. "Veterans of Foreign Wars ... ever heard of 'em?"

"Oh yeah, of course. So Ben's active with them?"

"He's more than just active, hell he basically runs the joint."

Spindler homed in. "So, you're a member, too?"

"Oh yeah, I'm one of 'em."

"What all does Ben do for them, run the meetings and such?"

"He does that and much more. The building itself is pretty run down, and he and some of us other vets try to keep the place running, as best as we're able."

"So the members do some of the repairs?" Spindler asked.

"We fix what we can handle ourselves, and raise money for repairs we can't."

"How do places like that raise money?"

"There was a time when we rented the hall out for functions, but not anymore."

"So nonmembers used to go there?" Spindler asked.

"Used to," Mungo said. "Back in the day we had parties and dances and wedding receptions and such, and that brought in good revenue, but that's long gone."

"So how do you guys get money now?"

"We have member dues, and do fundraisers like a spring carnival, bake sales and selling homemade quilts that some of the wives make," Mungo explained as the pump clicked off, and he hung up the nozzle.

"The dues alone, aren't enough to cut it, huh?" Spindler asked.

"No, at least not anymore. As we lose members, we lose the dues revenues along with them."

"Are some of them quitting?"

"Beg Pardon." Mungo asked turning back to Spindler.

"You said y'all are losing members, are they quitting?"

"No—they're dying."

"Oh … that's too bad," Spindler said. "So what kind of repairs does the VH … I mean the VW…"

"VFW," Mungo sighed as secured gas cap, and closed the hatch on his car that covered it.

"Yes, what do they need up there?"

"Like I said, the building itself is in bad shape, and the heat and air is shot, and the roof sprung a leak during one of the storms earlier this year. Everything there is like most of the veterans—old and worn out. We put off the things that we can, but the city inspectors keep breathin' down our necks, so we have to do some things just to keep from getting red tagged."

"I know what you mean, I have to deal with code enforcement at my store," Spindler said. "Has the building been tagged?"

"No, at least not yet, but no offense, it's cold out here, and I'm getting light headed from sniffin' gasoline fumes," Mungo said.

Spindler knew he had pushed the issue enough, and as he walked away, Mungo opened his driver's side door, and took a seat. He watched through his side-view mirror, as Spindler got in his car and drove back out on the highway. "I knew he didn't need no gas," Mungo grumbled.

Spindler left feeling he had what Pitzmyre needed, and after calling his contacts at the Bozeman Code Enforcement Department, he was anxious to give Pitzmyre an update.

"What'd you learn?" Pitzmyre asked.

"First of all, Ben's sentiments about Pitz-Smart are even worse than I imagined."

"What are you saying?"

"I'm telling you, the man has it in for us."

"I *really* hope that's not what you called to tell me," Pitzmyre replied.

"It's not, but I'm just warning you that he may be a tough nut to crack, but with that said, I may have the angle that you're looking for."

"What? A church or charity?" Pitzmyre asked.

"Ben's not a big churchgoer, but he does like using tools and doing woodworking projects and—"

"Stewart, everyone does that kind of crap in those small towns. What about the clubs, and charitable organizations? I mean, the man has got to do something with his spare time, for God's sakes!"

"I'm getting to that, it seems he's real active with the WVF ... or WFV ... I mean —"

"Is he into wrestling?" Pitzmyre asked.

"No, that's what I thought, at first. It's the foreign veteran's thing."

"The VFW?"

"Yeah, that's it!"

"I've heard of them," Pitzmyre said. "They're these places where these old farts go to drink and smoke and play cards and crap like that, however this is helpful, and here's what I want you do. Find out about their needs or what causes they support, perhaps we can suck Ben in with a donation."

"They're the ones with the needs."

"Who?"

"The VFW itself," Spindler said. "I was told that their building is falling apart and some of their equipment is shot, and they lack the money to make repairs," Spindler explained.

"How'd you hear about that?"

"First off, one of their members told me about it, but I also called the guys at Bozeman Code Enforcement. They confirmed that the place is a wreck, and they've been on the brink of getting tagged for quite a while."

"Tagged, as in red tagged?" Pitzmyre asked.

"Correct. The fella with the city said they've been going out there for a good while, and said they would've tagged it and shut it down by now, but they're real sympathetic for the old dudes that go down there."

"It's that bad, huh?" Pitzmyre asked.

"Apparently, and they do fund raisers to pay for some repairs necessary to just keep the doors open."

"That's good to know," Pitzmyre said. "So, what kind of fundraisers do they do—bake sales and that crap like that?"

"They do that and they sell some homemade quilts, too."

"How charming," Pitzmyre said sarcastically. "These people must be in some sort of a time warp, but here's the deal, you get hold of Ben Dingbat and tell him I want to meet with him. I have a regional meeting in Minnesota the second week of December, so let's schedule it around that."

"What do I tell him the meeting's about?" Spindler queried.

"As little as possible."

"He's bound to ask questions, though."

"I know, but don't volunteer any information. If he starts to quiz you about it, just tell him it's a proposition that will help the VFW and leave it at that," Pitzmyre instructed.

"Got it, boss."

"When does it thaw out enough there for that that golf course to re-open?"

"Joe, I've only been here a couple of years and I—"

"Stewart, I'm not asking for the exact date! Can you just give me a month, for Christ's sake?"

"I'm told late March, or early April."

"Okay, now you get that meeting scheduled, understand? Time's a ticking on the publicity clock and I want to get moving on this!"

Pitzmyre hung up, and Spindler wasted no time in finding Ben's home number and dialing it.

When Ben answered, Spindler said, "Good morning, this is Stewart,"

"Who?" Ben asked.

"Stewart Spindler, you know, the guy from Lone Wolf that gave you the golf rules the other day."

"The Pitz-Smart guy?" Ben asked.

"That's right."

"What do you need, Stewart?"

"I spoke to Joseph Pitzmyre a while ago. He's the founder and CEO of—"

"I know who he is," Ben interjected.

"He's asked me to set up a meeting with you."

"Joseph Pitzmyre wants to meet with me?" Ben asked with dismay.

"That's right."

"Now, why in the world would a guy like that want to—wait is this about my golf round?"

"Yes, it does involve that," Spindler said, "I don't know the details, but he's got an offer that he thinks will really interest you."

"I'd be happy if he and all the others around here would just let it go," Ben said.

"Hang on now, you did say the other day at the café that you were going to play the hole."

"I said I was *leaning* toward playing it and I still am, but I'd just like to be left alone about it until the time comes. Plus, I have a difficult time imagining me being interested in *anything* Mr. Pitzmyre has to offer," Ben said firmly.

"Don't dismiss it out of hand, Ben. I think you'll feel different about it after you hear him out."

"Is this why you've been looking up golf rules and quizzing guys like Mungo about me?"

Though caught off-guard by the question, Spindler knew well to answer honest and direct. "Yes, I had to know a few facts for my boss for him to put this deal together."

"I appreciate your candor, now tell me exactly what this is about."

"All I know is that it involves that veteran's club you're in," Spindler said.

"The VFW?"

"That's right, but I truly don't know anything beyond that," Spindler said. "But it's just a few minutes of your time Ben, and there's no obligation, and once it's done, and if it's not to your liking, you have every right to just walk away."

Ben's inclination was to simply decline, but he paused to think things through, and though he sensed that this involved a scheme designed ultimately to benefit Pitz-Smart, he nevertheless relented. "I suppose that if a man that busy wants to talk to me, I ought to do it, but he should know up front that the chances of me entering into any deal with him are as thin as that toilet paper y'all sell in your stores!"

On the day of the meeting, Pitzmyre's private jet landed at Bozeman's regional airport, and per his instructions, Spindler met him in a rented jet-black Lincoln Towne Car. Spindler greeted his boss on the tarmac, and then took the driver's seat, and the CEO took a seat in the rear. All windows of the car, except the windshield itself, were tinted so dark that as they drove, it all but obliterated the view of the scenic terrain, including the majestic mountain range. At Pitzmyre's request, Spindler detoured and made the first stop the VFW hall. When they pulled to a stop on the edge of the parking lot, Pitzmyre rolled down his tinted window, surveyed the property and said, "Shit! This place was a dump when they built it, and it's only gotten worse!"

"Yeah, and it's supposed to be a wreck on the inside too," Spindler said. "Do you want a closer look?"

"Hell no, look at that parking lot. I wouldn't drive even a rental, across that!"

"Seen enough?" Spindler asked.

"Yes, and I'd say they should be *very* desperate," Pitzmyre said gleefully as he raised his window.

From there, they drove straight to the Lone Wolf club to meet Ben, and as Spindler brought the car to a stop on the parking lot, Pitzmyre leaned forward and said, "So this is it?"

"What?"

"This," Pitzmyre said, pointing. "Is this the clubhouse?"

"Yes."

"How can they call this place a country club?"

"The building's a little dated, but serviceable, and you won't be able tell with all of the snow on the ground, but the course is a great lay out," Spindler explained while glancing at Pitzmyre's skeptical expression in the rearview mirror

As they made their way into the clubhouse, and toward the café, Pitzmyre assessed the interior, and his opinion of the property did not change. Spindler spotted Ben sitting at a corner table and waved, and Ben nodded then took in Pitzmyre's appearance as the two neared. The CEO had straight greying black hair that was slicked back terminating in a small ponytail. His skin, at least which showed, had a tanned, bronze glow a tone that few in that part of the country could sustain in the summer, and never in the winter. Everything he wore other than jewelry, was black, including a collarless shirt, jeans, pointy leather shoes, and a thigh-length, leather jacket.

When the two men reached Ben's table, Spindler made the introductions. "Ben, this is Joseph Pitzmyre, and Joe meet Ben Digby,"

"Glad to meet you," Pitzmyre said, shaking Ben's right hand with the exaggeration of using both of his. Ben glanced at Pitzmyre's perfectly manicured fingernails, noted his soft, smooth palms and fingers, and caught a whiff of an aroma akin to Emily's lotion—all of which spoke to him. "I've heard a lot about you," Pitzmyre said as the handshake finally terminated.

"I'm sure you have," Ben said, casting a quick glance in Spindler's direction.

"Ben, that golf round of yours was quite remarkable, it truly was a great thing you did." Pitzmyre said.

"Don't you mean almost did?"

"In my opinion, a seventy for seventeen holes, for a man of your age and handicap is quite an accomplishment, in and of itself."

"Excuse me, but can I get you fellas anything?" Cookie offered, but when each declined, Cookie returned to a table and resumed rolling a bin full of clean knives and forks into napkins.

"You see Ben, it was a great performance, but there's a little unfinished business," Pitzmyre said. "As you know, come this spring, your completion of this round is going to electrify this town."

"Mr. Pitzmyre, you should know up front, that I haven't committed to do anything come spring," Ben said, prompting Pitzmyre to stare over to Spindler with an icy glare. "I believe this has already been blown *way* out of proportion, and I honestly don't think the community could care less about me playing a single hole of golf months from now. With that said, can we just get down to what this is all about?"

"Sure, all we want is for you to agree to finish your round, just as soon as the hole is playable. When you do, Pitz-Smart wants to be a part of it, and give you the proper recognition you deserve."

Ben stared at Pitzmyre skeptically. "What exactly does that entail?"

"We simply ask that you let us use your name and image in some ads and on some banners that we'll display at the store and here at the golf course when the day comes. We would also like it if you could make a couple of public appearances at the store."

"What for?" Ben asked.

"It's just marketing, Ben. Publicity for us, and for you, and it's all intended to highlight the finale on the eighteenth."

Uninspired by the concept, Ben had heard enough. "Gentlemen, this thing has taken on a life of its own, and I honestly don't like it. I have received more letters since all of this started than I usually get in a whole year, and then there are the phone calls. That part has been so bad that I am actually considering changing my phone number, a number I have had for almost a half century. Publicity is your life blood Mr. Pitzmyre, but to me it represents a very unwelcome inconvenience."

Sensing a quick and disastrous end to the meeting, Spindler intervened. "Ben, the community would want it this way, and it'll be exciting for your friends, and fellow vets and all of us here at the club."

"I think Stewart's right, and believe those around this town will gravitate to it," Pitzmyre added.

"My friends might get a little enthused, but the public at large, I'm not so sure about that," Ben said. "You see Mr. Pitzmyre, the citizens here have real problems to deal with, including things like struggling to pay their bills and making ends meet."

"All the more reason to create a little excitement for them, right?" Pitzmyre encouraged, but Ben did not respond. "Look—I happen to believe that this *is* a big deal, and we simply want to be a part of it."

"And somehow, and in some way, you'll make money off of it, right?"

"Sure Ben, it's just business," Pitzmyre said. "After all, you were an entrepreneur and should understand that and I disagree with your assessment of the communities' interest in this."

"What do you know about this community?" Ben asked.

"Not a lot, beyond them not spending much money in my store, and I want to change that," Pitzmyre said, and Spindler sighed. "And while this community may have its own history and culture, at the end of the equation, it's made up of people, and I *do* know people, and I think there will be a lot of interest in this, in fact I believe that the appeal stretches well beyond the city limits of Bozeman."

"You may know people where you're from, but I know the people here, and they won't get all wrapped up in this."

"You think I'm overestimating the demographics?" Pitzmyre asked.

"No—I think you're underestimating them."

"Tell me this Ben," Pitzmyre said, "how do you think you got on a nationally broadcasted television show, and how did your story end up in a newspaper on my desk in Los Angeles?"

"Joe's right Ben, and you said yourself that you've been getting tons of calls and mail," Spindler said.

"Oh, the press can always hype things up and make more out of something than it really deserves, but all I'm saying is that the rank and file here are different."

"The press ran with it in the first place, because they recognized it as a compelling news story," Pitzmyre said.

"And if it makes the news again, you guys will be front and center to capitalize on it, right?"

"You caught me!" Pitzmyre said, raising his arms in surrender. "Guilty as charged, Mr. Digby!"

"At least you're up front about it," Ben said.

"Sure, there's no secrets here. I certainly did not come all the way out here to dupe you or put one over on you. I am simply an executive who is trying to do something good for my company. I owe it to the shareholders to think this way, but there is nothing emotional about this for me, I'm simply trying to get a struggling location back on track. We are a for-profit company Ben, and this is just every-day, run of the mill marketing, nothing more and nothing less. I just happen to think this would be a good thing for you too, but if you don't want to do it, I'll get on my plane and fly out of here with zero regrets and no hard feelings."

Ben rose from his seat. "Thank you for coming out here gentlemen, but I'm simply not interested."

Spindler's face showed panic and he darted his rapidly blinking eyes to Ben and back to his boss. The deal was unraveling and he feared that failure would somehow rest on his shoulders, but he also noticed that his boss was amazingly calm and seemingly unaffected by Ben's impending departure.

"Hang on now," Pitzmyre, said as Ben donned his old quilted jacket. "After all, you haven't even heard my proposal, and I traveled a long way out here to lay it out for you."

Ben's sense of hospitality compelled him to pause. "All right, let's hear it."

"I understand that you're a war veteran and a member of the VFW," Pitzmyre said.

"That's true."

"I couldn't help but notice that the VFW hall is in pretty bad shape."

"You went by there?" Ben asked.

"Yes, and I'm willing to donate ten grand to the VFW, if you'll play ball."

Spindler was stunned and Ben asked, "Ten thousand dollars—for the VFW?"

"That's right."

Ben shook his head. "I appreciate the offer, but—"

"Wait Ben," Pitzmyre interrupted as he retrieved a small black leather pouch from his inside jacket pocket. "Do me a favor and don't answer today, okay?"

"If you insist," Ben said.

Pitzmyre pulled a business card from the pouch and handed it to him. "This has my direct number on it. If you dial it, it will ring the phone right on my desk. All I ask is that you think it over for a few days and call me to let me know what you decide."

"Fair enough," Ben agreed.

"Just so you know the ten thousand is theirs whether you succeed with shooting your age or not."

"Let me get this straight—I play the eighteenth hole, and no matter what I score, the VFW gets that money."

"Yep, that's the offer, and I'll even put it in writing."

Ben shoved the card in his jacket pocket and asked, "There's more to this than just advertising, isn't there?"

"I'm a gambler Ben, and I'm willing to bet on you because I predict that if we partner on this, that it'll help bring in sales," Pitzmyre explained. "To get to where I am, you have to take a lot of risks, and I've always been willing to do that. I've won some and lost some, but overall, I've done pretty well for myself."

Ben placed the card in his pocket, bid them farewell and when he exited for the parking lot, Spindler turned to Pitzmyre. "What do you think the chances are?"

"Fifty-fifty."

The Ninth Hole

When Ben returned his house and walked into the kitchen, he said, "That brings back memories of—"

"K.P. duty," Emily finished.

"How'd you know that?"

"Because, you've said that most every time you've seen me peeling potatoes."

"Am I that repetitious?" he asked.

"Yes," she said smiling, "and I wouldn't have it any other way."

"You like repetition?"

"Of course! You see, most women thrive on security, and repetition is a big component of that."

"Sounds tedious to me, I mean with having the same things happening over and over," Ben said.

"Constancy and consistency leads to reliability, and that my dear and that adds to the all-important security."

"I'd find that dull and boring, but you don't?"

"Certainly not!" Emily said. "I take great comfort in knowing that, day in and day out, you'll greet me each morning, be here for me to take care of, and talk to me and to keep me company throughout the day," she said.

"You could get all of that from a parrot."

Emily grinned, wiped her hands on her apron and hugged him.

"Every woman wants and needs things in their lives that are constant and dependable, especially in a mate, and you my dear, are my precious constant."

"But what about spontaneity and serendipity?" Ben asked. "I've seen those words used on the cover of those ladies' magazines at the checkout stand. They say that spouses are supposed to be spontaneous and exciting, and I've never seen them mention constant and repetitious."

"Perhaps those characteristics are vital for twenty something year-old newlywed brides, but even they need a mate who's a constant over the long haul—even more than the romance."

"More than the romance, huh?" Ben asked.

"Yes, and truth be known, I think men are generally more romantic than women, but don't get me wrong, most women do need romance—at *any* age," Emily said, giving Ben's hand a squeeze. "But having a husband who's great in that department, but is likewise unreliable and unpredictable, is a recipe for a failed marriage or a miserable life."

"That makes sense," Ben said, "and just so you know, you are *my* constant."

Emily wheeled around. "So you find me tedious and boring!"

"What?" Ben uttered from back on his heels.

"You just said that *constant* to you equals boring and tedious, so you're saying that I'm just one big bore to you?" Emily asked wielding the potato-peeler.

"Wait! You said constant was good!"

"Yes, when it comes to husbands. Wives are supposed to be new and spontaneous,"

"I'm sorry, but I just thought—"

"I gotcha, didn't I?" Emily asked, grinning.

Ben exhaled, and said, "Yes, and I thought confronting Joseph Pitzmyre was a trying experience!"

"Oh yeah, how did your meeting go?" Emily asked, as she commenced slicing the peeled potatoes on a cutting board.

"Em, it was the darnedest thing I've witnessed, since I mistakenly wandered into a burlesque show in Paris." Ben replied, popping a piece of raw potato in his mouth.

"Quit that!" she said. "So what did they want?"

"Pitz-Smart is interested in using my image—can you believe that?

"What do you mean by that?" Emily asked.

"I don't know all the details, but it's all about this silly golf thing. They seem to think that if I play the hole, and they back me on the deal, it'll in some measure help their store."

"So they want to be on your side?"

"Apparently, plus Pitzmyre looks at this as some form of wagering, and sees backing me as a gamble of sorts ... I think ... I mean that part's a little murky. He also mentioned me making some store appearances."

"Pitz-Smart store appearances?"

"Yes, but I was so put off by all the whole rigmarole, that I just wanted to get out of there."

"You did turn him down, right?" Emily asked as she ceased her slicing and looked back at him.

"Sort of," Ben said and she stared at him curiously. "Let's put it this way, I didn't accept it," he said and reached for another slice of potato.

"You're going to ruin your lunch!" Emily said slapping the back of his hand.

"I just want a little snack."

"These are for scalloped potatoes, and not for snacking," she said. "So, how'd you leave it with them?"

"After I listened to his pitch, and said I wasn't interested, he gave me this," Ben said removing Pitzmyre's business card pocket and tossing it on the kitchen counter. "He asked me to think about it and get back to him in a couple of days."

"I would have thought you would turn him down outright, I mean how could they expect you of all people, to help them with their sales?"

"Oh, he knew better than that all right," Ben, said pausing to stare at the steam now rising from the boiling pot on the stove, "but the deal came with an incentive."

"What do you mean?"

"A big fat carrot on a stick, that's what," Ben said. "He offered money for the VFW."

"Oh … how much?"

"Ten thousand dollars."

Emily shrieked with excitement, but then noticed Ben's woeful expression. She knew he was troubled, and laid her knife on the cutting board and stood at his side. "Are you thinking about doing it?"

Ben ran his hand through his hair, took a deep breath and exhaled. "I hate to pass up a chance to benefit the hall, but I have my pride too, you know. You, our home and my pride are the only things of value I have left."

"But what if you agree and don't win that hole?"

"That's not a requirement."

"You mean the VFW will get all that money no matter what?" Emily asked and he nodded. "How'd they even know about the VFW?"

"Stewart Spindler's carefully conducted research—that's how," Ben said.

"They're manipulating you, aren't they?"

"Big time and doing a darn good job, and I think that's the part that eats at me most. They snooped around, asked all these questions about me, and searched for an angle. They needed a pinch point— something to leverage."

"And they found it in the VFW," Emily said.

"Right and ten grand is not the type of money you just ignore. That's more than we collect in dues per year these days," Ben said. "We do have so many problems down there, and that kind of money just might keep the hall open."

"Is it that bad down there?" Emily asked.

"Yes and the fact that you have to ask me that question speaks volumes."

"What do you mean?"

"You don't know the answer to that question, because you've not been down there to witness the problems first hand."

"Are you upset that I don't go down there anymore?" Emily asked.

"No, of course not. The place isn't suitable for anyone other than a bunch of hairy-legged old Jarheads and Gyrenes."

"But haven't you guys made a lot of the repairs?"

"We've done quite a bit of them, but some problems require permits and professionals, and with the dues diminishing, we're forced to dip into the operating account to pay for them."

"At least you have the funds to do it," Emily said.

"We do for now, but that takes away from our charitable budget. Every dollar spent on contractors is less for the other causes."

"What you all need are newer and younger dues-payers," Emily said.

"That's true, but to get newer and younger members, you need new foreign wars, and I don't want that either."

"Of course you're right," she said, "so what are you going to do?"

"I just don't think I can do it. As bad as things are down there, with all of us pitching in, and with the spring fundraisers, perhaps we can ride it out."

"What about the Christmas presents," she asked, referring to the VFW hall's longstanding tradition of providing gifts for children in the local shelters.

"We have money available, but only half as much as usual?"

"We can chip in, right?" she asked.

"Are you willing to do that again this year?" Ben asked as he perked up.

"Sure."

"Thanks, Em," he said and kissed her cheek. "It *really* is a good cause, and we should do it."

"I agree," she said, "now tell me about that burlesque show in Paris ..."

The following Thursday night was designated for the VFW's

quarterly business meeting. As was his custom, Ben poured over the books and financials, in order to address his fellow members. When he left for the meeting that evening, he was fully prepared to discuss, among other things, the fundraisers and their mounting budgetary woes. Ben served as the post's treasurer and secretary, and he recorded the minutes of each meeting. He was also the parliamentarian, and dutifully conducted each meeting according to the letter of *Robert's Rules of Order.* These meetings usually lasted thirty to forty-five minutes, but the members often lingered for several hours thereafter, playing dominoes, throwing darts and shooting pool.

The VFW hall was a rectangular building, the exterior of which was comprised of corrugated-metal panels, and their original bold, blue paint had now faded to a pale pastel. The white metal sign on the side of the structure faced the highway, and once bragged the name and post number, but those characters had faded to unreadable, vague smudges, leading many passersby's to mistake the building for an abandoned warehouse. A World War II era Sherman tank had sat for decades at the far edge of the pothole-riddled, shale-topped parking lot, and had blotchy white stars on the front and sides.

Inside the hall, nearest the entrance, members had framed up and sheet rocked a conference room. It and the remainder of the hall was illuminated, when the ballasts functioned properly, by long horizontal fluorescent lights hanging from metal chains attached to the steel-beam rafters. The building had no windows, and even when all the lights were on and operable, they only managed to cast an eerily dim ambiance.

At the opposite end of the conference room, the vets maintained a recreational area, featuring a shuffleboard table, a six-foot-long pool table and three dartboards adorned the wall nearest the rear emergency exit. Adjacent to that area was a lounge section with two, well-worn and stained couches and five tables with rusting chrome legs, with matching chairs. The centerpiece of the lounging area was the unreliable Zenith twenty-five-inch diagonal, Mediterranean-style console television.

Directly across from the seating section, decades earlier the members had installed a square area of darkly stained parquet floor tiles, which once served as a dancing floor. There was a time, back when the tiles were shiny and new, when the veterans applied a thin layer of fine sawdust to the surface to aid the gliding soles of fleet-footed two-steppers and waltzers. Years later though, those same members cordoned off the dancing floor with cautionary yellow tape, directing older vets around it for fear that one might fall on the slippery surface, or trip on a loose tile. A coin-operated Rock-Ola jukebox once provided the hall's dancing music, at a dime per song, but for years it had sat unplugged, dusty and facing the corner. Many of the interior walls displayed damage, and this was particularly true in the recreation area, where occasional disagreements over gaming contests, wayward darts, or launched cue balls had taken their toll.

The heating and cooling system once ably controlled the climate in the hall's interior but now, even when functioning at full capacity, it could only change the temperature in the poorly insulated structure a few degrees. This rendered the vets chronically vulnerable to the outside temperatures, particularly so during the frigid Montana winters.

As Ben neared the hall that evening, he noted several vehicles parked there, and two more following him onto the lot. The compromised suspension of Ben's old Chevrolet pick-up, popped, screeched, and jolted his bones as it traversed the lot, but he persevered and managed to park near the entrance. He exited his truck and it was then that he realized just how blustery the evening air was. After shaking hands with the two vets that arrived with him, Tom Kidd, a Marine, and Sailor, Jack Simpson, Ben led the way briskly toward the entrance.

When they entered the hall, the three men found that the temperature inside was not a vast departure from that on the outside. As they walked, each could still see their breath in front of them, but Ben was struck most by the absence of the other vets, only ten minutes before the meeting's commencement. Typically, by this time, he would have found the men gathered in the recreation area, socializing until the meeting convened, but on this evening, he saw no sign of them.

He stood perplexed, until a voice echoed, "Over here, Ben!" Turning back toward the entrance, Ben saw Cookie peeking through the slightly ajar door to the conference room. Unlike the rest of the hall, the conference room had low, insulated ceiling tiles, breached only by the chains used to suspend the lights. When its door was closed, the ceiling tiles and the solid sheet rocked walls, served to trap the heat, protecting the conference from the conditions in the remainder of the cavernous hall. The room featured a conference table and chairs, a small cherry-wood buffet, atop which sat a percolating silver coffee urn, and in the corner, stood a four-foot tall, artificial Christmas tree draped with silver icicles and green and red tinsel.

Ben and the other two vets headed in that direction, and once inside the conference room, they found all the early arrivals gathered at the conference table conversing. When the men noticed Ben entering, they delivered a round of applause, and he was congratulated for the golf round and the television interview.

"Thanks, fellas," the honoree said. "But what are y'all doing in here?"

"It's too cold out there!" Cookie said referring to the portion of the hall beyond the conference room door.

"You guys worried me," Ben said. "I thought the rapture occurred, and me and these two fellas didn't make the cut!"

"Maybe it did occur and *none* of us made it," Mungo said wide eyed, with feigned fright.

"I wouldn't worry if I were you, Mungo. I'm sure that among all of us, the Lord would want you up there for entertainment, if nothing else," Ben said taking a seat at the end of the table. It was then that Ben realized that even the conference room was uncomfortably cold and asked, "Cookie, I thought you were going to get here early and fire up the radiators."

"I did! With Alf and Kat spelling me at the café, I got here an hour and a half ago," Cookie, explained. "It just takes time."

Ben nodded, then confirming that they had the requisite quorum, albeit narrowly, he convened the meeting. He led an orderly discussion on the various items of business and took notes, though the final agenda topic was foremost on his mind. He handed each man a sheet of paper titled *Treasurer's Report*, and pulled no punches. "As you can see from the hand out, we have some major budgetary problems. We were nearly in the black for the third quarter, but we had to get the roof fixed from the storm. We should get most of that money back from the insurance company, so I'm not too worried about it, but the deductible alone put us in the red."

"That doesn't sound *too* bad," Mungo said, perusing the report.

"Yeah, it looks like we're at least treadin' water," Cookie agreed.

"Treading water's not enough," Ben replied. "We need to be in the black, and in a big way. There are expenses well beyond our normal fixed costs of utilities, rent and insurance. You all are well aware that we are facing repairs—some very expensive ones—some that we *must* do just to keep the building from being padlocked. There are the plumbing problems, electrical issues and the parking lot needs to be re-topped, to name a few. We have to do all of these things, while continuing to pay our normal bills, and trying to meet our charitable goals."

Cookie stared at Ben, with a furrowed brow. "So what are we going to do?"

"I don't know for sure," Ben conceded. "Ideally, I'd like to get all of these problems fixed and restore the hall to a place that people would once again want to come to."

"Hosting functions was the real money-maker," Mungo said.

"That's right, but we're the only ones who can stand to be in here—especially this time of year," Ben said.

"The summers are no walk in the park, either," Tom Kidd added.

Ben nodded and said, "That's true too, but we used to have money in reserve for unexpected expenses, back in a time when non-members, including our neighbors, wives and other family members would come up here for receptions and dances. With that income, the other fundraisers and dues revenues, we ran comfortably in the black."

"But even if we did all of that work, we couldn't compete with those new places with the ballrooms," Cookie said, alluding to two recently constructed chain hotels built out on the bypass highway. Each offered larger and more modern banquet facilities, and though both were much more expensive to rent, they had become the go-to venues for locals to host functions.

"I got an idea," Mungo said, grabbing the attention of the somber vets. "We could rob a bank!" Though, not in any respect helpful, Mungo's one-liner helped break the tension.

"In case this room is bugged," Ben said, looking upward to the ceiling tiles, "that was Mungo Thibodeaux speaking."

"But seriously, Ben, most of you fellas are on fixed incomes, but younger guys like me aren't," Mungo said. "Why not do an assessment on us workin' guys, like Lone Wolf does when they re-do the greens or bunkers, or need repairs to the clubhouse?"

"That's very generous, but the VFW is not a country club. We all earned our right to be members here and we're equal members, and we will pay dues equally," Ben said, "and besides, you, Cookie and Simpson are the only ones still workin' and Jack's old enough to retire but has too many ex-wives on the payroll to quit."

"They're each for sale fellas," Jack Simpson said, "just take over the payments!"

"Look—we're not standing at the abyss at this point, but it's in sight," Ben said, "I just wanted to get the issue on your radar screens. So, let's get past the carnival and the other fundraisers, see where we stand, and take it from there."

The men agreed, and with a proper motion, seconding and unanimous voice vote, the business meeting stood adjourned. Several members immediately left for their homes, while others headed to the recreation area. It was now slightly warmer in that section of the hall, but not enough so for the men to remove their coats and jackets. Cookie and two other vets joined Ben at one of the tables to play dominoes, three others headed for the shuffleboard table, where stacked cinder blocks replaced one of its missing legs. Four men began hurling darts, while Mungo stood at the pool table and in a bad attempt at a British accent, asked, "Billiards anyone?"

Mungo found a taker when fellow Vietnam vet, James Strath, picked up the gauntlet, saying, "I'm your man!"

Unlike the shuffleboard table, the pool table had all four original legs, but the threaded knobs at the bottom of each, necessary for leveling the table, were long since gone. Previous players had shoved matchbooks and sugar packets under the legs in unsuccessful attempts at gaining balance, however nothing had been done to remedy the three tears—one large and two small—in the table's stained green felt. Each of these felt imperfections, were a consequence of ill advised, and poorly executed, masse shots. On the floor, under the back right corner of the table, sat a sizable galvanized mop bucket, used to collect accurate shots that passed through the breach in the leather pocket in that corner.

Mungo placed the plastic triangle shaped rack on the felt, and he and Strath walked opposite sides of the table retrieving balls from the five functional pockets. Mungo tended to the two pockets on his side, and then emptied the bucket, and when all balls were placed on the table, it was then that Mungo realized that two were missing.

"Jimbo, we have a problem."

"What?" Strath asked.

"Take a look, the one and the twelve are AWOL."

"Did you check the bucket?"

"Yes, it's empty," Mungo, said, then they each re-checked their respective sides of the table, to no avail.

"Too bad, Mungo. I was looking forward to putting a drubbin' on you."

"Fat chance," Mungo said as he knelt on the floor, and looked in all directions for the missing balls. He found none and muttered, "Well, shit!"

"Hey! No cussin' in the hall," Ben scolded.

"Sorry, but we've been robbed!" Mungo yelled playfully.

"Say, since a stripe and a solid are missing, it's even. Do you wanna go ahead and play with thirteen?" Strath asked.

"Suits me, Jimbo," Mungo said cheerfully, while laying a dollar bill on the rail. "Buck a piece?"

"Sure," Strath said, adding his dollar on top of Mungo's.

They each retrieved one of the six cue sticks from the rack, set them on the compromised felt, and rolled them back and forth to evaluate the extent of the warping. The men tested another cue before selecting the least warped among them. Next, each grabbed a random ball, in order to lag for the honor to break. They struck their respective shots and Strath's was clearly hit best, but as his ball ricocheted off the opposite end of the table and headed back toward them, his ball snagged on one of the tears in the felt, giving Mungo the winning lag.

"That's too bad," Mungo said insincerely, "rack 'em up, Jimbo!"

Grumbling under his breath, Strath corralled the thirteen balls with the rack, and arranged them in numerical order, starting with the blue two ball. Mungo reached to chalk the felt tip of his cue stick, until he realized his cue had no such tip. He glanced at the other cues, including Strath's, and realized that they all shared that same misfortune. He shrugged, returned the chalk cube to the table rail, and grabbed the cue ball, which sported a few blue-green dots earned in an era when the cues had felt tips to be chalked. Mungo strategically placed the cue ball in a spot where a straight shot would avoid the felt imperfections. He drew his cue stick back and forth rapidly, preparing to strike the cue ball, until he noticed it slowly rolling away from him and to the right. He grabbed it, and chose another spot, but as he lined up the shot, the cue ball again moved ever so slightly away—and to the right.

"Jimbo, the table's a little cockeyed. How 'bout you steadying the cue ball for me?"

"What do you mean?"

"Put a finger on it and hold it in place until I can hit it!"

"Why should I, after all we're playin' for a buck?"

"Look—you're gonna have the same problem when it's your break, and I'll help," Mungo reasoned.

Strath relented, leaned his cue against the table, and when Mungo re-situated the cue ball, Strath placed his right index finger on the top of it, like the place holder would do to a football for a field goal attempt. Mungo took his sweet time taking aim, and with Strath sighing impatiently, he finally thrust his cue stick forward. Unfortunately, Mungo hit the cue ball with a glancing blow on the top half of the orb, which steered the blunt wooden tip of his cue stick upward and colliding harshly with the tip of Strath's finger.

"Son-of-a-bitch!" Strath yelped, before sticking his finger in his mouth.

"No cussin' in the hall, Jimbo," Mungo admonished.

Though not a strong shot by any standard, it nevertheless propelled the cue ball into the incomplete rack of balls, creating a clicking sound that echoed throughout the hall. Strath sucked on his throbbing fingertip as they each watched as the balls separated, but with the weak velocity of the shot, all of them remained on the opposite half of the table. As each ball slowed, both men realized Mungo had not pocketed any, and accordingly Strath removed his finger from his mouth picked up his cue, and said, "Too bad—it's my turn."

"Wait a second—they ain't done yet!" Mungo said urgently and loudly, while crouching forward and staring at eye level at the balls, while the others in the recreation area now trained their attention on the unfolding scene.

Strath dismissed the comment, but as the balls appeared to have reached its final position on the felt, each one gradually began rolling away from the men, and to the right. The leading ball reached the far right corner pocket, dropped through the breach in its leather lining, falling into the galvanized mop bucket landing with a loud *clang*. Then, a second one *clanged* and then two more fell, gradually followed by the remaining nine, and not to be left out, the cue ball joined all others, filling the deep bucket by more than half.

"Boys! I ran the table!" Mungo crowed, took a bow before his audience, and snatched the two dollars off the table.

As the evening wound down and the veterans trickled out, Ben found himself alone with Cookie, who sat watching Ben return the dominoes to their original cardboard box.

"With the budget issues, how are we going to do the gifts for the kids this year?" Cookie queried. "It didn't come up in the meeting and with the money so tight, I was just wondering."

"It's going to get done, Cookie," Ben replied.

"We have the money for it?"

"Yes, but only around half as much as last year."

"Oh ... I see," Cookie said somberly, "then we'll donate half as much?"

"No, we'll do the same as last year. I've already cleared it with Emily, and we'll make up the difference, and that's the reason I didn't bring it up in front of the men."

"That's not fair to you y'all, Ben. I mean, you two kicked in some last year."

"The kids are going to have Christmas," Ben said firmly and reached up to return the box of dominoes to a wooden cabinet.

"But, what about your retirement?"

"First off, I'm going to make some of the toys in my work shop, and as for the money, we can handle it," Ben said.

"I hope so, you don't want to outlive your savings."

"We'll be fine, and as they say, *you can't take it with you.*"

"Or like ol' Mungo once said, *there ain't no pockets in a shroud.*"

"Sounds like him," Ben chuckled.

"That's very generous," Cookie said, "and I'd like to kick in some money, too. The café is doing pretty good, and I—"

"That's nice of you Cookie, but maybe next year," Ben said.

"Can I ask you about the other day at the café?"

"What day?" Ben asked.

"You know, that morning when you met with Spindler and that bigwig from Pitz-Smart."

"What about it?"

"I couldn't hear much of the conversation, but it seemed like they were trying to get you to do something for 'em," Cookie said.

"It's all about finishing my golf round from last fall."

"Didn't it involve money?" Cookie asked.

"Perhaps you heard more than you thought," Ben said with raised eyebrows.

"Ben, I swear I wasn't eavesdropping!"

"I'm just teasing, but how'd you hear about the money part?"

"You ought to know that Stewart Spindler came to the café a couple of days ago and told me about them makin' you an offer."

"They offered money all right, and of all people, they want to use *me* to promote their stores."

"Is it true that some of the money was for the hall?" Cookie asked sheepishly.

"It's *all* for the hall."

"I'm sorry if I'm prying, but I just thought it was worth asking about."

"Of course—that was their intention," Ben said.

Cookie stared at Ben curiously. "I'm not following you."

"Don't you see? I don't jump on the deal and as a result they plant the notion in your ear, knowing you'll in turn ask me about it and apply pressure."

"Sorry Ben, I guess I played right into their plans, but I want you to know I didn't ask him anything about this, and I'd *never* try to pressure you into something."

"So Spindler didn't tell you the details about their offer?" Ben asked.

"He told me an amount."

"It's true they offered ten thousand dollars for the hall, and we would get the money whether I shoot my age or not."

"I really regret bringing it up," Cookie said.

Ben patted him on the shoulder, "Don't worry about it. If it hadn't been you, it would've been one of the others."

"This is your decision and yours only Ben," Cookie said. "We all know how you feel about Pitz-Smart."

"Thanks, but I don't sense that Pitzmyre's the type of man that takes no for an answer, and I'm sure he'll keep turning up the heat."

"Speaking of heat Ben, did you notice most of the guys kept their coats on all evening? Cookie asked. "These old radiators are shot."

"Thanks for not pressuring me, Cookie," Ben said, and his friend hung his head. "It's okay, I'm actually thinking I will play their game in order to get the money for the hall, but I'm gonna do it on *my* terms."

The Tenth Hole

*B*en awoke early the next morning, dressed, and committed himself to calling the Pitzmyre. He transferred the CEO's business card from his wallet to his shirt pocket, and because he had to wait to call on California time, he used the interim to retreat to his workshop. While there, he concentrated on the woodworking projects for the kid's Christmas gifts. He finished several, small wooden racecars, each of which he had crafted weeks earlier from wooden blocks, using a band saw, various sized chisels and sandpaper. He hand painted the sleek racers, and equipped each with fully functional rolling wooden wheels. When Ben returned to the house mid-morning, he informed Emily of his intention to cooperate with Pitzmyre in favor of the VFW.

"That's a good thing you're doing, Benjamin," she said. "I know that you struggled to come to this decision, and I'm proud that you would sacrifice so much for the vets."

"I'm not going to like it, but I suppose it's a small price to pay to help keep the hall up and running—you know it's the only place some of the old guys have to go, particularly the widowers."

"I know dear, and everyone's getting so old and feeble—present company excluded," She said. "Now, I'm leaving in a minute for my PTA meeting and I've made a bunch of sandwiches for the ladies, and I'll bring home the leftovers for lunch, okay?"

"Will there be any left overs? I mean some of those ladies are a little—"

"Benjamin!"

"Sorry dear, are the roads clear?"

"Clear enough to get to Claire Faulkner's house and back," she said and headed for the front door, with her tote bag in hand.

Well I might as well get this over with Ben thought, and he reached for the phone, squinted to read the small print on the business card, and dialed the number.

"Ben my man, it's great to hear from you!" Pitzmyre said with a sugary inflection that in and of itself caused Ben to regret his decision.

"Mr. Pitzmyre, I've thought this over, and I'll play the hole for the VFW."

"That's super! We'll get the—"

"Wait—there's more. I want an additional fifteen thousand, also without regard as to whether I shoot my age or not."

"Oh ... so gentle Ben wants in on the action, huh?"

"I should have known you'd think that," Ben said. "No, the other fifteen thousand is also for the VFW. We have a lot of needs, and I'm just trying to sweeten the pot."

"I see, hmm..." Pitzmyre pondered.

"It's take it or leave it offer."

"How about this, the extra fifteen grand is only if you *do* shoot your age?" Pitzmyre asked.

"So twenty-five thousand if I do, and ten if I don't?" Ben asked.

"Yes."

"Fair enough."

"Ben, you got yourself a deal! We'll need a contract, so let's get the basic terms ironed out between us. As we discussed in Bozeman, I want you to do some appearances."

"Tell me exactly what you mean by that."

"We'll spell it out in the contract, but it's simply coming up to the store when called upon for events and promotions," Pitzmyre explained. "So in addition to showing up to play the hole, I want six store appearances."

"I believe you said a *couple* at our meeting?" Ben reminded.

"True, but with adding fifteen grand to my risk, I think six is more than fair."

"I really don't understand why you would want me to do even one."

"Leave that to me Ben, so what do you say?" Pitzmyre said.

"The local Bozeman store only?"

"Of course."

"That's fine," Ben conceded.

"We'll get to work on the contract, which will also include our right to the use of your name and image for promotions," Pitzmyre added.

"Understood."

"That's about it then," Pitzmyre said, "you know what Shelley wrote about winter—spring will be here before we know it."

"Yes, I heard something about that," Ben said.

"Right, so we need to get moving on this, so I'll have our lawyers whip up a simple contract and send it to you, and once you've signed it, we'll get back with you on the details."

Exactly one week later, Ben walked outside to retrieve their mail, and had to use the butt of his pocketknife to chip ice off the mailbox lid to open it. Found among the junk mail and a couple of bills, was a thick manila envelope. Ben wondered if it was the Sears catalog he was expecting, but after turning it in each direction, he saw that the return address read *Pitz-Smart Legal Department, Los Angeles, California.*

Ben walked with the mail in hand back inside, and sat it all on the kitchen table. He lifted the large envelope, ran his finger along the flap that sealed it, and removed the thick set of bound papers and thought, *simple contract, huh?* He grabbed a cup of coffee, and sat at the kitchen table and began reading the terms and conditions of the agreement, focusing on the sections that covered what he and Pitzmyre discussed on the phone. He was no stranger to contracts, considering the insurance policies and supplier and vendor agreements, he routinely encountered running their business, but this was unlike anything he had ever seen, and he spent the better part of the morning navigating through it.

As best as he could comprehend, the document correctly reflected the financial aspects of their deal, limiting the promotional appearances to six, and it outlined the general nature of activities that they could call upon him to do during those visits. Though dealing with Pitz-Smart on any level was unsavory to him, he did not regard the description as unusual or particularly burdensome. He then read the portion concerning the use of his *name, likeness and image*, and this section likewise required several pages to describe. Though it was difficult to understand all of the legalese, it clearly limited that use to a specific time, from the date of the contract until the day after he completed the round, and that too seemed reasonable.

He signed and dated the contract and slid it into the stamped, addressed envelope that accompanied the package, sealed it and trudged back to the mailbox. Ben paused at the curb, knowing that by placing the package in the mailbox, it represented the proverbial point of no return, but he overcame all apprehension, slid it in the box, closed the lid and raised the red plastic flag. A few days later, Stewart Spindler called and the first of Ben's six appearances was scheduled.

On the morning of Ben's first trip to the Pitz-Smart store, Emily sat on a bench in front of her vanity mirror brushing her hair and asked, "So what do think they'll want you to do when you get down there?"

"I honestly don't know, but I agreed to do it, so I'll go down there and find out," Ben replied, while struggling to slip on his heavy, thick-soled, black boots.

"What time did they tell you to get there?" she asked.

"They said eight—what time do they open?"

"That's when they open," she said setting her brush on the vanity and turning to him. "Oh, Ben, you can't stand to even drive by that store, and now you have to go inside it and deal with their ilk?"

"It's not going to be easy, but I'll go down there and find out what they want for these so called *appearances*," Ben said. "I just have to keep reminding myself that it's all for the good guys."

"That's the right attitude, but for the life of me I don't understand why they're requiring you to do it at all," she said, returning to her brushing with long steady strokes.

"I know the *why*, but it's the *what* that I don't know. I'm sure they'll have me do something that will in some way, bring in business and along the way ease the minds of old folks around town."

"How does this affect the seniors?" Emily asked.

"By attaching their brand to one of them. It's like the hosting thing, I'm sure they hope the folks will notice how they're supporting an old guy like me, and convince seniors that Pitz-Smart cares about them."

"I hope they're not that calculating."

"There must be some financial gain to be had, or they wouldn't be doing it," Ben said.

"The thought of them profiting from you upsets me!" she said.

"Em, you've spent all of these years consoling me about them and encouraging me to accept their presence and now that I'm on board with 'em, I feel like I have to talk you off the ceiling."

She glanced at him in the mirror and smiled. "You're right. I'm just so protective when it comes to you."

"I know and I love it that you do, but I have to face the fact that our friends shop there, and some, like the Whitcombes work there, and many of our old customers are now their customers, and that's just the way it is."

"Well that's the healthy way to look at it, just put it all behind you, and let bygones be bygones."

Ben raised his right hand. "I hereby declare, that as of this very moment that I, Benjamin Taylor Digby, do let go of every negative thought, release all disappointments and relinquish every broken dream, except— El Dorado— that part I can *never* let go."

"Oh Ben, please don't say that," Emily pleaded. "You were going along so nicely until you threw in that last part."

"I understand, but there's a limit to everything, and I think I'm entitled to cling to a modicum of regret."

"Fine, but you beat yourself up over it too much, and I know that the way you feel stems your own protectiveness for me."

"You would have truly loved spending the winters down there."

"Perhaps, but it didn't work out that way, and I'm perfectly content with what we have here," Emily said. "You know, I think that it may be cathartic for you to go on down there and take their money, and you just might release even that last remaining resentment."

"Maybe you're right, I guess it gets down to the old *if you can't beat 'em, join 'em* thing, but broken dreams are tough to let go," Ben said planting himself next to her on the bench, and staring at her in the vanity mirror, as she concluded her hundredth stroke with the brush.

Their eyes fixed on each other's, and she said, "You were my one-and-only dream, and I knew that the first day I laid eyes on you in that old Woolworth's store, wearing that letterman's jacket, those threadbare trousers and brogan shoes. Now you go on down there and do this for the veterans knowing that, unlike Mr. Pitzmyre, you're doing it for all the right reasons."

"You're right," he said, kissing her on the cheek, and rose to his feet. "I'll do my part and keep my chin up."

"Do that, and perhaps when you get home, I'll do my part too," she said, smiling.

"Oh, is it what I'm thinking of?" Ben said, with his eyebrows bobbing up and down.

"Not that, you cad! I bought some ground beef to make a batch of chili!"

"Cad? It was the chili that I was thinking of!"

The Eleventh Hole

When Ben reached the bypass highway, and turned in the direction of the Pitz-Smart store, he tried to imagine what lay ahead. He drove onto the parking lot ten minutes ahead of schedule, and despite the early hour, he found his truck was only one of a number of vehicles converging on the parking slots closest the store's entrance. Having driven past the store on many occasions, Ben knew that it attracted a seemingly endless ebb and flow of patrons, but why there would be this many people arriving so early, baffled him.

Ben parked and stepped out of his truck, and found himself unavoidably merging with the flock of customers. They trudged as a mass toward the entrance, joining a growing congregation on the sidewalk in front of the store's locked doors. During the decades of running his hardware store, Ben occasionally encountered a customer waiting outside when he opened his doors, usually be holding a leaking faucet or a busted pipe, but he never opened his store to find casual shoppers gathered.

He waited amongst the bustling crowd, until a man wearing the obligatory red-and-yellow Pitz-Smart shirt approached the doors from inside. He was carrying a large ring of keys and as he neared, he kept a watchful eye on all of those huddled on the opposite side of the glass. The man stooped and disengaged the floor-level lock and rose to do the same for the lock at the top of the door, as the eager shoppers pressed closer to the glass. The customers began jockeying for position, and Ben glanced nervously to those nearest him and was reminded of news videos, of the mobs outside of stores the morning after Thanksgiving, and accounts of how shoppers were often injured.

The Pitz-Smart employee positioned himself in such a way as to stand as far from the door as he could, while maintaining a tight grip on the key that was now inserted into the top lock, a lock that once disengaged, would free both glass doors. The man concentrated on making the final twist of the key, and when the door was fully unlocked, he removed the key and scampered several steps backward.

The guests, including Ben, entered the store like water through a breached dyke, channeling straight toward four long rows of shiny, silver shopping carts. There was no shortage of these carts, but many customers eagerly competed for those at the front of each of the four rows. Other patrons who were larger, older or afflicted with physical challenges, vied for one of the dozen electric scooters, each taking a seat and weaving perilously through the throng and out to the sales floor.

Ben instinctively positioned himself away from the shopping cart frenzy, and froze. He felt like a rock in the middle of a free flowing stream, but moments later the flow of patrons ebbed, and he sensed he was safe. With the bulk of the crowd now inside the store, Ben ventured from the cart section to the main shopping area, and marveled as the seemingly endless rows of florescent lights were switching on in succession across the high ceiling. He took in the scope of the expansive sales floor, and was stunned by the store's vast interior, and with exception of a B-17 bomber hanger, he could not recall stepping into a space that large, ever. He was next drawn to the long rows of fully stocked shelves of merchandise, with television monitors mounted on the end caps of each, playing a loop of sales pitches and depictions of discounted merchandise.

Ben turned and noticed Mrs. Whitcombe, who was only one of several Pitz-Smart employees already tending checkout stands. Among the other employees on duty and customers ambling about,

Ben recognized other familiar faces, including some of his own former customers. He stood clueless as to where to go or what to do, and scanned the area for anyone who could direct him, and opted to return to the entry. He approached the employee that had braved the unlocking of the doors, who was now standing near the depleting rows of shopping carts. The man was surveying papers on a clipboard, and Ben noticed that his nametag identified him as *Leonard Duncan* and more importantly, under his name it read *Assistant Manager.*

"Sir," Ben said, trying to gain Leonard's attention, but to avail. "Excuse me, *sir*," Ben said louder.

"Yes," the man responded tersely, lowering his clipboard.

"Ben Digby, here."

"And?"

"I'm supposed to report here today for—"

"Oh, thank goodness," Duncan said, as his sour expression eased, and he shook Ben's hand. "I'm *very* glad you're here, but you should've arrived fifteen minutes ago and entered through the employee entrance—didn't the people with HR explain that?"

"HR?" Ben asked.

"Yes, Human Resources," Duncan clarified, but Ben's facial expression demonstrated an equal lack of familiarity with that term. "You know—personnel."

"Oh, I understand now," Ben said, "but I got here ahead of the time I was told to, and no one told me where I was supposed to enter."

"No worries—all's well that ends well, right Bob?" Duncan said with a slap on Ben's back.

"The name is Ben."

"Right, so are you ready to get started?"

"I suppose—what exactly do I do?" Ben asked.

"You haven't been through an orientation?"

"No."

"That figures," Duncan said, shaking his head. "It's not that complicated, and I'm sure you'll catch on quick—so follow me Bob, and we'll get started!"

"It's Ben," he reminded as they walked.

"Correct. Now, the main thing you need to know to serve as a host is to—"

"A host?" Ben said stopping abruptly. "I think there's been some mistake."

"Don't worry, Bob. All you have to do is greet the folks and keep an eye on the shopping carts, and when they get low, to make sure they get replenished."

"You want *me* to get 'em off the parking lot?"

"No, not you! All you have to do is pick up any phone, like the one on the wall over there, and punch the red button, which puts you on the intercom. Then, you page the stock boys to the front, and *they'll* round up the carts."

"Okay."

"Then, as each customer enters the store, you just need to greet them with a smile, and hand them a flier from that stack," Duncan said pointing to a metal rack holding a three-foot column of store advertisements.

"Do I just say hello or welcome or something like that?"

"Oh, no—we don't leave this part to chance," Duncan stressed, and he handed Ben a slip of paper with bold type reading: *hello and welcome to Pitz-Smart.* Ben read it and offered it back to Leonard. "No, Bob, you keep it so you can refer to it when need be."

"I think I can manage," Ben said, placing the paper back on Leonard's clipboard, and asked "Are you sure I'm supposed to host?"

"Yes, and you're tailor made for it. Thankfully, HR got that part right."

"All right," Ben said, as he headed toward the stack of promotional flyers.

"Wait, Bob!" Duncan intervened. "You've got to be in uniform!"

"Uniform?"

"Yes, it's mandatory—look around," Leonard said, pointing toward the employees stocking shelves and those staffing the checkout stands. "Everyone on duty, that's on the sales floor, has to be in uniform."

"Where do I get that?"

"Follow me, and I'll show you," Leonard said, and he led Ben around the corner to the customer service counter, where the store's newest host received his own bright red Pitz-Smart T-shirt, sized large enough to slip over his own clothes. The shirt featured a Pitz-Smart logo on the front, and the word *HOST* was emblazoned in yellow on the back. "Go ahead and put it on," Leonard instructed, and Ben removed his coat and scarf, and then slipped the shirt over his head. "Sorry Bob, but they haven't made you a name tag yet."

"I'm beginning to think I need one," Ben said.

"In due time. We don't usually print newbies a name tag until you make it a week or two."

"A week or two?" Ben asked.

"Yes. Now, leave your coat and scarf in this bin, and we'll get started."

"Leonard, I truly don't think I'm—"

"No time for chit chat Bob, we have an entry in need of a host!"

Ben, now in uniform sans the nametag, returned with Leonard to the main entrance. The training wheels were off, but Leonard remained close enough to assure Ben's proper execution of his duties. An older man approached, claimed a cart, and before Ben could utter his scripted greeting, the man exclaimed, "Hey, Ben! How the hell are you?"

"Fine, Sam," Ben responded. "How's the arthritis?"

"Pretty bad in this weather, but thanks for askin'."

"You'll find what you need for that in the Health and Beauty department on aisle twelve," Leonard interjected. Sam rolled his eyes and patted Ben on the shoulder, before entering the store.

As the next customer neared, Ben handed her a flyer and said, "Welcome to Pitz-Smart."

The woman nodded and after she passed, with flyer in hand, Leonard muttered, under his breath "You forgot *hello and*."

"Beg pardon?" Ben asked.

"You said *welcome to Pitz-Smart* but it's supposed to be *hello and welcome to Pitz-Smart,*" Leonard said, returning the slip of paper with typed verbiage back to Ben. "I knew I shouldn't let you go it alone."

"Sorry, Leonard," Ben said contritely.

Another familiar face entered, grabbed a cart, and halted upon seeing Ben. "What in the world are *you* doin' in here?"

"I guess I'm hostin', Morris," Ben said. "How's Fernie and the—"

"Ahem!" Leonard interrupted.

"Oh … hello and welcome to Pitz-Smart," Ben said quickly. "Now, how are Fernie and the girls?"

"They're just dandy Ben, and you and Emily?"

"All's well, thank you."

As Leonard stared on, Ben's acquaintance leaned over and whispered, "I never thought I'd see *you* in here."

"Me neither," Ben replied and the man nodded and continued into the store.

"You're a natural, Bob!" Leonard said. "We've had lots of hosts in and out of here over the years, but never one that gets greeted by the customers first!"

"What are you doing!" shouted a voice from behind them, and Ben turned to see Stewart Spindler rushing toward them.

"This is Bob, our new host," Leonard said. "It's his first morning, and he's doing splendidly!"

"His name is Ben, as in Benjamin Digby!" Spindler said, "He's our special guest for the Sporting Goods promotion—remember?"

"How odd, that's not on *my* sheet," Leonard said, holding up the roster on his clipboard.

"Damn it Leonard, that's yesterday's! Ben, please take off that shirt and come with me," Spindler said. Ben complied and removed the shirt, then handed it to Spindler, who then motioned for him to follow.

"If you take him, we have no host," Leonard protested.

Ignoring the comment, Spindler kept walking with Ben by his side and said, "Follow me up to my office, and we'll discuss what we're doing today."

Ben nodded, but had difficulty ignoring Leonard's sincere, but receding pleas from behind, and said, "He seems pretty adamant."

Spindler stopped, glanced back and sighed. "Oh hell ... Leonard's making a scene back there. Please just wait here for a second," Spindler said, and trotted back to his assistant manager, with Ben's host shirt in hand. "Damn it Leonard, this is Pitzmyre's deal, and you almost mucked it up."

"Sorry Stewart, but if you take him, what do we do for a host!"

Spindler shoved Ben's shirt into Leonard's free hand and said, "Here—you put this on and do it until a replacement arrives,"

"But, that's an entry level job!"

"Then you should be able handle it!" Spindler said, as he turned and walked briskly back to Ben. They continued together toward the rear of the store, and through a set of large metal swinging doors, then made a sharp left taking them down a long hallway. They proceeded past an expansive storeroom full of mostly boxed and palletized inventory. Present were employees moving about rapidly, with some maneuvering forklifts and hydraulic dollies between long rows of multi-level, stocked shelves, dutifully adhering to the boundaries marked by thick, bright yellow striping on the floor. Ben followed Spindler past the employee lockers and time clock, then up a flight of stairs to a group of offices, entering the largest, marked *General Manager.*

Spindler offered Ben a seat on the opposite side of his grey metal desk, and said, "I'm very sorry about the mix up—I just don't know about Leonard sometimes."

"That's all right," Ben said, "besides, I'd probably be more comfortable passing out flyers and saying hello to folks, than doing whatever you've cooked up for me."

"It's actually not much different—it's still a people thing, so let me explain what we're going do," Spindler said, then gave Ben a general overview of the events of the morning.

"So this amounts to a golf club promotion?" Ben asked.

"Essentially, take a look over here," Spindler, said rising and walking around his desk to a wide window. He flung open the curtains to reveal a panoramic view of the expansive sales floor, and stood peering down at the countless aisles, with his hands clasped behind him at the small his back, as a captain would standing on the bridge of a ship. Ben joined him at the window, and Spindler said, "Look over there toward Sporting Goods." Ben squinted and strained to see where Spindler was pointing, and the General Manager added, "Look just to the right of those red-and-yellow balloons."

Ben complied, and was drawn to a large banner that hung over a table reading, *Play Pitz-Flex, the clubs that record-setter Ben Digby plays!*

"What's Pitz-Flex?" Ben asked.

"It's our trade name for the golf clubs you'll be promoting," Spindler explained as he closed the curtains. "It's our deluxe line of irons and woods, and you just need to go down there and hand out brochures."

"Brochures for those golf clubs?"

"Yes and the objective is to sell as many sets as we can."

"I have a problem with the sign though," Ben said.

"What about it?"

"First off, I haven't set any record and secondly, I don't golf with those clubs."

"I know Ben, but like Pitzmyre said at our meeting, shooting a seventy for seventeen holes is a pretty remarkable, in and of itself. What's more, we firmly believe you *will* shoot your age come spring, and we want to demonstrate that faith to the folks."

"But you're talking about a prediction, and that sign is a statement of fact."

"Ben, you're looking at it all wrong," Spindler said. "It's what they call in advertising *puffery*, like a car dealership commercial saying *Deal of the century* or *Lowest prices in the world*. Everyone understands there's no way to substantiate those claims and that it's just hyperbole."

"One man's hyperbole is another man's white lie," Ben said.

"Let me ask you this, how many times have you walked off a seventeenth green with seventy on your card?"

"Never," Ben said.

"Sounds like a record to me."

"Fine, but what about the clubs? You're saying with that sign that I play those, and I've never heard of them, much less owned any."

"I can fix that!" Spindler said enthusiastically, and strutted toward a closet on the other end of his office. He flung open the closet door, and among the hanging umbrellas, overcoats, neckties and jackets, sat an oversized, black, leather golf bag with a full of set of golf clubs in it. The bag had a bright yellow-and-red Pitz-Smart logo embroidered on its side, and a golf towel attached to it by a brass ring. "Here you go Ben, your own set of our Pitz-Flex golf clubs."

"These are for me?"

"Yes, does that make you feel better about the banner?"

"Some, but isn't there some implication that I've actually used them?"

"Hyperbole Ben, hyperbole! Plus, we hope you *will* use them."

Ben stared at the bag of shiny new clubs. "How much you want for 'em?"

Spindler chuckled and placed his hand on Ben's shoulder. "Sorry, I should've made myself clear. These are yours as our gift."

"You're giving me a set of golf clubs?"

"Yes and the towel is yours too," he said proudly as he unclipped the brass ring, removed the towel and raised it to his chest, "it actually has your name on it, see?"

Ben stared at it. "It's very nice, but I think there's a typo."

Spindler quickly turned the towel around, stared at it and said, "Dingy? Ben Dingy? Well damn it all!"

"Well at least it was close," Ben said, as he selected the five iron from the bag, and gripped it in his customary fashion. After waggling it a couple times, the veteran golfer knew in an instant that these clubs represented what is known in the sport as a *starter set*—the cheapest available—usually reserved for youngsters or beginners, not yet committed enough to the game to invest in a quality set.

He returned the iron to the bag, and said, "Well, at least the bag's nice."

"The bag's actually mine," Spindler said returning the flawed towel to the brass ring without fastening it. "I had to put the clubs in something other than the cardboard box they came in, so I'll need that back before you leave the store."

"I see," Ben said.

"Now, before we get started, there's a couple of papers to sign," he said lifting them from his desk and displaying them to Ben.

"What are they?"

"Corporate mumbo jumbo mostly. The first one acknowledges your receipt of the clubs and that you're responsible for any taxes for accepting them as a gift."

"Taxes?" Ben asked, and Spindler nodded. "Will I owe taxes for taking these things?"

"The legal department forbids us from rendering tax advice, but between me you and me —I don't really think so."

"Thank goodness, because I—"

"But we always advise that you consult your own tax professional to be certain," Spindler added. "Now, the other document releases Pitz-Smart from any liability, for you getting hurt doing any of this promotional stuff, while on our premises."

"Hurt? Sitting at a table?"

"I hear what you're saying, but the lawyers insist on it."

"Look—I already signed a contract that was so thick that two grown men couldn't shake hands over it, so I don't—"

"Ben?" Spindler interrupted with a wry grin. "Did I just hear a little white *hyperbole*?"

Ben sighed and said. "Point taken, but why should I have to deal with even more contracts at this point?"

"One reason is that the contract you already signed—you know the *thick* one—says that you agree to sign and I quote *such other and additional contracts as needed,"* Spindler explained. "It's just two more signatures Ben, and we'll be under way."

Ben perused the documents and after confirming they were essentially, as Spindler represented, he relented, signed, and dated each. Spindler then retrieved a camera from his desk drawer and began loading film into it.

"What's that for?" Ben asked.

"Since you agreed we can use your image for store advertisements, I have to photograph this event to ... well ... make some images," Spindler explained. "So let's get down there shall we?"

Spindler put the camera strap around his neck, lifted the golf bag and led Ben out of his office and down the steps. He paused at the bottom of the stairs and handed off the bag to Ben. "I would like for you to carry the bag from here to Sporting Goods, okay?"

"All right," Ben said holding the club-heavy bag by the side handle and experiencing its full heft.

"I want those present here this morning to see you with it, and follow you through the store and all the way to Sporting Goods. You need to walk just as you do on the golf course, and this is going to create the right atmosphere to generate excitement. So instead of holding it like that, go with the long strap over your shoulder, with the bag crossways behind-you."

"Are you sure?"

"I'm positive."

"I mean this thing's awfully long and bulky and it would be a lot easier to carry by the handle."

"We want the folks to see, hear and feel golf, and then to buy, buy, buy."

"I wish I could go bye, bye, bye," Ben sighed.

"Trust me on this, it'll be great!" Spindler encouraged as he checked his watch. "I've got to get out there right away and make sure everything is set for your grand entry, but you take your time, and I'll meet you at the table."

When Spindler dashed away, Ben struggled to walk with the bag, which by itself was a load, but with a full set of clubs—even shoddy ones—it was unwieldy and awkward. Ben made his way slowly down the hallway and when he reached the double doors that led to the sales floor he stopped, and sat the bag upright on the floor. Ben released the small handle, then as Spindler instructed, he lifted the bag by the strap, placed it over his right shoulder, causing the bag to suspend behind him.

With that configuration, he needed all of the width of both of the swinging doors to exit out of the hallway, and on to the sales floor, and as he did he heard a page. "Attention Pitz-Smart shoppers," Spindler's voice boomed over the intercom, "local golfing legend Ben Digby is in the store and will be walking the aisles, with a golf bag containing his own personal set of Pitz-Smart brand Pitz-Flex golf clubs. He will be making his way toward our Sporting Goods department, so proceed straight over there, or follow Ben there if you see him walking the aisles. Once there, take time to greet Ben and get a set of your own of deluxe Pitz-Flex golf clubs, and as always, shop smart-shop Pitz-Smart!"

Ben shook his head and trudged onto first aisle he saw—aisle seven. As he lumbered past the stocked shelves, his challenged gait caused the large bag, with its rattling clubs, to collide with the displays on each side destabilizing the items atop them. Casualties on the right included bottled water, fruit drinks, and canned and bottled soft drinks. On the left, the collisions disrupted shelves of snack foods, including, salsa, bean dip, queso, chips and nuts. The pendulous golf bag simply knocked some merchandise over on the shelves, while other products fell from the shelves directly to the floor, or knocked adjacent selection off, creating a chain reaction, that produced a cascade of products crashing to the hard tiles below.

From behind him, Ben heard *kaboink, kaboink, kaboink* as the succession of plastic bottles hit and bounced on the floor. The contents of the plastic bottles of soda, suffered the assault well, with exception of turning the dark carbonated beverages into beige suds. Falling glass bottles on the other hand, produced a sharp shattering sound, and resulted in spreading puddles that engulfed the shards of glass. The aluminum cans presented an entirely different catastrophe, and though some that reached the floor experienced only dents, others breached and erupted. The latter were sent spinning and rolling while spewing their pressurized contents in multiple directions, coating not only the other items on the floor, but also those unaffected items remaining on the shelves. Ben heard the distinct hissing sounds as compromised cans danced on the aisle seven, releasing fountains of soda.

For the sake of the store's remaining inventory, Ben abandoned the charge to *walk as he would on the golf course*, opting to return to carrying the bag by the handle, stopping intermittently to alternate grips as needed when fatigue and cramping in his hands necessitated it. This approach allowed him to traverse successive aisles without further damage, but in the final department before Sporting Goods— Ladies Lingerie—Ben unwittingly exited that section with a large bright white Playtex girdle, plucked by the bag's open towel hook.

When Spindler witnessed Ben's arrival, he glanced at his watch then back to Ben. "What took you so long?"

Ben, noticing the girdle for the first time said, "I guess I just got hung up."

"That's not the way I asked you to carry the bag," Spindler observed.

"I realize that. I tried it your way, but it caused a few ... let's say ... difficulties."

"Fine," Spindler sighed, "Back up a few steps, and put the bag behind you the way I wanted, and let me get some snap shots of you coming to the table."

Ben was tired, sweating some and breathing heavily, but he complied and heaved the bag strap back over his shoulder. Spindler raised the camera to his eye, trained it on Ben and signaled him forward. As Ben walked, in compliance with Spindler's directive, the camera clicked rapidly, but from his vantage point, Spindler still could not see the dangling girdle through the lens. When Ben reached the table, the clicking of the camera ceased, and Ben eased the bag down to the floor, and tried to catch his breath while staring at boxes of Pitz-Flex golf clubs stacked high and long to the right of the table. Spindler resumed snapping photographs, including some of the congregating customers, and others of the boxes of clubs, and once satisfied he had sufficiently captured the photographic scene, he instructed Ben to take a seat at the table, and he gladly complied.

"Ladies and gentlemen," Spindler bellowed into a cheap plastic megaphone, "here's the guest of honor you've all been waiting for—Ben Digby!" Ben awkwardly acknowledged the polite smattering of applause, and Spindler continued. "As you all know, this man shot the greatest seventeen holes of golf this community has ever known, and did so in a blizzard. He plans to complete what he started that day, by playing the final hole when Bozeman's own Lone Wolf Country Club re-opens in the spring. When he does, we here at Pitz-Smart will be one hundred percent behind Ben, and believe wholeheartedly that he will complete the feat of shooting his age!" Some customers clapped, but Ben simply watched on anxiously. "I now direct your attention to these stacks over here," Spindler said pointing. "Each of these boxes contain a full set of our Pitz-Flex deluxe golf clubs, and just know that Ben here is the official spokesman for them and each of you—"

Ben tugged on Spindler's shirt gaining his attention, and whispered discretely, "I didn't agree to that,"

"What?" Spindler asked holding the megaphone away from them.

"That spokesman thing. I didn't agree to that."

"It's in the contract," Spindler said.

"Spill on aisle seven," boomed a page.

"I don't recall that, but I'll take your word for it," Ben said, "but I've never hit a single shot with those clubs, and those that know me—know that."

"Ben, no one here is going to know that, plus you can speak for a product without using it," Spindler argued, growing impatient with what he regarded as Ben's priggish point of view of marketing, and while the two bantered, neither had noticed that Mungo Thibodeaux was now standing in the crowd.

When Spindler turned back to the customers, he was greeted by Mungo's toothy grin, and trying to ignore him, he returned to the megaphone. "You see, these deluxe clubs are the perfect choice for the novice, the most experienced golfer or *anyone* just trying to get their game in shape." Mungo raised his hand and Spindler asked impatiently, "What do you want Mungo?"

"I have couple of questions. First, we all noticed that Ben's set of clubs came with a free girdle—is that what you meant about getting your game *in shape*?"

Spindler turned, noticed the dangling garment for the first time, and fired back. "No! Now as I was saying these clubs—"

"Pardon me, Stewart," Mungo interrupted while placing his hand on one of the Pitz-Flex boxes. "About these *deluxe* clubs, as you call them, are you saying Ben Digby actually owns a set?"

"As a matter of fact he does," Spindler, bragged. "Ben is the proud owner of the Pitz-Flex clubs sitting in the bag next to him."

Mungo put on his glasses, walked over to the large golf bag and removed one of the irons, and quickly arrived at the same qualitative conclusion as Ben, and asked, "Is that true, Ben? Are these really yours?"

"I'm the proud owner all right," Ben said with a wink.

"Huh, who'd a thunk," Mungo said, turning back to Spindler. "But are you saying that Ben Digby actually *plays* with these alleged deluxe clubs?"

"Excuse me, but you said a *couple of questions*, and I answered them!"

"The girdle thing was just a joke and don't count!" Mungo argued.

"Wrong! Joke or not, it was still a question," Spindler retorted. "Now back to Ben's golf feat. We here at Pitz-Smart—"

"Hey, what about it?" another customer asked. "Does Digby play golf with them or not?"

"I, er uh … you see … as I said Ben owns a Pitz-Flex set, and may play with them if he wants … now that he's the product spokesman … that is."

"So you admit that he don't play 'em?" Mungo pressed, and all eyes trained on Spindler.

"Let's get it straight Mungo, I never said he actually uses the clubs, okay?" Spindler said as sweat stains were spreading from the armpits of his cheap, light-blue dress shirt.

"What about that?" Mungo asked.

"What about, what?"

"The sign hangin' there!" Mungo said pointing toward the banner above the table. "That thing says right there, *Play the clubs that record-setter Ben Digby plays—Pitz-Flex!* So does he play 'em or not?"

"Well uh ... I think he ... um ..." Spindler stammered.

"I've known Benjamin Digby for many years, and I ain't *never* seen him—or anyone else for that matter—with one of those clubs in hand," Mungo said.

"Well, that changes today, and you all can be just like Ben here and become the owner of your own set of Pitz-Flex clubs, which are as all-American as ol' Ben Digby himself," Spindler said.

Mungo turned back to Spindler. "Did I just hear you say that these clubs are *all American?*"

"Yes," Spindler said tersely.

"I thought so," Mungo said, returning his reading glasses to his face. "It says right here on the box that they're made in Taiwan?"

Ben heard a smattering of muffled murmurs and snickering and stared down at the table to conceal his own amusement. Spindler's face flushed red and his eyes fluttered rapidly. "I was referring to ... um ... you know ... the classic American design of these fine, high quality golf clubs."

"Oh, that explains it," Mungo said, rolling his eyes.

"There's still a spill on aisle seven!" the pager repeated.

Spindler, taking notice of the page this time and seeing that several employees were now among those in the audience watching the promotion said, "Would you all get back to work and answer that page?" They obeyed and Spindler returned to the megaphone, and with one of the brochures in hand said, "As you see, we have several sets of Pitz-Flex clubs right here, and they're available at a special price to commemorate Ben's appearance here today. So step right up and greet Ben, grab one of these brochures and last, but certainly not least, pick up your own set of these miracle clubs, and remember to shop smart—shop Pitz-Smart."

"The only miracle around here is that you got Ben Digby to sit through this nonsense!" Mungo said.

Though it seemed much longer to Ben, the whole Sporting Goods presentation lasted only a matter of minutes, and all of those approaching the reluctant celebrity offered nothing but well wishes and kind words, however he felt ill at ease at the sight of customers picking up boxes of the clubs and heading for the checkout stands. When the crowd dispersed, Ben rose and began walking away from the table anxious to leave the store. Spindler was instructing a stock boy on the handling of Ben's new clubs, until he noticed Ben departing, and called to him. "Wait up, Ben! Where are you going?"

Ben stopped, and said, "Home."

"I need to speak with you about a few things in my office, before you go. Would you mind following me please?"

"Lead the way," Ben said reluctantly, and they started to the back of the store.

As they walked Spindler added, "Don't worry about your clubs, my stock boy will remove them from my bag, put them and the towel back in the box, take them up front, and Leonard will watch them until you leave." Ben nodded and followed Spindler down the main aisle, through the double doors and into the hallway.

"How'd you like being king for a day?" Spindler asked as they walked.

"To be honest with you, I still would've preferred hosting."

"Oh, come on Ben. It was great exposure for us, and you deserve all those nice comments the people gave you."

"If you say so," Ben responded and they trudged back up the stairs and into Spindler's office.

"The people really seemed to really like it, and we may have sold more Pitz-Flex sets this morning than we did all of last month. With that said though, I need a favor," Spindler added in a serious tone. "You know Mungo pretty well, don't you Ben?"

"I do."

"Going forward, I feel that this little arrangement of ours would work a lot better if he would keep his nose out of it," Spindler said, leaning on the sill of the large window with his back to the curtains. "Do you think you could have a little talk with him?"

"And tell him what? I mean your store's a public place."

"I understand that, and please know that I'm not barring him from coming here. Hell, I've actually never seen him in here before, but he happens to show up on a day when we're doing an important promotion with you."

"That is odd," Ben acknowledged.

"Yes and I just thought it would be helpful if you could kinda—you know—discourage him."

"Oh, Mungo was just being Mungo," Ben defended.

"I know, but he can be quite the smart mouth, and he could've compromised the full effect we were trying to achieve here today. Mungo is a swell guy, and all I'm asking is if you could just speak to him." Spindler said as he turned and opened the window curtains.

"I'll do that, but you know Mungo is a free spirit," Ben said.

"I realize that, but I just—" Spindler stopped in mid-sentence, as he peered down toward the sales floor, seeing employees mopping up piles of glass, goo and other debris on aisle seven, and yelled, "What the hell happened down there?"

Ben joined him at the window. "Whoa, that sure looks like a mess."

"Mess hell! It looks like a damn earthquake hit! Sorry Ben, but I've got to get down there and find out what's happening."

"You do that," Ben said.

"I've got more to discuss, and I'll be back, so make yourself at home," Spindler instructed, and then stormed out of his office and toward the stairs.

Ben waited by the window, and watched on as Spindler reached aisle seven and began pointing and barking questions to the employees. Ben used the diversion to make his break, and hustled to the bottom of the stairs, and out to the sales floor, consciously avoiding getting near aisle seven. He continued to the front of the store, and after retrieving his clothing from Customer Service, he made a beeline toward the front exit.

When he neared the area with rows of shopping carts, Ben saw Leonard, clad in his red hosting shirt, talking to customers and behind him, on the floor sat the box with his clubs. Ben's inclination was to leave the box where it sat, considering that he neither needed nor wanted the clubs, and desired to avoid any threat of tax consequences. He likewise did not want to risk Leonard engaging him in conversation, a delay that could allow Spindler to catch up with him, but then thought *hell, if I leave the clubs here, they'll just call me back up here to get 'em.*

Ben settled on the strategy of surreptitiously removing the clubs, and did so by easing nonchalantly behind Leonard, lifting the box from the floor, and then heading directly toward the exit. With clubs in hand, he walked hastily through the glass double doors, and as he did, he heard from behind him a loud beeping sound. Ben had never exited a store that used sensors to foil shoplifters, and he had no conception that the piercing sound from behind had anything at all to do with him. Following Pitz-Smart protocol, Leonard made an immediate radio call on his walkie-talkie, oblivious to the identity of the fleeing suspect. Ben was walking briskly, and as he neared his truck, he heard a loud male voice from behind yell, "Stop right there!"

Ben froze and turned to see a rotund uniformed man, approaching rapidly on an electric one-seater golf cart. As the man brought the cart to an abrupt stop, Ben set the box of clubs on the hood of his truck, and turned back to him in order to learn what he wanted. He noticed a patch reading *security* on the left sleeve of the man's white shirt, a shirt that he estimated was at least two sizes too small, and that he wore black slacks that strained to suspend his large stomach that cascaded over his belt line. Then Ben realized that the security guard was wedged between the cart's driver's side seat back and the steering wheel, but the guard kept his eyes trained on Ben as he rocked back and forth, struggling to free himself from the golf cart. Once liberated from the one-seater, he walked winded and warily toward Ben, with his hand conspicuously hovering over his holstered can of pepper spray.

"What can I do for you?" Ben asked.

"Start by answering the questions and not asking them," the man demanded between taking rapid gasps of breath. "I got a page that you set off the security alarm back there mister,"

"I'm awfully sorry about that, but what in the world did I do to set it off?"

"You walked out with that right there!" he said, pointing at the Pitz-Flex box.

"But why'd it go off?" Ben asked, beginning to sense the gravity of his circumstance.

"I think you know exactly why!"

Ben noticed that on the man's shirt, opposite the side with the badge, it read *S. Snead*, and said, "Mr. Snead, I truly don't understand what I did to set it off."

"Failin' to pay—that's what! You see, that box has a state of the art theft prevention strip on it that would have been disarmed if you'd bothered to pay for them," the security guard explained as other customers began gathering around the two men.

"You don't understand—these are mine."

"Oh?" Snead asked suspiciously, "do you have a receipt?"

"No sir, I don't," Ben admitted.

"Are you claiming you paid for 'em?"

"No, but—"

"Then you'll need to come with me, fella!"

"Come with you?" Ben asked and Snead nodded. "But these were a gift."

"Gift?" Snead smirked. "We here at Pitz-Smart call that takin' the old *five-finger discount*."

"What exactly are you getting at?" Ben asked.

"It's called *theft* mister, and Pitz-Smart takes it very seriously!"

"Mr. Snead, just go inside the store and find Leonard Duncan, he can explain the whole thing?"

"Leonard is the one that paged me to come apprehend you."

Ben tiptoed and looked over the gathering crowd and toward the store's entrance. "There he is right there with Stewart Spindler," Ben said, pointing to the two men talking as they walked out of the store, and glanced in all directions. "Go over there and ask them, and they'll explain everything."

"Oh, no. I'm not falling for that old trick!"

"Trick?" Ben asked.

"Yeah, I leave you here to go over there, and then you make your getaway," Snead said as he snatched the box off Ben's truck and placed it on his cart.

"You don't understand, this is all just a big mistake," Ben, pleaded as the number of observers grew.

"It certainly is, and the jails are full of people that have made such *mistakes*," Snead said, "so save the alibis for the police."

"Police! You're not serious, are you?" Ben asked.

"I'm dead serious, and I'm taking you into custody, and before I do, I'll need to pat you down for weapons."

"What in the hell are you doing, Snead?" Spindler yelled, while frantically pushing his way around the onlookers.

"Securing a crime scene—that's what."

"Crime scene?" Spindler asked.

"Yes sir, I caught this man stealing a set of golf clubs—the expensive ones too!"

"These clubs were a gift from me!" the red-faced General Manager said, as the color drained from the Snead's face.

"He was telling the truth about that?" Snead asked swallowing hard.

"Yes and how could you do such a thing?" Spindler asked.

"Don't worry about it Stewart," Ben said, trying for de-escalation. "Snead here was just doin' his job."

Spindler sighed with relief. "I'm sorry, Ben. What can we do to make it up to you?"

"Just let me go home now—I'm starvin'."

"Of course, that's a given. Anything else?"

Ben pondered. "Yes, just count today as two of the six appearances, and we'll call it square."

"That's a deal," Spindler said.

Ben nodded and quickly hopped in his truck, and as the crowd began to disburse, Spindler was exchanging words with Snead, until he saw Ben's clubs sitting on the security cart. Spindler lifted the box from the cart, and yelled, "Ben! Ben! You forgot your clubs!" Ben responded by revving all four barrels of the old Chevrolet's carburetor, turned the volume knob up on the radio, and pretended not to hear Spindler's plea as he fled the parking lot.

Once home, Ben walked into the kitchen and said, "The chili smells great."

"Thanks, I believe it's a good batch, if I say so myself." Emily said. "How'd it go at the store?"

"Honestly, I feel like I need to take a shower," he confided as he flopped into his recliner.

"Oh? Did you sweat or something dear?"

"Some, but it's mainly just from dealing with the Pitz-Smart folks."

"Was it bad?"

"You should have seen the circus they created, just for a golf club promotion. They paraded me out to the customers like some sort of big shot, and on top of that, they made me the spokesman for their golf clubs."

"Spokesman?" She asked.

"Yes, it's apparently in the contract I signed."

"Did the customers like it?"

"Oh, I suppose so," he conceded, "heck, some of them actually bought some of the clubs."

"Isn't that a good thing, after all that's what Pitz-Smart wanted, right?" Emily asked.

"It was good for Pitz-Smart—bad for the customers."

"Why is that?"

"They're lousy clubs, and I hate the notion that some might have bought a set only on my endorsement," Ben said. "They even wanted me to have my own personal set of the clubs."

"They expected you of all people, to buy a set from them?" she asked.

"No, they gave me a set. Believe me, I wouldn't pay money for 'em."

"Where are they—in your truck?"

"No, but that's a long story," Ben said. "Bottom line is I've had better mornings, and I do shudder to think of what they'll cook up next for me at that mammoth store of theirs."

"What'd you think of it?"

"The store?" Ben asked, and she nodded. He stared up to her wide-eyed. "It's unbelievable, I've never seen anything like the place."

"I felt the same way the first time I went in there."

"And the people sure seem to flock to it," Ben said. "Do you know that there was a crowd out front before the darn place opened?"

"I know that well, they're my competitors."

"What do you mean?"

"I'm quite sure many of them were my fellow coupon clippers, and that's why I too get there early."

"I can certainly understand that now, and it was a tad disconcerting being among them and the whole thing made me very anxious."

"Perhaps they got what they needed this morning and won't make you go back down there," Emily said.

"That'd be great, but I doubt it seriously. They've got as much as twenty-five thousand bucks on the line, and I'm sure they'll want to milk this for all they can."

"I thought the deal was ten thousand."

"When I agreed to do this, I negotiated with Pitzmyre to get more for the hall."

"That'd be fabulous, Ben! Why didn't you tell me?" Emily asked.

"I kind of want to keep that part under wraps."

"Why? The guys down at the hall will think you're even a bigger hero!"

"The problem is they only get the extra fifteen if I shoot my age, so please don't mention anything about it. The pressure is enough as it is, and if this gets out, it'll draw even more attention to it. I failed to grasp how I would react to all of this until today, and going down to that store was bad enough, but then there's all this pretense and subterfuge, it's just so unseemly to me."

"You're being exploited, aren't you?"

"There's no doubt about that. Hell I—"

"Ben!"

"Sorry, Em. I knew going in that I was to be exploited and even signed a contract spelling out how I was to be exploited, but I just couldn't imagine how I would feel about it."

"I'm sorry it's making you so miserable," she said.

Ben sighed, and said, "I'll be okay."

"I know you will," she said. "Did you see any friends or old customers down there?"

"I saw a few, including Sam, Morris Stenson, and Sandy Whitcombe cashiering.

"What about Dan?"

"I didn't make it over to the meat section to see if he was there, but you'll never believe who else was there."

"Who?" she asked.

"Mungo Thibodeaux."

"I may be at fault for that," Emily said. "Mungo called for you this morning after you left with something about the VFW hall, and I told him where you were—I hope you don't mind."

"No, it was actually the only aspect of this morning that was pleasant."

"Imagine that, you and Mungo Thibodeaux, at the Pitz-Smart store on the same day—now that's astonishing," she said.

Ben chuckled. "Yes, Satan can now take up ice-skating!"

The Twelfth Hole

*W*ith Ben now legally bound to playing the final hole, Joseph Pitzmyre needed to take his plan to the next level, by making it a publicity bonanza. He homed in on the local Bozeman press, placing a call to Brian Cotton, the Tribune reporter and the author of the original article on Ben's interrupted round.

"Cotton, here," the reporter answered.

"Brian, Joseph Pitzmyre calling."

"Okay," the reporter responded tersely, not recognizing the name.

"You report on the local beat there in Bozeman, right?" Pitzmyre asked.

"That's correct?"

"And you wrote the article about Ben Digby last fall?"

"Ben who?"

"Digby, the man with the snowed-out golf round at that Lone Ranger golf course there."

"Do you mean Lone Wolf Country Club?"

"Right," Pitzmyre said. "Don't you remember the old dude that almost shot his age?"

"Yes, I know what you're talking about now," Cotton said, "the wire picked it up, and the man landed a network interview out it."

"That's right, but did your paper cover Digby's personal appearance at the Pitz-Smart store there last Saturday?"

"I heard something about it, but no we didn't."

"Why not?" Pitzmyre asked.

"There's nothing newsworthy about the man going to a department store."

"Brian, Brian, Brian, you act as if his story is over, but it's a developing one. There is a lot to cover between now and the time Ben steps onto that eighteenth tee this spring to complete his round—you do know he's going to do that, don't you?"

"No, but if he does I'm sure we'll write something on it then."

Riled by Cotton's apathy, Pitzmyre said, "I sense you don't understand the gravity of this."

"With all due respect, we report news. This was news last fall, and it may be news again in the spring, but I don't see anything newsworthy in between."

"I couldn't disagree more. This is a *big* damn story in the making, and you ignore it at your own peril."

"Hey! That sounds like a threat—just who do you think you are?"

"Who do *you* think I am?" Pitzmyre challenged.

"You said Joe Pit-something or another."

"Pitzmyre! Pitzmyre! Listen here scoop, you are familiar with the advertising department there at your alleged newspaper, aren't you?"

"Sure, I interned there for a year before they made me a reporter."

"That figures," Pitzmyre said. "Brian, I am Joseph Pitzmyre, the founder and CEO of Pitz-Smart International. Before I called you, I looked it up, and do you know how much money I spend every week to advertise in that rag of yours?"

Caught off-guard by revelation, and the question, Cotton stammered, "Oh uh … yes sir, I do! I mean …um … I don't know the exact amount, but your company spends a ton."

"Yes we do, and now that I have your attention, I'm gonna to make some news for you. I am putting up a hundred grand that says hometown hero, Ben Digby, will do this thing."

"A hundred thousand dollars?" Cotton asked.

"Yes!"

"That he'll shoot his age?"

"Yes, yes!" Pitzmyre stressed.

"And you're putting it up for what exactly?"

"Let me spell it out for you, do you have something to write with?"

"Yes sir, I have a pencil and I'm ready," responded the now attentive reporter.

"Pitz-Smart believes in old Ben so much so, that we're willing to wager that he will succeed in shooting his age, and we'll post that sum—"

"The hundred thousand?" Cotton interrupted.

"Precisely, and we'll place that full amount in trust so that those who choose to bet against Ben, can deposit their own wager against ours."

"Hang on just a minute mister ... I mean sir ... please," Cotton, stammered. "I want to get this straight. You're going to put up the hundred thousand in trust, and you're betting up to that amount that Digby will succeed?"

"You got it, scoop."

"And people can bet against him shooting his age?"

"Yes, and this is a big damn deal, unlike anything that's ever happened out there, and as such, I want it to make big damn news—if you know what I mean."

"But who do you expect to be betting with?"

"All comers, Brian! You see, with our hundred thousand dollars in trust, at the Accel Bank branch located in our store there, people can go there and place a bet against Ben, and by the way, you need to mention Accel in the article."

"Wait now, I haven't committed to running a piece on this," Cotton said.

"Oh, you're going to run one, or I'll find another place to spend my advertising budget."

"But it's not my call, Mr. Pitzmyre. After all, I am responsible to an editor, and I have—"

"Brian, I'm not pickin' on you, I am actually trying to do you a favor, but instead of thanking me for this opportunity and embracing the concept, you're throwing up roadblocks. This is a *big* deal, and you and your paper need to treat it as such!"

"Okay, I got it. I'll write the story and try to explain the importance of it to my editor," Cotton said.

"Good, that's more like it," Pitzmyre said, "and if your editor gives you any crap about it, you direct him to me."

"She," Cotton said.

"What?"

"My editor—she's a she."

"No shit. Well, if she gets her pantsuit in a ruffle about it, give her my number and I'll straighten her out too."

"Okay, but I need you to explain the betting thing a little more—I'm not sure I understand all of that."

"I'm glad to do it Brian, as I don't want you to screw this up," Pitzmyre said, "so here's how it works. Any wrong-minded person—or business for that matter—that wants to bet against ol' Ben can simply post their money in the same trust account. Accel will keep a list of betters and the amount of their wagers, and if Ben does not shoot his age, then they get their money back plus mine, in the amount of their bet."

"Up to the hundred thousand," Cotton said.

"Right. On the other hand, if he succeeds in shooting his age, we get to keep it all, it's that simple."

"So they don't have to bet the full hundred thousand?"

"No, any amount will be accepted up to that maximum."

"I must say, this is very interesting."

"It damn sure is! Now I want that in your paper tomorrow, on the front page and out on the wire too, okay?"

"Yes, sir."

"Also include in the article that that the VFW stands to gain as much as twenty-five thousand dollars on this deal."

"The VFW post here?" Cotton asked.

"Right, and while you're at it, you need to mention that Digby is the official spokesman for Pitz-Smart's line of deluxe golf clubs, and use that word *deluxe*, since common people react to terms like that," Pitzmyre said and paused, until he heard a cessation in Cotton's scribbling. "Also, include the brand name of the clubs—Pitz-Flex," Pitzmyre demanded and spelled the trade name for Cotton then continued. "And note that these clubs are in stock and that they're only sold in our stores."

"With all due respect, I don't see how the clubs or the endorsement thing is germane to the story," Cotton said.

"It is, and you need to include it. Also, mention that Ben made that personal appearance at our store this past weekend, and that he'll make more like it between now and the big day."

"Got it sir," Cotton said, "and I'll put in the article that they can find word on Digby's future appearances in our paper?"

"Now you're thinking, Brian!" Pitzmyre said, "now take it from the top."

"Excuse me?"

"Repeat it back to me like you intend to write it."

Cotton cleared his throat and said, "Okay ... Anyone wanting to bet against your wager, could walk into the Accel bank and—"

"You mean, walk into the local Bozeman Pitz-Smart store, and go to the Accel branch located in there, right?"

"Yes, of course."

"This is very important Brian, so make sure you get that right in the article, okay?" Pitzmyre demanded.

"Yes, sir. So I could go to the store and—"

"The Pitz-Smart store, Brian! Shit man, do I need to feed this story to someone else?"

"No! I've got this," Cotton responded anxiously.

"All right then, take it from the top."

"Any takers can go to the local Pitz-Smart store here in Bozeman, then go into the bank—I mean, the Accel branch in the store—and if they want to bet against this guy—"

"Ben Digby," Pitzmyre said.

"Right, Ben Digby, and they can just pick an amount and deposit it in the trust account, and have a bet."

"Correct, but write it better than you just said it, okay?"

"Yes sir!"

Pitzmyre's call paid off the next morning when the front-page article detailing the story read:

LOCAL GOLFER GETS $100,000 VOTE OF CONFIDENCE FROM PITZ-SMART

President and CEO of Pitz-Smart International, Joseph Pitzmyre, has announced in an exclusive interview with the Tribune that Pitz-Smart is posting a wager in the amount of $100,000, that come this spring local golfer, Benjamin Digby, will make history. As we reported last November, Digby was playing the round of his life at our local Lone Wolf Country Club, when a brutal winter storm halted his play on the threshold of greatness by preventing him from completing the eighteenth and final hole. A par on the eighteenth would have given him the rarely achieved feat of shooting his age.

Sweetening the pot, Pitz-Smart has pledged as much as $25,000 to benefit our own local Veterans of Foreign Wars post, if Digby succeeds. This adds an additional level of excitement to an already exhilarating story. Digby is now the spokesperson for the Pitz-Flex brand, which is Pitz-Smart's deluxe line of golf clubs, which can only be purchased at their stores. Digby will be making future appearances at our local Pitz-Smart, like the one he did this past weekend—so watch for notices of Digby's forthcoming appearances, right here in your hometown newspaper.

That morning, Spindler spotted the article in the Tribune and immediately placed a call to Los Angeles.

"Yes Stewart, what do you want?" Pitzmyre answered.

"Boss, are you aware of the article about Digby in our paper," he asked.

"Of course Stewart, didn't you read the part about them interviewing me?"

"Sure I did, but I wanted you to know that not only did it make the paper, it was on the front page."

"Just as I demanded of its author," Pitzmyre bragged.

"So you called Brian Cotton directly?"

"Yes, and I practically wrote the piece myself, and it's going coast to coast on the wire!"

"I know Brian personally, why didn't you just have me contact him?" Pitzmyre sighed. "Because I needed it done right."

"But, a hundred grand, that's a ton of money to bet on a golf hole."

"It's chicken feed, if you think about it. First off, how many of those rubes out there have the money or the gumption to bet against ol' Dingbat?" Pitzmyre asked.

"Not many, I would guess."

"That's right, and consider the ton of free publicity we'll get by backing the old dude on this level."

"But what about that money for the VFW?" Spindler asked. "That's a lot, too."

"Sure it is, but think about it. The worst-case scenario is if Dingbat does shoot his age and no one bets, we have to pay the cash to the VFW, but in the process we'll get a write off and will look magnanimous."

"But what if people *do* bet against you and Ben *doesn't* shoot his age?"

"Then the VFW donation goes down to ten grand and I owe the amount of the bets, which you said yourself should be meager, if any," Pitzmyre explained. "And consider this, anyone wanting to wager, has to go to the Accel location right there in your failing store!"

"So?" Spindler asked.

"It's called foot traffic, dummy! All takers have to walk past all of that merchandise and advertising to place their bet. Who knows, perhaps a miracle will occur, and one of them will actually buy something, and if they do, who knows, perhaps lightening will strike twice, and they'll return and buy something else," Pitzmyre explained.

"I see, and along the way we get the publicity."

"We get that, and much more," Pitzmyre said. "Stewart, what demographic is always the last in any given community to get on board with our stores?"

Spindler thought for a moment, and then said, "Old people?"

"Old men, to be precise, and I'm sure that VFW hall is chock full of 'em. So the community will love us for supporting Dingbat, and it will help persuade the old folks to think differently about us."

"That's brilliant, Joe."

"Well—we finally have something we can agree on," Pitzmyre said, hanging up the phone.

After breakfast that morning, Emily opened the Tribune and was drawn to the front-page headline, and she perused the entire article, before walking to the breakfast table. She handed it to Ben, and stood anxiously at his side while he read it.

"My good Lord!" Ben said, clasping his hands on top of his head. "A hundred grand bet on this stupid golf hole!"

"Did you know anything about this?" she asked.

"No, I mean Pitzmyre mentioned that thing about being a gambler and all, but I didn't take it literally."

"The article also mentioned the twenty-five thousand for the hall," Emily added as she stepped back to the kitchen.

"Yeah, the cat's out of that bag on that too," Ben, lamented.

"It'll be fine, plus you're in the papers again, and everyone's going to be so excited," Emily said as she removed toasted bread from the mini-oven.

"That's all well and good, but this isn't about me, the game of golf or the VFW, for that matter—it's all about the almighty dollar."

"It's all about you, to me and your friends though, and at the end of the day, isn't that the most important thing?"

"I suppose so," he conceded.

"All you have to do is give it your best," she said and slid his breakfast plate in front of him. "Either way, the VFW will get much needed funds, so just set all that other nonsense aside."

"You're right, Em. You've always guided me to the bigger picture, but forgetting that a tenth of a million dollars is riding on your golf performance is easier said than done!"

"Oh my! When you put it that way, it does seem like a lot—do you think anyone around here would actually bet against you?"

"Who knows, it seems people bet on just about anything these days."

"What do you mean?" she asked.

"Get me the sports out of there, and I'll show you," Ben said and Emily leafed through the paper and removed the sports section, and handed it to him. Ben turned to the next to the last page of and asked, "You do know that the biggest football game of the year's coming up, right?" he asked and she nodded. "This is the pro football's game to name their champion, but simply watching it isn't enough excitement for literally millions of fans."

"Everyone knows that people bet a lot on which team will win, if that's what you're getting at," Emily said.

"Sure, but that's just the beginning, ever heard of the football propositions?" Ben asked.

"Are you referring to the girls at the hotels where the players stay? I did read about that in one of the tabloids."

Ben chuckled. "No, it's the proposition bets—here take a look," Ben said pointing to the betting lines in the paper. "Like you mentioned, people bet on one side or the other to win."

"Yes and they have the point thingy too," Emily added.

"Correct, that's called the point spread, and for this one, the favorite is giving four and a half points, meaning that team has to win by five or more for that side to pay off."

"So the other team could lose the game, but win the bet?"

"Yes and have you ever heard of the over and under?" Ben asked, and Emily shook her head. "It's right here," he said, directing her back to the sports page. "For this game, it's forty-four. So you can bet that the total score, for both teams at the end of the game comes, in over that figure or under it—thus the name. That particular wager is available for most any given game, but for this one, you can do the same thing for the halves and even each quarter."

"Hmm, so just waiting for the end of the game isn't enough for the betters."

"Right, and then you have other propositions, and they're over here," he said pointing. "You can bet on which team or even which player will score first, and if the first score is a touchdown, field goal, safety or defensive play, and the over and under on the total number of fumbles, interceptions, touchdowns, safeties, and field goals.

"My goodness, that's just plain crazy," Emily, said.

"Get a load of this, you can even bet on the outcome of the coin toss."

"What?" Emily asked in disbelief.

"That's right, you can lay money on whether the coin lands heads or tails," Ben said, "so you can actually win or lose a bet before the game even kicks off."

"That's nuts all right, but just how do *you* know so much about it, Benjamin?" Emily asked flashing him a suspicious stare.

He laughed. "Some of the guys at the hall used to bet with one another, and they talked about this stuff all the time. But the point is, people will wager on the strangest of things, so who knows if anyone will take a portion of Pitzmyre's bet or not."

The following morning, an unexpected source upped the ante, and in a big way, when Ferguson T. Knox, sole proprietor of Bozeman State Bank, weighed in. Knox, himself approaching his eightieth birthday, continued to manage the day-to-day operations of the bank, and in a public act of defiance, he captured his own front-page headline in the Tribune, reading:

THE BET IS CALLED – AND RAISED!

The article recapped Ben's golf challenge, Pitzmyre's initial wager and concluded with an excerpt from an interview with Knox.

"Hell no, I don't think he can do it! I'm nearing 80 years of living, and as such I haven't played that golf course in years, but I've seen Ben play, and it's never been pretty. The day that he played those 17 holes was nothing short of a fluke, and he should have played the last hole then. I am certain that whatever magic was in play has surely worn off by now. As such, I see Pitz-Smart's $100,000 wager and raise it another $50,000. Once we agree to the terms of the wager and know the final amount, my money will be deposited by sundown in that fly-by-night bank located in their store! Let's just see how behind Ben Digby, Joseph Pitzmyre is now."

The Thirteenth Hole

News of Knox's wager reverberated all the way from the mountainous peaks of Montana to the swaying palms of California. What began as a marketing ploy, with a defined risk, had just escalated greatly, and the ball was squarely in Pitzmyre's court. When the CEO learned of Knox's raise, he was more than agitated, and wanted answers and wanted them fast. Pitzmyre dialed his Bozeman location, and as the phone rang, he commenced chewing anxiously on a fingernail.

"Pitz-Smart Bozeman, how may I direct your call?" the operator asked.

"Get me Stewart Spindler."

"Who's calling?"

"Joseph Pitzmyre."

"Did you say Pitzmyre?" the operator asked urgently.

"Yes!"

"Oh dear," the operator said as she frantically fumbled with some papers until she located a typewritten bulletin, cleared her throat and recited, "Oh ... Mr. Pitzmyre, as CEO and founder of the Pitz-Smart International, I am honored to—"

"I don't have time for that shit," Pitzmyre said, "just get Spindler on the phone!"

"But I'm not through," she said.

"You're about to be through all right, if you don't get him on the line—now!"

"I am very honored to transfer your call, sir."

"Hello," Spindler answered.

"It's Joe, was that the same operator that I had trouble with before?"

"Yes," Spindler said, sensing his boss' renewed irritation, "did she not read the greeting I wrote for her?"

"Stewart, customers don't want to hear all that shit when they call your store!"

"It's not for the customers. I typed it out for her, for only when you call, I wanted her to ... you know ... be more respectful."

"I don't call your store to talk to the operator, Stewart. I just want her to transfer my damn call when I do."

"Sorry Joe, but I just—"

"Screw it—did you see the story about the bet from that banker prick?"

"Yes, and I was going to call you about that," Spindler said.

"What the hell's that old bastard doing?"

"I don't know him, but I hear he's rich, and I guess he's got money to burn."

"I assumed he has money," Pitzmyre said, "but why risk pissin' it away on this golf thing and make the locals out there hate him in the process, for lining up against Ben?"

"I have no idea Joe. I'm told he sits in that old rundown bank building, day in and day out, in his three-piece suit as if the place was teeming with customers."

"Does he not have a lot of customers?"

"No, according to Clive. He says that thanks to Accel and the other newer banks, Knox has a small customer base, and it gets smaller with each passing year," Spindler replied.

"It must cost him a fortune to keep that defunct bank open."

"I'm sure it does, and that's odd, considering that he has the reputation of being a stingy old miser."

"There's gotta be more to this than meets the eye and I want you to find out what it is," Pitzmyre said.

"Me?" Spindler asked.

"Yes, you!" Pitzmyre said harshly. "I have to know why he would risk his own personal money, and alienating what's left of his customer base. Is he just screwing with us, does he have it in for the Ben, or is it something else?"

"Do you want me to try to meet with Knox?" Spindler asked.

"Absolutely not! That would signal that we are worried, and he wouldn't likely tell you the straight skinny on it anyway. No, you're going to have to put your sleuth's hat back on and see what you can learn on the sly. My phone's going to be ringing off the hook with people wanting my response to this kook's call and raise, and I need to know what I'm dealing with before I do."

"Why do you have to respond to the raise part? The Tribune article made it clear that your bet was limited to a hundred thousand," Spindler said.

"Stewart, this guy challenged me, and did it publically, and if I stand on that limitation, it will make us look weak and petty and not truly behind Dingbat. The whole concept was making us look like we're standing up for this guy, and if we just blow this off it will backfire on us, and ruin what we're trying to accomplish—so I *have* to know what this is about, and need to know it pronto!" Pitzmyre said, slamming the phone down.

Spindler cringed at the abrupt end of the call and slowly lowered his phone receiver to the cradle. He needed information, and needed it quickly and opted to again resort to Cookie's Café, and he trotted out of the store and into his car, and then made a beeline to the Lone Wolf Country Club. Entering the café late morning, the urgency of his task quickly ceded to the smell of Cookie frying up hamburgers. It was the special of the day, and Spindler ordered a double meat with cheese and when Katrina delivered it, he became so engrossed in the culinary diversion, that he did not notice Ben sliding into a booth across the room.

Cookie made his way from the kitchen to Spindler's table, just as he was finishing off the cheeseburger, and asked, "How was it?"

"Delicious!" Spindler mumbled through his full mouth as he chewed. "It's the best I've ever eaten."

"Glad to hear it, Stewart."

Swallowing the last remnants of his burger, Spindler asked, "Say, Cookie, can I ask you a couple of questions about Ben Digby?"

"You can, or you could ask him yourself," Cookie said, nodding toward Ben who sat biding his time by thumbing through an issue of Golf Digest.

Crap, when did he come in? Spindler thought as he took a large gulp of his soft drink, belched and rose from his table.

"Do you need anything else?" Cookie asked.

Spindler shook his head, belched again and said, "Just add it to my account, please."

Sensing someone approaching, Ben looked up from the magazine and said, "Oh, hello Stewart."

"Good mornin' Ben. Have you heard the big news?"

"I read the article in the Trib, if that's what you're referring to."

"What do you think about that banker running up the bet like that?"

"I feel the same way about that as I did the original bet—I wish it hadn't been done," Ben said.

"You don't find it very exciting?" Spindler asked.

"No, I find it to be very stupid."

"I don't blame you ... this is all a little nutty to me too," Spindler conceded, "but Joe seems to know what he's doing, and it's not my money, so what the hell."

"That's one way of looking at it, I guess," Ben said.

"Mind if I join you?" Spindler asked.

"No, have seat."

"What'll it be, Ben?" Cookie yelled from the kitchen.

"I'll have the grilled meat loaf, and iced tea please."

"Sandwich or plate lunch?"

"The plate lunch please, I'm splurgin'," Ben replied, and turned back to Spindler.

"I'm just wondering what in the world this Knox guy is thinking—what's your theory?" Spindler asked.

"You're wondering, or is Mr. Pitzmyre?"

"We both want to know what's going on, and I was hopin' you could shed some light on it? I mean, does he have some grudge against you, or is it about us, or perhaps something else?"

"I truly don't know why he's weighing in on this, and it's certainly out of character for him. But, if I had to venture a guess, I'd say it's because he and I got mighty crossways when we ceased our business dealings."

"Were you a customer of his bank?"

"Yes, a longtime customer, and he had our personal and commercial accounts for my entire adult life, at least until we parted ways."

"How did that split come about—did it have something to do with your business?"

"Yes it did. Stewart, my only post military career was working at, and later owning, Big Sky Mercantile—a hardware store and lumberyard. We did well and for decades, until your company and others came along and began affecting the local businesses environment. When that happened, I simply wanted to have a chance to compete, and I calculated that with some capital to make some improvements to the store, and to have some staying power, I could ride it out until the novelty of new businesses like yours wore off."

Katrina brought Ben a tumbler of iced tea. "Here you go Mr. D and your lunch should be ready shortly."

"Thanks Kat," Ben said.

"My pleasure," she said. "Want another Coke, Stewart?"

"No, but thanks anyway," Spindler responded and Katrina began bussing tables.

"So, you needed a loan from Knox?" Spindler asked.

"Yes and in the worst way. In the past, it wouldn't have been a problem getting a line of credit for some float, however times were really changing here and becoming very uncertain for everyone. It all began when the bypass highway opened, as prior to that those passing through Bozeman had to travel Main Street, which took them through the downtown area."

"And downtown was where businesses like yours were located?" Spindler asked.

"Correct, and those businesses suffered a decline in customers the moment the construction barricades were removed and the highway opened, and the impact only worsened with the completion of your store."

"Mashed potatoes or peas?" Cookie yelled from the kitchen.

"Both please—I said I'm splurgin'," Ben yelled over his shoulder, then continued, "Word of your store's size, and prices spread through our community faster than a scandalous rumor, luring even the most skeptical to venture out there to have a look. Many that did became loyal shoppers, including many customers of the downtown stores. The initial symptoms of the success of new businesses like yours were subtle and difficult to detect and diagnose. Optimistic folks like me, felt that there were plenty of customers to share, and contemplated that Pitz-Smart would take the lion's share of those traveling through Bozeman, but once the new wore off, the bulk of the residents would remain true to the locals. But all of us began to experience serious symptoms, mostly in the form lost profits and declining cash flow, and it only worsened from there."

"So what'd you do?" Spindler asked.

"I did a lot of homework, and put together a detailed business plan and made a pitch to Knox. He listened, but in the end he didn't think my plan was viable."

"Did he explain why?"

"Yes. Through my situation and that of his other commercial customers, Knox had his finger on the pulse of the business community. He witnessed on a daily basis what the local retailers were up against, and as a result, he was not lending, especially on unsecured or what he regarded as *speculative loans*. At that same time, new banks were competing aggressively with his, and it became a vicious cycle—the capital dried up and that impacted businesses like mine, and with the lack of lending, Knox' interest income plummeted hurting his bank."

"Were bankers like Knox worried about getting stiffed on the loans?" Spindler asked.

"Sure, and unfortunately some of Knox' debtors did default, and a couple of them even filed Chapter Eleven.

"Did he fear that you'd file for bankruptcy?"

Ben bristled. "That word's not in my vocabulary, and Knox was *very* aware of that. He knew me well enough to know that I would *never* leave him holdin' the bag. I had banked with him for decades and never missed a single payment—on any loan—not one time. Through thick and thin, good times and lean, I always stayed current," Ben, said as Cookie sat his plate lunch in front of him.

"So you were you miffed when Knox wouldn't make the loan?"

"I was upset, for sure. You see, I was a *very* good customer, not his most affluent by any stretch, but certainly among his most reliable," Ben said, while using his knife and fork to cut the grill-marked slab of meatloaf into sections. After savoring his first bite, he added, "I realize in retrospect that Knox knew what I didn't know, or perhaps with my bullheadedness refused to recognized, and that was that stores like yours were successfully pricing us out. I learned from my own customers and friends that you guys could charge at or below my cost on items, and I couldn't compete, at least not in any sustained way. I knew price was important to the folks, but a lower price does not always equal good value, and I kept asking myself, *what about service and selection*. My store gave great service and knowing from customer feedback that you guys didn't, I had reason for hope."

"So you figured in the long run, that would make a difference?"

"Yes, naively so it seems. Back then, I figured it was important for a hardware store to have someone there to greet the customer, listen to their problems and provide solutions. I felt that loyalty and customer service, and a wider array of available parts, tools and other products, would ultimately prevail," Ben said, ate two more bites of lunch, then washed it down with another gulp of the iced tea. "You see, Stewart my customers typically required someone knowledgeable to direct them to what they needed, without having to spend hours in the process, and they seemed to appreciate a person that could offer tips on how best to complete the task. Most people darkening our doorway weren't there just to browse and casually shop, and more often than not they had a *real* problem, one that was important to them, and then there were the intangibles."

"Like what?" Spindler asked.

"Caring about customers and going the extra mile for them. After all, where were you guys when Cy Rogers, a father with a wife and five kids, lost his job and needed to carry some emergency home repairs on credit?" Ben asked rhetorically. "How about when old man Park's barn burned down after a lightning strike? We fronted him all the materials to rebuild so he could keep his dairy farm up and running and his family fed, while he spent two years fightin' an insurance company for reimbursement?"

"Pitz-Smart offers credit to the customers."

"Sure, assuming they qualify to get one of your cards, at nineteen percent interest."

"You heard about that too, huh?"

"Yes, and I think it's shameful."

"We don't make people charge things, they decide to do it, and for many it's the only way they can purchase what they want," Spindler defended.

"Don't get me wrong, I'm not blamin' Pitz-Smart for people making dumb decisions, God knows, there are some people out there that just can't be helped. But there are a lot of others that through no fault of their own fall on hard times and just need a hand up and we were there to give it to them."

"I hear you, but people are a risk, and we have policies to follow to make sure that someone is, you know—"

"Credit worthy?" Ben finished.

"Sure. We have to check their payment history, their credit rating and to verify employment."

"How does a man like Cy Rogers, running that family dairy farm, verify *his* employment, or credit history for that matter?" Ben asked taking another bite of lunch and Spindler simply shrugged. "You all need to consult some credit bureau, from God knows where, to tell you if someone is *worthy*, but I gave credit based on a familiar face and a handshake. Sure, I got burned a few times here and there—but it was rare. I could usually depend on the residents to work things out, without heavy-handed collection agencies. In my mind, it was just old-style, common-sense business dealings."

"I'm sorry Ben, but we're—"

"Don't apologize, hell your business model is obviously right," Ben, said as Katrina approached with tea pitcher. "But look, you didn't come here for a lecture, so what else do you want to know?"

It's a little late on the lecture part Katrina thought as she topped off Ben's tumbler, and began wiping down other tables and straightening the condiments.

"So I guess things didn't turn around like you thought?"

"That's right. Without funding my hardware store was bleeding the death of a thousand cuts, and I had to make tough decisions, some with great regret, including letting employees go. The first was a real smart and hardworking college student studying engineering, but being the last hired, he was first to go. That one was bad enough, but the next was a master plumber whose contracting business had also failed. He was four years from Social Security time and desperately needed the job to bridge the gap. I gave it to him, and he was a great asset to the store, but then I had to take it away. However, the third was the worst," Ben said as he sat his utensils on the plate and shoved his half-eaten lunch toward the middle of the table.

"Who was that?" Spindler asked.

Ben took a deep breath, exhaled and said, "She was a terrific woman and a great employee. She was a stay-at-home mom for two young girls until her husband, an Air Force reservist, died in a helicopter crash in a training exercise at Malmstrom. I took a chance on her, and she quickly got up to speed on the product line, learned how to handle the inventory, did some accounting and the customers truly loved her. I had her for twelve years, and cutting her loose was one of the hardest things I'd ever done, and when I did, she wept—but not for herself—but rather for me."

"That doesn't seem fair," Katrina whimpered.

"It wasn't Kat, but I kept them all for as long as I could, I truly did, and a small piece of me died with each one I let go. Eventually, it was just my wife, a part-time stocker-cashier and me, with a store full of inventory, and very few customers. That place was my life's work, and with the exception of squeezing in a round or two of golf per week here, I spent most every waking hour in that building, until the day came to shut it down and locked the doors."

"Did you and Knox part ways angry?" Spindler asked.

"I can't speak for him, but I was certainly disillusioned. I pulled my accounts, and went to another bank, but that was a small loss to him at that point."

"What'd you do with your inventory?" Spindler asked.

"Fortunately, a few of the wholesalers allowed me to return some of it and the full cost was credited back, less the shipping. I sold quite a bit of boxed inventory to other sources in the area, but at a great loss, and the rest I stored. I then used what was left in my operating account and a big chunk of retirement funds to pay off every penny of the store's debts."

"I can see why you'd have a grudge against him, but why would he have one against you?" Spindler asked.

"I'm not sure he does. You see, Knox is just generally cantankerous and always seemed mad at the world about something."

"Do you think he has a grudge against Pitz-Smart?"

"He never said anything to me, but it's plausible considering the impact businesses like yours had on him and his customers."

"How is it that Knox is still in business?"

"If you mean by *in business* operating at a profit, I not sure he is, but that bank is his life, just as my store was mine. The difference between us is that he could suffer periods of operating in the red and I could not, at least not for the long term. You see, Knox started with money, made a ton more, and though I don't know how much, I'm sure he still has a lot of it. The real head-scratcher for me is why he would risk so much on something so frivolous. He's always been very tight with money, so this wagering is truly out of character for him."

"Does he have heirs—you know—someone to pass his money down to?"

"I honestly don't know. He's always been a *very* private man, and in all the times that I met with him at his bank, I never saw as much as a family photo, and the topic never came up. But, considering he's such a notorious miser, I'm of the belief that he regrets all of this, and hopes Pitzmyre will put an end this foolishness for the both of them."

"You think?" Spindler asked and Ben nodded and took a swig of tea. "So why would he do it in the first place?"

"I'm no mind reader, but I think Knox saw Pitzmyre's bet in the Trib, wanted to make a public statement, flew off the handle and cooked this up as some form of settling old scores. But based on my history with him, I'm sure he regrets it and I think that he'd be content if all of this just went away."

Spindler thanked Ben, left the café for his car, and phoned Pitzmyre from his cell phone as he drove out of the parking lot.

"What'd you find out?" Pitzmyre asked.

"There's no love lost here Joe," Spindler said. "Knox feels the same about businesses like ours as Ben does, and there's friction between the two of them."

"Friction over what?"

"Their businesses dealings. You see, Ben was a longtime customer of the old dude's bank, but because of the influx of new competition, and Knox pulling the rug out from under Ben on some financing, it ended very badly for his hardware store. With that same competition hurting Knox' other customers, his bank also took a big hit."

"So the old banker is pissed enough about all this of this to raise my bet?"

"It seems so," Spindler said.

"What about alienating what's left of his customer base?"

"At this point, I'm not sure Knox gives a rip about his customer base, but with that said I don't get the impression he really meant it."

"The bet?" Pitzmyre asked.

"Yes, he's an old notorious cheap skate, and he reacted emotionally and rushed into it to this to make a statement, and now that he's done that, Ben thinks he would be content if all of this just went away."

"So this was just some sort of a tantrum on his part?" Pitzmyre asked.

"Something like that," Spindler said. "I'm willing to bet, if you'll pardon the reference, that if you offered to make this go away, he'd jump at it."

"And publicly embarrass us in the process."

"What are you getting at Joe?" Spindler asked.

"We went out on a limb to support Dingbat, and this Knox character raises the bet, and now hopes we'll just go wee wee wee all the way home? We'd be vilified for doing that, and I'm *not* fallin' for it."

"What are you going to do?" Spindler asked.

"I'm gonna raise Knox."

"Raise him?" Spindler asked, stupefied.

"That's right!"

"Joe, if you won't cancel the bet, why not just call him."

"If I do that, I'm stuck, and I don't want to get stuck with a hundred and fifty thousand dollar bet. I see raising him as the surest way to get Knox to back out, and when he does he'll look like the turd, and I'll look magnanimous, and it gets the bet back to the hundred grand, with a few penny-ante takers."

"Raising is a big risk, though."

"Poker's always risk," Pitzmyre said. "Now, I want a press release that will state that I call his hundred and fifty and raise him an extra hundred," Pitzmyre said.

"You're taking the bet up to two hundred and fifty thousand?" Spindler asked.

"This calls for a knockout punch and I think this is it! Based on your intel, he won't take it and this gets it back to where it started," Pitzmyre said.

"If you insist on raising him, why not just go up fifty thousand?"

"No, no, Stewart! That's bad poker, and if this guy had any *real* guts, he would've doubled my bet when he raised. By me only going up another fifty, it might tempt him to call, and I am not falling for that. Besides, there is something about an even quarter of a million dollars that makes this whole thing have a psychologically higher level of importance. Hell, if this works out right, the old prick might have actually done us a favor."

"How so?" Spindler asked.

"This little dust up is just the thing to keep this circulating in the media."

"Do want me to get the PR firm to do the press release?"

"Yeah, why don't you call them up and—wait! Ditch the press release, let's do a press conference! I want to do it myself, and I want it to happen there!"

"Here in Bozeman?" Spindler asked.

"Yes! I will fly in this Saturday morning to make my move. I have to be in Chicago on Monday, so I'll just add a stop there, so you get it set up, understand?"

"Got it, Joe."

"If we do this right, it will go coast to coast without paying those hacks at the PR firm a dime! Get as many folks as you can down to your store that morning, and we'll give 'em a show right there in the parking lot."

"We can't do it in the parking lot—it's still way too cold."

"Fine, get a company to come out and erect a tent on the lot, like the one they do in the spring for all that lawn equipment and the fertilizer crap."

"Okay, but how do I get the people down here?"

"Damn it, Stewart! Do I have to map out every detail?"

"Sorry Joe, but I just want to make sure it's done the way you want it."

"Start with some large signs that say a big announcement on Dingbat is coming. Invite *everyone* and make it a *big* deal. Offer free hot dogs and sodas, and crap like that, and perhaps throw in a door prize—people like those out there eat that up! Oh, and make ol' Dingbat come down there as one of his appearances, all right?"

"Okay Joe, I can handle it. Do you want me to let the Tribune know?"

"Of course, and if they give you any crap about running a story, let me know and I'll call that Cotton guy and straighten them out."

"Should I tell the paper that this is your response to Knox's raise?"

"Yes, but don't mention the amount, everyone will expect that I'm going to call the bet, and the fact I'm going take it even higher is going to be the big news maker! But, Stewart, I swear if the amount leaks out I'll have your ass."

The Forteenth Hole

*T*he Digby's were relaxing at home one evening, until their phone rang. Emily took the call, and when she alerted Ben that it was Stewart Spindler, he instinctively cringed, but nevertheless took the phone.

"Hello, Stewart."

"Good evening Ben. I'm sorry to bother you, but I need you to come down to the store on Saturday morning?"

"If it's about the golf clubs, I really don't want—"

"No, it's not about that," Spindler interjected, "It's just your next store appearance."

"Already?" Ben asked.

"Yes, there's a function down here that morning that I need you to attend."

"Stewart, I'm getting a haircut that morning."

"Please Ben, this is *very* important."

"Does this involve this crazy wagering thing?"

"Honestly ... yes," Spindler said.

Ben sighed. "Well I hope the function is to call off all this lunacy."

"I know you do, and I wish it were the case, but you should know that it isn't going away—in fact this is about Pitzmyre's response to Knox. He's coming back here in person to handle it and wants it to be a big deal, and he personally requested you be a part of it."

"Is he really gonna to take that bet?" en asked.

"I can't speak to any of the details," Spindler said, "but I really need you down there and after all, you've only done one of the six appearances so far."

"Two of the six," Ben corrected. "You gave me credit for two that first day, for getting arrested on your parking lot," Ben said, receiving a curious stare from Emily.

"You weren't arrested," Spindler said defensively.

"I beg to differ."

"No way, Ben! After all, I was there."

"So was I, and even your own security guard, Snead, said I was *in custody* and threatened to bring the police, so what would you call it?" Ben asked and Emily now looked disturbed.

"I don't know ... I think uh ... you were simply detained until things got sorted out."

"Well, from where I stood, it sure seemed like an arrest."

"Fine, just please don't say it that way—going forward let's settle on *detained*, okay?" Spindler negotiated.

"Suit yourself," Ben said.

"But I do agree this will be the third of the six appearances."

"All right, I'll do it," Ben said.

"Thank you very much," Spindler said. "So get down there at or before ten, and go to the tent on the parking lot."

"Tent?" Ben asked.

"Yes, there's one already being erected there."

"I'll see you there," Ben said, hanging up the phone then spent the next fifteen minutes explaining his *detention* to Emily.

Blustery winds and temperatures hovering just above zero greeted the Saturday sunrise. Notwithstanding, the areas roads were clear and safe, and as the sun rose, so did the temperature and by the time Ben drove onto the Pitz-Smart parking lot it had climbed into the low teens. As he exited his truck, he noticed numerous vehicles already present, and saw the large red and yellow tent on the far side of the parking lot, near the Pitz-Smart Garden Center. He exited his truck, and saw that parking lot light poles had banners atop them, each with messaging, but the wind had them flapping so rapidly that the words were difficult to discern. As Ben made his way closer to the tent, he heard loud music resonating from inside and could better read signs adorning each of the tent's canvas panels. Written in large letters the panels read: *"BIG NEWS ON BEN DIGBY!"* and others, boasted: *"FREE HOT DOGS AND SOFT DRINKS!"*

Unbeknownst to Ben, and others arriving with him, was the fact that attendees could only access the tent through a closed tunnel, made of the same canvas material as the tent, which spanned several yards connecting the tent to the entry of the store's Garden Center. This exclusive means of ingress required all seeking entry, to do so by proceeding through the main entrance.

Ben confronted the brunt of frigid air as he walked the tent's perimeter searching for the non-existent exterior entrance. Thinking he had simply missed the access, he backtracked, tugging and pulling on the canvass panels along the way, and others with the same quest were now joining him on the same fruitless journey. Concerned that he might be late for the event, Ben resorted to kneeling on the pavement and attempting to lift the bottom of some of the tent's panels, but found that each were anchored securely to the pavement, and would not budge more than a couple of inches.

"Hey! What do you think you're doing?" came a voice from behind.

Startled, Ben rose to his feet and turned in the direction of the voice, and saw Leonard Duncan and security guard Snead, walking briskly toward him. Each man sported serious expressions, and Snead had his hand near his canister of pepper spray. As they neared, Ben stood holding onto the tent with one hand while using the other to brush the parking lot debris from the knees of his corduroys.

"Answer me—what are you up to?" Leonard repeated, not readily recognizing Ben from the limited amount of his face exposed due to his scarf and his well-insulated corduroy hat.

"Look—Leonard, I'm just trying to find a way in there," Ben explained, pointing to the tent.

"Oh, I remember you! You're Bob the golf guy," Leonard said, and his expression softened, but Snead on the other hand, failed to make the connection, and still wore his frown.

"He looks shady to me, Leonard," Snead said. "I bet he was trying to break into the tent for the food!"

"Nice to see you too Snead," Ben, said as a growing number of people continued walking around the tent.

"I don't know you and you don't know me," Snead said.

"Don't you recall arresting ... ahem ... I mean detaining me on this same parking lot?" Ben asked.

"I ask the questions on this parking lot, buddy," Snead responded tersely.

"Ease off, he's all right," Leonard said, "and besides, why would he break in when it's a free event?"

"I learned in security school that you don't need a motive to commit a crime," Snead reasoned.

"Ignore him Bob," Leonard said. "If you're here to get your Pitz-Flex clubs, I've got 'em inside at customer service."

"Uh ... thank you, but I'm not here for that, but I do need to be inside there though," Ben stressed.

"See, I told you he wants in to get the free hot dogs," Snead said.

Ben shook his head. "It's not that, I was instructed by Stewart Spindler to come here for whatever the hell's going on in there this morning."

"You can't get in the tent from out here," Leonard advised.

"You're telling me!" Ben said, as other shivering shoppers with the same dilemma began gathering around them, hoping for direction.

"There's no outside entrance on purpose, didn't you see that?" Leonard asked pointing to a single plastic sign, attached to the tent. It hung well above eye level, and because it clung to the tent by a single Copper loop, the sign waived in the wind, challenging anyone to read *attendees must enter through the store.*

"Oh, I see," Ben, said.

"Stewart should've explained this, but he rigged it this way on purpose to make folks walk through the store to get in," Leonard said directing Ben and the others toward the tent tunnel.

"That figures," Ben mumbled.

"So you all will need to follow me to the main entrance," Leonard advised the crowd and they all trailed behind as Duncan and Snead lead them toward the store. The group ambled into the welcome warmth of the store's interior, meandered past aisle after aisle, before reaching the Garden Center, and finally passing through the tunnel and into the tent.

The music Ben first encountered outside was blaring so loudly inside, that he felt his ears aching, prompting him to return the wool earflaps of his hat downward. He took in the tent's interior, and saw people milling around, with most carrying plates of food, but he did not notice that in the middle of the mingling mass, stood Stewart Spindler.

When Spindler spotted Ben, he was immediately relieved that another important part of Pitzmyre's marching orders had been accomplished by his mere presence, and waved his arms frantically and competed with the music by yelling, "Over here, Ben! Over here!"

Ben heard his name being called, faintly, and looked in all directions for the source. He even lifted the flaps of his hat to aid in the effort, grimacing again at the volume of the music, before finally spying Spindler. He quickly repositioned the flaps and made his way to the GM.

Spindler was standing next to a three-foot high stage erected at the backside of the tent. They shook hands, and Ben looked at the stage and noticed a wooden podium, adorned with a Pitz-Smart banner tacked on to the front, and Spindler's plastic bullhorn sitting atop it. Next to the stage, on a long folding table, Ben saw two wide and deep stainless steel containers, each warmed by flames from small canisters underneath. One bin contained a bounty of hotdog wieners and the other had steamed buns, and together they represented the center of attention for most of the attendees. Also, present were four propane-fueled tower heaters, relied upon to create a tolerable warmth for the guests. Spindler tried to explain the agenda, but the music and commotion overwhelmed Ben's challenged hearing, and even leaning closer to Spindler, Ben only caught bits and pieces of Spindler's comments.

While Spindler struggled to communicate with Ben inside the tent, Pitzmyre's limousine had arrived on the outside. The uniformed driver opened the back door of the long black car, and Pitzmyre emerged, taking in the visual spectacle and feeling the brunt of the brutally frigid easterly winds. He, along with other arriving customers, likewise missed the poorly conceived entry instructions on the flailing tent sign, and wandered about the tent's exterior, seeking a way in. The more he and the others searched, unsuccessfully, the angrier he became. As had happened with Ben, Leonard and Snead eventually intervened and redirected them all, including Pitzmyre, to proceed through the store, heightening the CEO's ire. Once inside, Pitzmyre was none too pleased to make his way toward the Garden Center, flanked by common customers, each on a quest for free food.

Spindler had prearranged to have the canvass tunnel lined with a cadre of employees each with a copy of a photograph of the CEO, in order that they might recognize him instantly. They had bided their time awaiting Pitzmyre's arrival, and when he and others entered the passageway, a cashier spotted him first and alerted her fellow employees. As rehearsed each began to clap and cheer sycophantically, in a manner usually reserved for the arrival of a Third World potentate, but Pitzmyre ignored them as he walked, and strutted directly and rapidly into the tent's interior on a mission to find Spindler.

When Ben caught sight of the executive, he knew in an instance, that he had flown in directly from California, considering his white linen pants, partially unbuttoned lime green silk shirt and ecru-colored Nehru jacket. With his attire, along with his darkly tanned face, and neck and partially bared chest, he stood out like a neon sign amongst the locals. He strode, agitated and shivering across the pavement and toward Spindler, as he took in the tent's interior.

"Hi Joe! So what do you think?" Spindler asked grinning.

"It's fine, but what's with that blaring music!"

"Is it too loud?"

"Yes! Shit, it's giving me a headache."

"I'll get it turned down," Spindler said.

"No, turn it the hell off! I want to get this going and get out of this ice box you all call a town!" Pitzmyre demanded.

Spindler reached over and killed the chaos blasting from the stereo speakers, leaving only the noise of the boisterous and growing crowd. "Is that better?"

"Yes, but what's with there being no entrance from the outside?" Pitzmyre asked, parking his under-dressed frame next to one of the tower heaters.

"I arranged it where customers would have to walk through the store to get in here—I thought you'd like that."

"That's fine for them, but you should have made a way for important people to get in and out, without going through all of that shit!"

"Sorry, Joe."

"And a sign telling people where to go sure would sure be nice," Pitzmyre added. "There are customers ambling around out there, like a bunch of hayseed zombies."

"There is a sign," Spindler defended, "and contract security and Leonard are supposed to be directing people."

"It's not working, and I nearly froze to death trying to get in here!"

"I'm sorry, Joe. I just—"

"And how do human beings live in this climate?" Pitzmyre asked.

"It's actually not that bad today, Wednesday it only got down to twelve below."

Pitzmyre sighed and said, "I'm not here to discuss the damn weather, so listen to me carefully. First and foremost, you *have* to get someone to make me a way out of here, so that when I'm done, I don't have to waste my time walking through your failing store to get to my limo."

"I'll get that done," Spindler said.

"Good. Did you arrange for a door prize drawing?"

"I'm sorry, Joe. I asked, but the printer couldn't get the tickets done on such short notice," Spindler said.

"Fine with me," Pitzmyre said, "you drew a good crowd without it, and your store can ill-afford giving anything away. Is that guy from the paper here?"

"Yes, that's Brian Cotton over there," Spindler replied, pointing.

"Okay, I see him. Does that bullhorn work?" Pitzmyre asked, pointing to the dais.

"Yes, I used it the other day when Digby was here, and to be on the safe side I put in new batteries in it this morning."

"Fine. Where's Dingbat?"

Spindler leaned over to Pitzmyre and whispered, "He's right behind you."

"Shit!" Pitzmyre said.

"And you better not get too used to calling him that," Spindler warned.

Pitzmyre nodded, turned to Ben and shook his hand. "Thanks for coming down, Ben. I think you'll be as excited as we are about what I'll announce here today."

"I'm not so sure about that," Ben replied.

Pitzmyre frowned, turned to Spindler and whispered, "Did you tell him about the raise?"

"No Joe, I swear it!"

Pitzmyre turned back to Ben. "So what's your concern?"

"This has something to do with this wagering thing, and I'm very uncomfortable with it."

Pitzmyre patted Ben patronizingly on the shoulder. "Don't you worry yourself about all this betting stuff. As you'll see in a few minutes, I've got that part *well* under control."

With the music off, all necessary parties present and a sizable crowd congregated, Pitzmyre decided it was time to begin. Continuing to stand as close to the heater as he could without igniting his finely tailored clothing, he gave some last minute instructions to Spindler, finishing with, "You go on up on stage first, warm up the crowd and introduce Ben.

"You want *me* to do the introductions?" Spindler asked as his eyelids commenced to flutter.

"Yes, and describe all of the shootin' his age stuff and don't forget to mention the club endorsement, and after that, introduce me."

Ben overheard the exchange, and watched with amusement as Spindler's face became drawn and ashen, except for the rosy cheeks. Spindler somberly took the steps up to the stage—with the gait and expression of a condemned man ascending the gallows. Once behind the podium, Spindler turned and stared nervously at the mingling crowd. He was accustomed to speaking in conference rooms and to small groups of customers or employees, however with the size of this crowd, coupled with the gravity of the occasion and the presence of his boss he was unnerved, and it showed.

Spindler lifted the bullhorn from the dais, and turned away from the crowd while he played with the switches and knobs, attempting to activate it. Few of the guests even noticed the reluctant emcee's presence on the stage, but as Spindler manipulated each knob, he failed to bring the device to life. Growing frantic, he raised the bullhorn to his mouth and blew into the mouthpiece between each adjustment, hoping for some sound—any sound. Several attempts produced nothing audible, and Pitzmyre shook his head at the bumbling manager's display of incompetence.

"Hand it here Stewart," Ben said reaching upward for the bullhorn, and Spindler ceded custody to him. Ben used his pocketknife to pry open the plastic cover that concealed the batteries, and once exposed Ben surveyed the rows of C-cells, and quickly realized that they had been installed backwards. He rearranged them properly, snapped the cover shut, and nodded as handed the bullhorn back to Spindler, who returned to his manipulations. After several adjustments, a squeal emanated from the instrument, followed by faint sounds and Spindler decided to face his audience.

"May I have your attention, ladies and gentleman?" Spindler

said nervously, but the noise of the crowd drowned out Spindler's inadequately amplified voice. Clearing his throat, he said even louder, "Excuse me, ladies and gentlemen!"

Ben noticed that Spindler's natural voice projected further than the amplified version, and he again motioned to him. Spindler knelt with one knee on the stage, and leaned over to Ben, who said, "No one can hear you on that thing, Stewart."

"I know, but what do I do?"

"It seems to be on, so you just need to find the volume knob and adjust it."

"The volume, huh?" Spindler asked staring at the bullhorn.

"Yes, turn it up and don't touch anything else."

Spindler rose to his feet, and again turned away from the assemblage, located the volume knob and commenced twisting it. He glanced toward Pitzmyre and noting his agitated expression he said, "I'm trying to get it to work." Pitzmyre could not hear what Spindler was saying over the unabated crowd noise, shrugged shoulders, and watched as his General Manager continued to work the volume knob. Panicked, Spindler raised the bullhorn and yelled into the mouthpiece, "I'm trying to get this piece of shit to work!"

Spindler's frantic manipulations had succeeded in raising the volume—to the maximum—and his intemperate words resonated loud and clear throughout the tent, down the canvass passageway and into the Garden Center. The luckless store manager turned back to the crowd, and confronted a sea of silent hotdog-stuffed mouths agape, but at last he had the undivided attention every man, woman and child.

To that point, Mungo Thibodeaux had been stealthily biding his time near the food containers, loading up on the freebies, but he eased toward the stage just as the presentation commenced.

"Uh ... welcome ... ladies and ... um ... gentlemen ... and Pitz-Smart shoppers," Spindler said in a nervous voice, as his eyelids fluttered. "We have ... um ... some big news today. But ... uh, let me say that I hope you each ... um ... are enjoying the delicious hot dogs and the drinks that we, uh here at your hometown Pitz-Smart store has provided. Just know that everything that you are enjoying in here can be purchased right inside the store, where you'll also find ... um ... countless other great values."

Mungo quickly shuffled stage side, and while holding up a frankfurter from his cache of free hot dogs and asked, "Is that the big news—that y'all have wieners?"

"No, sir, I assure you our wieners aren't the big news!" Spindler uttered.

"Of course not," Mungo responded, waggling the one in his hand back and forth, "that would be the *small* news, right?"

Disregarding Mungo, Spindler continued in his nervous monotone voice, "There will be ... um ... a big announcement made here today, but first I would like to introduce you all to a couple of special guests. We ... uh ... have here with us ... a local fella, one well known to many of you, a man that come this spring, is going to make history. This special guest began a round of golf last fall that ... uh ... turned out to be the best he had ever played. Unfortunately, a winter storm prevented him from playing the eighteenth and final hole, but he is going to complete that round when the course reopens. When he does, a par or better will give him something almost unheard in the game of golf, and that is a score equaling his age. By the way ... uh ... this guest is also the official spokesman for our deluxe line of Pitz-Flex golf clubs. You will be able to pick up your own set of these clubs in our Sporting Goods department on your way out this morning, and as always shop smart—shop Pitz-Smart! So, without further ado ... um ... let's give a big Montana round of applause for our hometown hero, Ben *Dingbat*!" Another awkward hush fell over the crowd and Spindler glanced right to see the fury present on Pitzmyre's face. "Ben Digby, that is," Spindler corrected and the crowd clapped, and Ben reluctantly nodded.

"We also have with us the CEO and founder of Pitz-Smart International, who traveled all the way out here from ... uh ... California with some *very* exciting news for our community. So, I present to you

Mr. Joseph Pitzmyre." The crowd offered only a smattering of applause intermixed with muffled boos, as Spindler backed away from the podium, anxious to surrender it to his boss.

Though the reception was tepid at best, Pitzmyre swaggered onto the stage, and used his raised arms to silence the near silent throng. He forced an amiable smile, and surveyed the crowd as he removed note cards from the inside pocket of his Nehru jacket and lifted the bullhorn. "As many of you know, we here at Pitz-Smart are dedicated to bringing you the best quality merchandise at the—" Suddenly, there was a squeal and then Pitzmyre's voice could no longer be heard. His contrived cheerful expression changed, as he shook the malfunctioning bullhorn and tried again to speak into it.

"Sir," Mungo yelled. "If you have your receipt, you can return that inside for a full refund!"

Pitzmyre dismissed the snide remark and the laughter, and when he could not produce any further sound from the bullhorn, he tossed the device to the pavement at Spindler's feet. He then relied on his natural voice to address the crowd saying, "Let me get right to the point. I'm sure you've all seen the media coverage of the wagering that has taken place, concerning Ben's upcoming golfing feat." The crowd reacted with a murmur and nodding heads. "It seems that some around here don't believe that Ben can shoot his age come spring," Pitzmyre said, then paused to allow booing to play out. "However we here at Pitz-Smart believe in our hometown hero and feel certain that he *will* do just that, and I on behalf of Pitz-Smart International your neighborhood department store, put up one hundred thousand dollars as a sign of our faith in Ben. I know you all heard about that, and when we did, I invited all takers to bet against him. Since then, we received a few small bets from a handful of small-minded naysayers, with the audacity to wager against your friend here, Ben Ding ... dong ... Digby."

"Is someone at the door?" Mungo asked glancing in all directions.

Pitzmyre sighed in disgust, then said, "Among those lining up against old Ben was one Ferguson T. Knox, the mean old banker from

Bozeman State Bank. He took my hundred grand bet, but that wasn't enough, oh, no, no, he went even further, by *raising* it another fifty thousand! Can you believe that?"

The crowd booing resumed, making Pitzmyre think that he not only had the assembly amped up, but was also in some measure extinguishing vestiges community resentment. "As further evidence of our confidence in Ben, we've decided to respond to the banker's wager, and to do so in a *big* way." The crowd fell silent. "On behalf of Pitz-Smart, we see the additional fifty thousand and—" the approving crowd interrupted with hearty cheering and clapping, and Pitzmyre raised his hands for silence, this time out of true necessity. "Hold on now, I'm not through!" Pitzmyre urged and the crowd noise ebbed. "We not only see his fifty thousand, but we also raise the mean old banker, an additional one hundred thousand dollars!" This time the audience erupted into a thunderous clamor as Ben stared on dumfounded. "Yes, you heard right. Pitz-Smart, a fixture in this community, is placing a quarter of a million dollars on our hometown guy," Pitzmyre said. "We here at Pitz-Smart, hope each of you will watch your circulars and the Tribune for Ben's future public appearances at our store here, then come out this spring and support Ben at one of my favorite golf courses, the Lone Ranger Country Club."

"Lone Wolf," Spindler corrected.

"Yes, the majestic and scenic Lone Wolf club, where this spring Ben will most assuredly make history. Now, you folks enjoy yourselves in here and when you go on back through the store, show your own support for Ben by taking advantage of some of the tremendous bargains you'll find inside."

As Pitzmyre walked off the stage, he saw his limo driver beckoning him from a breech in the tent that Leonard Duncan had created for his exit. He walked in that direction, as some guests returned to mingling while the others began to orderly file into the tunnel toward the Garden Center, until another voice rang out.

"Wait just a doggone second! We're not done here!" rang a booming, deep baritone voice that brought Pitzmyre to a halt.

A well-dressed elderly man had made his way from the outside, around Pitzmyre's limo driver, through Leonard's breech and into the tent and was elbowing his way through the returning crowd as he walked toward the stage.

Pitzmyre maneuvered quickly back to Spindler and asked, "Who the hell is that?"

"I'm not sure," Spindler said as the man slowly and carefully ascended to the stage.

It was Ferguson T. Knox, and though it was a weekend, he arrived there attired in the fashion that most that knew him had grown accustomed to, with a black suit, white shirt, a red tie and a trench coat. The short, rotund, silver-haired banker had a round ashy face, wrinkled with age and sporting drooping bags under each eye, and small, oval-shaped spectacles balanced on his bulbous nose, which was glowing red from the ravages of the wintry conditions. The tension was rising as Knox brought his squatty frame to the podium, and most of those that were departing had filed back into the tent, including Ben.

"For those who don't know, I'm Ferguson Knox, the *mean old banker* about whom this man has referred this morning," Knox said pointing his right index finger at the CEO. "Just know up front, that I don't have anything against Ben Digby—hell, I've known him for decades. However, I also know his golf game too, and I just don't believe Ben's going to do this so called *golf feat*. So, with that said, I'll get straight to the point. I call Mr. Pitzmyre's two hundred and fifty thousand dollars and raise him another two hundred and fifty, for a nice—tidy— even half-a-million."

The crowd gasped in disbelief, before spontaneously erupting into a cacophony of applause and cheers. As Knox strutted off the stage, all present turned their attention to Pitzmyre, who stood stunned and perplexed. "Damn it Stewart, how did Knox find out about this event? Did you leak it out?"

"Leak it out? Joe, it was in the Trib, and there are banners all over about this—you said you wanted it that way," Spindler defended.

"This was a sucker punch, damn it! This old prick stood outside and sucked me in, and I fell for it, and it's all your damned fault!"

"My fault? Joe, I don't see how I'm—"

"I don't have time to argue with you right now—I have to act on this," Pitzmyre said, chewing on his fingernail, and considering all of the angles. The excitement inside the tent was palpable and the more he pondered the higher the anticipation and accompanying pressure rose. Pitzmyre seemed visibly affected in a manner unlike any way Spindler had ever witnessed, and all eyes were on the executive as he stepped back to the podium. He cleared his throat and composed himself to speak, but this time there was no need for a bullhorn, or even an elevated voice, as those assembled fell into a tense silence.

"Well ... uh ... ladies and gentlemen, it seems we have in our midst a true gambling man," Pitzmyre said, and he pulled a handkerchief from his pocket and dabbed the perspiration from his face and the back of his neck. He glared over at the grizzled old banker, searching for a signs of capitulation, but Knox' demeanor showed strong and resolute.

At Mungo's prompting, the audience began chanting: "Raise him! Raise him! Raise him!"

Pitzmyre again held up his hands to quell the enthusiasm, and while he calculated that another raise might just force Knox to back off, he could not take the chance on this competitiveness getting any further out of hand. "I think we have a good game now, and I remain one hundred percent behind Ben. On behalf of Pitz-Smart, I call the raise to a total of half-a-million dollars." The crowd roared its approval, and Pitzmyre added, "As promised, Pitz-Smart will post the balance of its wager in the Accel trust account, located right here inside our store, and I expect the banker man here will do the same. We hope to see you all in a couple of months to watch Ben step up on that tee and do this thing!"

Before Knox could say anything further, Pitzmyre hustled off the stage and toward the tent opening, glaring at Spindler as he passed, and once back on the parking lot he jumped in his idling limousine, and it sped away. Ben quietly fell in with the throng, and proceeded with the others, out of the tent and through the store, and he sighed with relief when he made it through the Pitz-Smart double doors without setting off the alarm.

When he reached the parking lot, and headed for his truck, a voice from behind yelled, "Hey, Ben!"

Ben cringed until he turned to see Mungo approaching, and said, "Oh, it's just you!"

"*Just* me?" Mungo said with mock indignation.

"Sorry, Mungo, I thought it might Spindler, or one of his cohorts."

"I certainly understand," Mungo, said opening his sizable paper sack and retrieving yet another hot dog.

"Still hungry, are you?" Ben asked.

"Uh huh, want one?" Mungo asked, extending the open sack, "I got plenty."

Ben peered down into the bag and saw hot dogs stacked on top of hot dogs. "No thanks, but it sure looks like you got your money's worth in there."

"Hey—they advertised free hot dogs, and I took them at their word. After all, they are a *fixture* in the community, right?"

Ben chuckled. "I hope you enjoy 'em."

"Enjoy 'em or not the price sure was right!" Mungo said grinning. "Are you sure you don't want another?"

"I actually haven't had even one," Ben said, "How are they?"

"Tolerable. About what you'd expect at a stop-n-rob or a Little League ball game."

"All right then, let me have one," he relented, and Mungo re-opened the paper sack. "Did you bring your own bag too?" Ben asked, as he plunged his hand in and fished out the hot dog on top.

"Yes, I came prepared."

Ben took a bite and chewed. "They aren't very warm, are they?"

"No, not anymore," Mungo replied. "Next time, I'll bring an insulated sack!"

Ben smiled, took another bite and concurred with Mungo's qualitative assessment, but mediocre or not, it was nevertheless a hot dog, and Ben finished his in three additional bites.

"A half a million dollars," Mungo said, shaking his head. "How do you feel about all of this?"

"I think these guys have more money than they have sense. The upshot is I only have three more of these so called *appearances* to make, and one hole of golf to play, and the VFW gets its money, and I get my life back."

"That's a nice thing you done for the guys, we all know you didn't want to."

"Thanks—God knows we can use the money."

"Say, if you think about it, let me know when you get drug down here for those other dog-and-pony shows."

"Don't you mean *hot* dog-and-pony shows?" Ben asked.

"Food's certainly a part of it, but to tell you the truth I kinda enjoy jerkin' their chain."

"Believe it or not, Spindler actually asked me to keep you away from these get-togethers?"

"No joke?" Mungo said, perking up.

"That's right, I really do think you get under their skin."

Mungo stopped chewing and his expression turned serious. "Now look Ben, if I'm causing *you* any trouble, I'll be happy to back off."

"Don't worry about it, as far as I know it's not in my contract to discourage people from attending."

"Under their skin, huh?" Mungo repeated cheerfully. "I sure do like the sound of that!"

"You really dislike these guys, don't you?"

Mungo bit into another hot dog, held his fist to his chest and belched and said, "I actually hate 'em. I know that the good book's against hatin' and all, but I don't think even the Lord contemplated these big giant phonies when he wrote it."

"You may be right, Mr. Thibodeaux. Enjoy the rest of your free hot dogs, you hear."

"Here, you want another?" Mungo offered extending the sack.

"No thanks, one was plenty."

Ben drove straight home anxious for a warm shower, and to apprise Emily of the turn of events. He wanted to get the news of the escalation in wagering off his chest and avoid her learning of it from another source. When he entered their front door, Emily was in the kitchen tenderizing a flank steak with a metal mallet and when she heard him, she asked, "How'd it go, dear?"

"You're not going to believe it," he said, joining her in the kitchen. "They had this giant tent on the parking lot, with a stage and free food inside and—"

"Oh, it sounds real nice reception, dear."

"Wait—I'm not through," Ben, said eager to purge himself. "Fergie Knox and Pitzmyre went head to head at this thing."

"Head to head on what?" Emily asked.

"The betting."

"I can't believe Ferguson Knox showed up at Pitz-Smart," she said.

"Well he did, to the parking lot at least," Ben said, then blurted, "and the bet's now a half-million dollars."

Emily gasped, the mallet fell to the floor and she turned and stared into Ben's eyes, searching for signs he was jesting. "It's true isn't it?" she asked and Ben nodded and retrieved the mallet for her. "My lands—this is just crazy!"

"It's certainly gotten out of control, that's for sure," Ben said.

"I can understand one of these high-flying, outsiders like Mr. Pitzmyre engaging in such nonsense, but for the life of me I can't figure Mr. Knox. Why, in the name of heaven would he, of all people get mixed up in all of this?"

"That's the half-a-million-dollar question, now isn't it?"

"How do *you* feel about all of this?"

"Arguably, it doesn't change anything for me. I mean, I still have to play the one hole, and the hall's going to get their money."

"Do you really view this with that level of nonchalance?"

"No!" Ben said chuckling and shaking his head.

"At least you haven't lost your sense of humor over it, but what do you really think about it?"

"I think this is the damnedest thing I've ever—" Ben said, and paused for her admonishment over his language, but Emily continued washing the mallet with soap and warm water over the sink. "Well?" Ben asked.

"Well what?" Emily responded.

"Did you not hear my indiscretion?"

"Oh, I heard you, but under the circumstances, I think I'll let that one go."

Ben smiled. "Thanks for the freebie."

"I am sorry you're caught in the middle of all of this, what's wrong with these men?"

"It's a cocktail of money, greed, grudges, maybe vendettas," he lamented, "but there's nothing I can do about it, so que sera, sera."

Emily frowned. "Did you learn that phrase from that burlesque show in France?"

"No, I learned it from Doris Day."

"Oh my ... I had forgotten all about that show," Emily said, reminiscently. "You sure have it for Mrs. Day, don't you?"

The Fifteenth Hole

With the wagering contract signed by both parties and every penny of each side's bet deposited in trust, winner take all, the excitement in Bozeman began to build. One morning, Emily stirred in the dark of night, wondering the time. She squinted to discern the numbers on their digital clock, and saw that it was only 5:40. Then, with the aid of beams from a full moon creeping though the blinds, she was startled to see Ben sitting in his pajamas, on the side of the bed and staring into space. Propping herself up on one elbow, she asked sleepily, "Are you okay?"

"Yes," he said turning to her. "I'm sorry I woke you."

"You didn't dear, but is there anything wrong?"

"Just a little restless—that's all."

Emily had witnessed this same scenario play out many times in the past, especially during the era when the gradual demise of their hardware store robbed Ben of restful slumber, and each time she posed the same question then, she received the same answer as on this morning.

"Can I get you anything?"

"No thank you," Ben said as he turned on the reading lamp attached to their headboard, reached into the nightstand and lifted an oblong box wrapped in bright red paper and bound with a pink satin ribbon.

"What's that?" Emily asked.

"Happy Valentine's Day," Ben said, handing her the box.

"Oh Ben, thank you for remembering me, especially in the middle of all this Pitz-Smart mess."

"You're welcome, but it's not much," Ben said, and Emily slipped off the ribbon, tore away the paper and opened the box to find a shiny sterling silver hairbrush.

She gasped, then said, "My goodness Ben ... it's beautiful."

"Do you really like it?"

"Like it? I love it!" she said, leaning upward and kissing him on the cheek. "Did you get it at Lehman's?"

"No, I picked it up while I was at Pitz-Smart," he joked, and she slapped him playfully on his thigh. "Yeah, I got it at Lehman's—Jamie Anderson sends her regards, by the way."

"Oh, that's nice. Gosh, I haven't been in there in ages," Emily said, sitting up and examining the brush under the lamplight.

"You used to go there a lot," Ben said.

"Don't be that way, I have every—"

"I know what you're gonna say, you have everything you ever needed, but I wanted you to have some of the things that you truly wanted."

"Stop it, will ya? I have everything I ever wanted," she said and began trying out of the new brush on her sleep-tangled hair. "So what's really bothering you, dear?"

"It's just all of this wagering stuff, I guess," Ben said followed by a long sigh.

"Look on the bright side, when this thing is over it will be golf season again," she said.

Ben realized that Emily had raised a salient point, one that with all of the distractions had escaped him. In the past, at this point in the year, he would have been anxiously counting down the days in anticipation the opening of the course. He perked up at the thought of returning to his golfing routine, but that naturally evoked thoughts of the club café.

"I think I'd like to go up to the club for breakfast—do you mind?"

"Oh, I see. The brush wasn't a gift, so much as it was a bribe!" Emily teased.

"A Lehman's silver brush for one of Cookie's fattening, artery-clogging meals sounds like a fair trade to me," Ben said.

"Now that you put it that way, the answer is *no*," she said in jest. "But seriously, Ben, I know it's thawed some, but it snowed again last night, and it's below freezing out there."

"It's only twenty-nine degrees," he said.

"You checked the thermometer?"

"Yeah, an hour or so ago.

"Well, twenty-nine is technically freezing," she said, then saw his expression and realized that a trip to the café could go a long way toward boosting Ben's somber mood. "Oh, go ahead and clog an artery, just be careful getting there and back."

Ben dressed quickly, headed out the front door and into his truck, and drove cautiously on the slippery roads out of their neighborhood. Though scientifically impossible, as he drove the road that led to the café, a Pavlovian response caused him to salivate and he was convinced he sniffed the aroma of frying bacon and sausage.

"Hey, Ben! It's great to see you," Cookie said watching his old friend easing through the café door.

"Likewise," Ben said, removing jacket near the kitchen. "Emily gave me a hall pass, and I chose breakfast here."

"Good! It's been awhile—how are things?" Cookie asked, wiping his hands on a dishrag.

"I'm fine Cookie, and you?"

"I'm good, but man, I've been hearing about all of this Pitz-Smart stuff. Is it true that the deal's at half a million bucks?"

"It's true all right, and all of the money is deposited," Ben said as he craned his neck toward the sink to check for drips from the faucet.

"You seem a little down," Cookie said, "is this thing gettin' to you?"

"I'm okay."

"Listen to me Ben, I'm your friend and have known you a long time, and I know when you're down."

"Cookie, if I wanted all of this doting, I would've stayed home. Now be a pal, and exchange the interrogation for two eggs in the skillet and all the extras," Ben said landing a playful slap on Cookie's shoulder.

"Coming right up my friend!"

Ben grabbed an abandoned sports page from a table as he passed, and then took a seat nearest the large picture window. He perused the paper until Cookie brought his breakfast, and sat it in front of him. Cookie watched as his friend stared pie-eyed at the two piping-hot, over-easy eggs, hash browns, three strips of bacon, and patty sausage. At that early hour, Cookie had only a few other customers and they each were eating, so he took the opportunity to catch up with Ben. "Mungo says he's been tormenting the Pitz-Smart guys."

"That's true, and he seems to get a real kick out of it," Ben said. "Say, has Stewart Spindler been coming around here?"

Cookie thought for a moment. "No, now that you mention it, he hasn't been here in a week or so, why?"

"I'd love to be a fly on the wall during the conversations he's been having with Pitzmyre, about all of this."

"You reckon they're sweatin' this thing?" Cookie asked, and noticed two diners had entered, and taken seats in a booth.

"Pitzmyre's wealthy, but they have to be back on their heels over risking this kind of money on a single hole of golf," Ben said as three customers neared the café door.

"One would think," Cookie said, "but everyone around here and guys down at the hall are sure excited about it."

"I haven't been over to the hall in a while, how are the fellas doing?"

"Everyone's hanging in there," Cookie said. "But pardon me Ben, it's getting' busy."

Cookie began taking the orders of the men in the booth, and Ben turned his full attention to his breakfast. He ate while enjoying the scenery, and soon he had cleaned his plate, and laid his silverware atop it. He sipped coffee while staring out the window and down toward the eighteenth hole. Though the sun was now creeping over the horizon, the mountains shadowed the eighteenth hole and the green remained illuminated only by the dusk to dawn spotlight. Consequently, Ben trained his gaze on the mountains, and watched as the colors changed the on them as the sun crept higher, but his tranquility vanished the moment he heard loud chatter and laughter from the outside.

The café door swung open abruptly, and Clive Jacklin and Billy Auchterlonie, followed by three more from their group swaggered in. Clive helped himself to five menus with one hand, and used the other to brush the light snowflakes off his long, fashionable Burberry coat. The five men took it upon themselves to string two tables together in the corner, and while they continued their loud conversation, they perused the menus. Ben on the other hand, returned his attention to the scenery and his warm mug of coffee.

A party of three entered and took seats in a booth near the entry door, followed by yet another man, who took a table for one close to Ben.

Ben glanced away from the scenery, and watched Cookie hustle across the room and place the two plates of food in front of the two men sitting at the table closest to him. Kat, having arrived for her shift, began it by circulating with a coffee pot filling and refilling customer's cups.

"Hey, how 'bout some service over here!" Jacklin yelled from across the room.

"I'll be right with you guys," Cookie said, then made sure that the two orders he just delivered were satisfactory to the men.

"Look, man!" Clive said pointing to his wristwatch. "We have *real* jobs to go to, you know."

Cookie excused himself from the satisfied customers, and directed Kat to take the orders of the three men seated near the entry, and he in turn walked to Clive's table. Ben refused to be distracted and returned his attention to the window, concentrating on nothing beyond his own personal satiation and the beauty of the sun rising further above the cobalt-hued peaks.

"How 'bout me?" asked the man sitting alone. "What do I have to do to get some coffee and a menu, huh?"

Flummoxed, Cookie looked over his shoulder and clinging to his manners, said, "Sorry, sir, but these guys came in first. There's a menu on the table next to you and Kat or I will get your coffee in a jiff."

"Fine, but make it snappy Cookie monster," the man said flippantly.

"Say, what kind of a name is Cookie, anyway?" Clive asked of the chef.

"Oh, leave him alone about it," Auchterlonie said, "hell, his folks probably named him *Kooky* and they just couldn't spell!"

Clive and the friends laughed aloud, while Cookie, ignoring the insult, stood with pencil and pad in hand, and asked, "So, what'll it be, guys?"

"Kooky, I'll have the special," one of Clive's comrades lead off.

"The special it is," Cookie said. "Hash browns or toast?"

"Hash browns."

"Okay, and for you, Billy?" Cookie asked.

Following his colleague's cue, Billy said, "Same for me, Kooky!"

"Clive?" Cookie asked as he scribbled on the pad.

"Spanish omelet and toast, Kooky."

"Say fellas, I know you're trying to be funny, but I'd really appreciate it if you'd just call me by my name," Cookie pleaded, and even Ben was now having trouble ignoring the disrespect being paid to his friend, and he shifted in his chair to gain a view of Clive's table.

"Suit yourself, but Cookie sounds like a girl's name to me," Billy responded. "Hell, if I had to choose between Cookie and Kooky, I think I'd pick Kooky."

Laughter again erupted and Cookie swallowed hard. "That's fine, but I go by Cookie, and I'd *really* appreciate it if you guys would just call me that."

"But, how'd you get a name like that in the first place?" Clive asked. "I mean Billy's right—it does sound like a girl's name."

"Well, you see guys, my real name is Carl, but I was a career cook in the Army, and *Cookie* is a common nickname used for military cooks," he explained and Ben noticed Cookie's face was reddened, and that his left hand holding the order pad was trembling.

"Did you hear that, guys?" Clive yelled to all present. "Ol' sugar cookie here marched off to war with a spatula in hand!"

Raucous laughter filled the café, until interrupted by the sound of Ben's right fist slamming the top of his table. The force of the blow was enough to lift his plate, silverware and the salt and peppershakers upward, then each came clattering down to the Formica surface, as Ben rose and headed directly toward Clive's table.

"Uh oh," Katrina said, pausing from writing her customer's order.

Cookie turned and saw Ben moving toward him, dropped the pad and pencil on Clive's table, and met Ben half way, holding up his hands to intervene, and said, "It's all right."

"It's not all right!" Ben said, through gritted teeth and continued on past Cookie.

"Mr. D!" Kat called out, but Ben was not deterred.

Now truly worried, Cookie took after Ben, and grabbed his shirtsleeve from behind and pleaded, "Ben, just take 'em with a grain of —"

"I'm fresh out of salt!" Ben snapped, pulled away from Cookie's grasp and did not stop until he was a few inches from Jacklin and his comrades. He struck a rigidly erect stance with his hands on his hips, and Clive and the rest of his tablemates lost their smirks and sat staring cautiously at the veteran.

"I'm going to tell you men something and you're going to listen!" Ben said firmly. "I don't know who or what raised you, but you don't have a clue about who you're making fun of here. Some of you might not have even been born in 1966 when a war was raging in a country that you will never step foot in. It was Vietnam, and there was a military encampment, supporting the troops executing Operation Hastings and—"

Jacklin interrupted. "Hey man, we were just trying to be funny."

"It's not funny!" Ben shouted, as Clive and the others with him flinched, and all eyes in the café were now trained on the unfolding scene. "Now—if you had been in the Officer's Mess tent that fateful morning, you'd have seen this man, Carl *Cookie* Harrington, taking a break from the kitchen, between the breakfast crowd and preparing for lunch. He was standin' next to a table of officers and as I recall, there were two captains, two majors, a lieutenant and a lieutenant colonel," Ben said glancing back to Cookie, whose nod confirmed the head count. "Each of the officers had just finished enjoying their meals, and Cookie was talking to the men, while transferring their empty plates to a large, heavy, stainless steel bussing cart at his side. Then there was a thud, and all of the men heard it, but Cookie was the only one with the vantage point to see what caused it. He turned to see a figure of a man, likely a uniformed North Vietnamese soldier, fleeing away from the tent. He had unpinned a hand grenade, tossed it through an opening in the tent, and it tumbled to a stop a few feet in front of Cookie. He could have just crouched behind the bussing cart, and saved his own skin, but training and character made him risk all of his tomorrows, to protect those other men."

"What'd you do?" Clive asked, turning to Cookie.

"Don't ask him!" Ben said severely, "he'd never tell you this story! Now you men would not understand this, but Cookie first yelled *hit the deck* then raced around the cart, grabbed the grenade, and threw it as hard as he could back toward the opening in the tent. Then and only then did he join the officers on the dirt, but unfortunately the grenade exploded in midair about forty feet away. They all took shrapnel, but since Cookie was the closest, he got the worst of it, and he and four of those officers stayed in the hospital for many weeks, but because of this man, they all survived the attack."

"How bad off was Mr. Harrington," Billy asked timidly, daring not to address Cookie directly.

"He took shrapnel in his lower back, his right side and the worst was the right thigh, where it nicked the femoral artery. The medics got there in time to stop the bleeding, and with several transfusions, they saved his life. Despite their best efforts, they could not remove all the shrapnel, and to this day, Cookie has to bring documentation to the airport or to the courthouse for jury duty, to prove why his body sets off the metal detectors. Even though he doesn't let on, and would *never* complain, he still hurts—a lot. Because of that, he often can't sleep through the night, but despite all of that, he's here day in and day out, serving the ungrateful."

"Did you get a medal, or something Cookie?" the solo customer asked.

Before the Cookie could answer, Ben said, "Thankfully, the army recognized Cookie's bravery, and he was awarded the Purple Heart and the Silver Star, and so you know, the latter is the third highest medal for heroism—and I think the man deserved the Medal of Honor!"

"What happened to the other injured guys," Clive asked.

Cookie finally spoke. "One of the majors was later killed in action, but all the others eventually went home."

"Five officers went home to start a new life and raise children, only because of this man's bravery and selflessness," Ben added as the newcomers sat silent, and some were embarrassed enough that they simply stared down at the table top. "So I said all of that, to say this. All military service performed honorably deserves respect and should never—and I mean *never*—be demeaned, no matter what job the military assigned. Now I have said my piece, and I realize you all are grown men and can do or say whatever the hell you want. You have that freedom—a river of blood spilled overseas, to assure you that freedom, but all I ask is next time you feel the urge to poke fun at my friend, I hope you'll suppress it, and simply thank him for his service." Ben turned, patted Cookie on the shoulder, waved to Katrina who was dabbing tears with a tissue, and walked out to his truck.

Early the next morning, the ringing phone startled Ben awake, and he answered it.

"Ben, I apologize for calling so early," the voice on the other end said, "but I need you to come in today."

Addled, Ben asked, "Who is this?"

"Stewart Spindler."

"So what do you want now Stewart?" Ben asked glancing toward his alarm clock.

"It's time for your next appearance."

"When?"

"I need you at the store as soon as possible," Spindler said.

"This morning?" Ben asked.

"Yes."

"Gosh, I'd really appreciate some advance notice."

"I understand, but something's come up over here, and it's very important, or I wouldn't calling you on such short notice," Spindler explained.

"What is it," Ben asked.

"It's hard to explain, so I'll need to show you when you get here, but rest assured it doesn't involve wagering, sales promotions or anything like that. We've brought something into the store for you, and Pitzmyre himself arranged for it, and he instructed me to get you in to see it right away."

"But Stewart, y'all aren't even near being open yet!"

"I know, but that's why I'm calling so early. I'd like to have you in here before the customers arrive."

"I see," Ben said, peering out their bedroom window, and seeing snow swirling around their back-patio porch light. "It's snowing pretty hard."

"We'll send a car over for you," Spindler said.

"When?"

"It's already on the way."

"All right ... I'll get ready," Ben capitulated and hung up the phone.

"Was that Mr. Spindler?" Emily asked drowsily and he nodded. "What do they want you down there for?"

"Don't know for sure, other than he says it's important," Ben said, slipping on his trousers. "They've got something cooked up over there, and he needs me to get down there even before the store opens."

"But it's not even sunup, and I certainly don't want you driving in the snow *and* in the darkness."

"They're sending a car for me. It seems Spindler dispatched it over here before he even called."

"That's presumptuous, isn't it?" Emily said.

"Very."

Once dressed, Ben peeled and snacked on a banana, while he paced between the kitchen and the front window, waiting for the arrival of the car. By then, the snowfall was so dense that, except for headlights, Ben could only see an approaching vehicle when it passed under the streetlight directly in front of their home, but soon one such vehicle slowed and stopped. Squinting to see out their window, Ben could tell that the man behind the wheel was straining to read the numbers on their mailbox. Convinced this was his driver Ben tossed the banana peel into the garbage, hustled into his old jacket and tromped out the front door. When he reached the car, Ben rapped on the side window with his gloved hand and the driver flinched, looked up at Ben, and unlocked the door, and as Ben took the passenger seat, he realized that it was Leonard Duncan behind the wheel.

"Nice to see you again, Leonard," Ben said. "Thanks for picking me up."

"My pleasure Bob," Leonard said and they shook hands, and then Leonard drove them out of the neighborhood and toward the bypass highway. As they drove, Ben could not help wondering what awaited him at the Pitz-Smart store, but he was not going to gain insight from his driver, who listened intently to country and western music blaring on the radio. Ben deduced that Leonard was an aficionado of the genre, considering that he sang along to each of the disc jockey's selections, all the way to Pitz-Smart parking lot. Leonard was belting out Cash's, Folsom Prison Blues—the live version—as he steered his car past the entrance to the store and toward the far end of it.

Leonard finally lowered the volume on the radio and advised, "There will be a lady waiting for you at the employee entrance and she'll take you to Stewart."

Ben nodded, and when they turned the corner, he saw the employee standing at the glass entry door, and she waved at Leonard then motioned for Ben. Ben thanked his driver, exited, and Leonard drove away to park his car. The young woman ushered Ben into the store, and as they made their way on to the sales floor, Ben noticed it was much dimmer there than his first visit, as at this time of morning only one out of every five florescent lights on the ceiling were on and glowing. He followed his escort toward the back of the store and into the coffee shop where Ben saw Spindler seated and pouring sugar into a Styrofoam coffee cup. Spindler saw them approaching and nodded to the employee who turned and walked back the direction of the employee entrance.

"How are you, Ben?" Spindler asked, and then sipped from his cup.

"Fine—I suppose," Ben said.

"Well, this thing has certainly become a big deal now hasn't it?" Spindler said, gesturing for Ben to take a seat.

"Yeah, by no fault of mine," Ben replied as he sat down.

"No one blames you for anything," Spindler said. "Have you had breakfast?"

"I had a little something at the house."

"Good, you really don't want to eat here," Spindler, whispered under his breath. "The coffee's drinkable, though—can I get you a cup?"

"No thank you, but Stewart I've got things I need to do today, so can we get down to business?"

"I know you're busy, but once you see what we've done here, I predict you'll like it and will actually want to come back," Spindler said, with Ben staring back at him dubiously. "So let me start with a question, how much practicing have you done this winter?"

"Practicing golf?" Ben asked

"Yeah," Spindler said taking another drink of the coffee.

"In the Montana winter?"

"I certainly understand the limitations here, but we don't want the old winter rust to set in, accordingly Pitzmyre wants to make sure you're polishing up on your game."

"Polishing up my—have you looked outside?" Ben asked perplexed. "I mean, Mr. Pitzmyre may not understand, but this ain't California and I *can't* practice. Oh, I've putted some balls here and there at home and taken a few practice swings on the carpet, when the wife's not lookin', but that's about it."

"I completely understand, and since you clearly can't go to the golf course, Mr. Pitzmyre thought we'd bring the golf course to you."

"I don't get you, Stewart?"

"Come with me and I'll show you," Spindler invited as he returned the plastic lid to his coffee cup, and tossed it in the trash can next to him. He rose from the table, motioned for the skeptical Ben to follow him, and they walked out of the coffee shop, and proceeded down the largely empty aisles, impeded only by the occasional employee sweeping or stocking shelves. They arrived at an area where the Valentine's Day merchandise once displayed, but now the fixtures and shelves were gone, creating an open area where Ben beheld a rectangular structure with a blood red velvet curtain in the front.

"What in the Sam Hill is that?" Ben asked.

"Come closer, and I'll show you," Spindler said, guiding Ben toward the curtain, and explained, "What you see in front of you cost a ton of money to rent, but I think you'll find it *very* interesting and helpful too."

"Okay," Ben said cautiously as he watched on as Spindler pulled aside the curtain to reveal a curiously dark room featuring a black velvet ceiling and walls, except the far end, which was covered by a floor-to-ceiling white screen. The floor of the chamber was made of green artificial turf, and Ben noted a black box with buttons on it, sitting next the turf on the right, and beside it was a rack of golf clubs.

"Welcome to virtual golf!" Spindler said proudly.

"Virtual golf?"

"Yes, that's what they call it," Spindler said, "and I must say it's pretty amazing."

Apprehensive about stepping fully inside the room, Ben kept his feet on the sales floor, while extending his neck to peer in through the opening. "Is it some sort of driving range?"

"It has that feature, but it's much, much more. What you're looking at is state-of-the-art computer technology."

"There's a computer in here?" Ben asked glancing around the interior.

"Indeed there is, and a very sophisticated one at that," Spindler said pointing to the black box with the buttons, and Ben ventured fully inside the space. "You see, the operating system in this console has the capacity of all the NASA computers combined when Apollo 11 landed on the moon." Ben watched as Spindler pushed buttons on the box, and in an instant, the white screen sprang to life with a vivid panoramic view of a golf course. "You can actually hit a regular golf ball into this screen and watch an electronic image of the ball's flight," Spindler explained.

"Really?"

"Yes, and very realistically too, and you can play real golf courses and get very accurate results."

"Y'all brought this contraption here just for me?" Ben asked, and Spindler nodded, "and you hit a real ball?"

"That's right and this setup is designed to assess the direction and spin of each ball you hit into that screen. It will detect a slice, a pull, a pull hook, fade, shank, shots hit thin or shots hit fat. It also senses how hard you hit it and the trajectory and calculates how far the ball should travel, and where it should land, and does it all in an instant," Spindler explained, snapping his fingers for emphasis.

"What happens to the real ball?"

"It just falls to the turf, here let me show you," Spindler said grabbing a four iron from the rack of clubs and then teeing up a ball. "Let's play the seventeenth at Pebble Beach, shall we?"

"Pebble Beach?" Ben asked.

"Yes, the computer software has over seventy major courses in the U.S. and abroad," Spindler explained while typing in a code on the console. Ben watched in amazement as the familiar image of the par three from the storied golf links appeared on the screen. It showed true and complete, with sand traps right and left and the Pacific Ocean in the background. "The hole is a hundred and eighty yards from this tee," Spindler said, as he addressed the ball with the iron in hand and took a cut at it. The ball slammed into the screen hitting with a thud and as described, it dropped to the plastic turf below. Ben watched as the screen showed the flight of the electronic version of the ball, and consistent with Spindler's real game, his shot faded right and landed in the rough fifteen yards short of the green. "I've seen that shot before," Spindler confessed.

"Well, I'll be," Ben, said astonished as the screen switched to a view of Spindler's ball in the thick grass. "This thing really works."

"Indeed it does," Spindler, said trading the four iron for a pitching wedge. "Since I'm in the rough, I have to take that into account and hit the shot a little harder."

"The computer knows you're in the rough?"

"Yes," Spindler said as he took a couple of practice swings before chopping down sharply on the ball. The lofted face of the club sent the ball high, striking the screen near the top, then landing near its companion on the turf. The virtual version of the ball arced high toward the faux California sky, before descending to the virtual green. It hit softly, bouncing three times before coming to rest beyond the flag on the fringe.

Spindler grabbed a putter that had a wire attached to it, connecting it to the computer console. "Putting is a little tricky, and you have to use this putter to do it, and there's a switch here on the grip that activates it," Spindler explained displaying it to Ben.

"I see. Is this the only club that has a wire like that?"

"Yes and look down here," Spindler, said directing Ben to a small window inset in the green plastic turf that featured laser lines. "This sensor in the mat detects the putter, and the lines assess the speed and direction of your putt. Those grid lines on the screen show the slope of the green and as you can see, this putt is downhill and breaks to the left. As such, I'll move the putter head softly and a little left to right and see how it goes."

"So for putts, you don't actually hit a ball?" Ben asked.

"Right, the putt is judged by the speed and direction of how the bottom of the putter head crosses those lines," Spindler explained as he steadied the putter behind the small window, drew it back and passed it over the laser lines. He accelerated the putter slightly harder than the shot required, but the virtual ball handled the break well, traveling from the fringe onto the green, tracking left and missing the hole by inches, before slipping four feet beyond it.

"This contraption really works," Ben said.

"It sure does, and as you see, it's a fantastic practice tool and pretty fun too. I admit I enjoyed playing it yesterday when the rep got it up and running and I've been here this morning since five-thirty getting in a few holes, before I even called you."

"You already seem pretty good at it," Ben said.

"Thanks, but it's pretty simple. Here, why don't you try to hole it out," Spindler said, handing off the electronic putter to Ben.

Ben stood where Spindler had, assessed the grid on the screen and found the line to hole to be a left edge uphill putt. He stroked it, and the ball headed on line for the cup, then lipped out, leaving only a tap-in. Ben holed it out from there, and an electronic scorecard emerged on the screen, logging a double-bogie five for the hole.

"Now try it from the beginning," Spindler said as he punched a button that returned the screen to the view from the tee.

"All right, but I'll need a three wood," Ben said.

Spindler glanced curiously at Ben. "Did you say a three wood?"

"Yeah, that's what I'd use for a shot this length."

"You need a three wood to hit a ball a hundred and eighty?" he asked and Ben nodded. "Okay, but I only have a driver and a five wood in here."

"I'll try the five," Ben said, and Spindler handed the club to him.

Ben placed a ball on the tee, took a couple of practice swings, and then paused. He took the club back and swung it quickly forward, striking the ball smartly into the screen and watched with fascination, as his virtual ball soared high and straight and on line with the flag, settling in the rough ten yards shy of the green.

"Look at that!" Spindler crowed. "You didn't warm up and still did better than me on your first virtual golf shot."

Ben nodded and traded the five wood for the pitching wedge, and lofted his next shot safely on the green. He grabbed the specialized putter, and Spindler watched on as Ben two-putted for a bogie. Spindler encouraged him play a few more holes, and Ben complied and seemed to acclimate well to the technology and equally important, he seemed to enjoy it.

"You see Ben, you can practice our eighteenth at Lone Wolf right here in the warmth of our store," Spindler said.

"This machine doesn't have our golf course on it, does it?"

"No, but the virtual golf rep and I assessed the layout of our eighteenth, and compared it with all of the par fours available on the console to find the closest one to it. We included in the analysis, the length and contour of the Lone Wolf eighteenth, the shape and topography of the fairway, factored in the creek and after all of that, the thirteenth at Eagle Crest is as close as we could get."

"I see," Ben said.

"Here, let me show you," Spindler said and punched in the code for Eagle Crest and then selected the thirteenth hole.

When the image emerged on the screen, Ben immediately noted the similarities, which he further confirmed when he played it tee to green. Spindler encouraged him to try it a second time, and when Ben finished, he asked, "Is this what you meant by bringing the golf course to me?"

"Precisely!" Spindler said.

"You all are certainly pulling out all the stops, aren't you?"

"Pitzmyre is determined to give you the best shot at doing this, and we don't have a whole lot of time left. This is a good way for you to hone your skills, and you're welcome to come down here anytime you want to practice."

"That's fine, but I have so many chores to do, then there's the weather and I can't—"

"Just come when you can, and we'll make this available to you."

"I don't have to come when the store's closed, do I?"

"No, I just wanted to introduce the concept to you without a lot of customers hanging around. Now that you've seen it and have a general understanding of what it does, you can come when you want."

"I see, but what about my contractual appearances?"

"I'm glad you brought that up. I cleared it with Pitzmyre, and you can consider all of them done, except for playing the hole, of course. But it's our hope that you'll *want* to come back, and practice."

"Even with customers here?"

"Sure, I'd actually prefer that."

"Mr. Pitzmyre must be awfully concerned to go to all of this trouble."

"Trouble *and* expense," Spindler said. "Like it or not, we're on the same side of this deal, and all we want is for you to have the best chance possible on that final hole."

"Okay, I will come up here when I can."

"That's great, but when you do, all I ask is that you give us a half hour or so leeway to get things set up. For now though, go ahead and try a few more shots—are there any other holes or courses you'd like to try?"

Ben pondered. "I've always wanted to play the eighteenth at Doral."

"Consider it done, but let me show you how this part works so you can do it yourself," Spindler said. He gave Ben a tutorial on keying in the codes from the list of available courses taped to the console, and once the course was selected, how to pick the desired hole. Ben seemed to understand it, and played another twenty minutes before deciding to head home.

When Leonard returned Ben back to his house, Ben thanked him and once inside, he found Emily reading the Tribune in their sunroom.

He explained the events of the morning, and his description of the virtual-golf chamber amazed her, almost as much as the enthusiasm he displayed in describing it.

"So that's what took so long," Emily said and he nodded. "I like that it gives you a safe place to get some exercise, without the temptation of fattening foods," Emily said.

"They do have that small cafe there, but there's no need to worry, apparently even Spindler won't eat there."

"Will you be going back up there to practice?"

"I think so, I mean you really ought to see this thing, Em. The computer has all these *real* courses programmed into it, and you can play the ones you want. I have to admit it's pretty darn interesting."

"Sounds like it. I'm glad to know that there's some aspect of this Pitz-Smart deal that you might actually enjoy, and I think you *should* practice down there—around your chores, of course."

The Sixteenth Hole

*A*s February neared its end, the Montana winter was gradually ceding to rising temperatures, and moderating conditions. As it did, the lower mountain snowcaps commenced to thaw, resulting in the predictable swelling of the Bozeman area streams and tributaries. With the improving weather conditions, the consensus among the Lone Wolf members was that the course could re-open as early as sometime in late-March.

Ben rose from bed early one morning and after completing a light slate of Emily's honey-dos, he retrieved their mail. As he walked back toward the house with several envelopes in hand, he found the temperatures and sunshine alluring. Feeling antsy, he quickly self-diagnosed an acute case of *cabin fever* secondary to *oatmeal fatigue* and pitched the findings to the chief pharmacist and she prescribed a breakfast at the club.

When Ben arrived at the café late morning he was pleased to see Mungo and Cookie, and that the only newcomers present had already eaten.

"Over here," Mungo said beckoning Ben to his table.

"Hey Mungo, how are you doing?" Ben asked taking the chair across from his friend.

"Right as rain."

"Good morning Ben," Cookie said he swept the crumbs out from under a table on the other side of the café.

"Hey there Cookie—can I still get breakfast?"

"Sure."

"Good, I'll take the usual with ham instead of bacon, please."

"You got it!"

"It's really warming up out there," Mungo said.

"Unseasonably so," Ben agreed, "it's hittin' close to forty today,"

"Hey Cookie, can you come over for a second, before you start on Ben's order?" Mungo asked.

Cookie nodded and leaned the broom against the wall, and wiped his hands on a dishrag as he walked to their table. Mungo leaned forward, and in a voice low enough for only the other two men could hear and asked, "Ben, Cookie told me that you really gave it to Clive and his bunch the other day."

"Yeah, I kinda flew off the handle at the way they were treatin' Cookie and wanted to put the ingrates in their place."

"You sure did that," Cookie said. "It's not often you see a table of newcomers speechless."

"I only wish I could've been there to see it for myself," Mungo said, ruefully and added, "and Cookie says you made him out to be the Audie Murphy of the Vietnam War!"

"In my opinion, he is," Ben said.

"Thanks for that, but I don't think ol' Audie would need his friends to do his bidding for him," Cookie replied.

"Come on, Cookie," Ben said, "we all know why you put up with them, and if you didn't need their business, they'd all still be recuperating in the hospital."

"But you delivered a knockout punch without laying a hand on 'em," Cookie said, "I'm sure it'll wear off, but since you dressed 'em down, these guys have been walking on egg shells around here."

"Good," Ben said.

When Cookie headed to the kitchen, Ben began introducing the virtual golf concept, describing the set up, and what it was like to play a hole, and explained the wired putter, but he found that his words alone did little to paint the picture.

"Let me see if I understand," Mungo said, scratching his chin whiskers. "You hit a normal ball?"

"Yes, a regular golf ball."

"It ain't got a wire connected to it?"

"No. Other than the putter, none of the equipment has wires," Ben explained.

"Did you use your Pitz-Smart clubs?" Mungo snickered as Cookie returned with Ben's coffee and silverware.

"No, I never actually got those, but they have a few *real* clubs in the velvet room."

"Those Pitz-Flex clubs are pretty bad, huh?" Cookie asked.

"Very," Ben said, and Mungo nodded his concurrence.

"But I read in that Trib article that they are *deluxe* golf clubs," Cookie said, stressing that adjective, as if with it the clubs could not be so bad.

"Have either of you ever known anything that was called *deluxe* that was worth as much as a tinker's damn?" Mungo asked

"Come to think of it, I can't recall a single instance," Ben said.

Cookie smiled and headed back to the kitchen, and Ben fielded more virtual golf questions from Mungo. When Cookie returned with Ben's breakfast, he joined the men at the table, and as Ben dined he continued his description of the concept to both men, but the more he explained, the less they seemed to comprehend.

"Cookie, I know you can't abandon the post, but Mungo if you want to come with me down there, we can get in a few holes?"

"Will there be any free food?"

"Mungo! You just ate a breakfast fit for a lumberjack!" Cookie said.

"That was forty-five minutes ago," Mungo, defended. "Plus, I don't have to eat what they have, while I'm there. Hell, the last time I went there, I lived on hot dogs for two whole days."

"I doubt they'll have anything like that, but there's only one way to find out, so are you in?"

"Sure," Mungo said eagerly, until a thought crossed his mind. "Do you reckon they'll want me down there with you?"

"I know for a fact they won't," Ben said, "but they want me there, so I figure they'll have to put up with you, to get me."

"Hot damn, let's go. It's been a while since I got under some skin!"

After Ben finished his breakfast, Mungo followed him out to his truck, and the two headed together straight to the Pitz-Smart store. Once inside, Ben guided Mungo over to the virtual golf room, where they found yellow ropes now cordoned off the area around it. Ben led Mungo inside the ropes, through the curtains, and into the chamber's dark interior.

"I can't see a damn thing in here!" Mungo said.

"Hang on," Ben said, reaching back with one hand to force the curtains fully open, while using his other hand to feel around for the computer console's power button. He managed to activate the console and the lights atop it flickered before becoming static, and with that illumination, and the light coming in through the curtains, a dim ambiance was cast in the velvet interior.

Mungo looked around wide-eyed. "Hell, I ain't seen a room like this since I toured Graceland!"

"The darkness helps to see the hole you're playing," Ben explained, and punched the buttons and pulled up the last course played.

"Wow!" Mungo said when an aerial view of a golf hole emerged on the screen. "That's pretty realistic."

"Yes, and it's very accurate, as you'll see," Ben said, and the two of them realized that shoppers had begun to gather at the ropes to watch on by peering in through the breach in the curtains.

Mungo stared at the screen, which showed rocky beach and foamy ocean next to the fairway and asked, "Is this Pebble Beach?"

"Yes, the ninth hole," Ben replied, pointing to the electronic score card, appearing at the bottom of the screen.

"The ninth, huh? Say—if you finish it, can we get a virtual beer at the turn," Mungo asked, drawing laughter from the small gallery.

"No, but if we did, I'm sure that you'd stick me with the virtual tab!"

Ben played the hole, and a couple more thereafter, and Mungo shared his enthusiasm with the concept. Ben, then keyed in the code to bring up the Eagle Crest course, and then selected the thirteenth hole. When the view from the tee emerged on the screen, Ben asked, "Look familiar?"

"It does, but I can't place it," Mungo said.

"This is the one that they want me to practice, since their research shows it's the closest to the layout to our eighteenth," Ben explained.

Mungo squinted as he carefully examined the image and said, "That's pretty close, ain't it?"

"It sure is, and you'll see more of it as I play," Ben said as he teed a ball, addressed it and swung. The ball struck the screen, and the crowd watched as the virtual version rose high, then arced downward, striking the fairway and bounding rapidly. It came to rest in the rough on the right side of the fairway, and the screen switched to a close up of Ben's ball and the obstruction presented by the trees that stood between it and the green.

"Is there a way to virtually kick it back into the fairway?" Mungo asked.

Ben smiled and addressed the ball with five wood in hand, aiming out to the left to avoid the trees. He struck the shot solidly and as intended, the virtual ball evaded the trees, took Ben's natural left-to-right bend, taking it back toward the hole, and came to rest over the creek and twenty feet short of the green.

"Nice shot!" Stewart Spindler said, parting the gathering of customers and entering the chamber. Stewart was thrilled that Ben had come to the store without compulsion of contract, and that the shoppers were taking in the exhibition, but Mungo's presence instantly threatened his enthusiasm.

"Hello, Stewart," Ben said. "How are you?"

"I'm doing great Ben, and I'm happy to see you here."

"What about me?" Mungo asked facetiously.

"Oh, it's always a pleasure seeing you, Mungo."

"Likewise, I'm sure," Mungo, responded with feigned cordiality.

"Ben, I wish you would have let us know you were coming," Spindler said. "I did mention you notifying us, remember?"

"Sorry, it kinda came up on the spur of the moment—do you want us to leave?"

Spindler glanced at Mungo. "One out of two would work."

Ben explained, "Problem is we drove here together, and I—"

"I'm just kidding fellas," Spindler said. "I've got some stock boys coming with some signs and some boxes of Pitz-Flex clubs, so feel free to play all you want."

Ben nodded and, three strokes later, he finished the hole with a bogie-five. He played the thirteenth hole four additional times, recording a bogie, double bogie, par, triple bogie, and Spindler took mental notes.

"Want to give it a whirl, Mungo?" Ben asked, needing a breather.

"Sure, assuming it's okay with the boss man here," Mungo said, and the two men turned to Spindler, who reluctantly nodded his consent, as his eyelids fluttered.

"What course do you want?" Ben asked.

"Let's see," Mungo, said cogitating. "How 'bout St. Andrews!"

"The one in Scotland?" Spindler asked.

"No, the one in Milwaukee!" Mungo said, rolling his eyes. "Of course, Scotland!"

While Mungo warmed up for his virtual-golf debut, Ben looked up the code, punched in the numbers, and soon the drab green, rolling landscape of the historic golf links appeared on the screen.

"Any hole in particular?" Ben asked.

"Yes, I'd prefer the eighteenth, if you please," Mungo replied with a poor Scottish accent, and continued his stretching.

When the image of the course's final tee emerged on the screen, Mungo selected the driver, teed up a ball and positioned his small frame over it. He eased the club back and then swung with remarkable force, striking the ball hard and propelling it into the screen. He and the others watched on as the computerized counterpart showed as an impressive draw that landed and rolled briskly down the hard, wide, and undulating fairway.

"Very nice," Ben said, and the growing gallery of customers gave a courteous golf clap.

"Thank you," Mungo said, and he took a bow before sizing up his second shot. The computer took the screen to Mungo's ball sitting on the fairway on a slight up slope.

"You're one sixty-seven out," Spindler said.

"That's to the green. I want to know how far it is to those buildings over yonder," Mungo said pointing to the computer image of the historic stone structures standing tall and majestic to the right of the fairway.

"Why?" Spindler asked.

"I just need to know to plot my strategy, that's all," Mungo said, and Ben snickered under his breath.

"It's two twenty-five give or take," Spindler estimated.

Mungo grabbed the five wood, and positioned himself to hit his second shot, but this time aiming well right. He swung the club, launching the ball into the screen, and the image of it rose high and soared long, until it careened off one the ancient buildings, and rebounded into a pot bunker to the right of the fairway.

"Now that's cool!" Mungo said, and the shoppers applauded robustly.

"That's enough of that!" Spindler intervened, snatching the club from Mungo and returning it to the wooden rack.

"What's the big deal, Stewart?" Mungo protested.

"Well ... uh ... you could've broken a window."

"Ain't y'all got virtual insurance?" Mungo asked.

Ben, feeling obliged to return to the objective, keyed in the code for Eagle Crest, and played the thirteenth no less than six additional times, and only once did he manage to hit the green in regulation and two putt for par. Spindler could not tell if Ben performed poorly because of the virtual format or if he was simply out of practice, but either way, he found it alarming.

Ben decided to stop for the day, and when he and Mungo emerged from the velvet chamber, their eyes had to adjust to the glare of the store's fully illuminated fluorescent lights. Spindler thanked Ben for coming, and as the two men walked toward the exit, they could hear bits and pieces of Spindler's Pitz-Flex sales pitch to the customers.

Over the next couple of weeks, Ben practiced at the store on four occasions, and Spindler either witnessed the performance in person, or studied the computer's performance log after each, hoping for signs of improvement. However, after every visit, he found little to provide optimism, and Spindler, having pledged to report any progress or problems to Pitzmyre, reluctantly dialed his boss' number.

"What—now, Stewart?"

"There's a problem with Digby."

"Did he die or something?" Pitzmyre asked, seemingly enthused by the prospect.

"No, nothing like that. It's his play Joe—it's not good."

"Is he not using the virtual golf?"

"Surprisingly, he's used it a lot," Spindler replied, "but he's simply not scoring worth a damn."

"What's he doing wrong?" Pitzmyre asked.

"His swing a nightmare."

"These old guys always play a little awkwardly," Pitzmyre said, "they all tend to swing real quick and choppy—you've seen that, right?"

"Sure, I've seen seventy-somethings take the club a quarter of the way back, and punch it forward with a sharp pop, and the ball sails low and straight, then rolls a mile on the fairway."

"Yeah, that's what I'm talking about, it's only natural as they compensate for their age," Pitzmyre said.

"Sure, but Ben's swing isn't anything like that," Spindler explained. "He hits these high fading shots that don't fly very far at all, and barely roll when they land. While his short game seems pretty good, he takes way too many strokes to get the ball to the point where he can use those skills."

"You didn't think it looked that bad the first day you reported."

"His swing looked a little off then too, but he seemed play better. Maybe it was beginner's luck, or perhaps he gets worse with the practice, but trust me Joe—it's not pretty. I have watched or read the results of Ben's play on the thirteenth at Eagle Crest countless times now. Even if you take out the shots where he hits a tree or puts it in the creek, he is still reaching the green more often in four shots, than two.

"A lot of bogies and double bogies?"

"Yes and worse …"

"Shit! He's making *some* pars on the hole, right?"

"Sure, but only one, and on a good day, two out every ten tries."

"Damn it! A half-million damn dollars on a ten to twenty percent chance!" Pitzmyre lamented.

"Yes, and that's on a machine with no wind, no crowd and no pressure," Spindler added.

"What's wrong with his swing?"

"Where do I start?" Spindler asked rhetorically. "One thing is he raises up some during the take away and shifts his weight to his front foot instead of the back."

"Front foot on the take away?" Pitzmyre asked.

"Yes."

"That's a beginner's mistake."

"I know," Spindler, said, "it's as if he's trying to compensate for something and just doesn't realize what he's doing. He also takes the club all the way back—beyond parallel—and brings the club down like a woodchopper. He fades or slices the ball on most shots over a hundred and twenty-five yards, and he couldn't consistently hit a fairway on a bet."

"Have you said something to him about it?" Pitzmyre asked.

"I considered it, but I'm afraid if I interfere, it'd only make things worse."

"Shit, you might be right."

"Should we offer him a golf pro to help? I mean perhaps getting some instruction might get him back on track."

"That's not a bad suggestion, but I think you raised a good point on the interfering angle," Pitzmyre said. "At his age, I'm worried if we screw with his head at all, his already shitty game will fall completely apart, and we can't risk that."

"What do you want me to do?" Spindler asked.

"You *have* to make sure he practices and gets back into the groove. I need him to do this thing, damn it, and it's not just my money on the line," Pitzmyre said. "Stewart, if this doesn't end well, I'm not sure I'll keep the presence in Bozeman."

"Don't say that Joe," Spindler pleaded, "all of this is stressful enough, without you threatening the store."

"Stressful for you! What do you think it's like for me? I have a fortune on the line out there *and* a failing store on top of that."

"But Joe, shoppers come here by the droves! Our foot traffic continues to improve, and I think the deal with Digby is a big part of that."

"Okay—you say a lot of people are coming in the store, but are they buying anything?"

"Our parking lot stays full, and people are—"

"You're not hearing me Stewart," Pitzmyre interrupted. "Your store reminds me of a shopping mall that opened just outside of Newark, before I moved out here from New York. We had actually looked at part of that tract to build one of our stores. The price was right, and there were plenty of households in the area, but the demographics and median income concerned us. On top of that, there was a large, established mall four miles up the road, which was an older property, but still popular, so we begged off on it. This commercial developer from Atlantic City ended up buying the whole damn thing and constructed a medium-size indoor mall. Stores big and small, signed leases and moved in, and when it opened, the parking lot stayed full and foot traffic was good. Fast-forward a year and half later and most of the stores had moved out, it got worse from there, and the mall is now a huge—ratty—flea market, and the developer lost his ass."

"What was the problem?" Spindler asked.

"First off, I was right about the demographics, but I still couldn't fathom why the mall failed so miserably—so fast. A couple of years later, I saw that sucker developer at an Association of Retailers convention in Vegas and asked him about it. He told me that there were several problems, but it seems that main one was that in the summer, these undesirables in the area would come there *only* to enjoy the air conditioning and avoid running up their own electric bills during the day. The reverse was true for the heating-oil bills in the winter. Very few of those people actually came there to shop and most didn't have the wherewithal to buy much if they were so inclined. They also made the mistake of building a small playground in the center the damn thing, and as a result, the mall became primarily a place for parents bring their kids, friends and relatives to hang out—for free—and enjoy the atmosphere. As a result of all those people hanging around there, day in and day out, the good paying customers, the ones that had two nickels to rub together stopped coming, opting instead to drive the four extra miles to the other mall."

"But what's that got to do with my store?"

"Like your location, this mall had plenty of *foot traffic*, in terms of humans coming in and out, but not a whole lot of *buying* was going on."

"You think some of the customers in my store, just come to hang out?"

"I think too many of those coming into your store are specifically not *customers*, and they do like hanging out there. It must be some sort of a novelty—a real treat—to come in to your store!"

"Why would they do that?" Spindler asked.

"Think about it, they get to enjoy free cable TV in electronics, watch fish swim and finches fly in the pet center, they get to bounce rubber balls around in the toy department, all the while enjoying a year 'round perfect seventy-two degrees. I actually think the only way to make your store profitable would be to institute a cover charge to enter or a two-purchase minimum, like they do at strip clubs here in Los Angeles. Stewart, we're standing up for this old dude, and I'm sure some people out there like that, but so far it remains to be seen if it's resulting in increased sales. The upshot is Dingbat seems to like the virtual golf, so hopefully he'll keep coming there and get his game back on track."

"The customers eat it up when he's here, and we've sold a lot of Pitz-Flex sets, but with that said, I'm beginning to think the virtual golf is hurting, and not helping him."

"I hear you, but we can't let the first ball he hits after all this time, be the tee shot on that eighteenth hole," Pitzmyre said. "He *has* to practice, and when he's there, make sure he's playing only the thirteenth at Eagle Crest and not screwing around on other courses."

"That's another issue, Joe. I noticed on the computer log that he's playing quite a bit on a whole different course."

"What, Pebble Beach, Harbor Town?"

"No, it's some course in Arizona called El Dorado," Spindler said.

"Never heard of it."

"Me neither, but he must have played it before, since he really seems to like it and sometimes plays all eighteen holes."

"First of all, you have to put a stop to that! I'm not spending all of this money to provide him with recreation, but just out of curiosity, what's he shooting on that course per round on it?" Pitzmyre asked.

"When you average it out, he shoots around his handicap."

"Mid-nineties, huh?"

"Yeah, mid to low," Spindler said.

"Hell, that round he shot last year was truly was lightening in a bottle, but that's why I favor him practicing."

"It's your money and your call, but I think it's a mistake. In addition, my Easter inventory will arrive next week and I really need the space back."

"Okay then," Pitzmyre relented. "Get the damn thing out of there and back to the manufacturer and cancel the lease!"

"Consider it done, Boss."

"Don't waste any time either—we had it on a thirty-day trial so just tell them that we changed our mind, and they can keep the deposit."

"Got it. I'll get Leonard and a crew of stock boys to dismantle it and box it up in the morning," Spindler said.

"Fine. Has it thawed out up there any?"

"It's still pretty cold and it snows some, but it's gettin' there," Spindler said.

"Are there any driving ranges open so Ben can hit some real golf balls?"

"No, not yet, but I don't think it'll be too much longer."

"Good. As soon as it does, make sure he gets some range time, and offer to pay for it."

"I'll talk to him about it, but you know he's done with his mandatory appearances," Spindler said.

"I realize that Stewart, but we're not asking him come to the store in a clown suit and pass out balloons! I just want him to practice—hell he ought to want to do that on his own."

"I'll encourage him, and will let him know we got rid of the virtual golf."

"What about the condition of the golf course?" Pitzmyre asked.

"When the weather cooperates, they're starting to work on it some, but it's still in real rough shape," Spindler said.

"How much more time do they need?"

"Depending on the conditions, the course as a whole will take about one and a half to two months, but the pro-shop guy, Chuck Duval, says they're focusing on getting the eighteenth ready first, and they're thinking, three or four weeks—weather permitting."

"Okay, let's set a date for Dingbat to play the hole, and to be on the safe side, let's go with the first Saturday of April, and get this thing done. Get me that Duval person's contact information, I need to send people out there to do a lot of advanced preparations at the course. Just run the date by everyone, and let's get this thing over with."

"Okay, Joe."

After contacting Duval, Knox and Ben, everyone agreed to the date, and during the weeks that followed, Pitz-Smart's corporate management and select contractors were at Lone Wolf, fulfilling Pitzmyre's vision of how the event should look.

The Seventeenth Hole

17

*W*hen the morning arrived for Ben to complete his round, Pitzmyre's jet landed before sunup at Bozeman's regional airport. News reporters, having been tipped off as to his estimated arrival time, gathered near the tarmac. Camera flashes and video camera lights illuminated the scene and captured the moment, as Pitzmyre grinned and waved, as he descended the stairs of his Gulf Stream aircraft. He walked briskly to an idling limo that would deliver him to the golf course to meet with Spindler and to oversee final preparations, and when he drove away, the media packed up and headed toward Lone Wolf.

While that was unfolding, Ben was in bed fast asleep. Emily stirred and rolled over and noticed that it was 6:45 a.m. She sprung to her feet and announced, "Ben, it's time to get up!"

Ben blinked his eyes and glanced at the clock and then to her and said, "You're right, I'll get ready."

A half hour later, Ben joined her at the breakfast table, showered, bright eyed and clean-shaven. Emily treated him to a plate of scrambled eggs, toast and coffee, and as he ate he asked, "Say, you're still goin' down there with me, aren't you?"

"Sure, assuming you want me to."

"I do," Ben responded.

"I'm going to be nervous, but I really want to be there," Emily said. "I'll get things done here, and get ready to go."

"Good, I'll brush my teeth and get my clubs."

"You seem to be at ease about all this … are you okay?" Emily asked.

"I'm tired of frettin' about it, and just want to get it over with."

Emily felt it best to conceal her own mounting anxiety, and opted to go about her normal routine as if this was just any other Saturday morning. Soon, the kitchen was clean and the dishes breakfast ware in its place, and Emily emerged from their bedroom dressed for the day.

"Do you think this looks okay?" Emily asked, modeling her light blue, calf-length skirt, white blouse, a light-blue sweater that highlighted her eyes, and a pair of low-heeled shoes.

Ben stood and walked over to her and wrapped his arms around her waist. "You look like the wife of a champion, my lovely constant."

She pulled a folded piece of paper from the right pocket of her dress and said, "While I was waiting for you this morning, I wrote you a limerick."

Ben smiled. "Let's hear it."

She unfolded the paper, cleared her throat, and recited:

There once was a golfing old coot,
A great round he did shoot,
Then the old golfer,
Accepted an offer,
and took Mr. Pitzmyre's loot.

"Thank you for that—I love it!" he said, with a peck on her cheek.

"You're very welcome, but we better get going, don't you think?"

"Yes, it's time," Ben said, and he lifted his bag of clubs and followed Emily to the side exit of their home. As they walked outside and toward their garage, they noticed that the morning clouds were dissipating, and though it was a cool morning, the wind had moderated and the conditions proved unseasonably comfortable.

They had decided to take Emily's car to the golf course, and with Ben's clubs secured in the trunk, he backed out of the driveway, and steered her sedan in that direction. As they drove, Emily continued her attempt to appear calm, but the closer they drew to the golf course, the more she struggled. She remained awkwardly silent, focusing her attention on the beauty around them—including the diminishing presence of snowcaps on the mountain peaks, and the small colorful buds of the wild Abelia shrubs growing along the roadside. However, this lapse into scenic tranquility evaporated the instant they rounded the corner and turned on to the road leading to the club parking lot.

"Oh—my—goodness!" Emily gasped.

As Ben drove, his eyes alternated glances between the road surface and the spectacle that lay ahead. There were endless colorful Pitz-Smart banners, and members of a high school band and a drill team lined the way from the edge of the parking area to the designated golf club drop-off on the perimeter of the lot.

"It's them! It's them!" the half-asleep band teacher yelled to his young charges. Having gained their attention he raised his baton and signaled the commencement of a shrill—off-key—rendition of the theme from the movie *Rocky*. As the band played, the drill team lifted and shook their pom-poms on each side of the drive, heralding the couple's arrival, Ben drove slowly, not so much to soak in the adoration, but rather to keep from running into any of those in the bustling throng.

The parking lot was near capacity, with more vehicles present there that morning, than Ben had seen in over a decade. Included on the lot were the vehicles and trucks for the news crews that had earlier captured Pitzmyre's arrival. Those same still cameras flashed and video cameras rolled, as the couple arrived at the bag drop. Emily sat speechless and petrified, as the throng converged, and their respective car doors were opened simultaneously.

When Ben emerged from the driver's side, he was met with outstretched right hand of a beaming Joseph Pitzmyre. "Welcome, Ben!" Pitzmyre's voice boomed as he turned toward the photographers to assure each lens captured the two together, hand in hand.

"Is this a golf event or a movie premier?" Ben asked.

Pitzmyre prolonged his vigorous handshake, and through his plastered on grin whispered, "It's just publicity, my man. Pure, solid-gold, publicity." Once the cameras captured the moment, and when the flashes subsided, Pitzmyre then and only then released his grip on Ben's hand. Ben walked to the back of the car and raised the trunk lid, removed his golf clubs and sat the bag on the wooden rack on the sidewalk.

Emily eased out of her open car door, and Ben took her by the arm, and escorted her around to the driver's side. "Mr. Pitzmyre, I want you to meet my wife, Emily."

"Nice to meet you, now you two need to follow me—we're on a tight schedule this morning," Pitzmyre said, leading the couple in the direction of the clubhouse as the crowd cheered and the band played on. Some of the reporters followed and shouted questions, but Pitzmyre lead the couple at a sufficient pace to prevent them catching up.

"What about our car?" Ben asked as they passed a stage with a podium like the one in the parking lot tent.

"My assistant is parking it."

"And my clubs?"

"Stewart will take care of them," Pitzmyre assured, "they'll be at the eighteenth tee when we get there."

"Why aren't we going with Spindler to the tee?"

"It's not time for that. There's an itinerary for this morning, and that comes later," Pitzmyre said, maintaining the brisk pace.

They neared the clubhouse, and Ben was surprised that they were being escorted in the direction of the door to the men's locker room, "You know this is the—"

"Yes, I cleared it with the club, and your wife can go in. Other than me and Spindler, no one else will enter," Pitzmyre said as he led the couple toward the entry door.

"Why not the café," Ben asked.

Pitzmyre stopped and turned to the couple. "Look—I don't want any distractions or anyone getting to you, understand?" Ben nodded and Pitzmyre ushered the couple through the door and into the locker room. "You will be isolated in here, and nobody will bother you. I have also arranged for the driving range and the path to it to remain clear, and no one else will have access, got it?"

"Understood," Ben, said.

"Do you have the score card?" Pitzmyre asked and Ben reached into his jacket and handed Pitzmyre the worn and crinkled original. Pitzmyre examined the card and re-added the scores, and Ben began warming up by doing some stretching. "That's good, Ben. You do whatever you need to do to get ready and then hit some range balls," Pitzmyre said and placed the scorecard in his pocket, then stepped to a corner of the locker room to review the handwritten notes on several index cards, and Emily took a seat on a bench by the lockers and remained eerily silent.

"Are you okay, dear?" Ben whispered.

She turned to him. "It's a bit overwhelming, but I'm hanging in there, how about you?"

"I'm good," Ben said.

"Here's the plan," Pitzmyre said, returning his notes to his jacket pocket. "You guys make yourselves at home and feel free to ask for anything you need. I'm just going to get out there and answer some of the reporters' questions and come back here, so don't go anywhere except the driving range, okay?

"All right," Ben said.

"Once I do this meet-and-greet with the press, you and I will go to the clubhouse, get into a designated cart and ride together to the tee," Pitzmyre explained, as Spindler entered. "As for you Mrs. Digby, Stewart here will get you out there separately."

"Thank you," she said.

Pitzmyre turned to Spindler. "Everything ready at the tee?"

"Yes Boss, but don't forget the shirt!" Spindler said, pointing.

"Oh, I almost forgot," Pitzmyre, said and he lifted a bright-red T-shirt off the top of a row of lockers and tossed it to Ben. "You'll need to pull this on over your clothes."

Though folded, Ben knew by the color scheme that it was Pitz-Smart apparel and said, "Look—I really don't want to wear this out there."

"It's in the contract," Pitzmyre said.

"Okay," Ben sighed, removed his hat and commenced pulling the shirt over his head.

"I'll see you in a little bit," Pitzmyre said, and when the CEO opened the door to leave, the Digby's could hear the clamor of the crowd and the blare of the horns from the band playing a poor rendition of the theme from *Chariots of Fire* until the door mercifully slammed shut.

"I don't like that man," Emily said, staring at the now closed door.

Ben glanced over to Spindler who shrugged and said, "Did Joe tell you that the driving range is open and cleared just for you?"

"Yes," Ben said.

"Feel free to head on out there—you'll find a large bucket of range balls waitin' for you."

"Thanks, Stewart, but I think I'll just wait it out in here with Emily."

"You don't need to practice?" Spindler asked.

"No, I don't."

"Have you gone to a driving range since we spoke about it on the phone?"

"I don't like to hit range balls," Ben explained.

"Suit yourself. I'll be back to get you soon, Mrs. Digby," Spindler said, and Emily nodded and he headed out of the locker room and toward the press conference.

"You gotta be kidding me!" Ben said as he stood in front of a full-length mirror attached to the end of a row of lockers, and stared incredulously at his image. Written in yellow on the front of the Shirt below the Pitz-Smart logo was *The Pitz-Smart Challenge* and Ben turned his body away from the mirror and glanced back to see *Ben Dingy—Pitz-Flex Spokesman* adorning the back of it. Duty bound to wear the shirt, Ben unbuckled his belt and began tucking the tail of it around his waistline of his corduroys.

"This is just one continuous commercial for Pitz-Smart, isn't it?" Emily said.

"That's their pattern."

"You know they misspelled your name, don't you?"

"Yes, that's also a pattern," Ben said.

Emily's emotions caught up to her and she teared up, and said, "I know that this is a big deal, but I don't want you to be disappointed," Emily said with a sniffle, "especially with all of this hoopla, spectators, bands and news coverage—I just didn't picture it being this way."

"Neither did I," Ben said, as he cinched the belt and took a seat next to her on the bench. "But you know, I've had my fifteen minutes of fame, and though I didn't invite it and it's been quite irritating in some respects, it's been nice in others. I've kind of liked some of the attention, and I have met some new folks and talked to others that I haven't seen or heard from since we closed the store. The papers have written about me and—"

"More than once," Emily added.

"That's true, and you and I were on TV. With that said, I would never want to do all of this over again, but win lose or draw, we'll move on and laugh about all of this someday."

"I'm glad to hear you say that, because I truly want this to be a positive for you. You have so many regrets Ben, and you *just* don't do regrets well," she said, and leaned into Ben's open arms, feeling at ease for the first time all morning.

"Don't worry about me, it'll all work out," Ben said.

Outside, the setting was anything but serene. Many attendees were claiming spots near the tee, along the fairway and around the green, while several others gathered at the wooden stage erected near the parking lot awaiting Pitzmyre's press conference. The marching band played on, and the crowd remained boisterous as Pitzmyre strutted up the steps to the stage, which featured a huge, colorful Pitz-Smart banner suspended along the full length of the backside of it. Once on the stage, he signaled the bandleader, resulting in an immediate cessation of the music.

Pitzmyre took the podium and greeted his audience. "Welcome to the Pitz-Smart Challenge! For the record, I am Joseph Pitzmyre, founder and CEO of Pitz-Smart International, and I am delighted to see so many Pitz-Smart shoppers and members of the media here with us today. I plan for this to be a brief, but informative question-and-answer session, but first I have some opening remarks."

All watched on as Pitzmyre pulled the notes from his jacket pocket, cleared his throat, and re-capped Ben's interrupted round of golf and the importance of the final hole, and the club endorsement. He took a sip from a bottled water from under the podium, and then added, "Standing to my right is Stewart Spindler, General Manager of our Bozeman location," he said and pointed to Stewart, who had arrived and was standing stage side with fluttering eyes and a wide grin. "Come on up, Stewart," Pitzmyre invited, and Spindler's grin widened and his ascension to the stage prompted an anemic smattering of applause. "You'll find Stewart, my right-hand man, at your local Pitz-Smart store, day in and day out, making sure that your shopping experience is a positive one."

Once atop the stage, Spindler walked behind Pitzmyre, hoping to be included in some of the camera shots. As he did, the strings attaching the large Pitz-Smart banner ensnared his foot. This caused him to stumble and simultaneously loosened the tie strings that allowed the left side of the banner to drop gently and silently to the floor of the stage.

"Say Pitzmyre! It looks like your right-hand man's—got two left feet," a voice rang out. Pitzmyre glanced in the direction of the comment, and saw that Mungo Thibodeaux had positioned himself among the onlookers. The CEO recognized him from the parking lot tent, and the comment and countless stares focusing on the scene unfolding behind him caused Pitzmyre to turn and witness Spindler's faux pas, and Pitzmyre whispered, "You dumb ass! Put the banner back up—now!"

"Sorry, Joe!" Spindler, said while sitting on the stage frantically struggling to free his foot from the tie strings.

Returning his attention to the gathering, Pitzmyre said, "Now, I'll open the floor for questions, and after that, we'll all need to move out to the eighteenth to watch history in the making."

"How do you like this weather?" a reporter on the front row asked.

"I love it!" Pitzmyre responded to the softball question. "I would say it's a perfect day for setting a golfing landmark, and it's because of weather like this, that I consider the great state of Minnesota my home away from home," Pitzmyre said.

"It's Montana, Joe," Spindler said, now removing his shoe to liberate himself.

Pitzmyre cleared his throat and said, "Yes—of course I mean the great state of Montana."

"Don't y'all sell maps down there at the Pitz-Smart?" Mungo yelled.

"Yes we do, little man," Pitzmyre, responded, "lowest prices in town on them too. That's not just true for maps, but for all of our electronics, clothing, hardware and food items. Who's next?"

"Speaking of food, where are the free snacks?" Mungo blurted out, looking in all direction for the stainless steel containers.

"Pardon me just a minute folks," Pitzmyre said and turned to Spindler. "Damn it! What's he doing here?"

"I don't know," Spindler said, having now freed himself and stood trying to reattach the banner ties.

"Get rid of him!"

"You want me to do that, or fix the banner?" Spindler asked.

"Both, damn it!" Pitzmyre said, and turned back to the crowd. "What else do you have for me?" A few raised a hand and Mungo raised two. Pitzmyre, ignoring Mungo said, "I call on my main man, Brian Cotton from the Tribune."

"Do you have a prediction for today?" the reporter asked.

"Good question, Brian," Pitzmyre said, taking another gulp from the water bottle. "The answer is yes, and I predict that Ben ... Ding Digby will shoot his age this morning, by parring the eighteenth hole of this magnificent specimen of a golf course, and when he does, Ben will become to golf, what I have been to retail, and that is a champion of the common man!"

"Give me an ever-lovin' break!" Mungo said, shaking his head. "You dare to represent yourself to be the *champion of the common man?*"

"I most certainly do."

"My—ass!" Mungo said. "I saw you on the news this morning arriving here on a private jet and didn't you roll up here earlier in a stretch limo?"

"Yes I did, little man, but you run along now and let the grown-ups talk," Pitzmyre said.

"I ain't goin' nowhere ... *common man*," Mungo said.

"What's your name?" a TV reporter asked, extending his microphone toward Mungo, and Pitzmyre rolled his eyes and sighed aloud.

"Mungo Thibodeaux is the handle, and I'm Pitzmyre's *left-*hand man."

"I assure all present that this simpleton has no connection to me or the Pitz-Smart brand, so let me get back to the point. Pitz-Smart is proud to have partnered with Ben and to be a small part of this momentous event."

"A small part? Jesus! All I see is Pitz-Smart written all over everything and Ben's name or picture ain't anywhere!" Mungo charged, and many in the throng nodded their agreement and stared to Pitzmyre for a response.

"Wait until you see his commemorative shirt, little man!" Pitzmyre defended.

"A T-shirt? Is that it?" Mungo asked.

"Yes, and it's a *very* nice custom made shirt with his name prominent on it, and you all can buy one of your own as a souvenir before you leave. But just know that what you see out here is simply the marketing part, but make no mistake about it, Mr. Ben Ding ... Digby—who by the way is a frequenter of our store here in Bozeman— has always been the focus."

"I dare you, or your right-hand man, to name one thing that Ben Digby has *ever* purchased at your store!" Mungo challenged.

Pitzmyre turned to Spindler, who simply shrugged, causing Pitzmyre to improvise. "Look—I said Ben frequents our store, and that's the truth. Apparently, not everyone who enters our location here buys something. Nevertheless, Ben agreed to collaborate with us and we wagered a hundred thousand dollars on Ben because we *believe* in him. But because a misguided old banker saw fit to raise the bet to a half-million dollars, we showed our confidence in Ben by taking that bet and did without hesitation."

"No hesitation?" Mungo asked. "Hell, I was there in that tent that morning old man Knox raised your bet—you were sweatin' up a storm."

The crowd stirred, and Pitzmyre held up his hands trying for calm. "Ignore this man folks, he's not right in the head."

"That may be true, but my eyes are fine, and when you pondered Knox' raise, you were as nervous as a virgin at the prison rodeo!"

"What does that even mean?" Brian Cotton asked.

"Well you see, down in Huntsville, Texas there used to be a prison rodeo that—"

"Forget about that!" Pitzmyre interrupted. "The bottom line is we called that bet to demonstrate our confidence in Ben, and that's the end of it! So, I remind you all to shop smart—shop Pitz-Smart. Now let's get this thing done!" Pitzmyre said, cutting his losses by putting an end to the press conference. He nodded to the band director, and the band lifted their instruments and launched into a rendition of *We are the champions.*

As Pitzmyre descended from the stage with Spindler in tow, he glanced back and asked, "What damn good are you?"

"What do you mean?"

Stewart, I didn't invite you on *my* stage to ruin my display, but you managed to do that and blow the photo op!"

"Sorry, Joe, it was just an accident."

"Everything about you is a damn accident, and how could you allow that loud mouth country hick to ruin my presentation?" Pitzmyre said as he paced rapidly toward the clubhouse.

"What was I supposed do?" Spindler said. "After all, it is a free country."

"It sure is Stewart, and you're about to be free of a job!" Pitzmyre yelled back to Spindler who now followed him at a distance. When they returned to the locker room, Pitzmyre saw Emily sitting alone at the table and said, "Ben must be over at the driving range, huh?"

"No sir, he's just in the bathroom washing his hands," she said.

"Did he get in any practice shots?"

Emily shook her head. "He said he didn't want to."

Pitzmyre pulled Spindler aside. "Why didn't you make sure he went out to the driving range?"

"I suggested it, but he said he wanted to wait it out in here with his wife."

"Oh, how sweet!" Pitzmyre mocked. "It's the biggest damn hole of golf he's ever played, and he doesn't even warm up!"

Ben entered wiping his hands on a paper towel, and Pitzmyre confronted him. "No practice time?"

"No, I usually leave my best shots out on the driving range."

"I see," Pitzmyre said. "What *did* you do to get ready?"

"You saw it, I stretched a little to loosen up my lower back—that's all I ever do."

"Okay then, let's get this thing going, Ben, you come with me," Pitzmyre instructed, then wheeled around, and walked to the back of the locker room, and held open a door that led to a hallway connecting it to the pro shop.

"I guess this is where we part ways," Ben said, placing his hands on Emily's shoulders and staring into her eyes.

Emily hugged him and whispered in his ear, "Just go out there and do your best."

"I will, and I'll be looking for you."

"Mrs. Digby, I have a cart outside, and on my way to the tee, I'll be dropping you off at a good spot by the green," Spindler said. "There's a Pitz-Smart employee with a shirt like Ben's, holding a place for you by the ropes."

Emily nodded nervously, and after Pitzmyre and Ben disappeared into the hall, Spindler led her out of the locker room and toward the cart.

The Eighteenth Hole

*A*nticipating an unnerving throng when they entered the pro shop, Ben was gratified to see only Chuck Duval, Cookie and a few other members milling around.

Chuck walked to Ben, shook his hand, and said, "I know you can do this, Mr. Digby."

"Thanks," Ben said. "I guess you're back from Bridger Bowl."

"Yes, sir, and I'm looking forward to another nice summer here," Chuck said as Pitzmyre stood at the pro shop door glancing at his watch.

"Me, too Chuck," Ben said. "I got a look at the eighteenth, and it appears you all did a fine job getting it ready."

"Thanks, we got real lucky with the weather," Chuck replied, then leaned toward Ben and added in a whisper, "Working with all of the Pitz-Smart people was the *real* challenge."

Next, Cookie shook Ben's hand. "I'd love to be down there with you."

"Don't worry, I know you have to tend to the café," Ben said.

"I'll watch from the window, and if I get a break in the action, I'll turn things over to Kat and head down there. Good luck, my friend."

"So long, Cookie."

"All right Ben, are you ready?" Pitzmyre asked.

"I was ready when I got here."

"Good. Now that's our cart out there, so come with me," Pitzmyre instructed and Ben followed him out the door, and they each took a seat in the four-seater with Pitz-Smart logos pasted on each side.

"Are you sure my clubs are down there?" Ben asked.

"Yes, they'll be waiting at the tee box," Pitzmyre confirmed as he directed their cart down the path that ran past the eighteenth green, then upward along the fairway, and to the tee. So thick was the crowd around the cart path, that as they drove, Ben had no chance of spotting Emily as they passed the green. As they made their way slowly past the spectators standing attentively on each side of the path, Ben was humbled by how enthusiastic and supportive they were, with most clapping and calling out words of encouragement.

"Still think I underestimated the public's interest in this?" Pitzmyre asked, glancing at Ben.

"Goodness no. I didn't know there were this many people in this town."

"This town? Did you see the license plates in the parking lot? There are people here from all over."

As the cart reached the eighteenth tee, they each saw Spindler and that next to him stood Ferguson T. Knox, who was conspicuously dressed in his dark, three-piece suit, standing with hands on his hips and wearing an unnerving grin. Ben glanced toward the tee box and saw large Pitz-Smart advertisement boards on two sides of it, and when he exited the cart, he spotted Spindler's oversized, black golf bag with its prominent Pitz-Smart logo, sitting next to the cart path.

Ben walked over to Spindler and asked, "Where's my bag, Stewart?"

"In the trunk of your car, you'll need to use mine to play the hole."

"That figures," Ben muttered.

"Good luck Ben," came a voice from behind, and he turned to see Mungo. "I'm rootin' for you pal."

"I appreciate that, Mr. Thibodeaux," Ben said smiling.

"Well, this is it," Pitzmyre said, rubbing his hands together. "Any questions Ben?"

"Yes, that bag does have *my* clubs in it, right? I mean, you don't have those Pitz-Flex clubs in there, do you?"

"Hell no!" Pitzmyre said emphatically. "The bag has every one of your clubs in it, from putter to driver—I wouldn't risk you using a crappy starter set for something of this importance."

"I see," Ben, said glancing toward Mungo.

"Deluxe, huh?" Mungo muttered.

"As a reminder, I'll need my bag back when you're done," Spindler added.

"I'll be sure to do that," Ben responded. "Say Stewart, did Emily get situated?"

"Yes, she'll be close to the pond at about ten o'clock as you face the green."

"Thanks for that," Ben said, and walked over to the bag and inventoried his clubs.

"Say Pitzmyre, is that the commemorative shirt you bragged about on stage?" Mungo asked while pointing toward Ben.

"Damn it! Don't you have anything better to do?" Pitzmyre chastised.

"Actually I don't, but what about it?" Mungo pressed as the crowd around them silenced for Pitzmyre's response.

"Yes, and you all should know that the shirt was custom-designed to honor Ben and commemorate today's event and are available for purchase," Pitzmyre said.

"Well, you ought to know, that the custom designers misspelled Ben's name."

Pitzmyre positioned himself behind Ben, read the typo and glared at Spindler, as his face flushed red, but tried to recover saying, "All the more reason to get one today, since they'll become even more of a collector's item once we correct it."

Ben, anxious to get under way, hefted the bag off the turf, threw the strap over his shoulder, and began walking toward the slope that led to the tee area, to the cheers of the onlookers, up and down the fairway.

Hearing the commotion Pitzmyre rushed to his side. "No, Ben! You're going walk the hole, but Spindler will carry the bag."

Spindler's head jerked up. "Me? I'm the caddy?"

"Yes!" Pitzmyre confirmed. "It adds to the optics to have one, plus no one in their right mind would ask a man Ben's age to carry that ridiculously heavy bag of yours!"

Spindler glanced toward Ben, who shrugged and ceded the bag to him. Spindler begrudgingly carried the bag the rest of the way up to the tee, while Ben surveyed the people standing around it. He saw some familiar faces, including some veterans from the VFW hall, each wearing some form of military togs. Several wore a portion of their old uniforms, while others wore dark blue caps or tee shirts honoring a ship they served upon, or a campaign in which they had fought. To a man, they stood erect with their arms at their sides and stared straight ahead. The reverence steeled Ben, and he acknowledged them with a nod, however, Ben's sense of inspiration turned to one of dread, when he noticed a group of the newcomers at the ropes. They were positioned only a few feet away, and front and center among them, stood Clive Jacklin, flanked by Billy Auchterlonie and a half-dozen of their colleagues.

When Spindler saw Ben staring in Clive's direction, he cringed and said, "Uh oh!"

"What's wrong," Pitzmyre asked.

"It's Clive and those guys over there with him."

"What about 'em?"

"The locals don't get along with guys like Clive and his pals, and there's a lot of bad blood between them," Spindler explained and Pitzmyre began moving toward the ropes, prepared to intercede if there was trouble.

Jacklin spoke first. "Good morning, Mr. Digby."

"Good morning to you too," Ben said, then realized Jacklin was wearing a pair of brown corduroy pants, similar to his own.

"Do you like them?" Clive asked.

"I like 'em just fine, but I've heard that they're really out of style."

"Oh, yeah? Well, don't tell these guys," Clive said as he moved aside to show that each in his group stood in solidarity wearing and an identical pair.

Ben smiled. "It'll be our little secret."

"Good luck, Mr. Digby, and just know we're *all* on your side," Jacklin said, and the others nodded.

Ben turned and stared down the familiar fairway, as the crowd ebbed to near silence. The grass on the fairway was a greenish brown, but was in remarkable shape for that time of year, and light dew reflected the bright sunshine, giving the fairway an eerie, glistening iridescence.

The tee of the eighteenth was elevated, and from there the fairway descended steadily to near its midpoint, where it leveled and ran only slightly downward from there to the green. The fairway was generously wide up to that juncture, but narrowed by more than half from there. It was at this mid-point that the natural, free flowing creek joined the right side of the fairway, and ran parallel to it until it crossed in front of the green and emptied into the small pond on the left. This time of year, the area's melting snow and ice infused the three-foot wide creek, causing it to flow steady enough to keep the greenside pond at capacity. The backside of the pond had a spillway allowing excess water to cascade over a concrete retaining wall and down to a larger tributary, providing a pleasant waterfall sound that on any other morning would have been conspicuous and pleasing to the ear.

Ben grabbed his driver from the bag, pulled a ball from his hip pocket and stooped to tee it, but Pitzmyre interrupted. "No Ben, don't use that. We've provided balls and they're in the bag, and Stewart will get them for you." Ben turned and looked on curiously, as Spindler reached into the side pocket of his large black bag and retrieved a sleeve of three, brand-new balls, and handed it to Ben.

"Do you think I'll need all of these?" Ben asked.

"Of course not," Spindler said. "Use one—hopefully—and keep the rest as souvenirs!"

"Souvenirs?" Ben asked, removing the first ball from the sleeve and noticed *The PITZ-SMART Challenge* printed in red-and-yellow letters on it.

Ben swapped his teed ball, with the logo version, handed the sleeve back to Spindler. He stood erect to address the ball, but again Pitzmyre interrupted, informing him that he needed time for announcements and that more Pitz-Smart golf balls were being distributed to the crowd. Ben backed away from the ball, and looked to down to those lining the fairway, then shook his head in disbelief. At various points along where spectators lined the fairway and the green, the girls from drill-team, now dressed in yellow-and-red plaid knickers and flawed Pitz-Smart commemorative T-shirts, were passing out sleeves of the logo balls from wicker baskets.

Next, Pitzmyre prepared to address the audience with a megaphone, not the cheap plastic version like the one that failed in the parking lot tent, but rather one that plugged into an extension cord leading from a small generator on the backside of the Pitz-Smart signboards. It was connected to a pair of large black speakers, elevated above the dewy ground by tripods, and they worked very well.

"Good morning, ladies and gentlemen," Pitzmyre said, his voice resonating strong and loud to the ears of most present and causing those closest to the tee, including Ben to wince, and some stuck index fingers in their ears to mute it. "I'm pleased to welcome our Pitz-Smart shoppers and golf enthusiasts from all over the country! We are all here to watch history as our hometown hero, Benjamin Digby, will complete the final hole of a round he started last fall. I hold in my hand the actual score card from that fateful day, and all scores are recorded, except for this one final hole," Pitzmyre said, raising the wrinkled and worn scorecard, high above his head.

When Pitzmyre paused to return the scorecard to his pocket, Ben took the opportunity to remove his fingers from his ears and address the ball. The crowd noise ebbed and Ben took the club back, but halted at the top of his back swing when he heard, "Wait up, Ben!" Pitzmyre urged off mic. "I'm not done." Ben sighed and again stepped away from the ball and bided his time.

Pitzmyre returned to the megaphone. "At the conclusion of this memorable event, and as you exit toward the parking lot, you'll pass a set of tables. There, you will be able to pick up a souvenir of this historic day, including T-shirts, like the one Ben Digby and these girls in knickers have on, sweaters, koozies and commemorative pin flags. Many of you are already holding a sleeve of souvenir golf balls, and for those who did not get your own commemorative set, simply stop by the souvenir table on your way out. Once there, you can purchase a souvenir or two, and pick up a certificate that you can take to the local Pitz-Smart store and redeem it for a sleeve of your own—while supplies last, of course. But remember, we make that offer *only* for those present who don't already have balls."

"So girls and Pitz-Smart management can't get a sleeve?" Mungo asked, close enough to the open megaphone for it to echo down the fairway.

"Shut up!" Pitzmyre said angrily as Ben, fed up with the endless hype, again addressed the teed ball.

"Joe's not ready," Spindler said.

"Well, I am!" Ben responded firmly as he concentrated on the ball, and the crowd up and down the fairway noticed this and fell silent in anticipation of the all-important first swing. Ben drew the club back, accelerated forward and – *kaplink!* – came the sound from his metal driver connecting with the garish promotional golf ball. The crowd roared as they watched the ball soar, until descending to the downslope of the fairway, and then bounding rapidly on the grass. The ball drifted to the right and scampered out of the fairway and was now running and hopping through the taller grass. A hush fell over the gallery as onlookers struggled to follow the path of the ball, and for those around the tee box, it was now out of sight. However, to all familiar with the hole, it was certain that Ben's ball was flirting with the creek, and when a gasp erupted from those closest to the ball's path, it signified the worst.

"It's wet," Spindler said.

"In the water?" Pitzmyre asked and Spindler nodded. Pitzmyre hung his head and handed off the megaphone to a Pitz-Smart employee. Ben walked resolutely off the tee box and trudged down the slope and in the direction of his ball, as Spindler followed behind Ben with the over-sized golf bag, and Pitzmyre trailed the two of them. As they neared the creek, the crowd parted to provide access to the men, and the only question in Ben's mind was how bad of a lie he had.

They stood at the edge of the gurgling creek, and a spectator pointed them to Ben's ball. Though the creek was full, the ball had stopped in a spot that was only two to three inches deep. Ben verified he was looking at the right ball, by the colorful writing, and noted that the top of the orb sat about a half inch under the surface of the flowing water. With hands on his hips, Ben pondered his strategy, as Pitzmyre joined him in assessing the predicament.

"What a pity," came a voice from behind, and Pitzmyre turned and saw Knox standing a few feet away, his arms folded, and shaking his head.

Ignoring the comment, Pitzmyre turned to Ben. "I had more announcements to make back there."

"Oh you did?" Ben asked with feigned dismay.

"Yes, wasn't done with them."

"Well, we were sure done with them," Knox said.

"No one asked for your two cents," Pitzmyre said, then turned back toward Ben and saw that he was crouching at the creek's edge and reaching for his ball, and said, "Wait! What are you doing?"

"Picking up my ball."

"Picking it up?" Pitzmyre asked anxiously.

"Yes,"

"You'll take a penalty stroke if you do that!"

"I realize that," Ben said, still crouching, "but I think I have to."

"No way!" Pitzmyre said.

"Oh, let him take a penalty stroke, for goodness sake," Knox, said facetiously.

"Stay out of this, old man," Pitzmyre said, and he turned back to Ben. "Taking a stroke is a *terrible* idea."

Ben's legs were now burning from squatting so he stood and faced Pitzmyre. "What would you have me do?"

"You need to play it where it lies!" Pitzmyre insisted.

"Are you serious?" Ben asked.

"Yes, you have to!"

"I disagree," Knox said unwelcomingly. "I myself would opt for the penalty stroke."

Pitzmyre, exasperated with sharing strategy discussions with Knox, ignored the unsolicited advice and asked, "Ben, would you follow me please?"

Ben complied and as the two walked away from the creek, Pitzmyre put his arm over Ben's shoulder and once out of earshot of all of the others said, "Taking a stroke is out of the question."

"Mr. Pitzmyre, with all due respect I don't think you get it."

"I do get it and you *have* to play it from the creek," Pitzmyre countered. "If you take a drop, and don't hit the green from there, you'll have to hole it from where it lands for the par."

"I understand, but you can't expect me to hit it out of flowing water."

Ben's reference to the flow of the creek inspired a new strategy. "Ben, did you happen notice that your ball was moving a little with the water flowing over it?"

"I don't know if it is actually moving or if the flowing water just makes it look that way," Ben said.

"The point is, with that flow we could ... you know ... use it to our advantage."

Ben stared at him suspiciously. "What exactly are you getting at?"

"All I'm saying is that the ball could be just hanging by a thread there. There may only be just some algae or perhaps a small pebble holding it in place."

"And?" Ben asked

"It could easily dislodge and if it did, who knows how far it would make it down the creek before getting snagged again. Hell, it could flow all the way to the front of the green with a little ... you know ... encouragement."

"And are you suggesting that I provide that encouragement?" Ben asked with raised eyebrows.

"Keep your voice down," Pitzmyre said as he moved closer to Ben. "Now think about it Ben, the people will have to back away from the creek for you to swing and you would just need to ... you know ... get the ball rolling so to speak," Pitzmyre said, but immediately detected Ben's disapproval. "Ben, there's a half a million bucks riding on this and you placed your drive in the drink by rushing your shot. That was a bad thing you did back there, and all I'm asking from you is a little remediation for your hasty mistake. So, if you could see your way to do that, and this works out in my favor, there will be a little more than a thank you coming your way in response."

"What is *that* supposed to mean?" Ben asked now riled.

"We're partnered on this, and let me just say that I'd make it worth your while if you could ... you know ... help this situation a little," Pitzmyre said with a wink.

"That's not gonna happen! You partnered with the wrong person for something like that," Ben said severely, having heard enough of the scheme.

"Shhh—not so loud," Pitzmyre said nervously. "It was just a thought—that's all. So what's your objection to just hitting it where it lies?"

"You *have* to think this through," Ben lobbied, not ready to accede to the risky strategy. "First off, this is a very complicated shot, and I can't properly address the ball without standing at least partially in the water. Then, assuming my toes don't fall off, and when I do hit it, I can't guarantee that I'm even gonna get out it out of the creek. On the other hand, if I take a drop, I will have a decent lie and can try to hit it on or close to the green and attempt to hole it from there."

"Let's go back over there and have another look," Pitzmyre said and they made their way back to the creek, and reassessed situation. After viewing it from all angles, Pitzmyre arrived at the same conclusion, but asked, "Can you reach the green from here if you drop it?"

"Perhaps, but it's certainly at the very outer limit of my length."

Pitzmyre turned to Spindler. "How far did he hit his drive?"

"How would I know?"

"You're his damned caddy, for God's sake!" Pitzmyre yelled.

"I didn't even know that until a few minutes ago ..."

"But don't you play golf here?" Pitzmyre yelled, and Knox chuckled.

Ben intervened. "I'm essentially at the mid-point here. I hit it one eighty something, I have about that left."

"So, with an elevated tee box, the use of a tee, and the down slope, you only got it halfway using a driver?" Pitzmyre asked.

"Yes, but I lost a lot of roll by hitting the rough and landing in the creek."

Pitzmyre shook his head rapidly. "Huh uh, Ben this is my money, and I say play it where it lies."

Anxious to get on with it, Ben acquiesced, took a seat on the large golf bag, and began unlacing his shoes. Once both shoes and socks were off and his corduroys rolled up above his ankles, he gingerly eased the balls of each foot into the edge of the creek, and the clear cold water flowed over his toes and portions of his feet, taking his breath away. Emily, tiptoeing, witnessed the unfolding scene from her greenside vantage point, and thought *Oh my Lord, he will catch his death of cold!* Breathing deeply and rapidly, until his feet and toes numbed, Ben took his stance over the ball.

"Three iron, please," Ben said, and Spindler promptly pulled it from the bag and handed it to him.

"Wait! Did you say a three iron?" Pitzmyre asked.

"Yes," Ben confirmed.

"That's not enough, you gotta use more club than that!" Pitzmyre demanded as Ben stepped back out of the frigid water and placed the golf towel over his now purplish, numbed toes.

"If I try to hit a wood out of here, I can virtually guarantee I won't get it out of the water."

"Can you hit that three iron to the green from here?" Pitzmyre asked.

"No," Ben said without hesitation, "I can't hit the green from this creek with any club. All I'm trying to do is advance the ball as far forward as I can, without compounding the problem."

Pitzmyre squatted, and peered down to the large golf bag on the ground. "I see you carry a one iron, why not use that?"

"I can't hit long shots with it."

"But that's what it's for!" Pitzmyre said with exasperation.

"Not for me, I'm *terrible* at hitting it."

"Then why do you carry it?"

"I use it to punch balls out from under ponderosa pines, and I also like to chip with it around the green in certain situations."

"I carry mine to hold up in the air during lightning storms," Mungo interjected, grinning.

Pitzmyre bit. "You actually hold a metal club up in lightning storms?"

"Yes. According to the great Lee Trevino, *even God can't hit a one iron.*"

"I wish you great success in trying to electrocute yourself, little man," Pitzmyre said, then turned back to Ben. "What about a two iron?"

"Don't carry one," Ben said.

"Shit ... I guess three iron it is," Pitzmyre conceded, and this time Knox did not say a word. Ben eased his feet back into the water and though still uncomfortable, he found it less so the second time. Though anxious to hit the ball and dry his feet, Ben nevertheless took a deep breath and forced himself to focus on his stance, direction and his grip on the club. In order to shake off the tension in his forearms, he waggled the three iron back and forth rapidly, and then steadied the head of the club over the ball, and slightly above the water's surface. Ben glanced toward the green, one last time, and tried to visualize his shot. He returned his concentration to the submerged ball, swung hard at it, and *Kersplash,* was the sound made as the club struck the ball, launching it from the rocky creek bed. Cold creek water rained down on those in the vicinity, including Pitzmyre who struggled to follow the path of the ball, as he wiped his face with his jacket sleeve.

Ben had struck the ball well under the circumstances, and it traveled high and, drifted slightly in the direction of the green, and countless hopeful stares followed its flight. However, the next sound heard was a loud *clack*, which signaled bad news to every golfer present, as unmistakable confirmation of the ball striking a tree. The drooping limb of a mature aspen had interrupted the ball's flight, and the crowd groaned as the ball fell down to the dewy grass below.

"Aw, that's too bad," Knox, said.

Ben again took a seat on the golf bag, and dried his numb and tingling feet with a golf towel, and once sufficiently dry, he donned his socks and golf spikes. He rose and parted the throng lining the creek, on his way to locate his ball. As he walked, Ben worried most that his ball had come to rest behind a tree or next to a tree root, but found getting to it a challenge of its own. Those spectators that had viewed the action to this point from the upper half of the fairway had funneled down toward the green, and the closer the men drew to the area where the ball would have fallen, the larger the crowd swelled.

"Stewart, you lead the way and create room for us," Pitzmyre directed.

Spindler obeyed and moved ahead of them, and used his body, and the large golf bag, to forge a path for the others to follow, and among those availing themselves of this passage, were Knox and Mungo. Once they reached the ball, some spectators voluntarily backed away, and Spindler politely shooed others, providing Pitzmyre and Ben room to study its position. Though the ball had fallen only twenty-five yards short of the green, it was nestled in the grass with the trunk of the large aspen standing squarely between Ben's ball and the golf hole.

"You got to get it on the green," Pitzmyre said.

"I realize that, but I sure would've preferred taking the penalty and having had a *real* shot—now I'm blocked."

"Oh my," Knox said having done his own analysis. "This is quite the dilemma, now isn't it?"

"He can do this," Pitzmyre said, then turned to Ben, "so what do you think?"

"I don't see any way to get it anywhere near the green by hittin' it straight on—the tree has me completely stymied."

"Hey, Pitzmyre! Don't y'all have chain saws down at that Pitz-Smart store of yours?" Mungo yelled.

"Pipe down!" Pitzmyre demanded as he walked the area, and then said, "You just need to concentrate on getting the ball on the green, or at least close enough to it for a putt or a short chip."

Ben did not react to Pitzmyre's manifesto of the obvious, and instead walked around the ball in search of alternatives. While Pitzmyre and the others likewise pondered and assessed, Ben settled on an approach and decided to act. He snatched the one iron from the bag and with it in hand, he addressed the ball, but for this attempt, he was aiming away from the green.

"What are you doing?" Pitzmyre asked frantically, as those in the gallery stood puzzled by Ben's strategy.

"Hitting my shot," Ben said without looking up, and nearby spectators instinctively backpedaled to get out of Ben's line of fire.

"But the green is over there—you do know that, right?" Spindler said, pointing.

Ben did not respond, and wanted no more debate or private conferences, and opted instead to take a couple of sharp practice swings while maintaining his aim. Committed to the shot, he accelerated the club downward striking the ball with a crisp and clean punch. The ball sailed low and fast striking the trunk of a nearby Douglas fir, knocking a chunk of its bark off as it ricocheted backward and in the direction of the green.

To everyone's amazement, Ben's ball landed on the other side of the creek, bounded along the ground, then scooted over a mound and onto the green. The crowd delivered a robust cheer, one that grew in intensity as the ball continued at a fast pace upslope before breaking in the direction of the flag. The gallery yelled its encouragement to the ball, and all eyes watched as it ball raced within inches of the hole, before coming to rest several yards up hill, near where the anxious Emily stood.

Pitzmyre, elated, high-fived Spindler as Ben trudged through the crowd, humbly accepting many pats on the back as he walked. He tromped over the wood-plank footbridge spanning the babbling creek and paced on to the putting surface. He spotted Emily, who subtly waved her right hand and Ben nodded and smiled and retrieved a dime from his pocket, and used it to mark his ball. He lifted the ball and placed it in his pocket, and began assessing his putt.

"Look how far away he is," Spindler said, as he and Pitzmyre reached the green. "It's close to forty feet."

"Yeah, but it's a putt at least," Pitzmyre said.

"True, but I know this putt, and it's *very* fast."

"It looks like it and check out the break," Pitzmyre observed. "How good is Ben's putting?"

"I've never seen him putt, except on the virtual golf."

"Shit!" Pitzmyre said. "This is a tough one, isn't it?"

"It is, but Ben doesn't seem too worried, though," Spindler whispered.

"He doesn't have half-a-million dollars riding on it!" Pitzmyre said, in a voice louder than he intended and was enough to draw the attention of those around the green.

"Nice!" Mungo said.

"Never mind that Ben—it's okay—you just concentrate on that putt," Pitzmyre, encouraged, as Knox stood stoically on the fringe of the green. "Get Ben his putter and don't forget the banner," Pitzmyre said, referring to yet another Pitz-Smart advertisement. This one read *PITZ-SMART-always backs the winners* and it was rolled up, and attached to a wooden sign that in the summer, served as a leader board during club tournaments. The plan was for Spindler to pull a string that would let it unfurl, but only if Ben parred the hole.

Spindler removed Ben's putter from the bag, and walked on the green and handed it to him. He then removed the pin flag from the hole, setting it out of the way on the putting surface, and returned to the back of the green to stand near the banner.

A tense silence dominated, until Knox yelled, "Hey, big shot!" Pitzmyre was startled and looked around for the source of the voice. "Over here Pitzmyre, it's me—you know—the mean old banker man," Knox said, waving his arms.

Pitzmyre spotted Knox across the green, and asked, "What do you want?"

Knox walked onto the green, stared directly at Pitzmyre, and in his loud, deep voice asked, "I couldn't help noticing how nervous you look—losing faith in the so called *hometown hero?*"

Pitzmyre's face flushed beet red, as he glanced to Ben, then back to Knox. "No ... uh ... of course not."

"That's an awfully long fast-breaking putt, don't you think?" Knox asked.

"Ben can make it," Pitzmyre said with feigned confidence, "but it's really not fair for you to rattle his nerves like this to gain an advantage."

"Hey, Ben!" Knox yelled. "Is he right—am I rattling your nerves?"

"No, but I would like to get this over with."

"Fair enough," Knox said, returning his attention to Pitzmyre. "Now, since you've gone wobbly on Ben's capabilities, I'd—"

"Not true! Not true!" Pitzmyre repeated firmly while shaking his head.

"Oh, please, you don't believe that, and I can see it in your eyes," Knox said. "I'll tell you what I'll do, since I'm convinced you've lost faith in Ben, I'll give you a break on the bet."

"You want to cancel it?" Pitzmyre said, trying to conceal his excitement at the mere prospect.

"Heavens no!" Knox said with a chuckle. "But what I *will* offer to do is flip the bet."

Murmurs permeated the crowd as Pitzmyre stood speechless, and trying to comprehend the offer. "Tell me exactly what you mean?"

"I mean just what I said—I offer to switch bets because unlike you, I do believe in Ben's ability to do this," the banker said.

Pitzmyre pulled Spindler aside and asked, "What're the odds of Dingbat making this putt?"

"While I assume he's a decent putter, even the best on the pro tour make this putt only once or twice in twenty tries. So, I'd have to say it's a long shot."

"I thought you'd say that," Pitzmyre said, with his mind processing in high gear, and as he did, the crowd commenced mumbling amongst themselves.

"You're not considering doing this are you?" Spindler whispered to his boss. "I mean, I know it's a long shot and all, and we're talking about a lot of money, but what about our public support of Ben?"

"What about it?"

"Joe, if you switch the bet, it'll be a public relations disaster, no matter the outcome."

"A half-million dollars buys a lot of public relations Stewart," Pitzmyre said, then walked on the green for another look at the putt.

"So what's it going to be?" Knox pressed, as Ben joined Spindler on the fringe to watch the exchange between the two executives.

"Just so we're on the same page, you're offering to make my contractual bet yours and your bet becomes mine, correct?" Pitzmyre asked, and the notion of him forsaking Ben, urged the mumbling spectators into much louder, grumbling of discontent.

"That's right. I had a feeling that something like this might happen, so I had this little ol' addendum to our contract drawn up that succinctly and plainly set's out that change," Knox said, pulling the document from of his suit coat. He unfolded it and handed it over to Pitzmyre, who despite the cool mountain air, was now sweating. The single-paragraph document acknowledged that once signed, their respective obligations from their original contract would reverse. As Pitzmyre read the document, he noticed that Knox had already inked his signature on the space at the bottom of the page in anticipation of Pitzmyre's capitulation. The CEO scrutinized the language, making the spectators even more restless at the looming betrayal.

Pitzmyre looked up from reading the document, with his mind made up, and simply said, "Deal!" Pitzmyre quickly added his signature to Knox' and handed the contract back to him. The crowd promptly erupted in a loud and sustained chorus of boos, replaced thereafter by a rapid, sustained series of splashes. Pitzmyre turned toward the odd sound and witnessed spectators taking turns opening the cardboard sleeves and hurling their commemorative Pitz-Smart golf balls into the greenside pond. Spindler stood with his mouth agape, while Pitzmyre and Knox added a handshake on the swap and walked away in opposite directions.

"I'm sorry, Ben," Spindler said under his breath.

"Don't be, Stewart. It's not your doing."

When Ben met Pitzmyre crossing the green, he asked, "I want to clarify the VFW part of the deal."

"That contract is still the same—they still get theirs," Pitzmyre confirmed tersely, as he continued on to the edge of the green and resumed his nail biting at Spindler's side.

Cookie had seen the commotion from the café window and his curiosity piqued. That interest coupled with a lack of unserved customers in the café, compelled him to place Kat in charge before heading out of the clubhouse. He trotted down the slope toward the eighteenth, and pushed his way through the crowd to stand next to Emily greenside.

Ben returned to his ball to the putting surface, picked up his ten cent marker and the crowd quickly calmed, providing him a respectful silence. Ben had always relied on his gut to guide him in decisions, both on and off the golf course, and was never known to spend much time surveying shots. However, five months of anticipation and a fortune now hinged on Ben's putter, and he took another glance at the slope and the break.

He then straddled the ball with putter in hand, crouched

slightly and slowly eased the putter back, and as he moved the club forward, Pitzmyre reached above Spindler's hand and pulled the string for the banner, and it fell with a conspicuous *whoosh* precisely as Ben struck the putt. Spindler and many others were drawn toward the sound, but immediately returned their focus to the path of the ball. They watched on as the ball rolled smoothly down the grade, breaking left and leveling out as it tracked nicely in the direction of the hole. As the speed of the rotation diminished, the ball seemed to move in slow motion and as it neared the cup, the spectators cheered. Their voices grew louder with each revolution, until the ball lipped the edge of the cup, and with the urging of centrifugal force, it lurched left finally settling three and a half feet below the hole.

The disappointed spectators groaned in unison, lapsed into a disappointed silence, then provided Ben an honorary applause for his effort. He respectfully tipped his hat, while Pitzmyre, on the other hand celebrated. The CEO embraced Spindler, then broke into a circular dance on the green, all the while waving the scorecard and repeating, "I won! I won! I won!"

Ben stood stoically, with putter in hand waiting for Pitzmyre's enthusiasm to subside, before attempting his bogie putt.

Cookie noticed this and, said, "Hey, you jerk, Ben needs to putt out!"

Pitzmyre stopped celebrating, turned toward Cookie, then to Ben and sneered, "What difference does it make now?"

"It means something to *me*," Ben said, "and if you want me to total and sign that card you're waving, I suggest you knock it off."

"Let 'er rip," Pitzmyre said flippantly.

Ben paused over the ball, and then ran in the putt, and Pitzmyre handed the scorecard to Ben, who wrote the score for the hole and the total for the round, and added his signature at the bottom.

"Nice miss, Ben!" Pitzmyre said ignobly, snatching the card out of his hand then walked over to Spindler who stood in celebration with other Pitz-Smart employees near the unfurled banner.

Ducking under the ropes, Emily hurried over to Ben and planted a big kiss on his cheek. "Sorry it didn't work out, but I'm very proud of you."

"Thanks, Em," he said.

She looked around and added, "You really drew a crowd, huh?"

"Yes indeed," Ben responded and removed his custom-made shirt, and laid it on the oversized bag.

"I'm surprised they didn't charge admission," Mungo said, as he and Cookie joined the couple on the green.

"Me, too," Cookie said shaking Ben's hand. "They'd have made a fortune, if they had."

"Don't give 'em any ideas guys," Ben replied.

"Congratulations on one hell of a round," Mungo said.

"And ten grand for the hall—that's a great thing, too!" Cookie added.

"Thanks, fellas," Ben said, then looked to Emily. "Well, I guess we better get going."

"What about your clubs?" she asked.

"I need to leave the bag here, so I'll carry them loose to the car."

"What about your souvenir golf balls and *custom-made* shirt?" Mungo asked facetiously.

"I won't miss 'em," Ben said.

"Want me to help get the clubs to the car?" Mungo asked.

"It does seem that my caddy has abandoned me," Ben said glancing the Pitz-Smart celebration, "but I think I can handle it."

"Okay, well since there ain't no free food out here, I'll follow Cookie back to the café," Mungo said, and he and Cookie bid them farewell and headed in the direction of the clubhouse.

Ben began pulling his clubs from the bag, and Emily said, "I can carry some." Ben handed off a few to her, but he kept most for himself, and as the couple walked from the green toward the parking lot, they heard Pitzmyre's loud voice from behind say. "Where's that fat, old banker?"

Spindler tiptoed to look over the disbursing crowd and saw Knox ambling off the course, and in the direction of the clubhouse. "He's over there, Joe," Spindler said pointing.

"Yeah, that's him all right," Pitzmyre said gleefully, "come with me—let's have some fun." Pitzmyre said. With Spindler and other Pitz-Smart employees trailing, Pitzmyre trotted around the exiting spectators and as he neared Knox, he yelled, "Hey old man, wait up!"

A number of spectators noticed what was unfolding and followed the Pitz-Smart team to see what would ensue. Mungo had likewise heard the commotion, and glanced in that direction, and said, "Cookie, let's go see what's up."

"What?"

"Look over there," Mungo, said pointing.

Cookie considered his café obligations, but he decided it could wait for a few moments more, and he and Mungo made their way toward the gathering. When they reached the others, they each noticed that Pitzmyre had gained Knox' attention and the crowd quickly encircled the men.

"Where are you going, banker man?" Pitzmyre asked smugly.

"To get a cup of coffee, if you must know," Knox said.

"Do you need a loan to buy it banker man?" Pitzmyre jibed receiving a laugh from his underlings.

"And just what do you mean by that," Knox asked.

"I wonder if you have enough money left for the coffee, I mean we have a little matter of a half million dollar bet, don't we?"

"Oh yes we do, and thankfully the funds are in trust," Knox replied, and turned to leave.

Pitzmyre grabbed the sleeve of Knox's suit jacket. "Hang on now, a fortune has just been lost here, and that's your only reaction?"

"Yes," Knox responded, jerking his sleeve from Pitzmyre's grasp, and again tried to walk away.

Pitzmyre, with the throng in tow, followed Knox. "That's it? Don't you have something you'd like to say?"

Knox stopped, turned the CEO and said, "Indeed, I do, but I'm not one to gloat,"

"Look, old man, losers don't gloat," Pitzmyre replied.

"Pitzmyre—you're proving that wrong as you speak!"

"Wait, wait, wait," Pitzmyre said, "are you trying to welch on the bet?"

"Welch? Are you kidding?" Knox said, guffawing loudly. "Why would I welch on a bet I won?"

"Imagine that, a banker that doesn't know simple math," Pitzmyre said to Spindler. "We switched the bet old man—don't you remember?"

"Oh yes, we did."

"What do you think's happening?" Cookie whispered to Mungo.

"Beats the hell out of me, but I'm beginning to think Fergie Knox might have dived off the deep end."

"Ben bogied the hole!" Pitzmyre said smugly, while pulling the crumpled card from his pocket and waiving it in Knox's face. "This here is the *official* signed scorecard, and it spells it out in Ben's own handwriting—what's your response to that?"

"I'll show you," Knox said as he reached into his jacket pocket, pulled out a folded piece of paper, and handed it to Pitzmyre.

"What's this?" Pitzmyre asked curiously.

"That there's what you call an *official*, certified Certificate of Live Birth for one Benjamin Taylor Digby," Knox said.

"What's the big deal?" Spindler asked.

Pitzmyre perused the document, lowered it and slowly turned to Spindler. "His birthday was two weeks ago."

"So?" Spindler asked.

"He's seventy-five—you dumb-ass!"

All present stood stunned, and murmurs ensued, until a strange sound emerged, which could only be described as wild cackling. The spectators turned in that direction and as the crowd parted, they saw Mungo, doubled over, and repeating between cackles, "He's seventy-five! He's seventy-five! Ben Digby's seventy-damn-five!" The crowd erupted in a roar of laughter, a sound that reverberated all the way to the parking lot, prompting Emily to stop and ask, "What do you think that was all about?"

"It's a long story Em, I'll explain it all on the way home."

The Ninteeth Hole

*T*hree weeks later, and at Ferguson Knox' request, Ben traveled to Bozeman State Bank. When he arrived, Knox saw Ben entering the bank by looking through a window in his office that provided him a view of the bank's lobby and teller stand. He rose from his desk, and beckoned Ben, and when he entered his office, Ben shook Knox' hand and accepted accolades for a round well played.

"I may have played a good round, but you played Pitzmyre even better," Ben responded.

"I suppose, but I still couldn't have done it without you," Knox said. "Have a seat."

"So what's this all about Fergie?" Ben asked taking one of two high back leather chairs on the opposite side from Knox' antique mahogany desk.

"I'll get to that shortly," Knox, said opening a large, leather-bound checkbook to a page marked by a folded piece of paper. He lifted the document, extended it toward Ben and said, "Before I forget I want to return your birth certificate, thanks for loaning it to me."

"No problem," Ben said slipping the document into his jacket pocket. "So just when did you think of the birthday angle?"

"It crossed my mind long after that morning in the tent, and it spooked the hell out of me. I seemed to remember your birthday being early in the year, and checked our bank records and found the date on some of our old forms. I felt certain that you would celebrate that birthday before the eighteenth could become playable, and though I was skeptical about you parring that hole, I likewise doubted you would double bogie it. Consequently, I drafted the bet swap addendum, in case you did a little *too* well that day. I was concerned that Pitzmyre would make the same birthday connection, but thankfully, he did not and as they say, *the rest is history.*

"You certainly covered all the bases, didn't you?"

"I tried to, and on that morning at the golf course, I had to play it out as it unfolded, and when you hit your drive in the creek, I figured I had it in the bag and wouldn't need the bet swap. But then you launched the ball nicely out of the drink, and I got a little worried."

"Even with it hitting the tree and being blocked?" Ben asked.

"Yes, considering your short game, and being only a few yards off the green, it was disconcerting, to say the least, and I must say, when you ricocheted that ball off the tree trunk and on to the green, I was back on my heels."

"It was pure luck," Ben confessed.

"Luck or not, it was a game changer, and I knew then that I *had* to get the bet swapped. Once I accomplished that, I had hoped you would just made that long putt, and render the birth certificate irrelevant, but when you missed, I was damn happy to have the one stroke cushion."

"I tried my best, but because Pitzmyre dropped that goofy banner, I pulled my putt a little, or I just might've sunk it."

"And leaving a three-footer—"

"Three and a half," Ben corrected.

"A three and a half footer for the bogie was a tad disconcerting too," Knox added.

"How'd you know Pitzmyre would switch the bets?" Ben asked.

"I didn't, at least until I saw him on that green that day. He was unnerved, and I could tell it."

"He did look bedside himself," Ben agreed.

"You know what really eats at Pitzmyre more than the money?" Knox asked and Ben shook his head. "It's the concept of losing and being out smarted in the process. He's not used to it Ben, and does not like it one little bit. The nervousness he displayed in the tent that morning I raised him, and on that eighteenth green, was not about the money—it was all about winning and losing."

"So Pitzmyre paid up, huh?"

"Yes, but it wasn't easy, he even unleashed his legal team on me."

"Oh?"

"Yes, and they tried a couple of outs, first saying the bet was based on you being seventy-four, since that's was your age when you started the round."

"It didn't work apparently."

"Nope," Knox said, detaching a check from the leather book. "It was a nice try, but the contract contained three little ol' words that sealed the deal in my favor. It clearly stated that the deal was based on your, and I quote, *then existing age* on the day the round was completed which, could only be interpreted as seventy-five. Then, they claimed there was an ambiguity in the original contract, but they drafted it, and did so with no input from me, and the law's clear that any ambiguity is construed in the favor of the non-drafting party."

"And that's you."

"Correct. They had no real way out, and I made sure of that."

"As I recall, that same language was used in my contract for the VFW hall."

"I'm sure it is," Knox said.

"Based on that, I'm definitely going to demand the full twenty-five thousand from them," Ben said.

"You should," Knox encouraged, "and if they try that same tactic with you, just let me know—I think I've got their number on this."

"You're a very shrewd, Ferguson."

"Shrewd, huh? Over the last couple of weeks, Pitzmyre has called me, let's see … devious twice, chicken … ahem … excrement three times, and a term that begins with 'A' and ends with hole," Knox said as he lifted his pen and began to write. "But more than the legalities, Pitzmyre knew he had more to lose by skipping out on the bet."

"The Pitz-Smart brand?" Ben asked.

"Of course. Backing out on you was bad enough, but welching on the bet that he made so publicly would not have been treated favorably in the national news."

"What the press *did* say was not very flattering," Ben said and Knox nodded, as he extended his hand holding a folded check.

"What's that?" Ben asked.

"The moment I decided to jump into this Pitz-Smart betting mess, I made a pledge that if it worked out to my advantage, I'd do something good with it," Knox explained. "The money was never for me, and was always about doing something for others, and this is for you."

"Money for me?" Ben asked.

"Yes," Knox said grinning.

"But why?"

"You helped by loaning me your birth certificate and you made that putt, and I want to do something for you."

"I'm sure you could've gotten the birth certificate on your own, and I—"

"Not true," Knox interrupted, "I tried the Bureau of Vital Statistics and they required your authorization."

"Either way, that's nothing to be rewarded for."

"Ben, I didn't get into this betting thing for me, I did it for you and for others that I intend to share this with, and I offer this to you in recognition of our years of friendship."

"I haven't always been so friendly," Ben said.

"Neither have I, and that's why I want you to have a token of my appreciation."

"Fine, give me a bank calendar, or a toaster or something—I always could use one those, but Fergie I can't take money from you."

"Here, I insist," Knox, said extending the check even closer to him, but Ben shook his head. "Ben, it's polite to reject a gift once, but it's considered rude to reject it a second time."

"At the risk of being rude, you said you wanted to do *good* with this money, how about a charity or something like that?" Ben asked.

Knox walked around his desk toward Ben and said, "I'm doing plenty of that already, and I truly want you to have this, and I won't take no for an answer," Knox said while slipping the check in Ben's shirt pocket.

Ben sighed. "I don't know what to say."

"Don't say anything, and just know that this makes me happier than you can imagine."

"Is this a part of the Pitz-Smart money?" Ben asked patting his shirt pocket.

"Yes, so don't concern yourself about it, the big shot and his big company will be fine," Knox said.

"I guess you're right, but that's a lot of money to lose on a technicality."

"Whose side are you on, Ben?" Knox asked. "Why, if I didn't know better, I'd think you've grown soft on Pitz-Smart."

"Not a chance, but I do feel a little guilty benefitting financially from all of this nonsense."

"Give me my check back, and I'll return it to Pitzmyre," Knox joked.

"I don't feel *that* guilty," Ben chuckled.

"Well, you shouldn't. After all, you didn't do anything except try your best to play the hole and let Pitzmyre make dumb decisions."

"That's true, and I really did want to shoot my age."

"You did!" Knox said.

Ben shook his head. "Perhaps under contract law, but not under my way of thinking."

"Fine, but don't fret about the money, it's just a drop in the bucket for Pitz-Smart—did you hear they may be closing their store?"

"I heard that rumor, but do you think it's true?" Ben asked.

"I don't know for sure, but I did pickup one of the casualties," Knox said, and pointed out his office window toward the bank's long, oak teller stand. Ben turned, peered through the glass and saw Stewart

Spindler, handling a customer deposit. "I'm actually glad to see that, Fergie. I sense that Stewart's a good man."

"I do too," Knox said. "So far, he's proved to be very reliable and a hard worker—did you know he actually has a finance degree."

"I did not know that, but did he hire on as a teller?" Ben asked skeptically.

"No, he's just in training. As my new Vice President of commercial lending, he has to be cross-trained on multiple functions in the bank."

"Wow, Vice President—already?"

"Aw hell, Ben. There's an old saying in the business that most everyone working in a bank with above a GED will soon be a GD-VP-PDQ."

"I've heard something about that," Ben said smiling. "But if they do close their store here, Pitzmyre really took a bath on this fiasco."

"Not as much as you'd think. Chain stores of that size, routinely open, relocate and close locations as a cost of doing business, but if they do pull out, that big empty building represents a good opportunity."

"Are you thinking about buying it?" Ben asked.

"Lord no, but it would make a dandy hardware store," Knox said smiling slyly.

"Not a chance, Fergie, those days are far behind me."

"Not so fast. That check in your pocket would make a good down payment on it, and I'd finance the rest—if you get it for the right price, of course."

"Down payment?" Ben asked. "Just how much is this check for?"

"Take a look for yourself," Knox said.

Ben retrieved the check from his pocket, unfolded it, read the amount, sat wide-eyed, and uttered, "A hundred and fifty thousand dollars?" he asked with his voice quavering like it did at the beginning of his network television interview. Knox nodded and smiled, but Ben shook his head and laid the check on the edge of Knox' desk. "That's awfully generous and very kind of you, but I just can't take that kind of money."

"I won't take no for an answer," Knox said standing his ground.

"I just don't understand ... I mean, why you would do such a thing?"

"You see Ben, guys like Pitzmyre and me, get caught up in ourselves and our businesses, so much so that that we often miss the bigger picture, such as Pitzmyre not thinking of the birthday angle or like when I was your banker," Knox said as his cheerful expression turned serious. "When you had troubles and needed my help, I treated you the same way I would any other depositor and ignored the years of history we had together. I let you down, and I hope I've redeemed myself," Knox said, extending his right hand.

Ben, teary-eyed by Knox's comments, stood and shook his hand. "I truly appreciate that, more than you know, but I realize in retrospect, you saved me from an even worse financial disaster."

"That's beside the point, and don't say anything more or you'll make me weepy. Just take the money and enjoy it," Knox urged, lifting the check and handing back to Ben. "Now don't feel obliged, but I'd most pleased if you'd let Stewart open you up a new account in which to deposit that check."

"That would please me too," Ben said.

"Now, it's none of my business, but what are you going to do with this Pitz-Smart windfall?"

"I don't mind telling you, and I'm already running the numbers in my head. Of course, I have to clear everything with Emily, but I think I'm going to collect the twenty-five thousand for the VFW and add half of this to it," Ben said referring to the check. "This will give them an even hundred thousand, and that should be enough to get the hall in tiptop shape. As for the rest I will use it to take care of a little unfinished business."

"Oh?" Knox asked.

"You see Fergie, what's left over out of this check, and with our savings, it just might be enough to get me and the missus down to El Dorado."

Knox thought for a moment. "I remember you mentioning that place—New Mexico, right?"

"Arizona."

"Ah, yes. *The Eden of the Southwest* as I recall, didn't you used to carry a post card?"

"Good memory," Ben said, and after placing the check in his wallet, he pulled out the well-worn El Dorado post card, unfolded it and tossed it on Knox's desk.

"It looks lovely," Knox said as he stared at the photo, "year round golf as I remember."

"Yes, and you've made it possible to for us to finally make the move, and Emily and I will be forever grateful."

"You deserve it, and I'm happy for you two. So you're going to sell your house here?"

"We can't do that. We have too much invested here, and Bozeman will always be our home, but spending the winters in Arizona is what we've dreamed of for many years."

"You're taking snow bird status, huh?"

Ben nodded and asked, "If you don't mind me asking, what are you're doing with your share of Pitzmyre's money—at least what's left of it?"

"I'm glad you asked, and don't say anything about it, but I have already earmarked a sizable portion of this bounty to donate, anonymously, to the VFW post. I hope that with your donation and mine that the hall will be restored to what it should be, and they'll have a tidy budget going forward. You see Ben, I realize that my race is almost run, and I need to do some things in preparation. I want this bank to continue without me, and I have some folks in place here, whom I think can take the reins. I also have a lot money and no one to leave it to when I am gone, and I've been picking worthy causes and unloading some here and there."

"I certainly applaud the choice, but why the VFW?"

"I have some unfinished business of my own," Knox said, unbuttoning the left sleeve of his starched, white shirt and rolling it up to reveal his frail, wrinkled bicep. Ben moved around the desk and saw a faded tattoo of the shield of the 101st Airborne.

"Combat?" Ben asked.

"Bastogne."

Ben grimaced and hung his head. "My good Lord—I never knew."

"Ben, I always admired what you did for the VFW, but I never got involved with them. I always wanted to leave the past in the past, and never had the stomach to revisit my tour through Belgium."

"But why the anonymous donation?"

"I want to join them there as a member—I think it's time—but I only want to be one of the guys and not some sort of rich old benefactor. I might just drop in on them from time-to-time, and when I do, I just want to be one of the men."

"They'd be lucky to have you, sir."

"Well, if you'll excuse me, I have customers to tend to," Knox said rising from his desk.

Ben glanced backward, looked through the window, and saw a couple now seated on an antique love seat holding hands. "Dan and Sandy Whitcombe?" Ben asked, turning back to Knox.

"Yes, they're here to re-activate an old operating account."

"For their meat market?" Ben asked, and Knox nodded. "Well I'll be ..."

WITHDRAWN BY WILLIAMSBURG REGIONAL LIBRARY

Printed in the United States
By Bookmasters